A
PEOPLE
CALLED
WE

PHILIPPE SIOWTU

DEDICATION

In memory of my sister Cecilia
Who loved to listen
To my stories
When we were just kids

CONTENTS

ACKNOWLEDGEMENTS

The major effects of nuclear explosions on the population, structures and economies of the United States were based in part on a report published by the Office of Technology Assessment, "The Effects of Nuclear War." (Allanheld, Osmun & Co., 1980.)

The underground city in the Carlsbad Caverns was inspired by the account of the Biosphere 2 experiment in "LIFE UNDER GLASS: The Inside Story of Biosphere 2" by Abigail Alling and Mark Nelson (The Biosphere Press, 1993.)

PART 1: WASTELAND

1 BERTRAND AND HIS CLOCKS

On a cold and rainy day, Bertrand walked into a gift shop in South Harrow, a suburb of London, to purchase an alarm clock. The year was 1971. As anyone would have imagined, the shelves displayed nothing but mechanical alarm clocks. The tiny but mighty radio transistor was discovered in 1947, but the radio alarm clock in use today had not been built yet. The digital alarm clock was unheard of at that time and the digital radio alarm clock with an integrated phone had not even been dreamed up. Throughout his life, Bertrand woke up without the help of any alarm clock. He had never owned an alarm clock and never had a need for one until his English landlord evicted him from his rented room for oversleeping and for not showing up for breakfast in the morning.

When he was a child growing up in his hometown city of Port Louis on the island of Mauritius, Bertrand had several natural systems to wake him up in the morning. First there were the big roosters living on a chicken farm across from the house his mother rented from the chicken farm owner. The landlord's wife managed the farm. Every day before sunrise, the roosters crowed and the hens cackled. The cocks' crow woke up everybody living close to the farm. The crowing and cawing sounded like symphonic music to Bertrand's ears, but he did not have to get out of bed every time the fowls squawked because he did not have to be at school until nine o'clock. So he slept on. Later the cacophony of the neighbors chatting with the bread man and bargaining with the fisherman woke him up for the second time. The itinerary merchants came by every morning carrying their products on bicycles to compete for the residents' purses. Their chatter cut through the clean morning air and traveled past the fluttering curtains adorning the windows to wake Bertrand up. After the merchants left, Bertrand fell asleep

1

again, but only to be woken up for the third time by the milkman trumpeting his arrival with a series of loud honks. Sometimes he could hear the milkman arguing with the Health Inspector who stopped him to test his milk for its wholesomeness. More often than not, the milkman sold watered-down milk and got fined for doing so. When the Health Inspector left, he covered his ears with his pillow and went back to sleep. Soon after, the vegetable merchants joined the bread seller, the fisherman and the milkman. Their voices turned the quiet street into a bazaar and drew him out of slumber for the fourth time. When the itinerary merchants left, the neighbor's kids came to play outside his bedroom. The small children always quarreled while eating their morning bread. They chose to sit in front of his bedroom door everyday. At first they quietly sat down on the porch to eat their bread and play with their toys. Then they started to punch and slam at each other, which seemed to be a habit that never died as the children grew up. The French doors rattled and jostled when the children bumped against them. The rattling and jostling woke Bertrand up for the fifth time. After the fight the children ran home to their mothers, crying and shouting: "Ma, he hit me first..."

Bertrand listened to the parents admonishing their children until their voices died down. He then went rock-a-bye anew. At seven o'clock his friend who lived next to the chicken farm quietly slipped into his bedroom and softly called out his name. The itinerant merchants traveling on bicycles brought vegetables, bread, milk and sometimes fish, but never fresh red meat or poultry. Anyone who wanted to have meat for dinner must travel to town to buy them. Since the residents in the neighborhood were too poor to own a refrigerator, the residents had to travel to town almost everyday to buy meat. His friend borrowed his bike every morning for his trip to the meat market. Every morning he nudged him up to let him know that he had borrowed his bike. Bertrand then woke up to acknowledge him and then hit the hay again. The final wake-up call, administered by his older sister, was one that Bertrand dreaded the most. The three-way alarm was repeated morning after morning. It never failed to jolt him out of bed. First, she scratched his tender feet with her long nails and turned his big toes 180 degrees around. This failed to wake him up. A few minutes later, she returned and grabbed him by his feet and pulled him out of bed onto the floor. After she left Bertrand climbed back on the bed and fell asleep again. When she returned and saw him still sleeping, her sister seized the pillow from under him and whammed his dozing head screaming: "Get up!"

At the sound of her angry voice, Bertrand scrambled out of bed and ran to the communal bathroom. His mother never used an alarm clock to wake her up everyday. Besides, even if she had wanted to, she could not afford to buy an alarm clock. Nonetheless, she still woke up at five o'clock everyday without fail to attend to her daily chores. So Bertrand grew up in a house with no alarm clock. There was never any need for him to own an alarm clock. His sister was the best alarm clock he ever had. That was until he left Mauritius on April 13, 1971 for London to further his education.

Within a few days of arriving in London, he landed a job with the Kodak Company in Rayners Lane. He was hired as a Cost Accounting Clerk and was paid £11 a week. He boarded up with an English couple living in Harrow-Wealdstone, which was a 10-minute ride by train or by bus from Rayners Lane. The couple had one little boy and one little girl. When the landlady took him upstairs to view his room, he walked straight into a small room. The box room, as the English people calls it, measured 6ft by 7ft, but it was adequate for him as he had nothing but the clothing on his back and whatever he carried with him to London in his suitcase. The single bed had pink covering on it. He put his suitcase on the bed, thanked the Landlady and started unpacking. He later learned that the bedroom belonged to the couple's daughter, and that the Landlady intended to rent the larger room next door to him. For £5 a week, the English landlady provided him with a bed, a warm breakfast, and two meals in the evening. The Landlady, who was a full-time housewife, served breakfast at seven o'clock, set up the table for dinner soon after her husband returned from work, and served supper just before they retire for the night.

Bertrand settled down in his new place which he found very quiet, very private and very comfortable. For the first time in his life, he took a bath in a bathtub and sat down in a toilet instead of squatting like he was used to in Mauritius. Unlike the communal kitchen which his mother shared with other three families and which was always filled with smoke, the kitchen was self-contained and clean. There were no roosters in the landlord's back yard to wake him up, no itinerant merchants to pull him out of Morpheus' arms, and no children to jostle him out of his slumber. In the morning the landlady came up the stairs and knocked on his door to let him know that breakfast was ready. At first the knocks on his door were quiet and muffled, but over time they turned louder and louder. One morning the landlord himself came upstairs to wake him up. He pushed the door wide open and burst into his room. The door slamming against the wall abruptly woke Bertrand up. The irate landlord pulled him up by his pajama top and shouted: "Do I have to fire a cannonball into your room in order to wake you up?" The terrified Bertrand clambered out of bed and mumbled an apology to the landlord. The landlord left the room fuming with anger. He ran down the steps and hurriedly left for work.

Still in shock, Bertrand stepped out of his bedroom and looked downstairs. The landlady stood motionless in the hallway by the stairs. She briefly looked up at him, wiped her tears and went back into the dining room. After that day the English couple never came upstairs again to wake him up. The couple ate breakfast without him and did not bother to save anything for him.

A few days after he jostled him out of his bed, the tall Teutonic landlord summoned Bertrand into the sitting room. It was a Saturday morning and the landlord was off work. His wife sat quietly on an armchair and looked down. On the previous night she did not say a word to him while they ate dinner.

"My wife wants you to leave," the landlord said in a grim voice. Bertrand was taken aback by the request.

"What have I done wrong?" he asked.

"We are English," the landlord replied. "We would like to spend the weekends by ourselves. Having you living with us seven days a week is getting to be too much for my wife. It's too stressful for her. She prefers to have someone stay with us on weekdays only."

"You did not tell me that when I inquired about the room," Bertrand protested. "Had I known that you only wanted a tenant for five days a week, I would not have rented a room from you. Besides, I don't have a family to go to on weekends. My parents live twelve thousand miles from here. Where shall I stay on weekends?"

"You constantly ignore my wife whenever she goes upstairs to wake you up for breakfast. She is very upset about that. It's ridiculous that we have to shout every morning in order to wake you up. The British people never have to shout for anything. Do you understand?"

"I understand. I will leave when I find a new place," Bertrand said with deference. "I'll start looking for another room to rent tomorrow. Give me a week or two."

"My wife is also upset that you have been urinating all over the toilet seat," the landlord added.

"Pardon me?" Bertrand exclaimed.

"I find it hard to believe that anyone would urinate on the toilet seat," the landlord continued. "It seems that you are deliberately doing it to upset my wife."

"I swear that I did not piss on the toilet seat," Bertrand demurred. "When I went to use the bathroom this morning, I saw your son urinating on the bathroom floor. That must have been him pissing on the toilet seat, not me."

The landlady blushed and hurriedly left the sitting room. That night Bertrand had difficulties falling asleep. He tossed and rolled in his bed for hours, upset at being evicted from his room. When he finally fell asleep, he dreamed that her landlady's large behind was stuck inside a commode floating down the Thames River. She drifted in the current towards London Bridge, waving a British flag in both her hands and singing 'God Save the Queen.' The British Army's elite Coldstream Guards waited on the bridge for the commode to bob closer to them. When the commode carrying her landlady finally was within firing range, the guards raised their riffles and fired at it.

The next day Bertrand left the house and started looking for a new place to stay. Since he did not have a car, he walked along South Broadway Street and scanned the 'ROOM TO LET' signs displayed in shop windows. He visited scores of newsprint stands, liquor stores and confectionery shops, and wrote down the phone numbers of prospective landlords on a piece of paper. After collecting a few telephone numbers, he stopped at a telephone booth to call the landlords and inquire about the rooms. When he called the first number on the list, an English woman answered the phone. The woman told him that the room was still available. Elated, Bertrand boarded a London Transport bus for Sudbury Town to view the room. When he showed up at her door, the English woman smiled and beckoned him into the house. Just then, a man whom Bertrand presumed was her husband, walked out of an adjoining room and stood next to her. When he saw that Bertrand was a colored man, he quickly said in an Irish accent: "The room has been let." The English woman turned to her husband and gaped in surprise.

"No, it has not," she stammered.

Her husband slammed the door shut on Bertrand's face. Disappointed and deeply hurt, Bertrand resumed his search and made appointments to view other rooms. He viewed a room in a house owned by a young Pakistani couple in Sudbury Hill. The Pakistani landlord told him that he would not be allowed to smoke in the room or bring in visitors. He also restricted him to just one bath per week. Bertrand was stunned at the unusual restriction on bathing. He agreed not to smoke or bring visitors to his room, but insisted on bathing every day. When the couple refused, Bertrand passed up on the room. He left the couple's house and boarded the bus to Harrow-on-the-Hill to view another room. When he knocked on the door, a turbaned Sikh greeted him and showed him the room. The carpet in the room, to his dismay, was loosely laid down and unclean. He inquired if the landlord could have the carpet tacked down and cleaned up before he moved in. The owner became irate at his request. He started to gesticulate and to shout at him, telling him to mind his own business. Bertrand became frightened and quickly left the house. He spent the next three days pounding the pavement and looking for a decent place to live, but was unable to find one as quickly as he would like to. By midweek he decided to browse the window ads in another area of town. His landlord did not seem pleased that he was staying another week. The following week Bertrand boarded the train to South Harrow to view another room. The landlord showed him a box room on the second floor of a two-story building facing a railroad track. The room measured 8ft by 6ft. It was furnished with a single bed, an armoire, a metal table and a wooden chair. The worn-out carpet was not tacked down, but Bertrand kept his mouth shut less the landlord would ask him to leave. The landlord, an Indian immigrant, was however very polite and was very eager to have him as a tenant. He pointed to the loose carpet and told him that he would have it replaced before he moved in. Despite its small size, Bertrand rented the box room from the landlord for £6 a week. Four other tenants already lived in the house. The tenants shared one bathroom on the upper floor and one small kitchen on the first floor. The kitchen was so filthy that when he returned to his old room, he sat down at his desk and wrote a poem to describe the filthy kitchen.

Soon after he found a new place to stay, Bertrand went shopping for an alarm clock. There were several clocks displayed on the shelves. They ranged from the old-fashioned alarm clock with two large bells mounted on top of the clock to more modern-looking clocks with cartoon characters on the clock faces. On one clock, a rooster pecked on the ground when the alarm sounded. On another, a soccer player kicked a soccer ball when the clock chimed. Bertrand purchased the alarm clock that produced the loudest rings: the Big Ben clock. The alarm clock displayed big roman numerals on its face, had two large bells mounted on the top of the clock, and rang eight times at interval of two minutes. The clock had a feature that Bertrand thought would be very useful in getting him out of bed. The alarm could not be shut off.

The following Saturday Bertrand moved out of the English couple's house. He had stayed with the English couple for less than three months. Moving to his new room was simple and quick. His possession consisted of one suitcase containing clothing, a box with some books in it, and a new alarm clock that he had named Clox. The English landlord, eager for him to leave, called a cab. He carried his suitcase and put it in the cab. Before bidding him good-bye, the landlord reminded him to tip the British cabby. "It's a British tradition," he said. "They expect you to give them a tip." His landlady never came out of her room to see him off.

For the first few days, Bertrand faithfully woke up to Clox's ringing. The loud ringing of the two bells jolted him from his deep sleep. When he went back to sleep after the first ring, the clock's second thunderous ring woke him up again. When he dozed off again, the third ring stirred him up. By the time Clox rattled its fifth ring, Bertrand could no longer put up with the awful noise. He got out of bed to get away from the clock and go to work. After spending a few weeks waking up to the sound of Clox, Bertrand began to examine the mechanical clock to find a way of shutting off the dreadful sound. The constant waking up and dozing off in the morning were wearing him off to the point where he became tired and sleepy during the day. He soon discovered that he could shut off the alarm by simply advancing the hour hand forward. Now that he knew how to shut off Clox's ear-splitting rings, he could stay in bed longer and savor a few more minutes of sleep. Then he started arriving late for work once again. He failed to wake up on time and he frequently went to work without brushing his teeth and without shaving. He was so afraid that he would be late for work that he wore his suit, tie and shoes when he went to bed so that he would be ready in the morning. But despite all his careful planning, he was always tardy for work. When the bus or the train was late making their routes, which happened from time to time, Bertrand did not get into the office until an hour and a half later.

Whether he arrived in the office on time or not, he was always sleepy and he had trouble staying alert during the day. His clothes appeared like they had just been washed and wrung dry. His hair was disorderly and his mouth was filled with a foul smell. Every morning he quietly walked past the other accounting clerks with his head down and prayed that no one would notice his tardiness. Sometimes he intentionally did not punch his timecard so that his tardiness would not be noticed when his Supervisor checks the employees' timecards at the end of the week. His Supervisor had however noticed that he frequently did not punch his timecard. He warned Bertrand that he would terminate his employment if he neglected to punch his timecard.

In the summer of 1971 Bertrand feared that his Supervisor would fire him for his frequent tardiness. He quit his job and enrolled in a Photography course at Harrow College of Technology and Art. To support himself while he went to college, he worked in a Wimpy Bar close to the school. Since his classes did not start until nine-thirty in the morning, he no longer relied on Clox's booming rings to wake him up. Consequently, he relieved Clox from its morning duty and incarcerated it in a dusty drawer.

The Wimpy Bar closed at midnight, but he did not leave the restaurant until all the customers had left and the place was cleaned up. The chef cleaned the kitchen area. The dishwasher lady cleaned and dried the plates and cutlery. The waiters and waitresses cleaned the tables, the ice cream machine and the two tall coffeemakers. Bertrand collected the garbage bags and took them out to the dumpster. He also swept the floor and refilled the condiment bottles. The night Manager cleared the cash register and tallied the day's receipts. After his work was done, Bertrand waited for the night Manager to take him home. The night Manager frequently hanged around the restaurant with his friends after closing time. Sometimes they just sat around to drink Turkish coffee and play poker. Sometimes they played poker until four o'clock in the morning. There were no buses after 11:00 P.M. and Bertrand could not afford the taxi fare. So on poker nights, he patiently waited for the poker game to end so that the Manager could take him home. Sometimes he walked home instead of waiting for the poker game to end. Most nights, he did not return to his dig until two o'clock in the morning. The other tenants were night owls and were all awake when he returned home. They would gather in someone's room and spend the night drinking or just talking. Working at night gave Bertrand the opportunity to meet the other tenants. The woman occupying the room next to him was from Edinburgh, Scotland. She was, like himself, a student by day and a waitress by night. A week after he had moved in, she woke up him up at three o'clock and asked him to fix a lamp in her room. He found that the lamp was unplugged. When he plugged in the lamp, the light came on. When he turned around to leave, he saw the young woman lying half-naked on a sleeping cot with her eyes closed. Her bedroom gown was lying on the floor next to the couch.

"The lamp is working now," he said.

"You are not supposed to plug it back. Turn it off," she snapped, without opening her eyes.

Instead of turning off the lamp, Bertrand walked up to the sleeping cot and gazed at her. The Scottish woman opened her eyes and removed her bra. Bertrand felt her legs shivering under him and he dropped down on his knees. Breathing heavily, he reached out to the woman's underwear and pulled it down her legs.

The Scottish woman was not always in her room in the evenings. Whenever she was in her room and he felt lonely, Bertrand knocked on the woman's door and asked her if she had anything that needed fixing. Sometimes the woman replied in the negative and closed the door. Sometimes she let him in and they spent the time together in her room. Her sleeping cot was small, so most of the time they spent the night together lying and sleeping on the floor. Then the woman disappeared for several days. She suddenly reappeared one night accompanied by a black man. The two of them spent the night going from her bedroom to the bathroom and vice versa. They slammed the door each time they returned from the bathroom and kept him awake all through the night.

The fellow living downstairs was an architecture student from Pakistan. He was very friendly, sometimes too friendly. He traveled every day to Central London to attend classes. After classes he frequently stopped at Trafalgar Square to capture a pair of pigeons to bring home for his dinner. He used breadcrumbs which he carried in his briefcase to attract the pigeons to him. While the pigeons pecked at the breadcrumbs, he took his hat off and slammed it on the pigeons. Then he stuffed the pigeons in his coat pockets and boarded the train back to South Harrow. One day a pigeon flew out of his pocket when the ticket inspector asked him to show his train ticket. When he tried to catch the pigeon, the second pigeon came out of his other coat pocket and flew around the train compartment. Instead of trying to catch the pigeons, he got off at the next station and returned to Trafalgar Square to catch another. In the evening the Pakistani student killed the pigeons and made pigeon meat curry. When he was done cooking and eating the pigeons, he came into Bertrand's room carrying a copy of the KAMASUTRA book of love. He made himself comfortable in his room and quoted love passages from the book. After quoting a passage, he calmly said to Bertrand: "Let's take our clothes off and try love position #13." When Bertrand refused, he undressed and climbed on his bed. Exasperated, Bertrand ordered him out of his room. Whenever the Pakistani man showed up at his door carrying the book of love, he refused to let him in.

Almost every night Bertrand found another tenant, a young Englishman, squatting amidst bicycle or television parts on the kitchen floor or in the hallway. When the Englishman was badly in need of money, he knocked on his door to try to sell him a refurbished TV set, a radio or a bicycle. For a reason unknown to Bertrand, the Englishman always had to have the money before daybreak. On one occasion, the Englishman woke him up at night to buy back a TV set that he had sold to him a few days earlier. The Englishman would not take 'No' for an answer and stood by his door until Bertrand gave him back TV set. One night the Englishman sold him a used bicycle, but he would not accept a check from him. The deal was too good to pass up, but Bertrand did not have any money in his room. He called the Wimpy Bar to check if the Manager was still in the restaurant. As he expected, the Manager was still in the restaurant playing poker with his friends. He rode the bicycle three miles to the Wimpy Bar to borrow money from the Manager. When he got there, the Manager refused to be distracted from his poker game. He made Bertrand wait an hour and a half before he finally loaned him £10 to buy the bike. When Bertrand finally rode back with the cash, the sun had started to peek out. When he returned to his flat, the Englishman was sound asleep in his room. The next day the Englishman sold the bike to someone else.

The tenant occupying the room next to the Scottish student was an Irishman. One night he woke up and left his room stark naked to use the bathroom. After using the bathroom he went into the Scottish student's room and tried to make love to her. She was sleeping alone that night. She ran out of her room and sought refuge in the Pakistani student's room. Thirty minutes later Bertrand heard a loud crash coming from the Pakistani student's room, then dead silence. When he inquired about the noise the following night, the Pakistani student told him that the bed frame came loose from the headboard while he made love to the Scottish woman. After that night, the Scottish woman disappeared again.

On several occasions, Bertrand found the Indian landlord in his room when he came home after work. Somehow he had found out that Bertrand had bought a new record player. Bertrand had a Ravi Shankar music album that he liked to listen to at night. The landlord sat on his bed and listened to the Ravi Shankar music. He moved and shook his head in rhythm to the music with his eyes closed. He was unaware that Bertrand was in the room until Bertrand closed the door. On another night the landlord waited for him in his room to inquire about two female tenants living in the adjoining house that he owned. He had noticed a large number of men visiting the female tenants every day. After watching the two women over several days, he concluded that the two black women were prostitutes. When he tried to evict them, one of the women surged at him and scratched his face with her fingernails. Then they started to beat him up. The two women punched and kicked him until he fell and rolled down the stairs. The following day, the landlord summoned the police to remove the two women from their rooms. When the policemen arrived, the women resisted the officers' eviction order.

Their kicking and screaming woke Bertrand up and he went outside to see what all the fuss was about. The landlord was in shock.

"They are whores," he explained to Bertrand. "They are bringing men in their rooms day and night. I had to call the police to get them out of my house."

A few days after the women were evicted, they suddenly showed up at the Wimpy Bar where he worked. The prostitutes recognized Bertrand and shouted profanities at him. They accused him of tipping the landlord about their true identities. The restaurant owner threatened to call the police, and they left the Wimpy Bar without causing any more trouble. The most taciturn tenant, an Ethiopian student from Addis Ababa, was also the noisiest. When everybody was sleeping, he tapped on his typewriter keyboard for hours and hours. Later he surprised all of us by announcing the he had written a novel which he had titled 'A Tale of Three Cities.'

During his last semester at Harrow College, Bertrand and a group of students went to Dorset to shoot a film. Their English instructor had kindly allowed them the use of his country dwelling, the Nutbloom Cottage in Hazelbury Bryans. Since they only had four days to complete the filming, it was imperative that they began filming early in the morning. Bertrand took Clox with him so they would have an alarm clock to wake up the crew. It was a bitterly cold and blustery winter. The cottage had no hot water and no heating. A small electric heater was they had in the cottage. There was a small fireplace in the living room, but the owner had advised the students that it was unsafe to use. Two pairs of footprints, one pair smaller than the other, were stamped in black paint on the wall above the fireplace. The students took turn to impose their feet on the footprints. They chuckled and commented on the footprints' clean lines, shapely toes, and tapered arches. In the minds of the students, the smaller tracks conjured up the image of a fairy princess, whereas the larger tracks reminded them of that man's cousin, Bigfoot. Someone guessed aloud that the woman's footprint was made by a visiting professor from Chicago. The professor frequently climbed on the table in the visual art laboratory and sat with her legs crossed to deliver her lectures. Her sitting posture and Midwestern drawl drew comments from one English student that the professor came from an eccentric Mafia family. He speculated that the two female footprints on the wall was her clan's stamp of terror. The small cottage had a kitchen and shower room in the back. The two actresses, on loan from a drama school in London, spent the night sleeping in the attic. The crew of six men, including Bertrand, slept in the living room. It was so cold in the cottage that Bertrand wore three layers of clothing to stay warm at night. He shared a bed with Maddox who was responsible for putting together the soundtrack for the film. Bertrand set up the alarm clock before they settled in for the night. Wilcox, the cameraman, and Box, the lighting technician, slept next to each other on the floor in the middle of the room. The assistant cameraman, Cox curled up in his sleeping bag in front of the fireplace. Lenox, who was assigned the tasks of creating the still photographs as well as cooking dinner for the crew, slept close to the door leading to the small kitchen. Maddox, instead of going to sleep, strapped his NAGRA tape recorder on his shoulder and left the cottage to record the sound of the birds and the wind. The students were filming 'The Night of the Soldier,' a ghost story written by Bertrand.

It started to rain soon after Maddox left the cottage. The rain forced Maddox to stop recording and return to the cottage. Before going to sleep, he played back the tapes to listen to whatever sound he picked up outside. He did not realize that the volume knob was accidentally moved to its maximum level. So when he pushed on the Play Back button, a howling wind from the tape jostled everyone up from their sleep. The bearded Box broke out of his sleeping bag and shook Wilcox up. The waggish Wilcox wallowed in his sleeping bag and turned to face the wall. The lean Lenox leaped out of his sleeping back and rushed into the kitchen to escape the howling wind. He feared that the wind had blown apart the antiquated cottage. The charismatic Cox chuckled and growled.

"Maddox, shut that machine off and go to sleep."

"I am going to in a short while," Maddox mischievously murmured, covering his lips with his index finger. He adjusted the volume down, covered his ears with a headphone, and continued to review the audiotapes.

The rain whipped the old cottage's stone walls and the wind bellowed and rattled the windows, sending chills down Bertrand's spine and causing his hair to stand on his head. The storm kept him awake for some time. When he finally fell asleep, he dreamed of headless medieval knights galloping on horseback and chasing him into the Dover Cliffs. Soon, the dark and ancient cottage was engulfed with the deep snoring of the students. Maddox finally removed the headphone from his ears and put the NAGRA tape recorder away. He climbed on the bed and slid into his sleeping bag. Bertrand had placed Clox on the windowsill above Maddox's head. In the still of the night Clox ticked the seconds away: "Tic toc, tic toc, tic toc..."

Early the next day Bertrand, was abruptly woken up by Clox's first ring. He turned on his side and clamped his sleeping bag around his neck to keep out the chilly air. Two minutes later Clox sounded the second ring. Maddox popped his head out of his sleeping bag and snarled: "Bertrand, shut that alarm clock off!" The bitter cold inside the cottage kept Bertrand inside his sleeping bag. He turned over and curled up in his sleeping bag to stay warm and to enjoy a few more minutes of sleep. Then the third ring chimed.

"Bertrand," Maddox grumbled. "If you don't shut off that alarm clock, I will throw it out of the window." Bertrand ignored Maddox's murmurs of discontent and hardly moved. When the fourth ring tinkled, Maddox stuck his head out of his sleeping back and screamed: "Bertrand, I mean it. Shut off that damn clock!" When the fifth ring clanged, Maddox stuck his head out of his sleeping bag and snatched the clock from the windowsill. His mouth foaming with rage, he threw it across the room. The clock hit the wall hard and fell close to Cox who was wrapped up like a mummy in his sleeping bag. It continued to tick away the time. When it suddenly rang again, the maddened Maddox climbed out of bed, picked up the clock and threw it into the kitchen. Maddox then crawled into his sleeping bag to sleep.

The noise finally stirred Cox out of his slumber and he stuck his head out of his sleeping bag to look at what was going on. He thought that the situation was rather hilarious and burst into a roar of laughter. Braving the biting cold, Bertrand climbed out of bed and stepped over the sleeping students to retrieve Clox. He shook it and brought it close to his ears. The clock was still ticking away the time. Bertrand climbed back on the bed and put it back on the windowsill. Then Clox jangled the seventh ring. Furious at the ear-rendering tintinnabulation, Maddox broke out of his sleeping bag again to reach out for the clock. Bertrand leaped to the windowsill and snatched it before Maddox got to it. He moved the hour hand forward to shut off the alarm. By that time everyone in the room was awake and laughing. The crew chef went to boil water to make tea and cook breakfast. The actresses climbed down the attic to prepare themselves for the day.

"It's time to get up, Maddox," Cox said, giggling and sliding out of his sleeping bag. "Come on, Maddox, get up! We have a long day ahead of us."

"I am going to in a short while," Maddox murmured. Thirty minutes later, while everyone was packing the camera gear and filming equipment in the cars, Maddox was still snoring. Cox went to wake him up.

"You were out all night recording the wind instead of sleeping," Cox reprimanded him. "Get up and let's get going."

"I am going to in a short while," Maddox muttered.

"What time do you want the alarm to go off?" Bertrand said, holding Clox up over Maddox's head and pretending to set the alarm.

"Don't you dare," Maddox mumbled. "I'll kill you if that clock goes off again." The crew left the cottage without Maddox to start filming.

It was not until they returned to Harrow a few days later that Bertrand found out that Clox had sustained some damage. The clock was still functioning and showing the time correctly, but it would only sound the alarm once. Maddox's morning madness had mauled his mission timer. Fortunately Bertrand no longer relied on Clox to wake him up. He received his Diploma in Applied Photography in 1974. He spent the next few months looking for a job. After a fruitless job search in London and several other cities, he gave up looking for a job in Film and Television and returned to the Wimpy Bar to work. Money was running out and he could not afford to stay unemployed for a long period of time. Bertrand tried to enroll at the Royal School of Art, the National Film School, the London Polytechnic, and the

London School of Journalism to supplement what he had learned at HTCA. His application was turned down by all these institutions. Just for kicks, he applied at the prestigious *L'Institut Des Hautes Etudes Cinematographiques (L'IDHEC)* to study Films. The French Film Institute invited him for an interview and he took the train to Paris for the interview. He took Clox along with him on the trip to Paris. It's ringing made quite a few train passengers furious. The interview turned out to be nothing more than exchanging a few words with a pair of students from the School. L'IDHEC turned him down, but he was not surprised. As he was unable to continue his education and he was also unable to land a job in his chosen profession, he continued to work at the Wimpy Bar at night. After work he spent his time writing and tapping on the typewriter keyboard until dawn. Then he would go to bed and sleep until mid-morning. Since he slept late, woke up late, and was never late for work, he had no further need for an alarm clock. On May 20, 1977 Bertrand married his girlfriend Clorox (born Chloe Ox.) Bertrand made an oral prenuptial agreement with Clorox whereby she would allow Clox to stay with them, no matter how loud the clock was. Clorox reluctantly agreed. Clorox was never fond of the Big Ben Clock. She complained that it was too loud. About two months after they were married, the couple migrated to America. Clorox did not want to take Clox with them to America, but Bertrand insisted that the old clock should go to America too. He had become attached to the clock, and it would break his heart to leave the working clock behind. So when they departed from England, Bertrand packed Clox in a duffel bag and carried it with him to Dallas where the old-fashioned mechanical clock would later meet his more sophisticated cousins. Clox was so thrilled about flying to America that it clanged with joy when the plane took off. A new life awaited the migrant Clock and its master in America. The travelling clock and his master and new mistress arrived in Dallas on July 7, 1977.

The first of Clox's American cousins was Radox, an analog radio alarm clock. His brother-in-law, Zhang Fu Ox gave the clock as a wedding present to Bertrand. Zhang Fu Ox and his wife Xie Zhu disapproved of his sister's marriage to Bertrand. Zhang Fu was a Dermatologist and Xie was a trained, but unemployed Chemical Engineer. Zhang Fu acted very much like the castrated male of domestic cattle. He ploughed tracks into the minds of Clorox so that the seeds of family discord would be sowed into them. The notion of a man contemplating a career as a photographer, filmmaker, or writer did not bode well with the priggish couple. For the next two years, the arrogant couple belittled and scorned him. The slim electric alarm clock was the first of its kind that Bertrand had seen and owned. He liked the idea of waking up to music in the morning, and he was thrilled to be able to choose between a buzzer and music to wake him up. Instead of the traditional sweeping hands, Radox displayed the time in large white numbers. The large numbers made it easier for Bertrand to see the time in the dark. Unlike Clox,

Radox did not require winding up each night. With Radox now stealing the limelight, the migrant Clox was tucked away in a closet.

Like most immigrants who arrived in America, Bertrand took the first job that was offered to him. Landing a job was more important to him than doing the things that he wanted to do. Two weeks after he set foot in Dallas, he was hired by a film-processing laboratory to process films at night. He worked from six o'clock in the evening till three o'clock in the morning and he was paid $3.10 an hour. Because he was already used to working nights while living in London, Bertrand adapted quickly to his new work schedule. He soon discovered that the TV stations in America transmitted their programs 24 hours a day. When he came back home from work, he stayed up and watched television until dawn. Sometimes he spent the night painting the walls or hanging wallpaper. Working at night eventually altered his circadian rhythms. Two months later Bertrand gave up the $3.10 an hour job at the film-processing laboratory on Prudential Drive for a better-paying job in a factory on Mockingbird Lane. The new job paid $750 a month.

His new job at the factory was erratic. One week he was working from six o'clock in the morning to six o'clock at night, and the next week he was working from six o'clock at night to six o'clock in the morning. On his days off he was frequently called to work when an employee did not show up. Whenever an emergency situation developed, his Supervisor summoned him back to work the moment he came home. As a result of working odd hours, Bertrand started to have difficulties falling and staying asleep. He felt sleepy whenever he drove to work, particularly in the late afternoon. Sometimes he could not keep his eyes opened while he drove to work. He frequently pulled into a gas station to take a short nap. When he worked on the night shift he had trouble keeping his eyes open. Bertrand befriended a technician working on the night shift. During their lunch breaks they withdrew into the lunchroom to eat lunch or drink coffee. After eating, they would both fall asleep. Later the night foreman walked in the lunchroom. He saw them sleeping at the lunch table and kicked at the chair closest to him, shouting: "You are fired!" to the sleeping technician. Bertrand woke up and watched frightfully as his work buddy got up and ran out of the building. After the incident, Bertrand started bringing Clox to work. He began to feel stressed out and depressed by his lack of sleep. He became sluggish and careless and eventually lost interest in his work. When things were not too hectic, he climbed on a catwalk and stacked empty cardboard boxes around him. Then he set the alarm clock and hid behind the cardboard boxes to steal a few minutes of sleep.

Bertrand began to have trouble sleeping at night when he was scheduled to work days. He stayed awake for long period of time, tossing and rolling on his bed throughout most of the night. His chronic sleeplessness woke Clorox frequently, and she too began to feel tired and groggy. Night after night, he spent long hours in the grip of unremitting insomnia. When he finally fell asleep, a tingling sensation in his foot caused his leg to jerk up, causing him to wake up again. About every two hours, his restless-leg syndrome jolted him back to consciousness. On a normal night the leg twitching woke him five or six times. His turning and tossing in bed exasperated Clorox. One night she gave him two sleeping tablets and begged him to take them. At first Bertrand refused to take the pills. He was afraid that the sleeping pills would make it harder for him to wake up. Clorox then pleaded with him to take one sleeping pill, but he still would not take it. Finally Clorox split the sleeping pill in half and gave him one half of the tablet. Again, he refused. She split the half tablet into two quarters and begged him to take one quarter of the pill. Bertrand reluctantly gave in and swallowed the morsel of sleeping pill with a glass of water. A few moments later he felt that the bedroom ceiling was caving in and turning on its side. His head started to spin, slowly at first, then at a rapid pace. The furniture whizzed at a furious pace around him, sinking and bobbing like a carousel. He was drawn into a deep black hole. The furniture was sucked into the black hole too. Then his mind blacked out and he found himself at the head of a group of commandos holding and securing a bridge spanned over the river where he spent his childhood. The commandos fought against invisible soldiers. Machine guns rattled and spit out red and orange flames, bullets hissed over their heads, and grenades exploded around them. Above them planes crisscrossed the sky. Bertrand stood valiantly at the head of his men. He provided cover to them while they crossed the bridge so that they could go fishing on the other side of the river. When they had all safely reached the other bank, the airplanes dropped tons of US dollar bills over them. He watched helplessly as his men drowned under the massive amount of greenbacks. Bertrand dropped his gun and retreated to higher ground. He waded in the paper money around him and raised his hands to fend off the deluge of paper money falling from the sky. Then he heard Clorox shouting: "Stop pulling on the blanket."

When he woke up in the morning, Bertrand felt that his eyelids were glued shut. He felt drowsy from the effect of taking the sleeping pill. Clorox pulled him out of the bed, but he dropped back on the mattress and wrapped his arms around the pillow. She wet a towel with hot water and wiped his face with it. Then she went in the shower stall and turned on the water. Bertrand rolled over the edge of the bed and onto the floor. With his eyes still glued shut, he slowly and painfully crawled to the bathroom. Clorox became terrified. "Are you okay?" she cried.

Bertrand opened one eye and looked at Clorox. "I told you that the sleeping pill will knock my senses out," he moaned. "You did not believe me, did you?" He heaved and dragged his body to the bathroom while Clorox watched helplessly.

"I don't think that you should take it tonight," Clorox said.

15

She watched him while he showered to make sure that he does not fall in the shower stall and hurt his head. "It was only a quarter of a pill," she added. "I wonder what one whole sleeping pill will do to you."

"Probably put me to sleep for two days," Bertrand replied, as the hot water and steam began to wake him up.

Whenever Clorox worked on the night shift, Bertrand placed heavy reliance on Radox to wake him up. Eventually not even the loud persistent buzzing of Radox could arouse him from his deep sleep. He tried waking up at the sound of rock-and-roll music, but the music rocked-and-rolled him back to sleep. Then he reverted back to the buzzer, but the buzzer's unpleasant tone irritated him. He frequently grumbled when the alarm clock wailed. "God," he moaned. "I am living in a big city and I have this cow right in my bedroom to disturb my sleep."

Working odd hours at the factory was causing him to lose sleep. He left the company and took another job as a shipping clerk at another company, Clean Data System, Inc. He was hired to work on the day shift. Bertrand decided to go back to College to learn computer programming. In the fall of 1978, he enrolled at the Dallas County Community College to pursue a degree in Information Systems. In 1980, he transferred to the University of Texas At Arlington to complete the degree program.

Four years after arriving in Dallas, Bertrand and Clorox divorced. Clorox complained that Bertrand was not earning enough money. She boasted that she was earning three times what he was earning and thus deserved a man who earned more than he did. It was, however, more than just the issue of money that broke down their marriage. Xie Zhu had constantly reproached her sister-in-law for marrying a bum. Another reason was that Clorox, soon after arriving in America, had succumbed to a materialistic lifestyle. She worshipped money, worked overtime at every opportunity to boost her income, and spent the extra money earned on material things. Bertrand was dumbfounded when she bought a vacuum cleaner with a canister cast like a piglet for $250. Clorox had never vacuumed the carpet since he had known her. Her kimono caught fire when she cooked breakfast for him while they lived in England, and she burnt their Turkey dinner on their first Thanksgiving Day in America. The Turkey looked like Yorich's head when Bertrand removed it from the oven. Because of their different work schedules, Bertrand rarely saw Clorox. He saw and kissed the faces of Clox and Radox more than Clorox's. The inevitable just had to happen. While he went to night school to study Computer Science, the crabby Clorox courted a two-legged jackass named Jox. Bertrand confronted her about her escapades with Jox, but she refused to break up her relationship with him. Instead she admitted that she was in love with Jox and would like to continue seeing him. She told Bertrand that being married to him should not stop her from dating another man. Unwilling to live with a woman who was cheating on him,

Bertrand subsequently filed for divorce. Clorox left and moved in Jox's apartment. A few days later, while he was at work, the jumbo Jox jockeyed into their house and hauled the furniture, the television set and stereo equipment away. They left behind his personal belongings, his dirty laundry, huge unpaid bills, a few unwanted items, his books and two alarm clocks. Bertrand and Clorox were divorced in May 12, 1981. As part of the divorce settlement, Bertrand would take custody of Clox and Radox.

Clox was now eleven years old and Radox had just turned four years. Together, they squawked, beeped and purred to wake him up and then put him back to sleep. They cheered him up when he woke up alone in the morning. A few weeks after Clorox moved out, Bertrand started a new job that required him to work during the day. Radox, which was not as robust as Clox, soon developed mechanical problems. Bertrand blamed Radox's frailty on the fact that the electrical clock was built in the USA. Clox, on the other hand, was built in Great Britain. It was in his opinion the strongest mechanical clock ever built by the British. It was not as big as the 13-ton Big Ben clock in the tower of the House of Parliament, but it was as strong as her. Even after it traveled 12 feet inside the Nutbloom Cottage and hit two walls, it kept on working. Sir Benjamin Hall, after whom the massive Big Ben clock was named, would have been proud of the smaller Big Ben clock.

Now that Bertrand worked during the day, he grew more dependent on his two alarm clocks to wake him up on time. Radox, unfortunately, was becoming increasingly weak day after day. The clock frequently displayed the incorrect time. Sometimes the hour hand and minute hand stopped going around. The radio sometimes would suddenly stop working or the buzzer would remain silent. Bertrand spent many hours tinkering with Radox to see what was ailing it. He discovered that the numbers that made up the time were printed on plastic cards like a Rolodex index card system. A mechanism inside the clock caused the cards to flip down every minute to show the new time. The cards jammed and would not flip down when the minute changed. He tilted the clock to one side to loosen up the cards, thus causing the hour or minute cards to flip over and show the correct time. But this worked for a few days only. Then the time would stand still again on Radox's face.

Bertrand had cultivated the bad habit of shutting off the radio or the buzzer on Radox when they go off. As a result of doing this, he began to be late for work again. He began to look for new ways to prevent him from falling asleep again after he woke up. First he positioned Clox close to the bathroom so that he had to get up and walk by the bathroom to turn it off. That did not work for after getting up and shutting off Clox, he returned to his bed and went back to sleep. Then he plugged a vacuum cleaner into a timer and directed the nozzle towards his face. He abandoned this idea when the noise and the air suction irked him. Radox finally stopped working in the summer of 1981. He was reluctant to spend his money on another alarm clock and for a few months relied entirely on Clox to wake him up. When Clox failed several times to wake him up, he finally drove to the mall and bought a new alarm clock. It was Bertrand's first Digital clock and he christened the new alarm clock Digitox. Digitox had a bright LED display screen that helped him see the time in the dark with his eyes half closed. Soon after the arrival of Digitox, Clox's health went from bad to worse. Its voice grew weaker and weaker. It clanged intermittently and for a shorter duration. It gasped for breath before reaching the finish line. Sometimes the mechanical clock stopped running in the dead of the night. The final blow came to Clox one night when Bertrand brought home a woman he had met in a bar. While they made love in his bedroom, the woman's body shook violently and bucked like a bronco when she experienced orgasm. Her sudden spasmodic jerks almost threw Bertrand off the bed. When the woman reached out for the nightstand for support, she knocked the lamp off the table. The heavy lamp fell on Clox and both the lamp and the clock fell down on the floor. For what seemed like an eternity, Bertrand clung onto the woman while she shook. When her body finally relaxed, he released his hold on her and picked up the clock to examine it. The British-built clock had finally gasped its last breath in an American bedroom. Before it died, it clanged a faint: "No Sex Please. We are British!" Fortunately, Digitox sat on another nightstand and was not damaged by the tempest the lurid and concupiscent woman brewed up in his bedroom.

When Bertrand examined the clock again a few days later, he discovered that Clox after all was not completely dead. He unscrewed the back panel and meticulously removed the clock parts. He cleaned and dipped the parts in machine oil to lubricate them. Then he carefully reassembled the clock. To his astonishment, the clock started to work again. In fact it worked better than before. But not for very long! As he drove through a small town late one night, Bertrand overtook a car in front of him without realizing that the car he had just passed was a police car. It was two o'clock in the morning and there was not another car on the street. Bertrand was returning home after spending more than three hours in the computer lab at the University of Texas at Arlington. He had to complete his computer assignment as it was due on the next day. When he overtook the police car, the officer immediately turned on his red and blue warning lights and pursued him. Baffled, Bertrand slowed down and drove in a parking lot. He thought that he must have annoyed the police officer when he sped past him. The police officer cautiously approached his vehicle while his companion walked around the other side with his hand close to his gun. Bertrand rolled his window down.

"I flagged you down because your headlight is out of alignment," the officer explained. "The right beam is too bright. It will need to be adjusted."

The police officer removed a notepad from his shirt pocket and started to write him a citation. "It's just a warning this time," he warned him. "If you don't have the headlight beam corrected the next time I see you driving around here, I will give you a ticket."

Just then the alarm on Bertrand's mechanical clock went off. The officer dropped the notepad and reached for his gun. "Watch out," he yelled at his companion. "He's got a time-bomb in the car." The second officer dashed to the car and pulled open the door with one hand while the other hand held a revolver.

"Freeze," the officer screamed. He pointed his revolver at Bertrand. "Come out now. Get out!" Terrified, Bertrand scrambled out of his car and raised his hands over his head. "Get down," the officer yelled. "Get down on the floor," Bertrand lied down on his stomach. "Who is in the car with you?" the officer shouted.

"It's Clox," Bertrand replied.

"Who is it?"

"It's a mechanical clock."

"The noise came from a clock?" The officer asked.

"The alarm just went off," Bertrand explained.

The second policeman flung open the passenger door and cautiously removed the clock.. "It's a clock with big bells on top of it," he said. "I have not seen anything like it for years. It is not a bomb."

The first officer relaxed and put his revolver back into the holster. He stared at Bertrand lying down on the ground.

"Are you nuts?"

"Maybe," Bertrand timidly replied. Clox suddenly clanged the second alarm while in the hands of the second officer. The officer dropped the clock and coiled back.

"Don't drop my clock," Bertrand screamed. The clock fell to the ground with a thud and broke into several pieces. Bertrand got back on his feet and picked the clock's casing up. "You broke my clock," he said to the second officer.

"You must be nuts," the first officer said.

"I think so," Bertrand replied.

"Do you always carry an alarm clock in your car?"

"It keeps me awake and alive."

Bertrand handed the police officer his driver's license.

The first officer finished up writing the ticket and handed it to him. They looked at each other and walked back to their patrol car. Clox had finally found death on the main street of a small US town. It was an undignified death for a clock that migrated to America to trumpet better days for its master. Saddened by Clox's violent death, Bertrand picked up the pieces of the clock and drove home with tears in his eyes. When he came home, he placed the clock pieces on the kitchen table and went to bed. The next day he reassembled the clock. When all the parts were put back together, he wound the clock and held it near his ear. There was no sound coming from the clock. The bruised Clox was silent forever. Unable to breathe life back into his mechanical clock, Bertrand laid it down to rest in the hallway closet.

In 1983 Bertrand reluctantly dropped out of UTA. Clorox had left him with a huge amount of debt, and he could no longer afford to pay the college tuition or buy the textbooks which sometimes cost more than the tuition itself. Clorox agreed to put their house up for sale. She however refused to continue paying the mortgage payments. Bertrand decided to borrow ten thousand dollars from a local bank so he could buy Clorox's share of the home equity. With a house payment, a car payment, the new ten thousand dollars loan, and an assortment of credit card debts, he began to have difficulties making ends meet. To alleviate his financial burden, he took over a newspaper route from a neighbor who could no longer do it. Everyday he woke up at four o'clock to start his newspaper route. After delivering the newspapers, which usually took one to two hours, he returned home to sleep. When Digitox sounded its high-pitched jingles, he was unable to wake up. On weekends, he had a hundred and sixty more papers to deliver. In addition to the extra papers, the Sunday edition was bulkier and required a longer time to wrap up and deliver. He had to make two trips in order to deliver all the Sunday papers by seven o'clock. When he first took the paper route, he calculated that the paper route would earn him an additional $300 a month. This amount would have been adequate for paying all the bills. Unfortunately, more than half of the subscribers did not pay him for the papers. He collected one hundred and sixty-five dollars in a good month, but had to spend a good portion of his evenings going from door to door to collect the money. Since he was still unable to pay all his bills with the money from the paper route, Bertrand took another part-time job in a liquor store working from 5.00 P.M. to 9.30 P.M. With so little time left for sleeping, he started to doze off during his paper rounds. He had difficulties keeping his eyes open and frequently stopped to sleep. He sometimes found himself tossing newspapers in unfamiliar streets. Many of the papers that he threw out of the window landed on top of the subscribers' cars. Sometimes the paper slid out of the plastic bag and flew in all direction before landing on the front yard. He often wondered how he could drive a car, sleep at the wheel, and deliver newspapers all at the same time. Strangely enough, no one complained about newspapers being scattered everywhere on the front lawns.

One evening, as he pondered in the kitchen about his sleeping problem, he heard a muffled sound coming from the bedroom. The noise stopped when he went to investigate. Ten minutes later he heard the noise again. The sound was coming out of the closet in the hallway, not from the bedroom as he had thought. When he opened the closet door, he heard his mechanical clock faintly sounding up the alarm. Clox had suddenly come alive again. But instead of ringing eight times like it used to, it rang only three times. The next day Bertrand took Clox along with him during his morning paper round. When he could no longer keep his eyes open, he parked his car away from the streetlight, set the alarm and went to sleep. All he needed was a short nap. When Clox tingled, he resumed his paper delivery. One morning he fell asleep at the wheel. His car continued to roll down the street, swerved into a driveway and crashed into a car. Fortunately he was not hurt. He called his Newspaper route Manager and explained what happened. The Route Manager promised him that he would take care of notifying the owner and filing a report with the police.

Clox's digital cousin, Digitox, had a very convenient ON/OFF switch for shutting off the alarm. The company that built Digitox also built in a snooze function that allowed Bertrand to shut off the buzzer by simply slamming his hand down on the button. The snooze function allowed him to enjoy a few extra minutes of sleep. The clock engineers even made the snooze button very large so that his hand could easily locate it in the dark. He only had to reach out his hand and hit it. They also added a switch for dimming out the LED display. But since he was shortsighted, the dimmed-out clock fooled him into thinking that it was all right to carry on sleeping. Digitox had a high-pitch alarm. Instead of emitting a merry ring like Clox or a melancholy moo like Radox, Digitox transmitted a sharp whistle that was painful to his ears. The high-pitch sound hurt his ears so much that every time Digitox went off, he cursed at the clock. When the power momentarily went out at night, the clock was set back to midnight and the alarm was turned off. He had very little trust in Digitox's ability to wake him up on time. In 1982 he purchased a quartz alarm clock to replace Digitox. The low production cost has resulted in a proliferation of the quartz clocks. Many cheap models were being imported from Hong Kong and Taiwan. Bertrand was fascinated by the inexpensive quartz alarm clocks. He named the new clock Quartzox. The quartz crystal clock was very accurate and very quiet. It did not need rewinding or maintenance, but the alarm system was not loud enough to wake him up. After just a few months in his bedroom, the hour hand fell off. A few weeks later, it stopped working altogether. Disappointed, he tossed the clock in the closet and never used it again. Once again, Bertrand looked to Clox for waking him up in the morning.

In February 1983, Clean Systems, Inc. was sold to a company in Santa Barbara, California. The company name was changed to Uniform Data Corporation. A few employees were terminated after the acquisition. Bertrand was among the few fortunate employees who were retained by the new company. After the divestiture of AT&T, telephones that combined an alarm clock, an FM/AM radio and a telephone began to appear on store shelves. His faithful Clox was now thirteen years old and Digitox was three years old. Clox had undergone three major surgeries and outlived Radox which died in 1981 at the age of four years. Despite being mauled by an

Englishman, blown away by an orgiastic woman, and disemboweled by an American cop, it continued to tick away the time in the company of his fancier cousin Digitox. Unfortunately, Clox's old age was starting to show in the clock's hands movements. On several occasions, Bertrand woke up and saw Clox indicating seven o'clock. When he arrived for work he found, with embarrassment, that he was two hours late for work. In 1984, fearful that his boss would fire him for his tardiness, Bertrand bought another alarm clock to replace Clox and Digitox. He called his new alarm clock and bedroom companion Phonox. Phonox was both functional and elegant. It displayed the time in a bright green color. It had an integrated AM/FM tuner and a telephone with contemporary look and feel. It was loaded with sleep features to keep anyone awake at night. The push-button telephone had a mute key to prevent the person at the other end from hearing him snore when he falls asleep while talking on the phone. It also had a handy button to automatically dial the caller back after he wakes up. The machine came with a backup battery to ensure that the clock would continue to work during a power outage. Phonox had a snooze button, a music button, a buzzer button and an alarm shut-off button. Bertrand was particularly exulted at the touch-sensitive snooze button. He did not even have to open his eyes to search for the snooze button when the alarm goes off. Instead, he reached out for the large, illuminated dial and lightly touched it to shut off the alarm.

After he brought Phonox home, he removed Clox from the nightstand and put it into retirement in the closet. He was getting tired at working three jobs, so he decided to give up the newspaper route. Many subscribers were not paying him for the papers, and he was weary of knocking on their doors to beg for his dues. He found it unbelievable that people who lived in $150,000 homes would not pay him $9 for the newspapers. Despite giving up the newspaper route, Bertrand continued to suffer from insomnia. Every night he stirred and heaved restlessly on his bed and stayed awake for long hours. When he finally nodded off, his legs twitched and woke him up. Night after night, he bore the maddening and unbearable pain of sleeplessness, lying and staring at the blackness around him and counting sheep in reverse. His restless leg syndrome woke him up every few minutes. When he finally fell asleep, he dreamed that he was lying naked on a bed in a field next to a busy interstate highway. Buses loaded with tourists sped by him. The tourists waved, cheered and snapped photographs of him lying on the bed next to the highway.

During his long hours of wakefulness, his mind raced over the past events of his life. He was disappointed with his achievement and deliberated for hours on end over his many failures. He was angry at his mother for not being a good mother to him and his brothers. He was angry at his father for neglecting them. He was embittered at his former wife for dumping him in favor of a white man, enraged at social injustice and inflamed by racism. He was afflicted by his inability to make friends. He was deeply troubled by his poor communication skill. He was displeased with the reluctance of the City Officials to raise a water meter that was buried under two feet of water in his front yard. He was unhappy that the City Officials would not repair his fence which started to lean after a three-foot wide storm sewer running under his back yard collapsed. One night he dreamed that the water meter was buried under ten feet of water. When he dived in the murky water to locate the shutoff valve and cut off the water flow, a powerful floodlight underneath the water blinded him and forced him back. In his sleep, he wandered into territories where he brazenly expressed his deepest longings and candidly conveyed his suppressed feelings. When he woke up, he was incapable of recollecting what happened to him, where he was, what time it was and why he did what he did. Several times he dreamed that he was killed. Once he dreamed that he was in Brighton. He stood on the shoulders of his friend and dived into the sea. When he landed on dry sand instead of water, he wondered where the ocean had drained into. Almost every night, just as he was about to fall asleep, he felt his body falling into an abyss. He woke up and held on tightly to the headboard so that he would not get sucked into it. When he realized that it was just another nightmare, he uttered a sigh of relief and went back to sleep.

Phonox did not make it easier for Bertrand to wake up in the morning. Its phone constantly rang at odd hours of the night. One night a registered nurse mistakenly dialed his number and shouted: "Dr. Mattox, Mr. Fox's heartbeat had slowed down. What shall I do?" He told the nurse that she dialed the wrong number. Later she called back again and yelled: "Dr. Mattox, the frail Mr. Fox is unconscious. What shall I do?" He told the nurse to check the number she had dialed. After that, she never called him again. Returning home one night after a tiring day at work, Bertrand went to sleep early. The moment he fell asleep, Phonox rang. When he answered the phone a woman at the other end said: "Whoever you are, I would like to say goodbye."

"You have reached the wrong number," Bertrand replied.

"It does not matter," she answered. "No one cares anyway. Goodbye." The phone clicked into silence and the dial tone came back. Bertrand was perplexed. The stranger had aroused his curiosity and he was unable to return back to sleep. He kept thinking about the night caller, wondering whether she was an insomniac like himself, or whether she was a practical joker. He thought that perhaps the woman was thinking of killing herself and wanted to let someone know. Just as he was about to doze off, Phonox rang again. Bertrand hoped that it was the woman who called earlier to say goodbye, but he heard the voice of a small child instead. The child said: "I love you, Mickey Mouse." Then she quickly hung up. Half an hour later, as he was beginning to fall asleep again, the phone rattled. He picked up the phone. Another child blurted out: "I am just calling to say I love you, Mom." Bertrand chuckled at the voice and replied, "I love you too, honey. Goodnight." An hour later, the phone rang again and jostled Bertrand out of his sleep. He let the phone ring so that the message recorder will pick up a message. "Come on, Murdox." the message began. "Pick up that phone! I know that you are there. Pick it up or else I'll come over to your house and butt your ass." He had no idea who the woman was and who she was talking to. He was glad that he was not Murdox. When the house was silent again, Bertrand erased the message from the recorder and went back to sleep. When he finally fell asleep, he dreamed that he was driving along Pope Hennessy Street in his hometown city of Port-Louis looking for the Cotton Bowl and the Texas Fairground. He learned in his dream that his brother was making plan to migrate to Canada. Later he dreamed that he was frying peanuts on the nightstand in his bedroom. When Bertrand opened his eyes the next morning, he saw with horror that it was past 10 o'clock. He had exhausted all possible excuses for being tardy. Instead of calling and excusing himself for being late, he sneaked into his office and hoped that no one would see him. His boss, however, had grown weary of his tardiness. He summoned him immediately to his office. Bertrand had never seen his boss so solemn until then.

"Bertrand," he snapped, "I am tired of listening to the customers' complaints. The same customer had called me three times this week to complain that no one is responding to her phone calls. What are you going to do about this?"

Bertrand looked shamefully down at his feet. "I will be on time tomorrow," he promised.

"You have told me that a dozen times," his boss earnestly reminded him. He looked fixedly at him for a long time without saying another word.

"I promise you that I will be on time tomorrow," the abashed Bertrand avowed.

Bertrand felt uncomfortable at his boss' glare and left his office to take care of the day's business. A colleague stopped him in the hallway and said: "We called you several times this morning but there was no answer.. We were concerned that you had an accident. Are you all right?"

"I am fine." Bertrand hastily said.

He nodded at the employee and thanked him for his thoughtfulness. Bertrand was disturbed that he did not hear the phone ring when his colleague called him while he slept. He did not know why he woke up when the nurse, the lonely woman, and the child called. But when his colleague called, he was sound asleep. He reflected that his windpipes must have collapsed while he slept. He thought that he must have stopped breathing when the phone rang or when the alarm sounded. For a brief moment, he thought that he might be suffering from obstructive sleep apnea or from another sleep-related disease. He quickly brushed off the thought and went on with the day's business.

That night, before going to sleep, the agonized Bertrand retrieved Clox from the closet in the hallway. He checked that the clock was still functioning and then packed a small plastic bag with a toothbrush, a tube of toothpaste, a comb and a towel. He then took a shower and changed into his work clothes. With a firm determination, he went to the garage, opened a storage trunk and pulled out a sleeping bag. He dropped the plastic bag and the sleeping bag in the trunk of his car and drove to work. He feared that his boss would fire him if he failed to report to work on time again. He no longer trusted Digitox or Phonox to wake him up in the morning. The only way for him to be on time for work was to sleep in his office. When he arrived at his office, he spread the sleeping bag by his desk and went to sleep. The small mechanical clock that had been his bedroom companion for fourteen years was by his side and stood ready to wake him up at the preset time.

In 1985 Bertrand returned to UTA to finish what he started in 1979. Since he no longer had the newspaper route and he no longer worked in the liquor store, he could devote more time to his studies. He was determined to complete the program and move on with his life. He was fearful that the company would eliminate his job position, and he wanted a more secure job. The nights he spent studying made him fall asleep quicker. He made it a habit to go to sleep at the same time each night and he avoided watching TV late at night. He woke up at the same time each morning and learned to rise up with the sun. After a while, he no longer had bad dreams and nightmares, and he no longer felt tired after waking up in the morning. Little by little, he learnt to become less dependent on his clocks to wake him up. In due time, he gathered all the alarm clocks except Phonox and put them away in the closet. Clox, the migrant clock no longer adorned his nightstand, and he did not miss him anymore. In August of 1987, Uniform Data Corporation was bought back by the previous owner of Clean Data System. The new owner handed pink slips to Bertrand and ten other employees. The downsized company then relocated to a smaller office. Bertrand and the laid off employees were asked to pack boxes and carried them to the new office which was situated about ten miles away. After the relocation was completed, Bertrand bade goodbye to his boss and left the company. He took with him one box containing his personal belongings. Among the contents of the box was one mechanical alarm clock. Bertrand later filed for unemployment benefits. He decided not to look for another job until after he completed his studies at UTA. On December 19, he received his Bachelor's degree in Information Systems, eight years after he started the program at the Dallas County Community College.

2 BOXING DAY

December 22

Matthew was hired to work as a store clerk in a department store late during the holiday shopping season. The store had initially hired fewer temporary employees than the previous year, but the unseasonably mild weather had prompted many people to leave their homes and head to the shopping malls. The department store hurriedly hired temporary help to deal with the unexpected surge in business. One of the new recruits was Matthew, a 17 yr old high school student. The HR representative assigned Matthew to work in the Electronics department after he completes his training. On his first day at work, Matthew joined a group of new employees in a conference room to watch three short videotapes about the company he was working for. The videotapes lasted about twenty minutes each. After watching the tapes, another HR person came to lecture the new recruits on safety procedures, store security and loss prevention. At twelve o'clock the new employees broke up the meeting for lunch. Matthew was too excited about at his new job to eat lunch. He walked around the store and examined the merchandises in the various departments. With Christmas only three days away, the shoppers crammed the aisles and looked for Christmas gifts for their families and friends. Store employees unpacked boxes and stocked merchandises on the shelves. Merry shoppers sifted through barrels filled with merchandises and searched for bargains. Not wishing to be late for the second leg of the employee orientation program, Matthew returned to the meeting room before his lunchtime was over. Ten minutes later, the HR person returned and inserted another videotape in the VCR. Matthew and the new employees silently watched the videotape. At the end of the video presentation, an employee training coordinator walked into the room. He ran a discourse on the payroll dates, employee discounts and rain checks. He then lectured to the new employees on the company dress code and the importance of good customer service.

"You, the employee, best reflects our organization," he told the new hires. "You must dress neatly when at work. Men must wear a tie and women must wear hosieries. Blue jeans are not acceptable. Male employees who are in frequent contact with customers must not wear their neckties loosely around their necks. You must be polite to the customers at all times because it's the customers' business that provides for your paychecks. Never forget that the customer is always right. If a customer is unhappy with her purchase, refund her money or exchange the merchandise. A happy customer will always come back; an unhappy customer will badmouth the store."

"Do we issue a refund to the customer even if nothing is wrong with the merchandise returned?" Matthew asked.

"Yes. Many people will buy on impulse. After they take the merchandise home, either they no longer desire the merchandise or they feel guilty that they had bought them. I once had a customer who returned four packs of underwear. He wore the underwear for more than a week before returning them to the store, but I gave him his money back." The training coordinator paused and drank some water. "I was mad, but I politely advised the customer that in the future he should clean his ass with soap and water before putting on the new underwear."

"Why did the customer return the underwear?" a new employee asked.

"I didn't ask him," the training coordinator answered. "In this business we don't ask why the customer returns the merchandise. We swallow hard and smile." The training coordinator pulled up the projection screen and taped a map on the white board. "Certain part of the store is off limit to customers," he said. "If you see a customer wandering in a part of the store that is off limit, politely ask him to go back to the main store. There are no cameras in these locations. Most of the times, the customers accidentally wander off into these places. You must always be alert and watch for shoplifters."

"What if the customer refuses to leave?" a new employee asked.

"Then tell the customer that a CNN television crew is doing a documentary about shoplifting in the store," the coordinator replied. "He will leave immediately. The restrooms are for the use of both the customers and the employees. There are no signs in the restrooms for requesting an employee to wash his hands before returning to work. Management thinks that the employees are smart and they don't need to be told to wash their hands. This store does not handle prepared foods. You won't start a biological warfare, kill or contaminate anybody if you don't wash your hands. However, I advise you to always wash your hands when you return to work. Twenty percent of the death in hospitals are attributed to poor hand washing. Besides, the storeowners frequently make unannounced visits to the store. They occasionally meet and shake hands with employees. They expect a clean handshake from the employees. We have signs posted near the restrooms requesting customers not to take merchandises inside the restrooms. The signs apply to employees as well as customers."

"Are the restrooms fitted with the kind of water faucets which require that they be held open with one hand while we wash the other hand?" a new employee asked.

"Yes. These faucets save water. What are you getting at?"

"I am just pointing out how difficult it is to wash our hands clean with these types of water faucets."

"I agree. You have to hold the water faucet open with one hand while you wash the other hand. It has been suggested before that the employee calls his Supervisor whenever he needs to use the restroom. The Supervisor can hold the water faucet open while the employee washes both his hands."

"Are there any cameras in the restrooms?" another employee asked.

"No," the training coordinator replied. "However, I can tell you that this company has terminated many employees for theft. There is a restroom at the back of the store strictly for employees' use. If the public restrooms are out of service, you may direct the customers to the employees' restroom.

"What should I do if I see an employee carrying merchandises to the restroom?"

"You have to consider what they are taking to the restroom. If the restroom is out of toilet paper, and they take a roll of toilet paper off the store shelf and carry it to the restroom, that's all right. However, the customer should inform someone at the customer service desk that there is no toilet paper in the restrooms. Shoppers wanting to try out new clothes will often mistake a restroom for a fitting room, so you have to point them to the right direction. Be alert for customers who walk into the fitting room wearing a blue dress, but leave the store in a white dress. In general, you kindly remind the customer that merchandises are not allowed inside the restrooms. Be particularly more watchful during the winter months when shoplifters wear oversized coats to hide shoplifted merchandises. When a customer buys something from the store, he is not only buying the physical good but also the service that goes along with the goods. Our pledge to the customer is that we will provide quality service to them until they are fully satisfied. By making that pledge, we have added value to the merchandise. Your patience dealing with an irate customer is value-added. So is the smile that you flash at him when he walks into the store. Being courteous to the customer also adds value to the merchandise. Never contradict, offend or neglect the customer. Let the customer vent his anger for as long as he wants. Listen patiently to their concerns and offer solutions to their problems. Never ever upset a customer. An angry customer always remembers a bad shopping experience and will not come back to the store again. Does anyone have any further questions?"

Matthew raised his hand. "How will I know if a woman has hidden merchandises inside her clothes?

"Do you have a high school diploma, young man?"

"No, but I plan to graduate next summer."

"Good for you. You will then be able to make an educated guess. Until then, all you can do is to make an intelligent guess."

The training coordinator pointed to the parking lot on the map. He pointed to areas where employees could or could not park their vehicles.

"The parking spaces closer to the store are reserved for our customers. They'll come in the store and give us their money quicker. The lights in the parking lot are turned off after all the customers have left the store. Employees generally spend some time in the store after closing time to tidy up. When you leave the store, the parking lot will be dark. Please bring a flashlight to work with you for your safety. The company is not liable for your personal safety after you leave the store."

The training coordinator then explained stock shortages, lane calls, and timecard regulations to the new employees. A few minutes later the HR representative returned. She handed a packet to the new employees. She pulled one form out of a folder and held it in front of the employees.

"This form certifies that you have read all the company policies and that all work regulations have been explained to you and understood by you. Please sign the form before you leave."

She then handed W2 forms for the new employees to fill out and sign, and gave each new employee the name of the Supervisor to report to the next day. Matthew was told to report to Mrs. Schroeder the next day to receive training on the point-of-sales terminals. The HR representative collected all the forms and wished the new employees well in their new jobs.

December 23

Matthew looked for the head cashier when he reported to work the next day. A checker pointed him to a small woman wearing a bright red blouse and a black skirt. When she saw him, she went to the office and came back with a cash tray. Matthew followed her to a checkout lane located further away from the bustling registers. The head cashier inserted a key in the POS terminal and verified that it was functioning properly. She loaded a blank roll of paper into the printer and pulled out a small training manual from underneath the counter. She opened the manual and pointed to the chapters that would be helpful to him.

"Always remember to pull the receipt out after you have rung up a sale," Mrs. Schroeder advised him. "Otherwise the paper will jam up the printer."

Matthew stood up to read the training manual since there was no chair near the checkout lane. Despite standing thirty feet away from the other checkout lanes, he could still hear the checkers greeting the customers and ringing up sales. He read in the manual that department codes identify the various departments while item codes identify the merchandises. He learned to distinguish between taxable and non-taxable items and practiced totaling and subtotaling sales on the cash register. He learned to distinguish between the employee-discount key, the non-taxable item key and the data-entry key. He canceled and re-entered sales over and over until he had memorized all the steps. When he completed the last set of practice exercises in the training manual, he threw away the sale receipts in a trash can. At that moment Mrs. Schroeder returned and asked him how he did.

"I think I did well," Matthew replied. "The POS terminal did not jam up on me."

"Good. Don't worry about the receipts. Come with me. I'll put you in an open checkout lane."

"Will I ring up sales for real?" he asked, feeling somewhat apprehensive.

"No, no, no," she quickly replied, shaking her head left and right. Matthew was relieved. "I will team you up with a checker so you can watch her in the course of her work. You can then ask her questions on things that you don't understand. It is all part of your training."

She took him to the express lane at the other end and left him with the checker. The checker introduced herself as Terri. A long line of customers stood in her lane.

"This is a very busy checkout lane," Terri warned him. "You have to be fast because the customers coming to this lane are always in a hurry. They don't want to wait a long time. If they have to wait for more than five minutes, they become obnoxious." Anticipating a long wait, the first shopper standing in the line shifted his body weight from his left foot to his right foot. He looked up and stared at the ceiling. "Sometimes the customer buys only one item costing a dollar or less, but they pay for them either with a credit card or write a check for sixty-five cents." The second shopper standing in line dropped his basket laden with merchandises on the floor in exasperation. "Credit card transactions take a longer time to complete," Terri continued. "The longer wait angers the other customers waiting in line. Customers see red when someone in front of them pays with a credit card or check. If a customer pays by check, you have to run a credit check on him before accepting the check. Sometimes you have to get the Supervisor to authorize the check. She may not be immediately available. So you wait for her to arrive and authorize the check. The trouble is until the Supervisor approves the customer's check, you cannot ring up another sale. If the customer's credit history is bad or the check is not approved, you have to void the sale. At that point you have to page for the Store Manager to come and cancel the sale. Until the Manager cancels the sale, you cannot ring up another sale. So you wait for the Manager to come and void the sale." The third shopper in the line looked at her watch and scanned the checkout area for a shorter line.

"The customers sometimes forget that the express lane is only for customers who have twelve items or less to check out. Nonetheless they still come through this lane pushing carts overflowing with merchandises. I don't usually count the items in the basket and I will not turn a customer away if he has more than twelve items in his basket. If a customer has more than twelve items in his cart, politely direct him to another checkout lane. If you don't do that then the customers behind him will be pissed off. They will cuss at you because you are making them wait longer." The fourth shopper in the express lane looked behind her. Seeing a shorter line, she hurriedly swerved her heavy cart out of the line and headed off to the shorter line. The shopper behind her stepped forward to take her place. Matthew glanced at the line snaking around the checkout lane and blocking the other shoppers. Amidst the cha ching of cash registers, shopping carts knocked each other and became entangled. Shoppers seemed lost as they looked for the end to a checkout line. "From time to time," Terri continued, "a customer will refuse to go to another checkout lane because he had already waited a long time. The customers behind him then get impatient because you are making them wait longer. Nobody likes to wait. Not too long ago, one customer was beaten up by another customer because he had more than twelve items in his basket." The fifth shopper in line shuddered. She decided that she did not need certain items and unloaded them onto a magazine rack nearby. The sixth shopper in the express lane felt cramps in his arm. He laid the basket on a stack of bottled beverages and rubbed his arm. "There is something else that you need to be aware of. An item does not always have a price tag or a bar code label on it. The terminal will beep no matter how many times you run it through the bar code scanner. You have to call the appropriate department to request a price check. By the way don't make the terminal beep more than three times otherwise the customer will tell you something that you already know." The seventh shopper in line counted two items more than the twelve items allowed in the express lane. She removed the two items from her basket and placed them in the basket sitting on the stack of bottled beverages. "The sale transaction cannot be closed until the price checker calls you back with the price," Terri explained. "So you have to wait for the price checker to call back with the price. While you are waiting for the phone call, the shoppers in the line become impatient and call you names in unheard-of foreign languages." The eighth shopper in the line decided that she had waited long enough. She left the cart behind her and headed to the store exit. The ninth shopper in the line pushed the abandoned cart to one side and took her position in the line. He sighed with relief that he was closer to the beginning of the line. "Some customers may change their minds after you have rung up a sale," Terri warned Matthew. "The customers may have picked up the merchandise on impulse or they don't have enough money to pay for it. You have to page for a Supervisor or the Store Manager to come and void the sale. Big-ticket items require that both the Supervisor and the Manager sign the voucher when a sale is canceled. It may take ten minutes before both of them show up. So you have to wait for the Supervisor or the Store Manager or both to come and void the sale. That further irritates the customers standing in line." The tenth shopper standing in line tore open a box of cookies. She handed a cookie to her baby daughter strapped at the rear of the cart and then looked around her for a shorter line. "The customers don't like to see the POS terminal jamming up or running out of paper while they are waiting in line. They have to wait while the paper is being cleared out or replaced. Make it a habit to check the paper supply in the printer frequently. Put in a new roll if the thickness is down to a quarter of an inch. You won't have to deal with angry customers if you do that. Let me see, what else do I need to tell you? Oh, always ask the customer if he prefers paper or plastic bags, and always put the customers' receipts in the bag with the merchandises. They may not like being asked if they like paper or plastic, but we have to ask. It's the company's policy to give the customers a choice of paper or plastic bags. Some customers do not care if we put their merchandises in paper or plastic bags. They don't care if the ground is filled with plastics that are not biodegradable, and they don't care if we deposit 200 million ton of garbage in the landfills every year. If the customer does not show a preference for paper or plastic, put the merchandises in plastic bags. Plastic is cheaper than paper. I am flabbergasted. Why give the customers a choice? If we are going to save the ecosystem, then let give everybody paper bags. When you give the customers a choice, chances are they are going to choose plastic over paper. This is not going to do any good to the ecology if some people are going to fill our landfills with plastics. Let me tell you something else about paper and plastic bags. The customers get irritated whenever you say: "paper or plastic?" They don't like to make decisions about something that they are going to throw away. They are not taking the bags home to eat them. Be always prepared for things like that." The eleventh shopper in the line opened her purse to see if she had enough money to pay for her merchandises. She closed her eyes and uttered a four-letter word. She reopened her eyes and looked inside her basket to see what items were non-essential and could wait for another shopping trip. She took out a box of Ant & Roach Killer from her basket and placed it on the cigarettes rack. Angry at having to wait in line, she peeled off the warning label 'CAUTION - Keep out of reach of children' from the box of Ant & Roach Killer and pasted it on a packet of cigarettes. Terri looked up at the line of customers and flipped the light above the Express lane off. "Sorry," she quickly apologized to the customers in the line. "This lane is closed for employee training."

A customer snapped at the cashier. He threw some packages on the counter and left the store.

"What did he say?" Matthew asked Terri.

"Don't pay any attention to him," Terri replied. "You'll get used to hearing all sorts of comments from customers in due time."

Seeing the long line of customers, Mrs. Schroeder opened up another checkout lane and beckoned the customers standing in the express lane to the opened checkout lane. The shoppers rushed to the new checkout lane, their carts colliding with each other.

"Has someone told you about ringing up credit card sales?" Terri asked.

"No."

"They should have. You will ring up many credit card sales in a day. I am surprised that nobody showed you how to ring up a credit card transaction. In any case, this is the slip that you will use. Watch me." She turned the light in her lane back on and beckoned some customers to her lane. Matthew watched her ring up sale after sale. Each time she performed a transaction, she slowed down and showed him what to look for in an item and what mistakes to avoid.

"Always ask the customer for his credit card first," Terri advised him. "Then set the card on the terminal in this slot. Don't let go of the slip while it is printing the sale otherwise it will slip off and end up in the bottom of the terminal. You won't be able to retrieve it without moving the terminal."

"I know. It happened to me while I was practicing at the terminal earlier," he said.

"I make it a habit to imprint the credit card number on the slip before I ring up the sale," Terri said. "It's so easy to forget. Without the credit card number on the receipt, the company cannot collect the sales amount."

Matthew watched her fingers furiously punching down on the keypad. She was fast, conscientious and courteous to the customers. She performed her task with the accuracy and precision of a machine. She occasionally greeted the customers by their first names and inquired about their families, but rarely looked at a customer directly. Her eyes were always fixed on the merchandises placed in front of her or on the POS terminal. Her left hand dexterously sought out the price tags while her other hand quickly and faultlessly keyed the item number into the terminal. She ran merchandises with a barcode over the scanner. Occasionally she picked up the phone and requested a price check. Despite her courteous greetings, she looked cold and impersonal.

"Do you know how to approve a check?"

"No," Matthew replied, shaking his head.

"They did not give you the phone number to call?"

Matthew shook his head to and fro. She dialed the number again.

"Don't go too fast," Matthew said. She re-entered the numbers, but Matthew was still unable to write the numbers down. He asked her to write the number down on a piece of paper for him. She replaced the phone back on its cradle and started to write the telephone number on a piece of paper. Her hand hesitated on the last four numbers. After several exasperating attempts at recalling the number from her memory, she lifted the receiver and slowly punched the phone number one number at a time. Her fingers remembered which numbers to punch, but her brain did not.

"Do we have to obtain approval for every check that we receive from a customer?"

"No. You only need an approval if the amount on the check exceeds twenty dollars and the check number is below five hundred. A check number over five hundred is an indication that the customer has an established checking account with her bank. A newcomer in town is more likely to have a new checking account. He is therefore a credit risk to the store. When you order new checks, the new check number starts off where the last check number ends on the previous checkbook."

"The checks on my checkbook start at number one," Matthew revealed.

"Have you moved or changed banks recently?" Terri asked.

"I opened a checking account with another bank."

"That's the reason why your checkbook starts at number one. Each time you change banks, the check numbers start all over again. I have seen checks numbered two thousand and over. You still have to get an approval if the check amount is over $100 irrespective of the check number."

"What about credit cards?"

"You don't have to obtain an approval if the amount of the purchase is less than fifty dollars. You must always check the number on the credit card against a black list irrespective of the amount charged." She pulled out two computer listings from a drawer and explained to Matthew how to look up for bad credit card numbers.

Mrs. Schroeder returned and requested Terri to close her checkout lane. She sent both of them for their lunch breaks. After watching and listening to Terri for two hours, Matthew was relieved to break off for lunch. He left the store and walked over to a fast food restaurant nearby. An employee he met during the orientation program asked him about his new job.

"Great," he answered. "My dad went to business school to learn about the 3P's of marketing. I just learned the 2P's of marketing in half a day."

"What are they?" the employee asked.

"Paper or Plastic," he replied.

"I think that they should rewrite the marketing books," the other employee said. "They should now teach the 5P's of marketing in business schools."

"Product, price, promotion, paper or plastic. Good idea!"

When Matthew came back from lunch, the head cashier assigned him to checkout lane #7. She requested Terri to watch over him. Mrs. Schroeder turned on the POS terminal and gave Terri a money bag and a drawer with rolls of coins in it. Terri took out a roll of banknotes from the moneybag and inserted them in the bottom of the drawer. She broke open a few rolls of coins and dropped them in their respective compartments in the drawer. She then closed the drawer. She punched a few numbers on the keypad and flipped the top open to check the roll of paper in the printer.

"Turn the checkout light on to let shoppers know that your checkout lane is open," Terri instructed him. Matthew looked around him for the light switch. "Under there," Terri said, pointing to the switch under the terminal. "Flip the switch to the right to turn the light on. Flip it to the left if you need change or assistance. When you flip the switch to the left, the light will flash and attract the head cashier's attention. The telephone is behind you."

Matthew flipped the switch to the right. At the sight of the light, four shoppers converged to his checkout lane. Terri pointed to a time and record sheet sitting on the terminal.

"Sign the sheet whenever you operate the terminal. Sign off when you close the checkout lane. Note down errors and cancellations on the sheet too." The line soon grew to nine customers.

"You are ready to go," Terri signaled to him.

Matthew greeted the first customer in the line. "Will it be cash or charge?"

"Cash," the customer replied.

He punched the appropriate code on the keypad. Picking up the merchandises one by one, he looked up the tag and keyed the information in the terminal. He pushed the merchandises to one side of the table after he had rung them up. When he had rung up all the merchandises, he pressed the Total key and communicated the total amount to the customer. He pressed another key to close the sale.

"Would you prefer paper or plastic?" Matthew politely asked the customer.

"I brought my own shopping bag," the woman replied, opening up a large canvas bag. Without looking at Matthew, she paid for her purchases and filled the canvas bag with the merchandises.

"You forgot to give her the sale receipt," Terri said.

Matthew looked at the terminal and tore off the receipt. He looked for the customer, but she had already left the store.

"Some people don't care to receive a receipt," Terri said. "Put it on the side in case she comes back for it later."

For two long and grueling hours, Matthew handled merchandises, tended cash, requested credit card or check approvals, and called for price checks. He was slow and clumsy. He frequently conferred with Terri on some items. The customers must have known that he was new on the job. One of them smiled and encouraged him. "You are doing very well," the customer said. Terri kept her eyes on the terminal all the times. She corrected or guided him whenever he was confused. Matthew was glad that she watched over him because he felt uneasy at handling other people's money. He was careless a few times, leaving the cash drawer wide open while he had his back turned to it. Terri quietly pushed the cash drawer shut while he packed the merchandises in bags. On two occasions she whispered to him to close the cash drawer.

The growing line started to make him feel uneasy. A young woman at the end of the line kept looking at him. Her constant glare made him nervous and he started to lose his concentration. When she finally got to the front of the line, she deposited two boxes in front of him. Matthew looked at the price tag on one box and punched the item number on the terminal. Terri suddenly realized that the line had grown too long and asked Matthew to step aside. Matthew gladly stepped out of the checkout station and let her take over.

"This is not right," Terri said, looking at the price displayed on the terminal." She looked at the second box and shook her head. "This price isn't right either."

The young woman stared at Terri without saying a word. Terri picked up the phone to request for a price check.

"The prices on the boxes are wrong," she calmly explained to the customer. Two minutes later, the price checker called her back and gave her the correct prices for the two items. "This item is $24.99 and that one is $39.99," she told the young woman.

The young woman protested and pointed at the price tags on the boxes. "The price tags on the boxes show $3.99 for this item and $9.99 for the other," she insisted.

"They are wrong," Terri explained. "These price tags don't belong on these boxes. It appears that someone has pulled off the tags from other merchandises and pasted them over the original price tags on the boxes."

The woman turned around and left. Terri put the two boxes underneath the checkout counter and attended to the next customer. The line began to shorten shortly after Terri took over the lane. When she had rung up the last customer in the line, she looked at Matthew and said: "Always expect that some customers will try to take advantage of a newly hired employee. They can tell that you are new at the cash register. You have to be on the lookout for these kinds of customers."

She then motioned him to stand behind the checkout lane.

Matthew preferred to attend to customers who tendered cash for their purchases. The credit card transactions took a longer time to complete because he had to obtain approval for credit card purchases over $50. Whenever he called for an approval on a credit card, he received a busy signal. Sometimes he received a recorded message informing him that he had dialed the wrong number. Terri called another number and learned that the credit card processing center was having problems with their computer. She later gave Matthew a new phone number to call should the computer goes down again. An hour later, Mrs. Schroeder returned and signaled him to close the checkout lane. Matthew signed off the time sheet. "I made four mistakes," he apologized to her.

"You are doing all right," Terri said. "That's normal for someone operating the cash register."

Matthew gathered the checks, charge receipts, discount vouchers and sale coupons in one bag. He wrapped the dollar bills with a rubber band and dropped them with the coins in another bag. He then put the two bags in a larger bag and took them to Mrs. Schroeder's office. Terri watched him as he dropped the large bag in a safe in the wall. They returned to the checkout lane to set up the terminal for the next checker. Terri pulled the drawer all the way out and removed the coin tray. She then set it across the drawer. "Anyone who wishes to tamper with the terminal will clearly see that the cash drawer is empty," she said.

Matthew was eager to go home. Ringing up sale transactions had mentally and physically worn him out. During his four hours manning the terminal, he dealt with two unpleasant customers. He had always been an honest and hard-working kid. He grew up believing that everyone in the world was honest like him. He could not understand why people would want to steal from the store. On his way out of the store, he met the employee whom he lunched with earlier.

"What did they make you do today?" he asked him.

"I learned what it is like working in a checkout lane."

"I cannot stand working in the checkout lane," the employee said. "It is not my kind of work. How was it?"

"The slow lane gives shoplifting a whole new meaning."

"How is that?"

"Price tag lifting," he answered.

"Some people will do anything to save a few bucks. That's Disgusting!"

December 24

When Matthew arrived to work, Mrs. Schroeder instructed him to report to Joe Cabbabe in the Electronics department. As he walked across the store to his new duties, the Store Manager greeted the employees through the intercom system. The voice coming from above exhorted the employees to make the day an even more successful day for the store. Joe Cabbabe was expecting him. When he saw Matthew wandering around in his area, he walked up to him and shook his hand. Joe Cabbabe was a short man with red curly hair and a beard. Matthew guessed that he was in his late twenties. The HR representative had earlier informed Matthew that Joe would be leaving the store after Christmas.

"You will be bombarded with questions from customers," Joe warned Matthew. "Read as much as you can on cameras, films, camcorders and televisions. A lot of the answers will come to you as you go about doing your work. Has anyone shown you around this department?"

"No."

"Let me show you our setup. It helps a lot if you know where everything is." Joe took Matthew on a tour of the Electronics department. He showed him where the cardboard box compactor is located and where damaged and returned goods were stored. He showed him the bins where mislabeled merchandises were temporarily stored. He took him to the storeroom and pointed him the type of merchandises stored there. Finally he walked him through the aisles and showed him the various sections in the department.

"If you can't find something, ask somebody," Joe said. "You can't be expected to know where all the items are shelved. This is a self-service department. We are not obligated to walk to a customer and assist him with his purchases. We are store employees, not commissioned salespeople. When a customer looks for something, we show him where it is located. But we let him decide if he wants to buy it or not. We do not engage in high-pressure sale tactics, which is how it should be. If the customer has questions about an item, answer him as honestly as you can or call someone who can help him."

Joe showed him the big and popular items - cordless phones, television sets, personal computers, video recorders and electronic games. He then stepped behind a booth enclosed by a glass enclosure on one side and a POS terminal on the adjacent side.

"We keep the cameras, electric shavers and stereo headsets locked inside these glass cabinets," Joe said. He pulled out a bundle of keys from his pocket. "I keep the keys with me all the times when I am on duty. The numbers on the keys don't match the numbers on the locks. We never had time to replace the locks. For cabinet number 2, use the key numbered 3; for cabinet number 3, use the key numbered 2. Got that? I don't know what the numbers are for the other locks, so you will have to try each one of them until you find the proper key. The big key is for the storeroom. Do you know how to perform a price check?"

"No."

Joe beckoned him to follow him to the cash register. "When a customer takes an unmarked item to the checkout lanes, the checker will call you and request a price check. If you are familiar with the item, just walk up to the shelves and read the price from the price tag on the item. If you are not familiar with the item, then you will have to look up the price in this book."

Joe pulled a heavy computer printout from under the terminal and put it on the top of the glass cabinet. Someone had scribbled 'The nightmare book' across the front page. "This is the computer printout for price lookup," Joe said. "We receive a new copy from the data center each week. Most of the times, the checker requests the price of the item only. She will provide you with the department number and item number." When Joe was certain that Matthew knows how to use the nightmare book, he tucked it back under the terminal.

"Have you gone through the merchandise recovery process yet?"

"No."

"In the store where I previously worked, the employees are not allowed to start the recovery process until closing time. In this store the Manager will announce when to start the recovery process on the intercom system. For the time being ignore the order unless you really have free time on your hands. The way sales have been going during the last few days, I doubt that you will have time to start the recovery process during the day. I don't like the system myself. I would rather start the recovery process any time I feel comfortable doing it."

During the recovery process, the store employees moved the merchandises to the front of the shelves so that the customers don't have to look for them. They also picked up alien merchandises which do not belong to the Electronics department and put them in carts. The carts were then taken to the front of the store. Later the store employees sorted through the merchandises and grouped them by department. After sorting the merchandises were then returned to their respective departments to be re-shelved. In addition to picking up and sorting the merchandises, the employees also picked up trash left behind by the shoppers. Matthew glanced at the floor around the Electronics department and noticed that it was free of trash.

"I try to keep our area clean," Joe quickly said.

After acquainting Matthew with the merchandises on the shelves, Joe took out a list from his shirt pocket and handed it to Matthew. The crowd of Christmas shoppers had started to file into the store. A shopper walked up to them and inquired about a television set. Joe directed him to a stack of boxes.

"I don't expect you to interact with the customers too much today since you are a new employee," Joe said. "This is the last day for people to do their Christmas shopping. I expect a huge crowd to show up." Joe then handed him the bunch of keys and sent him off to the storeroom. Matthew guessed that he would be stocking up shelves during most of the day. He wheeled the cart to the storeroom and picked out items from the shelves and dropped them in the cart. He crossed an item on the list whenever he removed it from the storeroom. When he could not find an item, he marked the item on the list 'Not Found.' When he had filled up the cart, he re-arranged merchandises on the shelves to make room for the new ones. The shoppers grabbed merchandises faster than he could restock them. They crowded around him and tore open packages to look closer at what's inside. Whenever they loaded a TV set or a camcorder on a cart, Matthew heard someone calling for Mr. West. He wondered who Mr. West was and why everyone was paging him. At 11 o'clock the store manager ordered the store employees to begin the recovery process. Matthew ignored the order since he was too busy stocking shelves. Joe had left the POS terminal and had been gone for over an hour. An Arabic man asked Matthew about cordless phones. He showed him where the phones were kept and went back to stocking shelves. The phone rang, but the two sale assistants were busy talking with customers. Matthew walked over to the phone to answer it. A woman wanted to know if her photographs had came back from the film-processing laboratory. He went over to the print bins and flipped through the stack of envelopes. A few minutes later, he picked up the phone and replied to the customer.

"No, Ma'am. They are not back yet. Could you please call back later?"

Two hours later, Joe returned and sent the two sale assistants off for their lunch breaks.

"Did you restock the shelves?" he asked Matthew. Matthew gave him his list back and pointed at the items that he did not find in the storeroom.

"These items are on order," Joe said. He glanced at his watch and then looked at Matthew. "It looks like the crowd has thinned out. Take your lunch break now." Joe went to help a customer load a TV set on a cart. As the customer left, Joe reached out for the phone and paged for Mr. West.

"Who is Mr. West?" Matthew asked his lunch buddy as the two of them left the store for lunch. "It seems like everyone is paging for him."

"He is nobody," his lunch buddy replied. "He is just an imaginary person."

"What? I don't understand."

"It's just a security measure. You call Mr. West when you see a customer carry a big-ticket item towards the store exit. The security guard will understand and will keep an eye on the shopper to make sure that he pays for the item before leaving the store."

A group of store employees ate or smoke on the sidewalk. The crowd of Christmas shoppers had drained the energy out of them. An older couple rested on a bench and refueled with potato chips and carbonated beverages. Matthew and his lunch buddy headed for the same fast food restaurant they visited the previous day. Christmas shoppers packed the restaurant and waited patiently in line to order their foods. After waiting for more than twenty minutes, they finally ordered their lunch and carried them out to eat. They walked back towards the store and joined the group of employees sitting on the sidewalk.

When Matthew returned to work, Joe sent him to the receiving dock to collect two pallets of electronic goods. Matthew used a forklift to bring the pallets to his department. After stacking the large boxes on the floor, he removed the smaller items from their cardboard boxes and arranged them on the shelves. When he ran out of space on the shelves, he took the merchandises to the storeroom. Once he was done stacking the shelves, he loaded the forklift with the empty cardboard boxes and went to the compactor room to shred them. After watching the machine chew up the cardboard boxes, he returned the forklift to the receiving dock. At two o'clock, the Store Manager once again asked the employees to pick up alien goods from their respective departments. Matthew took a cart full of alien goods as well as an alien child he found wandering in the aisles to the front of the store. He came back with another cart filled with small boxes. He examined the boxes to ascertain that they were not opened before putting them back on the shelves.

"Do you know how to operate the POS terminal?" Joe asked him.

"Yes, I do."

Joe handed him the keys for the POS terminal. "If you need any help, call Mrs. Schroeder." Joe then left for his afternoon break.

Most of the shoppers chose to go to the checkout lanes at the front of the store. The slower pace allowed Matthew to do several things at once. He answered the telephone, stocked up shelves, rang up sales, and picked up after the inconsiderate shoppers. He responded to calls for price checks, fielded customers' questions and helped them locate particular merchandises. He helped customers load TV sets on carts and paged for Mr. West when they headed towards the store exit. At four o'clock the store Manager again instructed the employees to begin the recovery process in their respective departments. Matthew ambled down the aisles amidst the shoppers and recovered alien merchandises dumped here and there by shoppers who had changed their minds. At around five o'clock Joe reappeared and told him that he could leave. Matthew went looking for his lunch buddy, but he had already left. He walked by shoppers frantically looking for that perfect gift for their friends and families. They were too focused in their shopping to wish anyone a merry Christmas. The store employees were all too busy or tired to wish each other a merry Christmas. Disappointed at not finding his lunch buddy, Matthew left the store and went home.

December 25

After eating breakfast and spending some time with his parents, Matthew stepped into his father's Mercedes and drove to a Refuse Center on the outskirts of the city. Christmas lights adorned the roof of houses and wreaths in traditional green and red colors hang on doors and porches. Matthew imagined families in the houses exchanging gifts and wishing each other a merry Christmas. His father had asked him on Thanksgiving Day what he would like for Christmas. He vehemently told him that he did not want any Christmas presents. To convince his parents that he did not want anything for Christmas, he gave away all the presents that he had received over the years - computers, video games, stereo systems, tennis rackets and bikes. He decided that he would no longer accept any gifts from his parents during the Christmas Holidays, and he gave them no explanation for his request. His parents were stunned. They had a difficult time understanding the sudden change in him and they spent many agonizing nights wondering what they did wrong. Nonetheless they respected their son's wish and abstained from putting up and decorating the traditional Christmas tree. They too decided that they would not buy Christmas gifts for each other.

The Refuse Center was located about fifty miles from his home. The gravel road leading to a landfill where truckloads of waste were dumped everyday was closed. A rusty chain and padlock held the double gates leading to the landfill secured. Matthew parked the Mercedes sedan on the side of the road and crawled through a small opening in the wire fence. Half a mile down the gravel road, he was met by the stench emanating from the nearby landfill. He carefully removed a dust mask from his jacket and covered his nose with it. Later, feeling uncomfortable breathing through the mask, he removed and threw it away. He came upon a mountain of black, brown and white plastic bags covering an area the size of twenty football fields. Some garbage bags had burst open and spilled their contents. Others were pecked open by birds or torn open by stray dogs. Matthew climbed over the waste piles and looked at the site where human beings come to discard ever-diminishing resources. He pulled a broomstick protruding from a heap of refuse and poked at the trash bags to reveal their contents. A fascinating array of objects spilled out at his feet. Poking at the refuse with the broomstick, he brought out into the open bundle of newspapers, pens, pencils, diskettes, tin cans, glass and plastic bottles. He ventured deeper into the wasteland and stepped over books, clothing, a tricycle and several plastic buckets. He could see several cans of paint, some empty, some still full with paint, a number of gallons of oil, syringes, an ironing board and a rusty barbecue grill. He was amazed at seeing shovels, a couch, bed frames, broken vases and toasters piled atop each other. He picked up a pair of eyeglasses in perfect condition to examine it, and then threw it back into the waste. He stopped to look inside a 5ft long bathtub filled with rainwater. In the bottom of the tub, he saw paper plates, foam cups, broken window glasses and a garden hose. Further away, he saw hundreds of battery cells with the acid oozing out from them and lying amidst toys, hats, animal carcasses and rusty tools. He stepped over a long wooden ladder sitting across the piles of garbage. At the end of the ladder he found plastic spoons and forks, plastic milk jugs, a leather handbag, a computer keyboard, broken picture frames and a table lamp. Aluminum cans and bottles littered the landfill. A television picture tube sat on top of a mattress slit on its side. He picked up a golf club and swung at a trash bag. The bag burst open, spewing its contents in the air. He jabbed at the waste with the golf club to reveal aluminum foils, disposable diapers, scrap wood, dolls, and rags and used condoms. A few feet away from him a stack of lawn chairs sat next to an empty propane tank. He tripped on a roll of telephone cable and landed on pieces of electrical wiring and a pair of broken telephones. Two stray dogs foraging into a pile of foods took off when he approached them. He prodded in the refuse with the golf club and uncovered a leg of ham, roasted chicken, and three slabs of turkey breasts.

Matthew suddenly realized that he was not alone in the landfill. Not far away from him, four men patiently sifted through the refuse. The two stray dogs came back and stopped to feast on the leg of ham and roasted chicken. Above him, large flocks of birds circled over the pile of trash. When the four men saw him, they stopped rummaging through the refuse and stared at him. Matthew was astonished to find homeless people in the landfill on Christmas Day. When he stepped closer to the homeless people, he realized that one of them was a woman.

"I am amazed at all the things that people throw away," he said to the woman.

"Yeah, yeah," one of the men muttered.

"Merry Christmas," he wished them.

The woman was surprised at his greetings. "Is it Christmas already?" she asked in disbelief.

"Yes. It's Christmas."

"Oh, Lord!" she exclaimed. She turned to the man closer to her. "Jerome, did you hear what this young man just said? It's Christmas. He came to the landfill to wish us a merry Christmas."

"I ain't going to celebrate Christmas," Jerome answered in a low voice. "I know nothing about Christmas."

The woman was overjoyed. "Of course you know about Christmas," she said, extending her arms and hugging him. She wished him and the other two men a merry Christmas. The two other men were in shock. They mumbled "Merry Christmas" to each other.

"Did you know that you could go to the Salvation Army compound downtown and enjoy a free Christmas dinner?" Matthew said. "They will also give you some Christmas presents."

"No, sonny," the woman sighed, slapping the air in front of her with her right hand. "We have everything we need here. This is our home, our kitchen, our living room, do you see? We shop here for all our daily needs all year round and everything is free." She opened up her arms over the landfill and exploded in a raucous laughter. "I am not going to pay department store prices anymore."

"The Salvation Army can also provide you with free clothing and blankets," Matthew added.

"The army?" the woman asked. She pointed to her companion. "He spent his entire life in the army, but look at him now. He doesn't even have a place he can go home to. This landfill is his home. I am not getting any blankets from the army." She went back to rummage in the waste pile and wrestled a candleholder from under a pile of garbage. She suddenly became suspicious of Matthew and stiffened up.

"What is a white kid doing in the landfill on Christmas Day?" she interrogated him while she eyed him with distrust.

43

"I work in a department store," Matthew explained. "Thousands of people came to the store and bought all kinds of things for Christmas. I was curious as to what people do with them after they take them home."

"Put them right in here," the woman said. She pointed to the sea of garbage around her. "See for yourself."

"Yes, Ma'am," Matthew acknowledged. "You are right. This place is like a department store." He pointed at the other end of the landfill. "That area looks very much like the Electronics department in the store where I work."

"It's a department store where everything is free," the woman said, bursting in an explosive laughter. She pointed at another end of the landfill. "See that area over there? That's the kitchen department. That's where I found all my cooking utensils. On the other side you'll find the Bedding and Linen department. Do you need bed sheets or curtains?"

"Oh no, thank you," Matthew replied. He walked towards the homeless people, but they stepped back from him and held their garbage bags tightly in their arms. "What do you want from us," the frightened woman suddenly said. "We have no money. Leave us alone."

"I mean no harm," Matthew reassured them. He sensed that they were afraid of him and stepped back. He turned away from them and sank knee-deep in the refuse. The woman called out after him: "Are you sure it's Christmas Day?"

"Yes, Ma'am," Matthew hastily said. "Today is December the 25th. The infant Jesus was born on this day."

"Merry Christmas," she wished her three companions again. The two men farthest from her returned her greetings softly. Her companion looked puzzled. He shook his head and muttered: "I know nothing about Christmas." The homeless woman unearthed an antique feather Christmas tree with real goose feathers from underneath a pile of garbage. She planted it into the garbage and pushed down on it to keep it from leaning. The woman and her companions trudged around and dug out an armful of Christmas decorations each from the waste piles. They hanged Santa figurines, delicate glass beads, cherubs, fluffy cotton snowmen, cardboard elves and glass balls on the tree. They adorned the tree with strings of antique glass beads, German glass ornaments, ribbons, candles, tinsels and such. They dangled figurines dressed in flowering red, green, orange and gold robes on the branches. The woman wrapped Christmas decorations around her neck and shoulders. She hanged wreaths, Christmas lights and snowflake trivets on her companions. She gave one of the men a silver-plated cherub salt-and-pepper set, a cranberry server with glass dish to the second man, and a set of twelve Noel coolers to the third man. She turned to Matthew and said: "I have something for you too." She put a Santa's nightcap on Matthew's head, decorated him with garlands, swags and red velvet bow ties. Then she gave him a decorator tabletop clock. "Batteries are not included," she quickly said, laughing. The men looked around them for gifts to give her. The first man gave the woman a red and green holiday sweater. He handed out Christmas bath accessories to Matthew, Christmas rugs and doormats to his companions. The other two men gave Matthew a brass umbrella vase and an antique brass firewood basket. Matthew was humbled by their generosity. He was amazed that the gifts the homeless people had given him came from the landfill.

"Thank you very much," he said apologetically to the homeless people. "I am sorry I don't have anything to give you."

"Nonsense," the woman said. "You just gave us the most wonderful gift of all: Christmas Day." The woman then hugged her companions. "Let have some foods and drinks," she said. The three men intoned, "Yeah, yeah. Let's eat."

The woman opened a sack and brought out an assortment of meat, vegetables, bread, cakes and cookies. The men returned to their shopping carts and came back with bottles of wine and liquor, paper plates, paper towel and plastic knives and forks. They sat in a circle on the garbage sacks. The woman divided the foods among them while the men poured liquor in paper cups. She gave Matthew a plate of sliced ham, yam and cut green beans.

"No!" Matthew protested, pushing the paper plate away from him. "I don't want to take all your foods." He rose up to leave.

"Please," the woman insisted. "There are plenty of foods for all of us. It's Christmas time." Matthew took the plate from her and sat down. He stared at the foods without touching it.

"Eat and drink up," one of the men said. He handed him a half-empty bottle of whisky.

Matthew raised the bottle up and wished the group a merry Christmas. He then drank the whisky. He stared at the homeless people eating. These people, he thought, ate foods picked up from the garbage cans every day. If they did not die from eating the foods, he probably wouldn't either. Not far away from them, the stray dogs fought over the leg of ham. Matthew slowly took a piece of ham with the plastic fork and put it in his mouth. It tasted just like ham. He smiled at the woman and took another mouthful. The liquor worked up a Christmas spirit in the homeless people and they started to sing Christmas carols. Matthew gleefully joined in the singing. The dogs scavenging in the landfill added to the merriment by barking and yapping. The woman pulled out an old dilapidated radio from a trash bag and fumbled on the buttons. The radio crackled, fizzled and popped. Then music poured out of the speakers. She stood up and took Jerome by his arm. They embraced and danced on the mound of waste. The two other men formed a pair and joined in the dancing. They whirled and stomped on the garbage bags. The trash bags broke open and garbage flew around them. Matthew laughed and cheered them on. He clapped his hands and pounded his feet.

More garbage bags burst open and spewed out more trash. He stood up and kicked up the loose garbage in the air. They held hands and formed a circle and stepped round and round. The radio suddenly went dead. The woman tapped on it a few times. It momentarily came alive, and then went dead again. She threw the radio into the landfill. The other two homeless men looked around them. The first man pulled out a rusty trumpet from underneath the garbage while the second man picked up a drum. The two men blew and beat up a cacophony of sounds with the discarded musical instruments. They spent the day drinking, eating, dancing and laughing in the sea of trash. Like children engaged in a pillow fight, they chased and pounded one another around the landfill with the trash bags. An hour later, they became exhausted and laid down in the trash to catch their breath. They passed the bottle of whisky around and recounted tales of Christmas past to each other. Suddenly, a loud shriek broke the peace in the landfill. Matthew got up and saw the homeless woman curled over Jerome.

"Don't leave me now," she screamed. "Don't leave me now!" The two other men stared at the motionless body lying in the trash. They were overcame with fear and stepped away from their lifeless companion. The homeless woman desperately hanged on to Jerome, screaming and crying loudly. She leaned back and clasped her face with both her hands and lamented "No, no, don't leave me now, don't leave me now."

Matthew zipped open the homeless man's jacket and applied CPR to the unconscious man. He frantically pushed down on the lower part of the man's chest. He opened his mouth and cleared his airways and then pressed down again on his chest. After several agonizing minutes trying to resuscitate the homeless man, he yelled: "Call for an ambulance." The two homeless men stared back at him. "Come on, go get some help," he shouted. The woman sobbed and rolled in the refuse.

Matthew applied mouth-to-mouth resuscitation to the homeless man, but to no avail. The homeless man had suffered a heart attack and died. He gave up trying to revive him and broke down in tears. The woman crawled up and sat next to Jerome. She gently caressed the dead man's face and removed the Christmas decorations from around her and placed them on him. The other two homeless men moved forward and did the same. The woman swayed and fell over the piles of garbage. Matthew helped her up.

"He loved this place so much," the woman said, clinging to Matthew. "This is the only place that he had truly called his home. He said to me once that when he dies, he wants to be buried here." The woman detached herself from Matthew and gathered her belongings. "Homeless people in this country are merely throwaways," she tearfully added. "The landfill is where throwaways belong."

"We can't leave him here," Matthew protested. The woman slowly walked away from her dead companion. The two homeless men picked up their garbage sacks and followed her. They went back to their shopping carts and dropped the garbage sacks on them. They slowly pushed the shopping carts in front of them and sang a farewell song to their dead companion. Matthew watched them depart from the landfill with tears in his eyes.

Matthew came out of the wasteland and drove back home late in the afternoon. The sidewalks were lined with trash bags. He imagined the bags filled with Christmas wrapping paper, cardboard boxes that once contain Christmas gifts, foam padding, plastics, beer cans, excess foods and empty liquor bottles. He surmised that by sunrise the following day every home in America would have at least one trash bag out on the sidewalk. The trash generated by the Christmas festivities would add 45,000 tons of waste to the 350,000 tons of residential and commercial solid waste that are dumped into the landfills each day. The Christmas gifts that people had spent so much time and effort looking for would someday find their way in the landfills too. If his fellow Americans, who produce nine times as much waste as Africa or Central America, could reduce their wastes, the landfills could be freed and put to other uses. He envisioned the landfills converted to music parks with giant musical instruments towering over them. Cute cottages would dot the parks' landscape and provide shelter for the homeless people. Music would flow out of the musical instruments day and night to entertain them. Children would visit the homeless people in their rooms inside the mushroom-shaped cottages and bring foods, clothes and other gifts to them.

December 26

Matthew had trouble finding an empty parking space when he drove into the store parking lot. Two fire trucks were parked close to the store, but he saw no fire or any smoke coming from the building. An ambulance was parked behind the fire trucks. He drove to the rear of the store and parked his car next to the receiving dock. He came to work earlier than usual so that he would be prepared for the crowd of shoppers filling the store on the day after Christmas. Nothing had prepared him for the long line of shoppers waiting for the store to open. The line snaked all the way to the rear of the building. The shoppers patiently stood in line and chatted with each other. Some sat down on lawn chairs they had brought along with them. A few shoppers covered with blankets squatted on the sidewalk. A stream of cars and trucks stopped in front of the store to unload returned merchandises. Matthew walked into the store using the rear employee entrance and was met by Joe Cabbabe.

"It's going to be a busy day," he warned him. Matthew followed Joe to his office at the back of the store. Once seated in his office, Joe informed him that he had temporarily assigned him to work behind the Returns counter.

"I don't expect a lot of people buying electronic goods today," he said. "The shoppers will be returning merchandises and looking for marked-down items. All the Christmas merchandises have been marked down. Soon you will see shoppers stampeding in every direction to snatch up anything in their way. The customer service department will need a lot of help dealing with shoppers returning stuffs. Have you worked in customer service before?"

"No," Matthew replied. A head of cabbage on Joe's desk caught his attention.

"We've set up a special window at the customer service desk for handling customers who return television sets and other electronics goods. I would like you to man it. This will give you some experience working directly with customers. You must remember not to say too much today," Joe reminded him. "We are committed to the customers' complete satisfaction. Almost everybody in America did not like what he or she had received for Christmas. They will be in the store today to return or exchange unwanted gifts. Where I came from, we exchange gifts on Christmas day, but leave the gifts under the Christmas tree until the next day. Leaving the gifts under the tree add to the holiday spirit. On the day after Christmas, which we call Boxing Day, we open up the presents and play with the new toys or wear the new clothes. Well, Boxing Day in America is not for opening up Christmas presents. It is an unofficial National Holiday for shoppers to fight over discounted rolls of Christmas wrapping paper and ornaments." Joe pulled out a hard hat from out of a cardboard box and handed it to Matthew. "Wear this hard hat," he advised him. "You will need it soon. Lots of projectiles will fly over your head when shoppers fought over marked-down items. I don't want you to get hurt. You will see some nasty fist fights today. Please stay out of these fights. You must never interfere between two shoppers fighting over a roll of Christmas wrapping paper. I have seen the best boxing bouts of my life in this department store. The best boxing matches are between shoppers on the day after Christmas. Do you like to watch wrestling, Matthew?"

"I am not into violent sports, Sir," Matthew replied. "I don't even like to watch football. I like to read."

"You'll like the sport when you see a couple of shoppers fighting over a marked-down pair of pantyhose. The best part of the fight is when the wrestlers pull off each other's pantyhose to carry home as a trophy. At the end of the day the store will be filled with returned merchandises. A decision will then have to be made by each department as to what to do with the returned merchandises. They could be marked down and put up for sale later, or they could be repackaged and put back on the shelves. We can elect to give them away to charitable organizations, or we can dump them."

"Dump them?" Matthew asked, puzzled. "Dispose of them in Wasteland?"

"I don't care where we dump them, but we dump them," Joe sharply replied.

"They can be marked down and put back on the shelves," Mathew said.

"This is not a day for asking questions. Don't say anything that will aggravate the shoppers. For some people the Christmas holiday season is a very stressful time, and returning unwanted gifts add to the stress. The shoppers will be so stressed out that they would need a whole month to recuperate. Some customers will leave this store with black eyes and bruises. Some may even leave the store on stretchers. Don't make it more stressful for the shoppers by asking them too many questions. Don't embarrass the customers by asking them personal questions like 'did you use soap and water before trying on the new underwear?' The shoppers are very conscious that there are dozens of other customers listening to their complaints. Let the customer do all the talking and just listen. Today you will need all the patience you can garner to deal with the shoppers. If the customer wants a refund, issue a refund ticket to them. Write down the amount to be refunded on a voucher and point the customer to the refund windows. This procedure ensures that we attend to as many customers as possible. You won't have to deal with money or credit cards yourself."

"Yes, Sir," Matthew said. Joe frowned and sniffed at the air around him.

"I smell something rotten in this room. Can you smell it?"

"No, Sir, I don't smell anything," Matthew stammered.

"We must not add to the shopper's agony by being rude to her. Don't forget to thank the customer for her business and always ask the customer to come back again."

"I will."

"God, this smell is awful. I wonder where it is coming from. Good luck, Matthew. It's been very nice working with you. I'll check back with you every now and then just to make sure you are fine. Did you have a good Christmas?"

"Yes, I did. Thank you Sir."

Matthew pointed at the head of cabbage on his desk. "Could the smell come from this cabbage, Sir?" he asked.

"I don't think so," Joe answered. "I picked it up from the grocery store this morning. Did you go anywhere for Christmas?"

"I spent Christmas Day in Wasteland, Sir," Matthew replied. "I mean, the landfill."

"Good for you. I have to say, my knowledge of geography is pretty poor. I haven't been to too many places myself. Is that the low-lying southwest region of France that is covered with furze and heath?"

"No, Sir. That country is named Landes. This former wasteland is now a pine and oak forest. You ought to take a tour of the neighborhood landfill someday, Sir. It has everything that this department store has."

"I plan to travel a lot when I retire."

When the doors opened, a wave of bargain-hungry customers poured into the store. The excited shoppers stampeded in every direction and knocked down toys, gadgets and clothing from shelves and racks. They shoved each other and grabbed everything with a SALE sign on them. Tempers flared and fistfights erupted. As usual, they fought over rolls of Christmas wrapping paper, boxes of Christmas decorations and other drastically marked-down merchandises. Matthew pushed his way through the frenzied crowd to get to the customer service desk. At the service desk he saw shoppers lined up to return shirts, shoes, neckties, electrical appliances, power tools, television sets, radios, cameras, camcorders and binoculars. He quickly took his place at the window specially set up for customers returning electronic goods. He smiled to the first customer in line and beckoned her to his window.

"This television set is all trash," she complained. "I want a full refund for it."

"Did you bring the receipt with you?"

The woman fumbled in her bag and retrieved a crumpled up piece of paper. She handed him the receipt. He looked at the date on the receipt.

"Ma'am, you bought this TV set two years ago?" Matthew raised his eyes and stared at the woman.

"Yes, I did," the woman replied without showing any sign of embarrassment.

"What's wrong with it?" he politely asked her.

"Nothing," the woman replied. "It's a wonderful machine, but the TV programs are full of violence. There is so much killing in this box that they make me sick in the stomach when I watch them. My children, on the other hand, get very excited watching all this senseless violence. I think my children really enjoy watching acts of violence on television. This bothers me a lot. The TV networks also show all these soap operas during the day. I waste my whole day watching them. After watching them, I hardly have any time left to take care of the housework. Have you ever watched a soap opera?"

"I have not," Matthew replied. "I imagined it must be heart-breaking watching them."

"I cry every time I watch them," she sobbed. "I cried when I go to bed at night. My husband thinks that I have lost interest in our sex life and he accuses me of deliberately crying to avoid having sex with him. My doctor warns me that too much crying is bad for my eyes. Can you see all these wrinkles around my eyes? My doctor says that the wrinkles appear because I cry too much. He recommends plastic surgery to tighten up the skin around the eyes. He says that the surgery will make me look younger too.."

"I imagine that it will be expensive, but you have to have it done, right? Do you have an estimate from your doctor?"

"Yes, I do," she replied. She took a physician's estimate from her handbag and gave it to Matthew.

"Let me see," he pondered. "You purchased the TV set for $413.46 inclusive of the sales tax. The plastic surgery will cost you $8,219. Is that correct, Ma'am?"

She nodded and dabbed a tissue paper under her eyes to dry off the tears.

Matthew added the two numbers on his adding machine. "Your refund is $8,632.46," he said. He wrote the total amount to be refunded on the ticket, signed and handed it to the woman. He then pointed her to the refund window.

"If you would just go to the line over there, you will receive your money back. Thank you for your business. Please come back again."

The next customer pushed a cart with a TV set on it.

"What can I do for you, Sir?"

"My son died after he spent the night watching this filthy box," the man said.

"I am very sorry about your son's death," Matthew said.

"He was my only son," the man continued. "He was such a clever boy."

"Is the TV set faulty?"

"Yes," the man screamed. "It killed my son. They showed a movie a couple of weeks ago in which a man went out and robbed a bank. The robbery was brilliantly executed and the robber escaped with over a million dollars. The TV set made the robbery looks like a child's play. My son thereafter went out to rob the bank in our neighborhood the following day. The security guard at the bank shot him."

"Did you bring the death certificate?"

The man gave him a picture of his son and a death certificate. "He was the smartest kid in the whole neighborhood," the man lamented.

"I am sure he was," Matthew sympathized.

"He was only thirteen years old. He would have been fourteen next month."

Matthew checked the refund guideline manual for accidental death. "Our underwriters have limited the payment on your son's life to $20,000. I wish I could offer you more, but I have to work by the store's rules."

"This will not bring my son back," the man complained.

Matthew wrote down the amount to be refunded for the TV set. On the next line, he wrote the amount of life insurance benefit payable to the man for the lost of his son. He approved the refund ticket and handed it to the customer. He then pointed him to the refund window.

"If you would just go to the line over there, you will receive your money back. Thank you for your business. Please come back again."

The third customer complained that the TV set she had bought had ruined her life. "My husband," she complained, "spends his entire time sitting in front of this box. When he is not watching television, he is sleeping. He has not taken me out since we bought this TV set. He had not said a word to me during the last six months. Can you believe it, he no longer remembers the date we were married. When I ask him if he still loves me, he said he loves watching football more than anything else. Oh, what an insult! Do you think I look like a baboon?"

"Not at all," Matthew said.

"My husband has gone blind as a result of watching too much television," the woman continued. "He thinks that I am a baboon and he feeds me bananas. I am suing for divorce. I am keeping the house and all the furniture. I spent more than $3,000 on attorney's fees to have him evicted from my house. I blame all my misfortunes on the TV set that I bought at this store. I want my money back."

"We'll be glad to refund your money, Ma'am," Matthew promised. He wrote the amount to be refunded to the customer on the ticket, signed and handed it her. He then pointed her to the refund window.

"If you would just go to the line over there, you will receive your money back. Thank you for your business. Please come back again."

A woman wheeled a TV set on a cart towards the service desk. "This TV set makes me feels so inadequate and unwomanly," she complained. "It makes me feel that every woman in the world but me is beautiful. All the women that live in this box have pretty faces, beautiful legs and full breasts."

"I understand," Matthew acknowledged. "Would you like a refund?"

"I want to undergo surgery to augment my breasts," the woman added. "I want to look like one of the women on the TV screen."

"I don't blame you. Watching these people on television does make one feel left out, isn't it? They all have the perfect body, live in luxurious homes, and dine at lavish restaurants. All I ever eat for lunch is hamburgers and I buy my clothes at discount warehouses."

"I want to improve my appearance and enhance my self-image."

"Do you have an estimate from your physician?"

"Yes, I do. I also have an estimate for an ultrasonic liposuction." the woman tended Matthew a receipt and a surgeon's estimate for enlarging her breasts and removing unwanted fat from her waist and thighs.

"Okay. You purchased the TV set for $384.16. The silicon transplant and liposuction will run you $18,420. Is that correct, Ma'am?"

The woman nodded. Matthew added the two numbers on his adding machine. "Your refund is $18,804.16." He wrote the total amount to be refunded on the ticket, signed and handed it to the woman. "If you would just go to the line over there, you will receive your money back. Thank you for your business. Please come back again."

The next customer walked up to the service desk with one arm in a sling and his head wrapped up in a bloodied bandage. He leaned on a walking stick and looked confused and shaken.

"What in the world befell you?" Matthew asked the customer.

"Too much noise," the man said. "There is too much noise in this box and my neighbor does not like it. I want a full refund for this TV set. It is the source of all my problems."

"We'll be delighted to refund your money if you don't like the set," Matthew said.

"There is just too much noise coming for the TV set," the man repeated. "I can't hear the noise myself, but my neighbor who lives in the apartment unit above me thinks that the noise is too loud. The noise disturbs him. He is always lecturing to me about noise pollution, which doesn't quite make sense to me. He says that I violate his Constitutional rights."

"Did your neighbor do that to you?" Matthew asked, pointing at the bandage on his head.

"Yes. He came crashing down from the ceiling as I was watching this box. I thought it was an earthquake. First, a broomstick shot through the hole in the ceiling and hit me in the head. Then my neighbor plunged into the hole and landed on me. He screamed that the fucking TV was too loud and fussed about his constitutional rights."

"I understand," Matthew sympathized with the customer.

"He wanted me to turn down the volume, but I could not find the volume knob on the TV set." The man removed a remote control from his jacket. "This gadget came with the TV set. It has all these pretty buttons on it, but every time I press a button, my neighbor screamed: 'Turn the fucking volume down.' I want to return the TV set for a full refund."

"You did the right thing by bringing the TV set back," he told the man. He took the remote control from the customer and wrote $4,020.79 on the refund ticket. The amount included the refund on the TV set, the customer's medical expenses, and damage to the ceiling in his apartment. He gave the man the refund ticket and then pointed him to the refund window.

"If you would just go to the line over there, you will receive your money back. Thank you for your business. Please come back again."

"What did you say?" the man shouted.

"Take this ticket to the refund counter," he shouted back into the man's ear.

"No, I am not buying another TV set from this store again."

The line grew longer by the minute. The shoppers returned TV sets, personal computers, camcorders, telephones, alarm clocks, cameras and binoculars. One customer brought back a camera and complained that whenever he looks into the lens, he sees the picture of a nation floundering in enormous debt. A young man returned his binoculars because wherever he points the binoculars to, he sees a woman being raped. A mother returned her radio-alarm clock because every two minutes, the alarm reminded her that a child is being abused in America. A grandmother blamed the telephone she bought from the store for her accident. She complained that the telephone rang while she was in the shower stall. When she ran to answer the telephone she slipped and broke her leg. Several women took back the telephones they bought from the store because they constantly received obscene phone calls. A woman returned her personal computer because it had turned her marriage into a 'ménage a trois.' Another woman blamed a microwave oven for burning her scalp when she tucked her head inside it to dry her hair.

When the line thinned out Matthew returned to the Electronics department. He had issued refund tickets for 43 TV sets, 19 personal computers, 9 cameras, 5 binoculars, and dozens of video recorders and telephones. He had approved refunds totaling more than half a million dollars to the shoppers who returned these merchandises. At the Electronics department he found Joe sitting in his office, busy carving out a doll from the cabbage head.

"Now comes the fun part," Joe said. "Boxing Day isn't Boxing Day until the shoppers get into a real boxing match. Get a folding chair for you are about to see the fight of your lifetime."

Joe finished carving out the cabbage head. He took a plastic doll from his desk and separated the head from the body. He covered the cabbage head with guacamole paste and attached it to the plastic body of the doll. He then dressed the doll in a Holiday outfit to finish off his creation - the Cabbabe Patch doll. He lifted the phone from its cradle and activated the intercom system.

"May I have your attention," he announced to the shoppers. "The last Cabbabe Patch doll in the store is about to be given out free to our loyal customers in five minutes. The giveaway will take place in the toys department. No purchase is necessary to participate in the giveaway. The Cabbabe Patch doll will be tossed out at the crowd of shoppers, and the shopper who catches the doll will get to keep it. Good luck and thank you again for shopping with us." Joe put the phone down and grabbed a folding chair. He headed for the toys department followed by Matthew.

"Put on your hard hat," Joe advised Matthew.

About two hundred shoppers had gathered around the toys department. The crowd of women and children was tense. They sighed with relief when the waiting was finally over. Joe appeared before them and raised the Cabbabe Patch doll over them like a trophy. The shoppers gasped and bit at their nails. Eyelids flickered and eyeballs rolled as Joe swept the doll over his head for everyone to see. Some women clasped their hands together and said a prayer to the Virgin Mary. A woman's legs shook uncontrollably and she fainted. A store employee carried her off.

Matthew opened up the folding chair and Joe stepped on it. "Here it is, the last Cabbabe Patch doll," Joe announced. "At the count of three I will toss it over the crowd. Good luck." He swung his arm and brought it to rest behind him. The crowd stood still. Two hundred pairs of eyes were glued to the Cabbabe Patch doll. Joe counted to three, and then he flung the Cabbabe Patch doll over the crowd. The shoppers shrieked and scrambled to the direction of the throw. They knocked and pulled at each other. A few shoppers were knocked down to the floor as they scrambled for the doll. They crawled between the shoppers' legs and frantically looked for the doll.

"I got it, I got it," a woman shouted. She held the doll above her head. A woman came from behind her and snatched the doll from her. In the ensuing melee, merchandise racks were knocked down and toys started to fly around. Matthew pressed down on his hard hat to prevent it from falling off. Two shoppers landed on the doll at the same time. They each pulled on it and the cabbage head popped loose from the plastic body.

"It's mine," the first woman screamed, clutching the plastic doll body closed to her. The second woman stared at the cabbage head. Her face and hands were smeared with Guacamole paste. She shook off the green paste from her fingers and broke into tears. Two men came forward and surrounded the woman clutching the headless plastic doll to protect her from the other shoppers.

"Where is the doll's head?" one of the men said, looking around him.

The winner looked at her doll. "I don't care if it has a head or not," she said. "It's so cute." She held up the doll to her face and kissed it. Her red lips turned green with guacamole paste. Store employees began cleaning up the mess created by the fight over the Cabbabe doll. Paramedics tried to revive a man who got caught in the melee. They loaded him on a stretcher and carried him to an ambulance. A few feet away from them, two shoppers began to argue over a pair of marked-down pantyhose. They pulled on the package until the thin cardboard wrapping tore up. Then they pulled on the nylon stocking until it stretched ten feet apart. One of the women slipped and let go of the stocking, sending the other woman careening down on a rack of clothes. She stood up and held the hosiery above the head. "I have it, I have it," she victoriously bellowed.

"The American people like to win," Joe remarked. "The ecstasy of victory is more important than the value of the prize itself."

They walked back to the Electronics department. "What do we do with all the TV sets that have been returned to the store?" Matthew asked.

"Put them under the sledgehammer," Joe replied. "Sometimes it is cheaper to dispose of the merchandises rather than ship them for checking and repackaging. Occasionally, the store will hold a sale on the returned merchandises, but these sales have not generated enough interest in the past. The guys in receiving sometimes select and deliver some of the merchandises in working condition to the poor people in their communities." Joe pointed to a sledgehammer behind a glass enclosure in the back room. "Have fun!" He said to Matthew. "You may go home when you are done cleaning up." Joe walked to a door marked 'EXIT' and pushed it open. He left without looking back. Matthew stared at the sledgehammer behind the glass door. His lunch buddy walked in and pulled him by the arm.

"I thought that you did not come back after Christmas," he said.

"They put me to work at the service desk."

"I had this T-shirt printed for you as a Christmas present, but you had already left when I looked for you."

Matthew removed the T-shirt from the bag and unfolded it. His new friend unbuttoned his shirt and showed him the print on his T-shirt.

"Voila," he said with a grin.

WASH HANDS
BEFORE
RETURNING TO WORK

3 THE DREAMS OF ALFRED SHOEMAKER

For generations the Shoemakers engaged in the calling of their forefathers, that is to say, making and mending shoes. During the 1950's the shoe repair trade boomed as people took their shoes to the shoemakers' repair shops to have the heels or the soles replaced when they were worn out. By having the shoes repaired, their owners kept and wore their shoes longer. Alfred Shoemaker had, as tradition dictated, dutifully followed in his father's footsteps. He began his apprenticeship in his father's shoe repair shop in Rochester, New York. When he became skillful at his trade, he moved to Texas. He opened his own shoe repair shop in a little town North of Dallas. While still in his prime, Alfred worked hard to establish his business. He later met and married Adele, the daughter of another cobbler. They had two beautiful sons whom Alfred hoped would one day follow in his footsteps. When debtors began calling on him, Alfred suddenly realized that his shoe repair shop was not generating enough income to pay off his mounting debts. The number of customers who brought their shoes to be repaired had dwindled down to just a few each day. Each morning, before setting out to his shoe repair shop, Alfred discussed the state of his shoe repair business with Adele. They argued over the debt that kept getting larger and larger.

"People are not bringing me their shoes to be repaired anymore," Alfred lamented. "They threw away the old shoes and bought a new pair whenever they are worn out or are in need of repair. They no longer want to have them fixed because it's more convenient for them to buy a new pair."

"You are charging too much for repairing their shoes," Adele remarked.

"I only charge a customer $28 to replace the soles and heels," Alfred replied. "Anyone can afford that, but people would rather spend twice as much on a new pair than have the old shoes repaired." Alfred threw his arms up. "This doesn't make any economic sense," he cried out.

Alfred stood up and paced around the kitchen. "I don't know what else I should do," he said. "I am thinking of closing down the shoe shop and try another business. I no longer want our children to follow in my footsteps. They deserve to live a better life than us. I will break away from tradition."

"I still think that you are charging too much for shoe repair," Adele said. She picked up the breadcrumbs on the table and dropped them on her empty plate.

"Last week two servicemen came by to repair the air conditioner in the shop," Alfred continued. "The older of the two men pulled on some electrical wires causing the capacitor to blow up. I swear that the capacitor was still working before he pulled on the wires. He claimed that it was bad and he charged me $375 for getting the air conditioning unit working again. Now I need to have ten customers to bring me their shoes for repair so that I can pay the Air Conditioning Company its dues."

"You did not tell me that," Adele said.

"I am sorry," Alfred said. "I had other things on my mind."

"I had to call the plumber this morning," Adele said. "The toilet stopped up."

"What was wrong?"

Adele sighed. "He said he did not find anything wrong, but it stopped up again after he left."

"How much was it?" Alfred asked.

"I paid $175 for the first call. I called the plumbing company back, but they said that the second service call would be billable. They said that the problem was not related to the first service call."

"Great!" Alfred walked into the living room and returned with the phone book. He quickly flipped through the yellow pages until he reached the shoe repair section. He then pointed to a box advertising his business. The advertisement read: 'Shoe repair while-U-wait. Reasonable Price.'

Alfred scratched his head and leaned against the refrigerator. "I must think of a new way to attract more customers to our shoe shop," he pondered aloud.

"I don't think it's your ad," Adele said. "I think that you are too honest. You should add some extras to the service to get more money from the customers. After all the A/C service technician deliberately blew a capacitor. He charged you for a new one, did he not?"

"You mean, cheat the customers out of his hard-earned money? No, I will not. I am an honest shoemaker. I will not charge my customers for something they did not order."

"They won't notice," Adele insisted. "If you drill a hole in the sole, you can charge the customer for a new sole. They won't notice that the hole was not there before."

"No, I won't do it. That's unethical business conduct. That's robbery."

"A lot of companies are doing it nowadays," Adele said.

"I am in the shoe repair business," Alfred vehemently protested. "I am not repairing automobiles. If I were a car mechanic, I will do unneeded work on the car and charge the customers more, but I repair shoes. If I charge more for the service, the customers will never come back to pick up their shoes. Then I end up with more shoes than I have room for in the shop. Have you been in the shop lately? There are shoes everywhere. People brought them in to be repaired, then forgot to come back for them. How can people be so forgetful?"

Adele pulled the yellow pages towards her and scrutinized the ad. "Do you have to repair the shoes while the customers wait?" she asked. "Ask the customer if he could drop them at the shop and pick them up later. You could probably get more shoes repaired if you don't have to repair the customer's shoes immediately."

The phone rang. Alfred picked up the phone. "Yes, yes, I know," he shouted in the telephone mouthpiece. "Okay, okay, don't worry. You'll get your money, all right?" He hung up the phone and cussed. "It's the leather factory," he said. "They are threatening to sue us in order to recover the leather I bought from them. What were you saying?"

"I said that you should ask the customer to drop his shoes instead of making them wait for them," Adele repeated.

"Most of my customers have only one pair of shoes," Alfred explained. "If I don't fix their shoes right away, they will be unhappy. They can't go to work without wearing shoes."

"That's their problems," Adele said. "You should not have to worry about that."

"Yes, I do worry about their feet as much as I care about their shoes," Alfred said. He smiled. "The shoemaker's trade is not all about leather and heels, but also about the health of his customers' feet."

"You get too involved with your customers' feet," Adele said. "You have to get their business, not their feet."

"Their shoes and the comfort of their feet are my business. If I don't pay attention to their feet, they won't bring me their shoes. If they don't bring me their shoes, I have no business." Alfred glanced at the clock on the kitchen wall. "I am late," he exclaimed. He went around the kitchen and picked up several pairs and piled them into a bag. Adele watched him until he had picked up the last pair of shoes.

"How many pairs?" she asked.

"Six," Alfred replied. "I mended six pairs last night. I will earn enough money to pay last month's gas bill."

"I have never heard of any shoemaker who brings his work home," Adele said. She grabbed the meat tenderizer from the counter top and looked in awe at the bent knives and forks around her. She took a can opener from a shoe and threw it into the kitchen sink. She stared at the meat tenderizer and sighed. "This is the third meat tenderizer you have ruined this week," she said. "Will you please stop using my kitchen utensils to repair your shoes?"

"I got to run." Alfred rushed out of the kitchen. Adele stared at the pieces of leather on the kitchen floor. "The whole house stinks," she yelled after him. "Tell your customers to wash their feet more often." She turned towards the door and threw the meat tenderizer at her husband. He ducked at the projectile and ran out of the house.

Later in the evening, Alfred returned home with a new load of shoes needing repair. He walked into the kitchen and deposited the sack of shoes beside the door. Adele set the table up for dinner.

"We'll have taco salad for dinner tonight," she said.

"Good," Alfred replied. "I am starving." He dropped his heavy frame on the chair and gulped down a glass of milk. "Where are the boys?" he asked.

"They are outside playing around as usual. They could not wait for their hard-working papa to come home to have dinner with him." Adele took a shoe and filled it with her salad preparation. She then set it in front of her husband. Alfred's eyes popped out at the sight of the shoe filled with the salad. "What is this?" he gasped.

"Your dinner," Adele answered. "We are having Taco salad tonight."

"You are serving my dinner in a shoe?" Alfred asked, eyeing his wife with astonishment. "Where are all the plates?"

"I have to put up with all the smelly shoes that you bring home every night," Adele shrugged. "I want you to know how I feel."

"I am sorry. I'll try to be more sensitive. I will not bring too many of them home." Alfred emptied the salad on a plate and threw the shoe behind him.

"How was business today?" Adele asked.

"Getting worse by the day," he replied. "Fewer customers came in today. I am deeply sorry about the smelly shoes. It never occurred to me that the smell was bothering you."

"Can't you spray them with some odor-killing substance before bringing them home?" Adele begged.

"I will think about it," Alfred answered. "I am losing sleep about the business. Two of my creditors came in the shop today and demanded to be paid immediately."

Adele reached out and touched his hand. "I know how you feel," she said. "Would you please try not to think about it tonight? You are always talking about money, work, shoes, and nothing else."

"I watched hundreds of people walk by the shoe repair shop today. Only thirteen of them wore leather dress shoes," Alfred sadly said.

"That's pretty sad." Adele moaned.

"One old lady walked by the repair shop wearing house slippers."

"No wonder the soles of her shoes never wear out."

"A group of religious people dressed in orange robes stomped on the sidewalks barefooted and chanted that no one buys and wears shoes anymore.

Adele sighed and bit her fingernail. "Christ's shoes were taken away from him when he was crucified," she said.

"The office ladies carry their leather shoes in a bag while they walk to work in cheap rubber shoes," Alfred continued. "Once inside the office, they change back into their leather shoes. The sole and the heel of the good shoes just never wear out. When will I ever get to repair their shoes?"

"I am so sorry."

"This is what is hurting the shoe repair business," Alfred moaned. "How will I ever carry on with my shoe repair business if the heels and the soles never wear out? No one takes their rubber-soled shoes to be repaired when they wear out. People just go out and buy a new pair." Alfred covered his face with his hands and sobbed. Adele leaned over the table to comfort him.

The night was clear, crisp and cool. The house was quiet except for the clock that chimed every fifteen minutes on the hour. Alfred finished work on the last pair of shoes and retired into the bedroom. He quietly lied down on the bed by his wife. His smelly feet woke Adele up and she buried her face into her pillow. "I wish you would wash your feet before going to bed," she murmured. "They really smell bad."

"I am too tired to take a bath," Alfred replied.

"That's not fair," Adele said. "Why do I have to put up with your smelly feet every night?"

Alfred sighed. He climbed out of bed and went to the bathroom. Shortly afterward he returned and climbed back into bed. Adele raised her head from her pillow and turned to him. "You couldn't have taken a bath so quickly," she said. "I did not hear the water running in the shower."

"I am tired and worried about the business," Alfred protested. "My smelly feet should not bother you tonight." He turned around and closed his eyes. Adele sniffed the air around her and then crawled down to her husband's feet to smell them.

"What is this smell?"

"I rubbed L'Eau de PO perfume on my feet," he replied. "They should not bother you now."

The perfume aroused Adele and she began to kiss Alfred's feet and legs. Eventually she climbed over him and made love to him.

The next day Alfred poured a few drops of L'Eau de PO in the shoes he had repaired to dispel the smell inside. He packed the shoes in his duffle bag and left for work. When he arrived at his shoe repair shop, he found a customer waiting for him by the door. The customer wore a pair of designer sandals.

"I really need to have my shoes back today," he begged.

"They are ready."

"I have a lunch date with the most beautiful woman in the world and I don't want her to see my ugly feet."

Alfred looked at his customer's feet as he unlocked the front door to his shoe repair shop. "You should trim your toe nails more often," he told the man. "Your toe nails won't grow crooked, and you will have healthier toes. Women like men with beautiful feet. I found that out last night. My wife kissed my feet all throughout the night. Now, I can't even keep my eyes open." Alfred winked at the customer and beckoned him inside the shoe shop. He removed a pair of shoes from the duffle bag and laid them down on the counter. He took a rag from underneath the counter and polished the shoes until they shine. "I stayed up late last night to work on your shoes," he said. "You should consider buying another pair so that you'll have shoes to wear on emergencies. I have a few reconditioned pairs that you may like."

"I can't afford a second pair of shoes," the man said. "I have too many credit card bills to pay and quite a few girls to please. How much do I owe you?"

"Thirty-two dollars," he said. The man paid him and left the shoe shop with his shoes. Alfred went to the back of the shop and began his daily routine of repairing shoes. Piles of shoes were stacked around the room. He had spent long hours reconditioning the shoes, but their owners never came back to claim them. He took a pair and ripped out the soles, then affixed new soles to the shoes. He had few shoes to mend, so he repaired the same pair of shoes over and over to stay busy. Tearing the shoes apart and fixing them again made him forgot that his trade was fast disappearing. Occasionally a customer came in to claim his shoes, but hardly anyone brought him their shoes to be repaired. During the day a few old people came in the shoe repair shop to keep him company. They sat in the waiting room and chatted with him until they fell asleep.

By mid-afternoon Alfred became weary of sitting alone in the dark and smelly back room. He carried a stool outside and sat down on it. Then he took his shoes off, crossed his leg and rubbed his toes. He watched the pedestrians walk by, making notes of the types of shoes that they wore. Hardly anyone wore leather dress shoes. Shortly afterwards a woman stopped by him and sniffed at the air around her. Alfred greeted the woman.

"It's a beautiful day. I can smell the flowers already," Alfred remarked. The woman looked down at his feet.

"You have lovely feet," the woman replied. She dropped down on her knees. "Let me rub your toes," she said.

The woman's kindness touched him. He declined her offer, but she grabbed his feet against his will and massaged them ferociously. She threw her head back and closed her eyes. The fragrance on Alfred's feet had aroused her and she started to kiss his toes. Alfred pulled his feet back and pushed the woman away from him.

"What are you doing?" he screamed. The woman looked at his shoes and pointed at them.

"The shoes, how much are they?" she said.

"Do you want to buy my shoes?" Alfred stammered. "They are not for sale. I have some better shoes inside the store. If you would like to come inside, I'll show them to you. They are really nice. Do you need a new pair for your husband? "

"No, no," the woman said, pulling him by his shirt. "I want these shoes. How much do you want for them?"

Alfred laughed. "They aren't worth much, Ma'am," he answered. "I've had them for years. A customer brought them in for repair several years ago, but he never came back to claim them." Alfred picked up the shoes and turned them upside down so that she could see the worn-out soles. "See? There are holes in the soles. You wouldn't want these shoes. I have better ones inside the store."

"I want to buy them," the woman insisted.

Alfred scratched his head. "Oh, I don't know," he said. "They are not for sale, but if you insist, you can have them for ten dollars."

The woman quickly pulled out a bundle of banknotes from her purse and handed them to Alfred. She snatched the shoes from Alfred's hands. "If you could wait just a little longer, I'll put them in a box and gift-wrap them for you," Alfred said. The woman shook her head and walked off with the shoes. Alfred looked at the notes in his hand and suddenly realized that she had given him $200. He ran after her and yelled: "Ma'am, you gave me more than what I asked for them." The woman waved a taxicab to a stop and climbed into it. Alfred stood dumbfounded on the sidewalk, watching the taxicab as it sped down the avenue and eventually disappeared.

"Two hundred bucks for a pair of worn-out shoes," he muttered. "It's definitely my lucky day!"

As the day drew to a close, Alfred picked up some shoes and dropped them in his duffle bag. He promised Adele that he wouldn't bring home too many pairs, but the unfinished pair had to be ready for the customer the next day. Alfred switched off the light in the back room, emptied the cash register, and put the day's receipts in a money pouch. At that moment the front door opened up, and a young man dashed into the store and embraced him.

"Thank you, thank you very much for fixing my shoes," he said. Alfred remembered that the man came earlier to pick up his shoes. "Whew, what a good time I had!" he said, grinning. I owe it all to you." The man reached out for his wallet and drew out a $100 note. He slipped it into Alfred's hand. "She took my shoes off to kiss my feet and we made love in the back seat of my car," he added. "You are absolutely right. Women love a man with beautiful feet. She fell in love with my feet the moment she took my shoes off. Have you ever made love in the back seat of a Volkswagen Beetle?"

Alfred pointed his thumb at his chest and frowned. "Me? Can't you see that I am a big man? If I make love to a woman in the back seat of a VW bug, they'll have to cut the top off to get me out."

"There is far more room in that car than you can think. Hey, if twenty-three college students can cram into it, I don't see why it would be a problem for you."

"Twenty-three college students did not make love in the VW bug," Alfred retorted. The man waved him goodbye and left the shop.

Alfred glanced at the one hundred dollars note. He turned off the light and, for a short moment, stood still in the dark. He slowly shook his head to and fro. "What have I done differently today," he whispered.

Adele had his dinner spread out for him on the table when he arrived home. "I am not hungry," he said. He dropped the duffle bag at the foot of the table and headed for the bathroom. "I am going to shower and then go to bed. You wouldn't believe what happened to me at the shoe repair shop." He removed his shirt from his back and handed it to Adele.

Adele cuddled up to him. "You don't have to take a bath now," she said. "You look so tired. Come and let me massage your feet. You'll feel better afterwards." She led him into the bedroom and closed the door behind them. She made him lie down on his back and removed his shoes. Then she reached for a bottle of L'Eau de PO from the nightstand and rubbed the fragrance on his feet. She gently massaged his feet and sniffed at the fragrance. The smell of the fragrance excited her and she unbuttoned his trousers. For a long time the shoe repair business had preoccupied the shoemaker. His constant worries had impacted their love life and he felt guilty and remorseful. He cried softly as his wife made love to him.

"Tell me what happened to you in the shop?" Adele asked. Alfred leaned over the bed and reached out for his pants. He pulled out a handful of bills. "I earned $300 in just one day," he said. "My customers are going crazy over my shoes."

"I am crazy over your feet," Adele replied, turning over and kissing him. "I hope that nobody tried to kiss your feet."

"A woman tried to do just that," Alfred answered. "I could not believe that she did that in the street and in broad daylight. I broke away from her, but she would not leave me alone. She wanted to buy my old shoes and I reluctantly let her have them. She paid me handsomely for them too." Alfred held the money over Adele's face. She took the money from his hands. "Bring me more shoes tomorrow, and I'll help you repair them," she said.

"I thought that you were tired of looking at shoes and smelling them."

"We can put some sparks back in your customers' love life," she softly whispered.

Adele underhandedly poured L'Eau de PO fragrance in every pair of shoes that her husband brought home. Alfred's customers soon discovered that the fragrance in their shoes aroused sexual desires in their partners. Women became fixated on their partners' feet and men suddenly found that the shoes made them attractive and desirable to women. Words spread out that Alfred Shoemaker could shine one's shoes as well as one's love life. More customers started to bring their shoes to Alfred for repairs and business started to pick up at the shoe repair shop. People brought in their brand new shoes to Alfred to be repaired. "This is crazy," Alfred said to a customer who brought him a new pair of shoes for reconditioning. "There is nothing wrong with these shoes. Why do you want them reconditioned?"

"Oh," the customer replied, "the shoes are all right, but when you work on them, they turn my wife on. I think the smell of leather and the sweat from your hands excite her."

For a while the shoe repair shop thrived. Alfred earned enough money to pay off his creditors and support his shoe repair business. He even had some extra money left over to spend on extravagances. One night he came home and surprised Adele with a boxed gift. When Adele opened the box, she found a beautiful hat inside. Adele became fond of the hat and wore it to church on Sundays. People just could not stop marveling at the hat with the little leather shoe on it. Then, without warning, Alfred's shoe repair business took another downturn. People became preoccupied with AIDS, the economy, pollution, the high divorce rate, and the high cost of sending their kids to college. They sought to distance themselves from the reality of everyday life by stepping out of their shoes. They left their shoes at home and walked barefooted to demonstrate their disapproval for high taxes, government waste, crime and corruption. Suddenly it became fashionable to go about without footwear. People walked in the public parks barefooted, went to work barefooted, watched movies in theaters barefooted, and dined in restaurants barefooted. Men and women courted and married without wearing shoes. Athletes competed against one another without wearing shoes, and lawyers battled each other in courtrooms without wearing shoes. Worried politicians roamed the country and begged the American people to wear shoes again. The fad shook the entire shoe industry. Shoe manufacturers freely gave away all the shoes they had in their stockrooms in order to save on inventory costs, but people refused to take them. Shoe retailers offered free condoms with their shoes, but nobody came forward. The shoe manufacturers paid huge sum of money to have their shoes hauled away and destroyed, and many of them filed for bankruptcy. The poor nations of the world begged the US government to donate the shoes to their poor citizens. Congress, however, forbade the shipment of shoes to undeveloped nations. The politicians feared that the countries receiving the shoes might use them to build weapons of mass destruction or start a germ warfare. The barefoot trend that swept the nation signaled the end of the shoe-wearing custom in America and the collapse of the shoe-manufacturing industry. It severely impacted on Alfred Shoemaker's shoe repair business. Shoemakers and retailers met in emergency sessions to discuss on how best to utilize the massive surplus of rubber and leathers. While they debated, a new industry developed and took the country by storm. People began to adorn their feet with beads, chains, trinkets, jewelries, flowers, and anything that would make their feet look different from another pair of feet. Jewelry shops offered toe-piercing service so that rings can be fastened to the toes. A whole new array of supporting industries sprang up. Manicurists suddenly found themselves in the lucrative business of making up feet. Plastic surgeons joined in the bandwagon and performed surgeries on toes to shorten, lengthen or beautify them. The conversation in bar rooms, discotheques and restaurants turned to feet and feet ornaments. Nightclub owners staged 'BEST FEET', 'BIG FEET' and 'SEXY FEET' contests. Television stations ran commercials showing women's bare feet to advertise cereals, jewelries, perfumes, mattresses and clothing. Trendy restaurants attracted diners by adding such items as 'CHICKEN A LA FOOT' on their menus. Restaurateurs encouraged their patrons to stretch their feet up on their tables while waiting for their foods. The food servers occasionally joined in the foot display to satisfy customers' curiosities. In the restaurants and shopping centers, signs reading 'No Shoes, No Service' were taken down and replaced with new signs reading 'Patrons wearing shoes will not be served.' Across the country angry mobs burnt and looted establishments still displaying signs of 'NO SHOES, NO SERVICE.' Owners of establishments still displaying the old signs were frequently dragged outside, stripped off of their shoes, and forced to parade down the street with their shoes hanging around their necks. It became acceptable for employees to lay their bare feet on their desks during working hours. Beautiful and sexy feet became the traits by which an employee was judged for job promotion.

A major section of the population however did not embrace the new foot craze and divided the country into two opposing groups. One group advocated the use of footwear in public places, while the other group wanted to disband the use of shoes in American society. The group that favored the use of footwear in public places banded themselves into a citizen action group and called themselves the United Safety Footwear League. The group became known as USFWL. This group maintained that shoes must be worn for safety and civility. Its members argued that the shoe-wearing custom was a long-established tradition. This tradition distinguishes civilized people from the shoeless animals and savages. On the other extreme, the Anti Footwear League, which became known as AFWL asserted that the first man never wore shoes and all humans are born shoeless. The AFWL argued that the resources used in the manufacture of shoes should be utilized in ways that would benefit society the most. They argued that the resources should be used to make footballs. It strongly criticized all government programs that give shoes to the homeless people. It contended that the money spent on shoes should be spent on building homes for the homeless. It advocated new laws condemning footwear in schools and public places. One segment of the population, unable to side with either group, formed a new group called the Neutral Footwear League. This group was frequently referred to as the NFWL. The NFWL dictated to its members that they wear one shoe only. They recommended that the shoe be worn on the foot that is most likely to take the most stress while engaging in normal day-to-day activities. Within the NFWL body, the members became embattled with one another on which foot to wear the shoe. The NFWL ruled that its members should be free to wear the shoe on either foot. After several weeks of bitter arguments, the dissident members broke away from the NFWL and formed their own groups. The left-wing group advocated that the shoe be worn on the left foot. The right-wing group advocated that the shoe be worn on the right foot.

The AFWL furiously campaigned for an amendment in the U.S Constitution that would give the people the right to wear or not to wear shoes in public places. When White House employees began to arrive for work without wearing shoes, the President ordered an emergency session of Congress to address the shoe issue. Congress eventually enacted a new law requiring all federal employees to wear shoes at work. When a group of students refused to wear shoes in the classrooms at a University in Ohio, the Ohio State Governor called in the National Guards. Angry students walked out of the classrooms to protest their rights. Soldiers went in with raised batons and cocked riffles. They beat the students who walked about without shoes. The students threw books and backpacks at the guards. The guards threw smoke grenades and fired at the students. When the smoke lifted, four students were killed and several others wounded.

Amidst all this turmoil Alfred Shoemaker suddenly found himself with an obsolete trade. He courageously hung on to his trade while the lawmakers and the citizens hotly debated the issue - To wear or not to wear shoes! Adele had begun to lose interest in him and his shoe repair business. Her children became avid followers of the AFWL and refused to wear shoes at any time. Alfred's clientele dwindled down to just a few dozen loyal customers. Each day Alfred and Adele argued over his meager income. The money he earned repairing shoes was barely sufficient to buy the basic necessities of life. Alfred was hounded by his creditors and pursued by real estate agents and property developers wanting to tear down the shoe repair shop and build a mega mall.

"Sell the damn shop," Adele exhorted him every day. "There is no longer a need for a shoe repair shop in America. For heaven's sake, Al, you have to find another way to earn your living. We need money to feed and buy clothing for the children now."

"I don't want to sell," Alfred replied.

"Please," Adele pleaded.

Alfred refused to close down the shoe repair shop and give in to the Real Estate developers. Under constant pressure from Adele, he finally agreed to set up a foot accessories stand in one corner of the shop and let her manage it. On weekends Adele scouted the flea markets looking for odds and ends appropriate for adorning feet. She displayed her finds in the shop corner and sold them to customers seeking novelties to adorn their feet with. The sale of toe rings and ankle bracelets enabled the Shoemakers to live decently for some time.

While watching the news on television one evening, Alfred saw a clash between the members of the USFWL and the AFWL. The demonstrators hurled shoes and screamed profanities at each other. The police kept the two groups apart to prevent another bloody footwear war. News clips showed representatives from Arizona and Massachusetts meeting to discuss new proposals to end the shoe crisis. The new proposal called for the Federal government to suspend all form of economic assistance to the States who supported the banning of shoes in American society. The proposal also gave unlimited power to law agencies to enforce a new law requiring people to wear shoes in public places. Alfred turned off the TV set and went in the bedroom. He sat on the bed and buried his head in his hands. Adele came in the bedroom to comfort him. She leaned her head on his shoulders and took his hand in hers.

"You must change career now," Adele whispered. "It won't do you any good to hang on to old customs and traditions. The world is changing and people's needs are changing. You must find yourself a new trade before you are too old to work. Footwear is gone forever. The world is headed in a different direction and shoes will not be found and used again where it is heading. In a few months there won't be any shoes for you to repair. Give up your trade now."

"I am a Shoemaker," Alfred moaned. "I have mended shoes all my life and I don't know anything else." He bent over his knees and clasped his head with both his hands. "It's my trade, my only trade."

"You are being a fool," Adele said sternly. "There won't be any shoe-mending to be done anymore. You are just being stubborn. You must now find something else to do."

Alfred raised his head and stared at his wife. "What can I do?"

"You can try plumbing or carpentry."

Alfred stood up and looked out of the window. He turned around and faced Adele.

"I am a Shoemaker, Adele. Don't forget that! Generations of the Shoemaker family had engaged in the business of making and mending shoes and that's how it will remain in my family." His voice shook and Adele shuddered. She had never seen him in this state before. "I am the son of a shoemaker and my children will be shoemakers. I will die a shoemaker."

"You will be a dead Shoemaker soon if you don't listen to reason," Adele warned him. "Your time as a shoemaker is up. You must find another trade."

Alfred stubbornly refused to change trade. He stayed up all night thinking about ways to get the American people to start wearing shoes again. Then he slept the whole morning away. His late sleeping infuriated Adele. She patiently continued to work in the shop selling beads and trinkets to the fashion-conscious customers. She became abusive and frequently yelled at customers who walked into the shoe shop looking for foot novelties. Her bad temper kept the few remaining customers away from the shop.

When Adele's station wagon broke down, she called her husband and asked him to pick up the boys from school. It was a very hot day and the temperature was a sizzling 104 degrees Fahrenheit. Alfred arrived at the school early and waited in his car for the boys to come out of the classroom. A television crew filmed a program in the parking lot for the TV station's evening news. A member of the TV crew cracked an egg onto the hot asphalt. The lens of the TV camera pointed at the egg as it sizzled, cracked, popped and fried. At the same time workers from a nearby factory began to file out of the gates. They walked barefooted towards their automobiles in the parking lot. Alfred felt his stomach churned as he watched the shoeless workers walked by him. "If I could convince these people to wear shoes again," he mused, "I can be back in my shop doing what I love to do." A certain peculiarity about the workers struck him. Instead of walking, they hopped about the parking lot like rabbits. He also noted that they hopped on one foot, then on the other foot, all the way to their cars. It suddenly dawned on him that the workers' feet were getting fried on the hot asphalt. Like lizards that alternately raise their feet up to avoid the scorching sand, the factory workers hopped to their cars on one foot to avoid burning their feet.

"Fashion!" he muttered. "These people are out of their minds. They can avoid all this pain if they wear shoes." His boys ran out of school, hopping across the parking lot on one foot. They quickly got into the car.

"The asphalt is burning hot," one son yelled.

"My feet are burning," the other son screamed.

"How are your feet?"

"Fine," the boys answered back. His sons' feet were covered with blisters and calluses.

"You are all crazy," he told them. "It does nobody any good to walk around barefooted, especially on a hot day like this. Why don't you wear your shoes?"

"It is cool to go shoeless, dad. Nobody wears shoes anymore. You are out, old man."

"It is cool to have hot feet? Is that how they teach you to speak at school?"

"You are behind the time, Dad."

The blisters and calluses on his sons' feet worried Alfred and he spent the next morning thinking about the health of his sons' feet.

"What's the matter?" Adele asked him. "You haven't said a word since you got home last night. Are you mad at me because I asked you to pick up the boys from school?"

"How can I convince the American people to wear shoes again?" he said, more to himself than to his wife.

"Shoes, shoes, shoes," Adele burst out. "All I hear you talk about these days are shoes, more shoes, and nothing but shoes. I hope you are not losing your mind."

"If I can convince the American people to wear shoes again," he muttered, "I will save my trade."

Adele sighed and shook her head. She cleared the dining table of the dirty plates and carried them to the sink.

"That's it," Alfred yelled, jumping up from his seat. "I've got it!"

Adele dropped the dirty plates on the floor. The plates shattered into several pieces and flew in all direction. Furious, Adele screamed "Look what you made me do." She pointed at the pieces of the plates on the kitchen floor.

"Re-invent the shoe," he told Adele. Alfred sat down and smiled. He closed his eyes and clenched his teeth. "We have got to re-invent the shoe," he murmured. "People don't buy shoes to keep their feet warm and dry. They buy shoes so they would feel masculine or feminine; rugged and different; sophisticated and glamorous. I need to make buying shoes an emotional experience for the masses. I need to sell excitement, not shoes, to the American people."

"Go and re-invent my foot," Adele angrily said. "Look at all this mess."

"Honey," her husband begged. He clasped her arms. "People are burning their feet walking across a hot parking lot. If we can sell them a pair of shoes without forcing them to forgo fashion, we can be back in the shoe business. I must re-invent the shoe, redesign its shape and redefine its function. People will buy my shoes as long as I do not violate their individualities. I will promote the new shoes as having one specific use only. I will make a pair of shoes that people can wear just for walking, another pair for dunking basketballs, and still another pair just for running."

"Al, this is not going to work," Adele said. "Nobody is wearing shoes anymore, can't you see that? Nobody will buy your shoes, no matter how you make them."

"They will," Alfred insisted. "My customers won't have to be runners to buy my running shoes. They will buy and wear them because they will make them feel like they can run and win the Boston Marathon. I will make basketball shoes that will make teenagers feel that they can jump up and touch the top of the Eiffel Tower."

"I am telling you that nobody is buying shoes these days."

"I will make shoes for walking, shoes for biking, shoes for dancing, and shoes for making short trips to the bathroom at night."

"Wearing shoes for making short trips to the bathroom at night?" Adele shuddered at the thought that her husband might be losing his mind.

"I will call the new shoes 'bedroom slippers.' I will make loafers for husbands to wear when they want to loaf around the house. And, oh! Remember that little boy who lives down the street and who was born with deformed legs?"

"His legs are crooked," Adele said. "He won't look good or walk straight in anything that you make for him. The poor lad will never be attractive to women."

"I will make him a pair of boots that will make him look like one of them bow-legged wranglers in Texas. He will have many women chasing him in no time. He'll be country stepping in my new boots all the way to the altar. We will call these shoes Cowboys boots."

"I still think that your idea won't work."

"I will use green leather to make my shoes. I will make them in various colors, like burgundy, pink or pastel."

Adele frowned. "Honey," she said, "Nobody wants to wear shoes nowadays. Who will want to wear pastel-colored clogs?"

"Clogs," Alfred exclaimed. "Good idea. I will make clogs so that employers can hear which employees are coming to work on time and which employees are leaving early."

"People had given up wearing shoes altogether, Alfred," she said passionately. "How are you going to convince them to wear shoes again? It is useless, Al."

"I will design platform shoes for short women who want to appear taller. I will make shoes for people with one leg shorter than the other. I will build tiny shoes for women with big feet."

"What?"

"I know what you are thinking, honey. The women won't mind a bit. Neither calluses nor bunions will stop them from buying the tiny shoes that I will make just for them. Every woman in America will buy the shoes that won't fit, and every woman who will wear my shoes will feel like she is Cinderella. I will make Mules for idiots to wear, Oxfords for college professors, Topsiders for boaters, Islanders for tourists, and Bostonians for the inconsiderate drivers in Boston. I will build 5,285 shoes as a remembrance to all the teenagers killed by guns in America."

Alfred could hardly sleep at night. Various news media reported that the barefoot craze had harmed hundreds of thousands of feet. Frequent clashes between the NFWL and AFWL had resulted in more damage to the members' feet. Medical journals warned that shoeless people were more prone to suffer from broken toes, splintered toenails, twisted ankles, cuts and bruises, and snakebites. Bumps and gnarls on feet became common among people who walk barefooted. Toenails frequently turned yellow, white or brown. Hospitals recorded a disturbing increase in injuries and damage to the feet. Tens of millions of people, particularly young children, were suffering from various kinds of foot ailments, acquired while walking around barefooted. The reports gave Alfred encouragement to pursue his dreams.

Alfred absorbed himself in his new endeavor night after night. He brought shoes home and tinkered with them at night. To test his new shoes for their strengths and for their abilities to withstand hot or cold weather, he put the shoes inside the freezer, submerged them in hot water, and cooked them at high temperatures. To see how quickly they would dry, he placed the shoes in the microwave oven. To test their strengths, he coated the shoes with honey and left them outside for the squirrels to gnaw at. On rainy days, he left shoes outside to collect rainwater. When the rain stopped, he measured the water that had collected inside the shoes and sized the shoes according to how much rainwater had collected inside the shoes. He assigned a size 4 to a shoe that held four ounces of water, a size 22 to a shoe that held twenty-two ounces. For people who didn't like to wear new shoes, he hung a dozen pair of them in his backyard and fired lead pellets into them. At night he woke up to examine Adele's feet. Then he slipped a pair of his new shoes on her feet to see how they will look when worn.

After months of tinkering with his shoe prototypes, Alfred bought all the shoes that the shoe manufacturers did not want anymore. The shoe manufacturers were happy to give him their shoe inventory. He had the shoes delivered to a warehouse. When the warehouse filled up, he had them dumped in his back yard. Adele almost fainted when she came home one evening and saw a mountain of shoes stacked up two-story high around their house. She had to climb over the new obstacle in order to enter the house. Squirrels made their homes inside the shoes. Later raccoons, skunks and snakes joined the squirrels and built homes inside the shoes. Before long a flock of vultures and a pair of bald eagles landed on the mountain of shoes. The snakes feasted on the skunks and the squirrels. The vultures swept down on the raccoons and other animal carcasses. The bald eagles waited until the snakes had fatten themselves up, then swept down on them and carried them off for their own dinner. Each day the flock of bald eagles grew larger and larger. One day a bald eagle swept down on a child looking for raccoons in the shoes and carried her off. The neighbors alerted the police; park rangers were immediately dispatched to the Shoemakers' house to investigate. They refused to shoot at the bald eagles on the ground that the birds were on the endangered species list. Police later found the child on a hillside two miles away from the house. To protect the eagles' chicks, troopers fired tear gas at the girl. The child was overwhelmed by the dense smoke. She finally ran away from the nest, coughing and rubbing her eyes. The police then cordoned off the site with tapes. The park rangers went to the nest and examined the eagle chicks to ensure that no harm was done to them. The little girl, badly shaken and in tears, ran to her mother.

"I hope that you all get buried alive under a ton of bird shit," she screamed at the park rangers. A black bird perched on a bough above the nest crowed and flipped up its tail. A streak of white and green gooey substance zipped through the air and landed on a park ranger's face.

Alfred theorized that people would not mind wearing shoes again as long as they could continue to wear their feet ornaments. He sprayed his shoes with various colors of hues and stitched various kinds of ornaments on them. Then he sutured his name in bold letters on the shoes and called his new creation the *Alfredo Simplex.* He rearranged the furniture in the shop repair shop and in spite of Adele's objection, ejected the foot accessories counter from the shop. He then ordered a new sign for the shop front. When the sign was delivered, he had it hung above the shop main door. The bright new neon sign reading *Foot Decor Shoppe* immediately attracted the attention of window shoppers. Customers camped out in front of the shop so they could be the first people to buy the new shoes when the doors opened. On opening day, a horde of teenagers rushed to the store and bought the highly visible shoes. Fistfights broke out inside the shop over the new shoes. Affluent people who wanted to project a new image flocked to Alfred's shop and snapped up all the shoes from the shelves. The new line of shoes gained total acceptance among consumers. People, particularly those concerned about the safety of their feet, wanted them and were willing to pay a high price for them. In just a few weeks Alfred sold more than a million pair of his new shoes. People loved the new shoe design and the added protection that the new shoes provided to their feet. The new shoes were fashionable, functional and practical. They required no polishing or cleaning. Foot writers and reporters all over the country praised the *Alfredo Simplex* line of shoes as the most creative footwear ever invented since Julius Caesar and his soldiers swept across Gaul wearing toe armor. Reporters scrambled to Alfred's shop to interview and photograph him. Pictures of Alfred and his shoes appeared in newspapers and magazines all over the country. Demand for his new shoes surged. To meet the new demand, Alfred moved his shoe retail shop to a larger store and, in a move that stunned the nation, bought all the shoe companies that were struggling to stay alive. He brought all the idle shoe factories back to life and hired back several thousands of factory employees who were laid off during the barefoot craze. Within just a few months, *Foot Decor Shoppes* mushroomed across the country. Alfred Shoemaker became a millionaire and a celebrity. The newspapers dubbed him the new shoe magnate and praised him for reviving the shoe manufacturing industry in America. He was lauded at every business functions for his creativity, inventiveness and persistence. Politicians, businessmen and podiatrists acclaimed him for saving the nation's feet and setting new standards for style and comfort in footwear. They commended him for the country's highest civilian honor, the Presidential Medal of Freedom. Wherever he went, he was greeted with signs of 'ALFRED SHOEMAKER FOR PRESIDENT!'

The USFWL welcomed the return of shoes in American society. Its members unanimously approved of the rebirth of the shoe industry. Disgusted and jealous at the success of the *Foot Decor Shoppes,* the AFWL intensified its campaigns to ban the new shoes in public places. Its leaders organized a march to Washington, D.C to speak out against the shoe revival and threatened to order a nationwide strike to protest the sale of the new shoes. The NFWL sent out orders to its members to join in the march to Washington, D.C. On the appointed day, which became known as the Million Shoes March, tens of thousands of marchers wearing one shoe on the left foot walked to the Nation's Capital. They were later joined by hundreds of thousands of jeering marchers wearing one shoe on the right foot. Then, with a loud roar and amidst the sound of cracking bones, the NFWL marchers clashed with the AFWL marchers.

Alfred joined the marchers to look for ideas for a new line of shoes to complement the *Alfredo Simplex* line. He went to the convention as a spectator to collect market data and to look for new ways to sell more shoes. When the crowd streamed into Washington Mall, he noticed that the marchers limped. The noise distracted him. He soon forgot the reason why he came to the convention and mingled with the marchers. The crowd cheered when the NFWL chairman, wearing one shoe only, limped his way to the stage and took the podium to begin a long discourse on the ill-effect of wearing shoes. The marchers clapped their hands and shouted their approval and support.

"We decry the invasion of foreign-made shoes in our land," the NFWL chairman concluded. "We must resist any attempt by any foreign nation, friend or foe, to force upon us the old, unacceptable, and demeaning practice of wearing two shoes when we would rather wear just one shoe. We will fight anyone who wants to take away our right to wear or not to wear shoes, and we will use nuclear bombs against anyone who dares take our rights to wear one shoe only."

The crowd frantically applauded. The conventioneers slowly began to file out of Washington Mall. They left behind them a million shoes that were littered all around the city streets. Homeless people quickly moved in to begin scavenging the shoes. Soon the shoes were sold at street corners as the Million Shoes March souvenirs. A dark limousine driven by Secret Service Agents drove up to one shoe hawkers and purchased a box full of the shoes. It then sped to the White House. Alfred returned to his shoe laboratory and pondered over the observation he made of the Million Shoes Marchers. Podiatrists had discovered a curious growth on the hip of people who wore only one shoe. The lump, which they had termed the footloose syndrome, occurred predominantly among the NFWL activists. Since they only wore one shoe, the foot wearing the shoe stood higher on the ground than the foot without shoe. This created an imbalance in the person's stance, which some podiatrists referred to as SSE (shoe side effect.) The effect caused the person to limp. Gradually a hump formed on the hip above the foot wearing the shoe. There was no remedy for the abnormality and the deformity can only be corrected if the person wears two shoes. Worried about the health of the nation's feet, Congress appropriated a hundred million dollars to commission a study on why the American people had stopped wearing shoes. Congress later released a 1000-page report to publicize its findings. The report stated, among others, that the American people had stopped wearing shoes because they have deep mistrust for their government.

Alfred immediately saw in this foot abnormality an opportunity for him to expand his line of footwear. He knew that people afflicted with the footloose syndrome already owned one shoe and would not purchase a new pair of shoes. He could sell them only one shoe to correct the footloose syndrome. By buying just one shoe from him, the consumers would save the taxpayers millions of dollars in useless government study and research. Thereupon Alfred introduced a new line of shoes which he designated the *Alfredo NF*. The new shoe was uniquely designed for the person who already owns one shoe. The *NF* line, the *NF* standing for Neutral Foot, was a revolutionary concept in shoe design and marketing. It was designed to be worn on either the left or right foot and to complement any existing shoe. The public was enamored with the new shoe and rushed to the *Foot Decor Shoppe* to snap up the new model. For the first time since shoes were invented, consumers could comfortably walk into a shoe shop and buy one shoe only. The success of the new shoe line was far greater than what Alfred had envisioned.

The NFWL eagerly bought into the new shoe concept. The USFWL was delighted with the new shoes and was overjoyed to see more people wearing them. The USFWL leaders concluded that they had successfully accomplished their mission and disbanded. The AFWL saw its membership trickled down to just a few members. Finally, AFWL officials conceded that they have lost their battle to make people reject shoes and merged with the NFWL. The new group changed their name to the National Footwear League, thus continuing to be known by the American public by its abbreviated name, the NFWL. It continued to support the shoe-wearing public and to promote shoe uniformity and regulation. It aggressively lobbied Congress to enact more laws to protect Americans' feet.

Alfred continued to dream of making better shoes for the consumers and he frequently stayed late in his shoe factory to work on a new shoe design. During a visit to one of his shoe shops, Alfred saw a customer lingering around the store. Intrigued, he approached her.

"I have difficulties attracting suitors," she timidly said to him. "I thought maybe your shoes would get me some attention."

Alfred saw an opportunity to sell more shoes to women. "I think I may have just the shoe for you," he told her. "Could you come back in about two weeks? My engineers are working on a new shoe prototype."

"Certainly," she said with a smile. "I knew that I can count on you to create something that all women want - a pair of shoes that will attract men to us." She winked at Alfred and left the store.

Alfred lost no time in assembling his shoe designers. For days and nights, they brainstormed and wrote down ideas for a new shoe design. When they finally emerged from the meeting room after three days of brainstorming, they had compiled dozens of drawings and specifications for the new shoes. The shoe designers thereafter shut themselves in their shoe laboratories to create the new shoe prototype. At the end of the week, they had the prototype completed and ready to be tried by the customer. The shoe designers christened the new shoes the *Alfredo Amore*. The designers wanted the shoes to accomplish just one function: to attract the opposite sex. Working on the principle that unlike poles attract, the shoe designers encased powerful magnets of pure magnetite ore in the heels and the toe lining of the new shoes. When the people wearing the new shoes are within the sphere of influence of the magnetic forces, the shoes would attract one another.

When the new shoes were ready, Alfred invited the woman back to the store. In the presence of reporters and television cameras, he presented the new shoes to her. Watched by dozens of photographers, TV news cameramen and reporters, she slipped the shoes onto her feet. Unknown to her, Alfred had hired some male models to wear the new shoes as well. As she paced up and down and around the designers of the shoes, the shoes began to attract one another like iron fillings are attracted to a magnet. The attraction became stronger as she walked closer to the male models. The magnetic shoes drew her to the male models and she tumbled into the arms of a handsome man. The onlookers applauded and cheered. "Come on, give her a kiss," the onlookers urged.

"Wow," the woman sighed, blushing. "I have finally found you." She put her arms around his neck and whispered: "Now that I have found you, I won't let go of you." She pecked at his cheek. The onlookers clapped their hands and shouted approvals.

The photograph of the woman hugging and kissing a man in a shoe shop appeared in newspapers all around the country. TV stations reported the story of a woman who found love in a shoe store. After the newscast, people rushed to Alfred's shoe shops to buy the new shoes that would bring them eternal love and happiness. Animal welfare proponents welcomed the new shoes. Before the new shoes made their appearances, men and women looking for suitors used dogs to attract each other. The dog sparked conversation between the dog owner and the other person. These eventually lead to dates and wedding bells. But once the couple married, they abandoned the dog or dropped it off at an animal shelter. Soon after the new shoes were introduced, the number of marriage licenses soared to a record high number. Hospitals around the country reported an unusually large number of new babies. An increasing number of lonely people found it easier to find new partners while wearing the new shoes. Patients waiting for long hours in doctors' offices for their dental or medical appointments found that time went by quicker when they wore their love shoes. The gloomy visits to the dentists turned into amorous adventures. Grocery stores and book stores, encouraged by the news that a couple fell in love in a shoe store, organized food and book reading parties to attract single people. The single people showed up in drove wearing the love shoes. When the parties ended, they left the stores in each other's arms without purchasing anything. The stores complained that the parties did not result in any significant grocery or book sales. They concluded that people who were infatuated with one another had no time to cook, eat, read or shower. The stores eventually stopped organizing the parties.

Following the success of the love shoes, Alfred's designers introduced a new series of smart shoes. His factories built a new pair of shoes for the mail carrier to fight off fierce dogs on their daily mail deliveries. The new shoes, named the *Postmaster*, had a built-in electronic device in the heel. It emitted an ultrasound pitch that was inaudible to the human ears, but irritating to the dogs' auditory senses. Whenever a mail carrier wore the shoes to deliver mail, the attacking dog ran off and disappeared. For some time no one knew where the dogs went. Then visitors to the Yellowstone National Park began to see an unusually large pack of dogs inside the park. Upon further investigation, park officials determined that the dogs ran to the park to escape the mail carriers. To control the dog population inside the park, the park rangers used a tactic known as reverse discrimination. They dressed up like mail carriers and wore the *Postmaster* to hike the trails. At the sight of the mail carriers, the dogs ran off and headed for other National Parks. The *PrimaCare* shoe line, which Alfred had specifically designed for nurses, was well received by the Health Care community. A feature built in the shoes alerted the nurse whenever she had been standing on her feet for too long. The shoes checked and slowed down the development of varicose and spider veins on the nurses' legs. The new shoes brought male patients to the hospital rooms and joy to the accounting department. People with high blood pressure were relieved when Alfred designed a special pair of shoes, the *Magnetoe,* just for them. The magnet in the special shoes keeps the iron in the blood cells down in the lower part of the body and away from the heart, thus reducing the risk of a heart attack. Alfred had been concerned for some time about the high incidence of teen pregnancies. He once watched fishermen in waders fish the streams. The waders protected the fishermen from the cold water, floating debris, and the sharp barbs of flying hooks. It also allowed the fishermen to fish in deeper waters without getting wet. Alfred thought that if the wader can keep water out, it could be made to keep hands out too. He ordered his shoe designers to look at the wader and to model a new pair of women boots after it. He mandated that the new boots should be fashionable enough to be worn by a fashion-conscious teenage girl, but tall enough to keep her date's roaming hands from her thighs. A few months later, the new *Chastity Boots* were introduced to the press. Parents liked the computerized lockable chastity belt around the hips that only they could unlock. The extra safeguard gave the parents peace of mind whenever their teenage daughters went out on a date. They could dial into the belt's memory from a remote workstation to unlock the chastity belt should an emergency arise. Teenage girls became enamored with the new boots and eagerly bought them. Soon after the *Chastity Boots* were introduced, the number of teenage pregnancy dropped drastically. Alfred's designers introduced the *Monitor* shoe line to help people control their weights. His designers attached two electronic scales underneath the shoes to monitor and store the person's weight. A quartz display on top of the shoes displayed the weight of the person. The designers realized that some people's waistline might obscure the screen from view; they offered as an option a monitor that can be stored in a pocket or purse. The shoes could be programmed to beep whenever the wearer's weight exceeded a weight limit initially set in the computer's memory. Another version of his *Monitor* shoes monitored the wearers' own drinking excesses. The shoes beeped when the wearer could not walk in a straight line for thirty seconds. It automatically dialed a taxicab for the intoxicated person. Drunk drivers who wore the new shoes were indebted to Alfred for saving their lives.

The shoe manufacturing industry turned into a high-technology industry. Alfred Shoemaker's factories constantly introduced new models of shoes, each model more sophisticated than the previous ones. His shoe designers became shoe engineers. The engineers made extensive use of microchips, fiber optics and rare metals in shoe manufacturing. Engineers and mathematicians now made up most of his research staff, with machinery doing most of the stitching and gluing. Alfred spent most of his time going over design specifications with his shoe engineers, researching and testing new materials. One night Alfred examined a shoe prototype in his office. Suddenly the shoe slipped through his fingers, glided up in the air and landed softly on the floor. He thought that his imagination was tricking him, picked up the shoe and put it back on the table. Feeling tired after working sixteen hours, he left the factory and went home.

The following day Alfred revealed to Adele that his engineers were looking for the ultimate shoe.

"The new shoes will change the way we commute to work every day."

"You are now a multi-millionaire," Adele remarked. "You should be thinking about retiring now."

"I have merely reinvented the shoe and added some useful functions to them," Alfred said. "What the world needs is a totally different kind of shoes. Until now the shoes go where the feet take them. I think that the shoes should carry the person instead of the person carrying the shoes strapped to his feet. When I have developed such shoes, I will have found the ultimate shoes. Its ultimate function will be to move people about quickly, effortlessly and economically. What our society needs are flying shoes."

"You want to make flying shoes?" Adele dropped her toast and stared at her husband. She became fearful that her husband had developed an enormous greed for wealth and that the greed for wealth had driven him on the verge of insanity.

"That's right," Alfred said. "I will make shoes that can fly. After all, we have flying saucers, so why not have flying shoes? This technologically-advanced mode of transportation will reduce the impact to our precious environment. We will no longer depend on the automobiles to move us around. We will reduce our dependence on oil, decrease traffic fatalities, and eliminate traffic congestion and air pollution in our cities. The world would then be a safer place to live and raise children. The flying shoes will be the invention of the century. They will reduce oil consumption in America by 220 million barrels of oil per day. They will stop the 250 million used tires in the country's backyard from increasing up any further. The new shoes will eliminate the need for the 10,000 junk yards now spread across the country and save eleven million vehicles from being scrapped and dumped in the landfills each year."

"Honey, I think that you should take a vacation," Adele sympathetically suggested. "You haven't had a vacation since you gave the world the first *Alfredo Simplex* shoes. You have done enough already for the American people."

"I want to fulfill my dream. I am looking for the shoes that will give the people of this country a happier, healthier and freer lifestyle."

Alfred's engineers applied space age technology to his flying shoe prototypes. They altered their geometry, shaped them to cheat the wind, and added wings to them. They built miniature gravity-canceling devices into the shoes to make them float and ultimately fly in any direction. To make them even lighter, they experimented with various types of lightweight materials. They designed the new shoes to operate on the unlimited supply of solar energy, hydrogen and oxygen.

Alfred was convinced that his engineers could turn the flying shoe concept into reality. He envisioned that people would wear the new shoes to commute to work every day, travel to far away land, and explore inaccessible sites. He saw in his mind people flying into the sky, crossing rivers and scaling peaks.

He imagined thousands of people hovering over the Interstate highways, gliding into the future, and starting a new era in mass transit. People would no longer have a need for the automobiles. The automobiles would be scrapped and their parts put to other use. Oil would be conserved and saved for future generations. There would be no more traffic deaths, no massive carbon monoxide gases to pollute the atmosphere, and no noise to shatter the peace of the day. Commuting time would be drastically reduced and the ozone layer would be left intact to provide warmth to earth's inhabitants. People would breathe a cleaner air, would have more money to spend on other goods, and would have more time to spend with their families. His flying shoes would raise the standard of living in America to a new height.

Words that Alfred Shoemaker was manufacturing a new pair of shoes to replace the automobiles spread like wildfire even though his engineers and designers were sworn to secrecy. The automobile manufacturers panicked and became fearful that the auto industry would be relegated to the bottom of the economic scale. The automakers knew that if the flying shoes become reality, nobody would buy cars anymore. Oil companies became terrified at the prospect of having to shut down their oil refineries, close thousands of gas stations, and lay off thousands of employees. The automakers and the oil companies banded together and secretly attempted to convince Alfred Shoemaker to drop his new project. They offered him millions of dollars to shelf the entire project so that they could continue to build cars for the masses, but Alfred refused to give in to their demand. Soon after spurning the automakers, he started to receive threatening phone calls and death threats. Several fires started mysteriously at his factories and a bomb exploded and blew his car to pieces. Fortunately Alfred was not driving the car when it blew up. The FBI offered him protection, but he declined and continued to work on his flying shoes. One night a lone gunman took aim at him when he walked out of his office. The powerful shot threw him against a backdrop of a very common American scene, but he miraculously escaped the attack. The bullet grazed his imagination, pierced his ego, and shattered his entrepreneurship. The brutal assault on the free enterprise system angered the people who strongly condemned the attack. After the attempt on his life, Adele pleaded with her husband to give up on the flying shoes. Alfred reluctantly abandoned and shelved the project. He eventually sold his factories and retired.

Many new shoe factories sprang up to continue Alfred's legacy. In due time, the footwear market became saturated. Increase in labor costs slowly began to erode profits, forcing many companies to shut down their factories and lay off workers. They later reopened new factories in Asia and South America to take advantage of cheaper labor in those countries.

Walking in a shopping mall on a busy Saturday afternoon with Adele, Alfred was saddened to see so many foreign shoes on display in shoe shops.

The shoes were manufactured in China, Taiwan, Korea, Indonesia, Mexico, Brazil, Spain and Italy. He was disturbed that his country manufactured few shoes. His ingenuity helped bring the shoes back in American society, but the foreign countries were reaping the benefits. He was, however, content that the shoe companies had adopted his shoe design philosophy and carried on his dreams. He contemplated men and women walking around in hiking boots and tennis shoes. He watched grandmothers loafing around in loafers, janitors mopping the floor in work shoes, and young men loitering around in sandals. He observed young couples walking in comforters, students studying in sneakers, teenagers shuffling about in basketball shoes and senior citizens walking in deck shoes. Two youths sailed by them in their maritime shoes. A woman waltzed past them in her dancing shoes. A couple glided by them in their slides and a sneaky-looking man sneaked by them in his sneakers. A young mother with a baby strapped on her back sauntered by them in clogs; tiny booties protected her baby's feet. Alfred smiled at the sight of people wearing the shoes that he had earlier dreamed about making. He smiled even though he knew that the teenager wearing the basketball shoes would never dunk a basketball, or that the woman wearing the hiking boots had never been on a hiking trail. He smiled when he saw a man wearing running shoes standing still at one corner of the mall. He pictured children putting on soccer shoes to play soccer, businessmen donning golf shoes to play golf, and athletes slipping into cross-trainers to start training. When Alfred and Adele walked by the ice-skating rink in the middle of the mall, they stopped and sat down on a bench to watch the children skate around the ice rink in their ice-skating shoes. Not far away from them, a teenage girl clad in chastity boots cuddled against her boyfriend. They kissed while the young man's fingers fiddled with the control pad on the chastity boots. A group of religious people dressed in orange robes and wearing sandals beat on drums and twirled around. They celebrated the return and the wearing of shoes by people of all ages.

Two Mall Security Guards appeared and ordered the dancers out of the mall. Alfred and Adele looked at each other and smiled. They hugged one another, happy to be together and watching the world go round and round on shoes.

4 SILENT KILLER

The smokestack suddenly appears in my sight
Towering mightily over the cityscape
On a fine day with good sunlight
Neither the eyes nor the mind can escape
From the imposing structure

At first I saw just a streak
Almost invisible, but so sleek
A few seconds later
The thin lines lather
Into a huge ball

With great momentum, it leaves its kingdom
Like a lone prisoner craving for freedom
Surging and rolling into a glob of pelt
As smoothly as scribbling with felt
On fine paper

Expanding out of the colossal structure
It shapes into two hands stretched out in laziness
But before long it takes on another figure
Becoming a gymnast performing physical fitness

In between acquiring a new form
It loops when it climbs toward the constellation
It plumes when it abruptly changes its orientation
It wafts when it meets the North wind

It twirls when caught in a whirlwind
It fumigates when it hangs motionless
It lofts when it breaks its ghostly stillness
And surges upwards sans uniform

It soars into space
At an increasing pace
But I was not mislead
By the vanishing lead
For I know that before sundown
What goes up will come down

Copper will tarnish the water fountains on the school grounds
Zinc will oxidize the metals on the church playgrounds
Cadmium will find its way into our drinking water
Silver will crystallize on more than a cucumber
Antimony will spoil many a family picnic
And a child will collapse from licking arsenic
But what's more frightening than these earth-damaging pollen
Is that a silent killer called Lead is stalking innocent children

My name is Hong. I once worked in a lead smelter plant. My job was to clean the contaminated water before it is released from the holding tanks and into the adjoining river. I left the company in late 1978 after working there for less than 11 months. After I left the company I thought little of the company or about what I did in the company. In the summer of 1984 my health started to fail me again. I was ordinarily an energetic man and I hardly ever went to see a doctor. The last time I saw a physician was in the spring of 1978 when I applied for life Insurance. I was required to provide proof of good health to the insurance company in order to obtain life insurance coverage. The doctor gave me a clean bill of health, and the insurance company sold me a life insurance policy. My health suddenly began to deteriorate during the summer of 1984. I turned weak, lost my appetite, and I lost interest in my work and hobbies. My sickness lingered on for days. I thought that my declining health was due to poor eating habits and lack of exercise. People all over the country had embraced the new fitness craze. Health clubs were bursting to the seams with people who had joined in the momentum. Determined to shake off my morbid disposition, I joined a fitness club and began an exercise routine in an effort to lift up my spirits and chase away the sickly sensations. Three or four times a week, I worked out in the early morning and ran about four miles after work. Two weeks after I started to exercise, I recovered from my morbid disposition and felt energized and spritely all over again. The symptoms that I had previously felt disappeared as suddenly as they had appeared.

In the spring of 1985 the medical symptoms that I had felt the previous year suddenly returned. I lost my vigor and my enthusiasm for exercising. My weight dropped from 147 lb to 133 lb. Sometimes I felt so weak that I lied down on the couch for several hours at a time. Concerned at the drop in weight, I made an appointment to see a doctor. When I arrived for my appointment with the doctor, the nurse gave me a medical form to fill out. I filled out the medical form and then waited for the doctor to see me. After waiting for thirty minutes, the nurse beckoned me to an examination room. She asked me to remove my shoes and step on a scale. She noted down my weight and measured my height. Then she ushered me into another room to record my blood pressure, body temperature and pulse rate. She wrote down the medical information on a clipboard, told me that the doctor would see me shortly and left the room.

A few minutes later the door opened. The doctor walked into the room with a stethoscope strung around his neck and holding the clipboard in his left hand. He closed the door behind him and extended his right hand to me.

"Good morning," he greeted me, smiling. "I am Doctor Heimdall. How are you doing today?"

I stood up to shake the doctor's hand and replied that I had not been feeling well. Doctor Heimdall sat down on a stool and began to read the nurse's report on the clipboard. He read the report aloud, stopping every now and then to ask me to clarify something on the report.

"And all of a sudden you don't feel well?" Doctor Heimdall asked, with a puzzled look on his face.

"Yes. I started feeling sick only recently."

"Have there been any changes in your eating or sleeping habits?"

"No."

"Work habits? I mean, are you doing anything different from two weeks ago?"

"No."

"Have you had any problems sleeping at night?"

"Sometimes I do."

"Are you eating right?"

"I think I am."

"I see that you had previously seen a doctor in Minneapolis. Why in Minneapolis?"

"I applied for a job with Northwest Airlines. They sent me to Minneapolis for a medical check."

"I see. Did the doctor find anything wrong with you?"

"No."

"How long ago was that?"

"About six months ago."

"Tell me again the symptoms that you are experiencing."

"I feel lethargic and listless. I have no interest in play, and I have a poor appetite. I feel clumsy and cranky. I don't seem to be able to shake the feelings off."

"I would like to see your medical file. Could you request that it be transferred to me?"

"Yes."

"Sit down on that couch."

Doctor Heimdall asked me to show him my fingers. He plucked and pulled on my nails one by one.

"Your fingers look and feel all right. Take your eyeglasses off."

I removed my eyeglasses. Doctor Heimdall flashed his penlight into my pupils. He then asked me to pull the tail of my shirt out of my trousers and raise it high up to my chest. He ran his fingers on my back, my stomach and my chest.

"Roll your sleeves up," Doctor Heimdall ordered. I rolled up my sleeves. The doctor examined my hands and my arms. He asked me to lie down on my back. Then he pressed down hard on my stomach. "Has your pace changed?" he asked.

"No."

"You are not exerting yourself at work, are you?"

"No, I am not."

"Do you feel that you are under stress?"

"No."

"Everything looks fine. I don't see anything wrong. Maybe I'll find out more when I receive your medical report from Minneapolis. Did they do a blood test?"

"The nurse pricked my finger with a needle that looked like a hollow glass tube. She sucked up a sample of blood."

"That's not a blood test. She did that in order to determine if you are anemic. In order to conduct a blood test, the nurse would have to draw blood out of the vein in your arm. Did the nurse do that?"

"No."

"Oh, well! Then I will recommend that we have a blood test done first. We can do it now if you want."

"I would rather wait until you receive my medical file from Minneapolis."

"Is anyone in your family diabetic?"

"Yes, my mother. I don't know how long she had it."

"Diabetes is a hereditary disease. It is possible that you could have it too, but we won't know until we have conducted a blood test."

"I haven't had it for thirty-five years. Why will it suddenly show up now?"

"One never knows when it is going to hit. Some folks don't find out about it until they are 65 years old. I am not suggesting that you have diabetes. All I am saying is that it is a hereditary disease, and it is possible that you have acquired it too. You said that you have been in good health during most of your life. All of a sudden you come to me and say: 'I am feeling down in the dump.' Doctor Heimdall lowered his arms by his sides, opened his mouth, and stuck his tongue out "Yak! Just like that. That tells me that there is a slight chance that you may have the disease. But let us not get too hasty about this. As I said earlier, I want to do a blood test and check your blood sugar."

Later I called the medical center in Minneapolis to request that my medical file be transferred to Doctor Heimdall. When I heard nothing from Doctor Heimdall three weeks later, I called his office. The nurse told me that they had not yet received my medical file from Minneapolis. I called the medical record nurse in Minneapolis to ask for my file again. The nurse explained that she had not processed my request because she had been very busy. I got angry at the nurse and snapped at her.

"My life may depend on the information contained in the medical file. Could you please process my request right away?"

The nurse hastily replied that she would send the file to Doctor Heimdall immediately. Doctor Heimdall reviewed my medical file, but he found nothing in the file that would explain my illness. The report also confirmed that the nurse in Minneapolis did not take a blood sample. Doctor Heimdall then arranged for me to come back to his office for a blood test. Ten days later I returned to the doctor's office to have my sugar level checked out. When the results of the blood test came back from the laboratory, Doctor Heimdall called me at home to inform me of the test results. He was aware that I was hard of hearing and spoke louder than usual when he explained the test results to me.

"Everything looks fine in the report. I see that you are suffering from a hearing lost, but that should not worry you too much. I recommend that you have your hearing checked out every now and then. Your blood count is normal. That means that your red and white blood cells are in the normal range. However we noticed something interesting in your file. There are a large number of tiny red cells in your blood. This is an indication that your red blood cells are not fully grown. For one reason or another, the red cells in your blood don't develop fully, a condition known as thalassemia. This could mean that you may be deficient in iron. Your sugar count is 113, which is slightly above the maximum range of 110. I would not worry about it. I calculated that it is roughly two percent above the maximum range. So hell, what is two percent? Nothing, absolutely nothing! I would definitely say that you do not have diabetes and, for at least tonight, you can sleep peacefully and not worry about having the disease."

"What's thalassemia?"

"It's a blood disorder that leaves you deficient in iron." The doctor's voice became alarmed. "I read in your medical report that you have been exposed to lead. I am concerned about that."

"That happened a long time ago."

"How long ago was it since you were exposed to lead?"

"A few years ago. I was working in a lead smelter then."

"I would think that the lead has left your system by now. More than two years ago?"

"Yes."

"Were you directly exposed to the lead's fumes?"

"Yes, I was. We worked 12-hour shifts. We were given masks to wear while at work."

"Did you wear the mask all the times?"

"Not really. It was very uncomfortable. Some of us hung the mask around our necks. We would pull them up and cover our mouths whenever a Plant Supervisor walks by."

"I strongly advise you to have your lead count checked out. Now, tell me exactly, what were you doing in the lead smelter?"

"I was a Water Filtration Technician. My job was to oversee the water filtration process and to ensure that the water leaving the plant is free of lead and other contaminants."

"Were you working close to the smelter? What did you do when you were working inside?"

"Yes. I went in the smelter every hour to check the level of the discharged water in the sumps. One does not have to be inside the smelter to breathe the lead fumes. Dust particles were everywhere. They were on our shoes and on our work clothes, in the office, and on the break room floor."

"I definitely recommend that you have your blood checked for lead toxicity. What kinds of symptoms are you experiencing now?"

"I experience fatigue and shortness of breath. I feel like I want to go to sleep. Sometimes I feel discomfort in my chest. The skin on my arms is very sensitive which I think is very odd. I just don't feel energetic like I used to be."

"Could you call the receptionist and make an appointment to see the nurse? I would like the nurse to draw out another blood sample so that we can have a lead count."

When I arrived at the doctor's office for my second appointment, the nurse asked me a battery of medical questions.

"What's ailing you today?" the nurse began.

"The doctor asked me to come back to have a blood sample drawn," I answered, surprised at the nurse's question.

"Have you ever had tuberculosis, Cholera or chicken-pox?"

"No."

"Had anyone in your family had tuberculosis, Cholera or chicken-pox?"

"No."

"Had you had any back injury?"

"No."

"Have you been sick off work during the last twelve months, and if so, how many days?"

"Yes. Two days."

"Have you undergone surgery for any medical reason?"

"Yes. I had gum surgery performed to cure an attack of periodontitis."

"Has anyone in your family had diabetes?"

"Yes, my mother."

"Do you drink alcoholic beverages? If you do, how much alcohol do you consume a day?"

"I drink occasionally. Two or three drinks a week."

"Do you smoke?"

"Not anymore. I used to smoke just about a pack of cigarettes every week or so, but I gave it up several years ago. I was never a heavy smoker."

"Are you on medication?"

"No."

The nurse felt my pulse and inserted a thermometer into my mouth. She recorded my blood pressure and weight again. At that moment Doctor Heimdall walked into the room.

"How do you feel?" he asked.

"Not too good, not too bad," I answered, tilting my head left and right.

Doctor Heimdall made a gloomy face and rocked his fingers in front of him. "So so," he said. He sat down on a stool and opened up my medical file from Minneapolis.

"Everything looks good except for what I have told you over the telephone. Repeat to me the symptoms that you have been feeling."

"I feel lethargic and listless. I have no interest in play, and I have a poor appetite. I feel clumsy and cranky. Sometimes I feel a burning sensation around my chest. The skin on my arms is very sensitive."

"Your blood pressure is normal. Your weight is not far off from the last recorded weight of 139 lb. I would not worry about the slight loss in weight. Your sugar count is 113, which is above normal, but only by a count of 3."

"Do you think I should take a glucose tolerance test to check if I have diabetes?"

"I don't think it will be necessary. The AMA does not recommend a GTT done for men. This test is only recommended for pregnant women. The amount of sugar above the maximum range is insignificant. I definitely rule out diabetes. What worries me is the fact that you have been exposed to lead fumes."

Doctor Heimdall asked me to sit down on the edge of a bench. He took a pronged instrument and slammed his palm on the back of the handle to cause it to vibrate. Then he touched my ankle with the device. "Can you feel the vibration?"

"Yes."

"Tell me when you feel the vibrations stop." Doctor Heimdall repeated the test on the ankle of my left foot and on my knees. He then tested the reflexes on my knees by hitting them with a rubber mallet. He examined my fingernails and looked for blisters around my hands and arms. He looked very disappointed at not finding any blisters on my arms and hands.

"Everything looks fine."

"Do you think that I am suffering from a vitamin deficiency?"

"I don't think so. No one suffers from vitamin deficiency in America. If you have been eating well like you said, you should have all the vitamins that your body requires. There is such an abundance of fresh foods in this country that it is unlikely that anyone will lack vitamins, even if one subsides on vegetables alone. You do eat fruits and vegetables, don't you?"

"Yes. Could my trouble be related to a lack of sleep?"

Doctor Heimdall shook his head from left to right. "You have been sleeping that way for ... how long? Twenty years? You never had this happen to you before. No, I don't think that your ailment is sleep-related."

"Can my ailment caused by overworking in the gym?"

"No, I don't think it has anything to do with your workout. I'll order more blood tests to determine if your blood contains an abnormal level of lead."

Doctor Heimdall took me to a nurse sitting at a laboratory bench outside the examination room.

"Grab a piece of paper and a pen," he ordered the nurse. The nurse opened a drawer and fumbled through vials of different sizes and color. "We are going to need from him 10 millimeters in royal blue, 20 milliliters in lavender, and 20 milliliters in black." The nurse jotted down the blood requirements on a notepad. She opened a drawer and removed a vial with a royal blue lid, one with a lavender lid, and another with a black lid.

"I think I'd better leave before you drain me out of all my blood," I said, grimacing.

"We'd better hurry up before he runs away," Doctor Heimdall quickly said.

"Do we need 10 milliliters in Amber?" the nurse asked.

"Forget about the amber for now."

The nurse tied a black rubber band around my upper arm and felt the blood vessel with her thumb.

"You have good veins. That makes it real easy for me to draw blood from you."

The nurse inserted a needle into my blood vessel. She drew 10 milliliters into the vial with the royal blue lid, 20 milliliters into the vial with the lavender lid, and finally 20 milliliters into the vial with the black lid. When I returned home that night, I opened an old Hutchinson's New 20th Century Encyclopedia, (seventh impression, October 1968) to read up on the chemical that might be the cause of my poor health.

"**LEAD**, one of the four most used and produced metals, the end product of the uranium-radium and thorium series, symbol Pb (from Latin plumbum), atomic weight 207.21 and atomic number 82. Known since prehistoric times (mentioned in Exodus), it is a bluish-grey, and the heaviest, softest and weakest of common metals; it lacks elasticity and is a poor conductor of electricity. It is one of the cheapest shields for radioactive sources, and is widely used in plumbing (some roman pipe drains are still in use), for containing corrosive liquids, for biological shielding, for cable coverings, storage batteries, ammunition and low-melting alloys. It is also used in the manufacture of lead tetraethyl, an anti-knock additive to petrol, and in paints, especially white lead (basic lead carbonate), sublimed white lead (lead sulphate), red lead (lead oxide), and chrome yellow (lead chromate). Galena is the principal ore from which lead is obtained by a roasting process. Some lead salts are used in medicine as antiseptics and astringents."

I read from a more recent encyclopedia that "Lead is a cumulative poison. As a cumulative poison, lead enters the body from lead water pipes, lead-based paints and gasoline."

The thought that I might be suffering from lead poisoning prompted me to visit the lead smelter where I worked in 1977 and 1978. The following

Sunday I nostalgically drove along Mockingbird Lane and retraced the route I used to follow each day on my way to work at the lead smelter. The scenery along the route had not changed much. There were the usual buildings, business parks, strip malls and gas stations. As I drove further west, I noticed that the once narrow street was being expanded into a divided highway. When the construction zone ended, the road narrowed into a dusty street that ran over a narrow bridge. I remembered the day when, just past the bridge, I pulled behind a disabled car to assist a motorist in distress. Another car with two men inside stopped in front of the disabled car and waved me off. The men shouted: "Drive on; we'll take care of the lady." I felt a little suspicious of the two men, but nonetheless drove off. The street widened into a two-lane road once I crossed the bridge. For the next few minutes I drove by rows of dilapidated houses and dirty old storefronts built of mangled tin sheets. I remembered stopping at a gas station one day to fill up my tank. When I went inside the store to pay for the gasoline, I saw a huge revolver sitting on a shelf behind the clerk. Out of curiosity, I asked the clerk if the handgun was loaded. The clerk turned around and, to my complete surprise, handed me the loaded handgun to examine. It was the first time that I had held a real and loaded gun in my hands. Fearing that the gun might accidentally go off in my hands, I quickly handed the gun back to the clerk. After I left the gas station, I wondered why people are so callous as to hand a loaded handgun to a stranger. On a clear day one could see the smokestack towering above the lead smelter and bellowing dark and thick smoke into the sky. Sometimes I could see the red light flashing on the smokestack before even crossing the bridge. On a windy day the wind blew the lead particles and deposited them everywhere around the smelter. The neighborhood had not changed much as far as I could see. It was the same old neighborhood with the same old houses. I leisurely drove on South Westmoreland Avenue and pondered, like I did six years ago, at what point Mockingbird lane becomes Westmoreland Avenue.

Some merchants had set up shop on the sidewalk just before Singleton Boulevard. A crowd of five or six people browsed through racks of colorful clothes and piles of handbags, hats and belts displayed on the sidewalk. I had never seen vendors peddling their wares along the streets near the smelter during the time I worked there. When I drove up to the smelter, I saw that the large gates at the entrance of the smelter were chained and padlocked. The site at the corner of Westmoreland Road and Singleton Boulevard enclosed the lead smelter building, the smokestack, the water filtration house #1, the holding tank, the offices of the plant managers, laboratory, shower stalls and lunch room. It suddenly dawned on me that the smelter was recently ordered by the city to shut down its operation. I remembered reading about it in the Dallas Morning News. I also remembered that the community of predominantly black, low-income people living around the Smelter resented the plant's closing because the plant was a major source of jobs for the residents. Some residents were happy that it finally shut down because they were tired of living in the shadow of the smokestack. The site was bounded on the North and the East by the Trinity River, on the South by Forth Worth Avenue and Davis Street, and on the West by Walton Walker Boulevard. Seventeen thousand people lived within a three miles radius of the smokestack. For more than forty-five years, they toiled, breathed, wed and raised their children under a plume of lead dust.

After I realized that the smelter was closed, I turned around and drove home. Halfway along Westmoreland Avenue, I changed my mind and drove back to the plant. I was struck by nostalgia and wanted to see the place where I spent long days and nights toiling in lead dust. When I pulled into the parking lot in front of the personnel office, I saw just one car in the parking lot. During the time the smelter was operating there were usually seven or eight cars parked in front of the personnel office. Six years ago, I walked into the employment office and applied for the job of Water Filtration Technician without knowing what the job title meant. The interviewer gave me some exercises to test my eyes and hands coordination. After the tests the nurse gave me a medical examination. While I waited in the personnel office, I was struck by the appearance of a group of employees in and outside the building. They were dressed in dark blue pants and light blue shirts. They wore work boots smeared with a layer of brown dust. Their heads were covered with blue hats, but what puzzled me was the strange looking object hanging down their necks. At the time I did not know what the object was and why everyone had one hanging around their necks. On my first day at work my Supervisor handed me one of the objects. It was only then did I come to know that the object was a face mask to be worn while working in the lead smelter. I glanced at the company name at the entrance of the parking lot. The contaminated air had corroded not only the dreams and hopes of many families living around the smelter, but also the company's name and logo, the parking lot sign, and the paint on the building. I walked to the second plant situated about 400 yards away from the first plant. The second plant housed the battery wrecking house, a warehouse, the workshop, the administrative building, and the water filtration house #2. A large pond occupied the center of the plant. It acted like a holding tank for the contaminated water discharged from the battery wrecking house.

The grass was thick and green alongside the administrative building. I was not sure if the grass was greener because of the recent torrential rains or because the soil around the plant was cleaner. A wire fence was erected around the grassy area to prevent passersby from stepping on the grass. A 20ft tall fence blocked the entrance to the site. On the other side of the fence was a guard house. The gate was secured by a chain and padlock. I saw a trailer inside the gate, but there was no one in sight. Trucks once drove through the gate day and night to deliver their loads of poison. The site was once active with employees wearing white, green, blue, yellow or orange hats. The lab technicians wore green hats whereas janitors wore orange hats. The employees with the yellow hats maintained and repaired equipment in the plants. The blue-hat employees worked in the smelter and the battery wrecking house. The plant Managers and Supervisors always had on their heads gleaming white hats. It had always seemed to me that the white hats worn by the plant Managers and Supervisors were always shinny and spotless whereas all the other hats were soiled with mud, lead or paint. Sometimes it was hard to distinguish between a blue hat and a green hat because of the dirt covering them. The yellow hats were covered with brown specks, but the janitors' orange hats were the dirtiest. I frequently saw the employees going about their business with their masks hanging down their necks instead of being worn around their faces. The masks were very uncomfortable to wear. Employees removed them from their faces at the slightest opportunity. They removed their masks when they had to wipe the sweat off their faces, when they wanted to be heard amidst the machine noise, or when they had to drink or eat. I did what most employees did; I walked around the plant with my mask hanging down my neck instead of around my face. No one had told me when I was hired that I should wear my filter mask at all time. Most of the time I had it strapped around my neck. A small step led to the employee parking lot. It was the first time that I saw the parking lot devoid of automobiles. When the plant was in operation, the employees parked their vehicles in the parking lot and walked to the smelter at the corner of Singleton Boulevard and Westmoreland Avenue. The employees covered the lower part of their faces with their hands as they walked from the parking lot to the smelter. They did not put on their masks until they were inside the plants. I was surprised at the clear visibility around the plant which used to be shrouded by a thick dense cloud of dust. I walked up to the wire fence to have a closer look inside. The overhead door at the warehouse was open, so I gathered that there were people inside the plant. When I worked at the plant, the pond was always full with brown acid water. I had spent many long hours during the bitter winter months walking along the pond, checking the water level, repairing broken pipes, and making sure that the pump did not stop or freeze. I was curious to see how deep the pond was. I felt an urge to climb over the fence and jump on the other side, but I was afraid that a security guard might shoot at me for trespassing. I looked for an opening in the fence, but found none. From where I stood I could see the water filtration house #2. There was still a pallet of filter material on the platform overlooking the mixing tank.

Disappointed at not being able to enter the plant, I walked back to the lead smelter. I remembered stopping at the Missouri Pacific Railroad tracks at dusk to watch the sun go down. The railroad tracks glistered every time it rained. While crossing the railroad tracks I suddenly remembered that the tracks ran next to a concrete pit into which the pond overflowed. The overflow then drained into a creek. I followed the railroad tracks to the concrete pit. I found the concrete pit, but there was a wire fence around it to keep people out of the property. The soil underneath the fence had eroded, creating an opening beneath the fence. The opening was big enough for someone my size to crawl into. It appeared that someone had previously used the opening for there was a railroad tie across the creek just beneath the fence. After a moment of hesitation, I stepped over the railroad tie and crawled underneath the fence. Once inside the plant, I could see the entrance to the battery wrecking house. The doors were closed, but I remembered what the battery wrecking house was like inside because I had walked inside the building hundreds of times.

The used batteries were crushed in large vats to separate the lead from the casing. After washing, the lead slag and scrap were transported to the smelter where they were heated to separate the lead from the scrap. The lead was cast into ingots and the battery casing chips were dumped into walled areas and later sold as by-products. The chips inside the walled compartment sometimes reached 20ft high. Employees at the plant frequently took the chips home and spread them around their driveways and gardens. The acid from the batteries and the water used to clean and separate the lead from the battery were discharged into the pond. The contaminated water was then pumped into a series of ammonia pits to neutralize the acid before it was pumped into the water filtration house #2. The neutralized water flowed into a large trough with a rotating drum for filtering out contaminants. A vacuum pump sucked the contaminated water through a 3" thick filter cake on the outside of the drum. The cake filtered out lead, arsenic, antimony, copper, zinc, silver and cadmium particles from the water. After filtering, the decontaminated water was then pumped into the storm line. As the drum rotated, a blade near the cake's surface shaved off the filter cake with the contaminants trapped in it. The shaved sludge fell into an auger which directed it into a hamper. Whenever the hamper filled up, I summoned a forklift driver to haul it away. I never knew what the plant did with the sludge, but I had seen the forklift driver dump the sludge at a remote site inside the plant. When it rained, the contaminants in the sludge mixed with the rain water and drained into the ground. The filter cake was held to the drum by vacuum suction. During power outages, the drum stopped rotating and lost the vacuum suction. Without vacuum suction, the filter cake fell in the trough. The trough had to be emptied and cleaned, and a new filter cake had to be mixed. When the filtration process was interrupted, water cannot be filtered. The pond then overflowed and the untreated water spilled into the adjoining creek. The pond, as I had suspected, was dry. It had rained heavily during the previous week and the ground was still muddy.

During the eleven months that I worked at the plant, the pond was always filled with the coffee-colored water. The liquid ammonia tank stood directly across the battery wrecking house. The concrete pits were empty and the wiring connecting the pH sensors to the control panels were broken and loose. When the pH level of the water dropped, the siren inside the control panel wailed to alert the technician who might not be close by. The wailing siren often infuriated the employees working in the battery wrecking house because they had to notify the technician on duty to come and shut it off. Eventually someone pulled off the wiring from the siren and no one bothered to connect it back to the pH sensors. The siren remained silent till the day I left the company. I walked around the liquid ammonia tank and saw that the secret bypass line was still lying underneath it. My Supervisor, Wayne built the secret bypass line to dump untreated water into the storm line when the pond filled up. This happened whenever the battery wrecking house operated on an extended shift or whenever the contaminated water was not being treated fast enough. Whenever the pond filled up, Wayne hooked up the secret bypass line to dump the untreated water in the storm line. He arranged the U-shape line so that its ends could be hooked quickly when the pond fills up. The city inspectors monitored the water overflowing into the river by using sensors strategically located along the overflow path outside of the plant. It fined the plant whenever an illegal overflow had occurred. We circumvented the sensors by discharging the untreated water directly into the storm line. The secret bypass line was used when rain or melting snow threatened to overflow the pond, or when mechanical or electrical failures impeded the neutralization and filtration process. The illegal discharge of untreated water took place between 6 PM and 6 AM on weekdays because the city inspectors were least likely to visit the plant during these hours. I was frequently ordered to hook up the bypass line on Friday nights and let the untreated water flow into the storm line during the weekends. The pH of the water in the pond ordinarily registered between a pH of 1.0 and 4.0. Heavy rain or snow sometimes diluted the water to a pH of 5.0 which was still lower than the normal level of 7.5.

I followed the water line along the pond. The line was built of 10ft long PVC pipes and connected together with rubber tubes and clamps. The uneven ground, the rush of water inside the pipes, and the changing temperatures frequently caused the rubber connectors to separate from the PVC pipes. I carried a pair of screwdrivers, a pair of pliers, and several spare clamps with me whenever I inspected the lines. I carried a flashlight on my nightly inspections so that I could see the pipes. The water filtration technicians were provided with gloves to protect their hands, but the gloves hindered the repair. Besides, they always got wet with the acid water whenever I repaired a line. I smiled as I remembered the maintenance workers who befriended me just so they could have my wet gloves. I did not have to pay for my gloves. I could go to the supply store and get a new pair at any time. The maintenance employees, on the only hand, had to purchase their gloves. They kept and wore the worn-out, contaminated and dirty gloves for as long as they were usable. One of the workers was a short, chubby Mexican who barely spoke English. He sometimes sneaked behind me and stole my gloves from my back pockets.

During the first winter that I worked at the plant, I was assigned to work on the night shift. One night I discovered that the water pump had stopped. Since the level of the pond was low, I decided not to restart the pump. Wayne had not trained me on the proper procedures for draining the water pump when the temperature dropped below freezing point. That night the water inside the pump froze. The water inside the line at low points around the pond also froze solid. For several days, the temperature remained below freezing point, but the acid water from the battery wrecking house continued to pour into the pond and gradually filled it up. Working at single-digit temperatures, the maintenance crew used blow torches to melt the ice inside the water pump and the pipes. Pipes that were filled with ice were disconnected and replaced with new ones. When the pump was cleared out of the ice and restarted, the water line burst at several points due to some ice still remaining inside the line. Later in the afternoon, Wayne summoned me into his office.

"I ought to fire you for allowing the pump to freeze," he snapped. "You should have drained the water out of the pump before shutting it off."

I felt guilty that I caused all the problems with the pump and water lines, but in my mind disagreed that I should take all the blame. Wayne never told me that I should drain the pump when the temperature drops below freezing point. I was embarrassed at my mistakes and I remained silent. Wayne was so furious at me that I thought that he was really going to let me go. Without taking his eyes off me, he leaned back on his chair and put his muddy boots on his desk. He brushed his long hair off his face and put his hands inside the pockets of his pants. Then he smiled at me.

"Relax," he said. "I just wanted to tell you that I don't give a shit about this job. I am breathing lead fumes every day and, who knows, I'll probably die of lead poisoning some day. Do you think my Manager cares? None of them give a shit about what happens to you or me when we are out working around the pond. Did you see anybody wearing a white hat around the pond?"

I followed the water line to a small shed at the edge of the pond. A pair of water pumps, painted in silver, was bolted to a concrete pad. There used to be just one blue pump during the time I was employed by the company. There was no shed protecting the pump from the elements then. The second pump was probably used as a backup whenever the first pump broke down. I remembered that on one cold, icy day in January, Wayne ordered me to walk into the pond to retrieve a pipe section that broke away from the pump. It had snowed during the previous days and the area around the pond was covered with snow. When the sun melted down the snow, the pond filled up rapidly and threatened to submerge the water pump. The plant managers summoned a mobile crane to lift the pump to higher ground, but the crane did not arrive until two days later. When the pump was finally lifted up to higher ground, the PVC pipe drifted away in the pond. There was no spare pipe available, and it had to be retrieved for restarting the pump otherwise the pond would overflow. It was a very cold and wintry day and the water in the pond was freezing cold. Wayne stared at me and pointed to the drifting pipe. He did not say a word, but I understood from the look in his eyes that he wanted me to retrieve the pipe. I hesitated to walk into the pond.

"Are you going to go after it or shall I push you into the pond?" Wayne suddenly shouted.

Unconcerned for my own safety, I stepped into the pond and waded towards the drifting pipe. When the icy water rushed into my boots, I hastily retreated to the shore. Wayne pointed at the suction pipe and yelled: "Go get it!" I waddled back into the pond and caught the pipe. The water reached up to my crotch. I heard my teeth clatter and my arms shiver as I pulled the pipe towards me. The maintenance men laughed at me as I waddled in the pond. Wayne quickly grabbed the pipe from me and secured it tightly to the pump with a clamp. Later he tied a rope around the pipe so that it would not drift away again should the clamp comes loose again. As I stood quivering with cold, Wayne laughed and remarked: "I don't think the water is acidic at all. The snow must have neutralized the acid to some degree." I rushed back to the washroom to change into dry clothes. The skin on my legs was covered with spotty red marks, but I felt no pain. That night, Wayne had me connect the secret bypass line to discharge the untreated water into the storm line and lower the level of the water in the pond. After that day the intake pipe would always come lose and fall into the pond. The vibration from the pump frequently loosened the clamp and the pipe would float into the pond again. Wayne later acquired an old canoe to use in such eventuality, but the canoe sank to the bottom of the pond on the first day he used it.

I stood at the overflow pit thinking over the days I spent stacking up sandbags inside the pit to prevent the pond from overflowing into the creek. The overflow pit measured 6ft by 4ft and was 2ft deep. It was designed to prevent sandbagging. The mouth of the pit was only 1ft wide. Wayne ordered me to crawl into the pit and stack sandbags at the bottom to prevent the overflow from reaching the creek. I remembered the hardship I endured working inside the pit. For hours, I dragged sandbags weighing 60lb each into the bottom of the pit to build a wall. Then I piled sandbags around the mouth of the pit to block off the rising water and prevent it from spilling into the pit and overflowing into the creek. When Wayne returned to check on my progress, he smiled and patted me on my back. He was overly impressed by the watertight sandbag wall. What I remembered the most on that day was the weather. It was a sunny, beautiful and uneventful day. On that peaceful day, I did not have to deal with the elements, machine breakdown, equipment failures, broken water lines, power outages, or uncooperative employees. After seeing the wall of sandbags inside the pit, Wayne softened up and revealed himself under a different light. Until that day, he had always appeared to me as a cold, uncaring man. What impressed me most about him was his ability to fix things up by using what little resources was available to him. The water filtration department, in his mind was a drain on the company's financial resources as well as a pain to the Plant Managers to manage. He confessed that he had great difficulties securing funds for improvements around the pond and in the filtration buildings.

I returned to the hole underneath the fence and crawled back out. I was happy that no one saw me inside the plant and I walked back to the smelter at Singleton Boulevard. I stood at the gate and tried to catch a glimpse of the smelter and surrounding structures inside. The guard house was empty and the plant was deserted. Water rushed out from under the gates and flowed into the street. A few years ago, whenever water rushed out into the street, the siren blared and maintenance workers rushed around madly to prevent the water from reaching the street. I remembered the night when the sump inside the smelter overflowed. The lead-contaminated water quickly filled the yard and flowed out into the street. The siren that alerted us of a machine breakdown was still on the wall above the entrance to the smelter. The siren frequently went off at night. Whenever the siren wailed, the panicked night foreman rushed back and forth and shouted orders to the maintenance crew. The men stacked sandbags across the gates to stop the water from running into the street. The maintenance crew scurried around looking for the source of the overflow and shutting off valves inside the smelter. It was not the first time that the sump had overflowed. The lead-contaminated water inside the sump was pumped to a 20ft high holding tank. From the holding tank, it flowed into the water filtration house #1 where the lead particles and other contaminants were filtered out from the water before it was discharged into the storm line. I recalled the day when the overflow pipe inside the sump became clogged, causing the water in the sump to overflow into the yard and into the street. A big man from the maintenance crew held a water filtration technician by his feet above the hot water while he tried to unclog the overflow line. His head dangled just a few inches above the hot, steamy and contaminated water while he inserted a broomstick into the line to clear it.

Inside the water filtration house #1, the filtered water flowed into a 2ft wide well standing about 4ft above the ground. The outflow pipe to the storm sewer line was located at the bottom of the well. Every two hours, I collected a few samples for the lab technician. I used a plastic cup tied to a string to draw the samples from the well. The lab technician would then test the samples for traces of contaminants when he arrives the next day. One night the plastic cup broke loose from the string and became stuck in the mouth of the outflow pipe. The water level inside the well quickly rose and threatened to spill over. If the filtered water had overflowed, the overflow would flow back to the holding tank. The holding tank was over 80 percent full and halting the filtration process would cause it to overflow. I sought the help of the maintenance men on duty, but they refused to go inside the well. In desperation, I called Wayne to seek his advice. I felt bad that I had to wake him in the middle of the night, but I did not know what to do. After I explained to him the situation, he mumbled: "Get inside the well and break the plastic cup." He then hang up and went back to sleep. When I returned to the filtration house, the water inside the well had risen to 2ft above the discharge pipe. The two maintenance men were as useless as tits on a boar. They just stood around the well and watched the water rise without raising a finger. They had no idea how to clear the plastic cup from the mouth of the pipe. I momentarily diverted the water discharge from the rotating drum back into the trough and jumped into the icy water. I knelt in the bottom of the well and pried at the plastic cup with a screwdriver. The icy water burned my thighs and buttocks, but I continued to pry at the plastic cup. To my horror, the plastic cup flowed deeper into the pipe, and then remained stuck. The water in the well continued to rise and covered my hips. Then I heard the water gurgled and gushed into the pipe, carrying the broken plastic cup along with it. The water level immediately began to drop. Unable to endure the cold water anymore, I scrambled out of the well and rushed to change into dry clothes. Behind me the maintenance men laughed at seeing me wet. It was the second time in a month that the maintenance men had mocked me for endangering my own safety on the job.

Behind the water filtration house #1 stood the shower stalls reserved for the Plant Supervisors and Managers. The shower stalls had doors and were less crowded. Non-white employees, who were mostly black and Hispanic, used the shower stalls in an adjoining building. The shower stalls in that building had no doors or curtains. Sometimes one or two black employees stopped by my stall to watch me shower. Soon after I began working at the smelter, I noticed that Wayne used the shower stalls reserved for the Plant Managers. I was uncomfortable showering under the glare of the black and Hispanic employees and eventually started to use the Managers' shower stalls. Every week the nurse posted the employees' lead count on the bulletin board next to the lunch room. Employees with lead level higher than normal were ordered to stay home until their lead level dropped below a certain level. Wayne once recorded a lead level of over 30 mg and had to stay home until it dropped below 30 mg. The highest lead level that I ever recorded in my blood was 26 mg.

I remembered that I almost got into a fist fight with a forklift driver. When I first started at the plant, the Water Filtration Technicians were not allowed to drive forklifts. They relied on the forklift drivers in the smelter to provide them with a steady supply of filtration materials. The bags of white powder were transported by forklift from the warehouse by the battery wrecking house. They were stacked on the platforms in the filtration house at both sites. The platform could accommodate four pallets at a time. When the supply ran low, the technicians asked a forklift driver to bring a pallet or two from the warehouse. The forklift driver did not like doing it and did not always remember to bring the filter materials. Judging by their reaction, they did not like to take orders from the lab technicians. Sometimes the filter materials were not brought to the filtration house on time. Consequently the technicians and the forklift drivers frequently engaged in shouting matches. When I arrived to work one morning, the filter cake on the drum in the water filtration house #1 was less than a quarter inch thick. The holding tank was nearing the 90% mark and there was no filter on the platform. I was concerned about the rising level of water in the holding tank and I immediately requested a forklift driver to fetch me a pallet. Mixing a new filter cake would take an hour and a half. I kept asking the forklift driver to bring me some filter, but he kept telling me that he was busy. When he finally brought the filter to the filtration house an hour later, I lost my temper and got into a shouting match with him. Overwhelmed by the pressure of keeping the filtration drum running, I broke down into tears and ran to the shower room. I showered, went home and never came back to work again. I had finally succumbed to the intense pressure of keeping the water filtration houses running smoothly from day to day. I could no longer put up with the noise, the dust, the pressure, the workers inside the smelter, and the indifference of the white-hat people.

I susceptibly walked around the smelter to look at the changes that took place since it was closed down. I saw that bulldozers had scrapped off the contaminated soil from a vacant lot and replaced the soil with sods of green grass. Two earth moving machines were parked on another site across from the smelter. I was pleased that remedial work was finally being undertaken to reverse the damage done to the environment by the lead smelter. Having seen all that I wanted to see, I returned to my car and drove home.

Doctor Heimdall did not call me back until three weeks later. The laboratory had recommended that other tests be performed on my blood samples. When Doctor Heimdall finally called me, he informed him that my lead count was 13 micrograms which was considered normal in an adult. I sighed with relief. The laboratory had also recommended that I should be tested for chronic lead toxicity, but Doctor Heimdall thought that it was unnecessary because I was no longer working in the lead smelter. He started to explain to me the effect of inhaling lead fumes."

"Acute lead toxicity, which I don't think apply in your case, is a life-threatening disease that can also lead to severe brain damage," Doctor Heimdall explained. "We found your blood count to be normal. At the recommendation of the laboratory performing the tests, we evaluated the hemoglobin in your blood and found the presence of mycrocytes, some very tiny red blood cells, in them. We also checked the ferritin level in your blood, which is the best test available to determine if you are deficient in iron, and we found that your iron level to be normal. We could quantify, by separate tests, the different types of hemoglobin in your blood, but I don't think that it will be necessary. Generally speaking, from all the tests that we have performed so far, I am inclined to say that you are a healthy person. I suspect that you may have acquired Thalassemia-minor. If that is the case, there is nothing we can do about it. There is no cure for Thalassemia-minor. Taking iron vitamins will not solve anything. Thalassemia-major, on the other hand, is a killer-disease and occurs predominantly among children. There are different varieties of Thalassemia-minor and they occur among certain people with different background. I don't think that I need to do any more tests on you."

"There is something in my throat that bothers me," I said. "I wonder if it has anything to do with my ailments."

"That may be something else. If it continues to bother you, come by my office, and I will take a look at your throat."

A few days later, I went back to see Doctor Heimdall to have my throat examined. He did not look pleased at seeing me again.

"Tell me again, what is wrong with your throat?"

"I feel a lump in my throat and I have difficulties swallowing."

"When did you feel the lump in your throat?"

"About the same time I felt the symptoms I described to you before."

Doctor Heimdall examined my finger nails, my eyes, my ears, my hands and my arms. He asked me to remove my necktie and to unbutton my shirt. Doctor Heimdall then palpated my neck and throat.

"There is no visible inflammation in your throat," Doctor Heimdall concluded. "I don't feel any lump in your throat. You are coming to me with a different kind of symptoms each time. Your condition is not so simple that I can give you some medication to stop your ailments. The lab did some tests on your thyroid, but the tests are positive. I will request one more test in order to check the level of your thyroid's stimulating hormones. Then we will go from there. Your thyroid glands may be inflamed. If that is the case, the inflammation might have given rise to a goiter, which is a swelling of the throat. The thyroid glands secrete hormones which profoundly affect your physique and temperament. The goiter then may be the reason why you are feeling weak and tired. We will first check your TSH level. There are other tests that we can also do, but they will have to be performed at the hospital.

We can take a scope and look down inside your throat, or we can take an X-ray of the esophagus while you are swallowing water or foods to get a picture of what are going inside your throat."

Doctor Heimdall drew a picture of my gullet on an Aldactazide note pad and traced out the path of the foods going around an obstacle. He then took me to the nurse and ordered her to draw 10 milliliters of blood from the vein in my arm. Before I left the doctor's office, Doctor Heimdall assured me that the result of the blood test will be known to me in three days. Fourteen days later, Doctor Heimdall called me to confirm that my TSH level was 1.5 and normal. He then suggested that I see Doctor Adonati, a throat specialist, for an in-depth examination of my throat. I suddenly remembered that about the same time I had felt the lump in my throat, I almost choked on a piece of chicken bone. I remembered that I swallowed the piece of bone down because I was unable to cough it out.

"It's quite possible that the bone had punctured your thyroid glands. I suggest that you see Doctor Adonati. He may see something in your throat that I might have missed out."

Doctor Heimdall gave me a phone number to call. The following day I made an appointment to see Doctor Adonati at a nearby hospital. Due to unforeseen circumstances, I was forced to postpone the meeting with Doctor Adonati until two weeks later. When I finally went to visit the specialist, it started to rain. The rain stopped when I arrived at the hospital. After walking through a maze of corridors, I entered a spacious waiting room lined with bamboo furniture. On the wall was a plaque with Doctor Adonati's name on it. Next to the plaque were two arrows pointing to opposite ends. The first arrow pointed to the office of Doctor Amenraji. The second arrow pointed to the office of Doctor Jagannathi. The services of the three specialists were limited to the practice of Otolaryngology. A nurse greeted me and asked me to fill two sets of medical forms. After I had completed the medical forms, she led me into a very small room with barely enough room to accommodate two people. A chair and a stool sat in the middle of the small room. I sat down on the stool, but after the nurse left, I pondered on the seating arrangement and concluded that the stool was for the Doctor to sit on. Before the doctor arrived, I rose up from the stool and sat down on the chair. A hot-bead sterilizer and various kinds of instruments rested on top of a metal cabinet next to several small bottles containing gly-otic fluid, cortisporin, coly-onicin and hurricane gel. An air regulator, a buzzer and a transilluminator were built into the table; two kinds of scopes hanged down from the side. Fifteen minutes later, Doctor Adonati walked into the room. He had a small flashlight strapped to his forehead like a coal miner. His face was wrinkled with age and his lips were as pale as ale. Doctor Adonati inserted a long rod with a mirror at its end into my mouth and slid it over my tongue down into my throat.

"Say aaaaahhhh..," Doctor Adonati said.

"Aaaaahhhh."

"Good. Now say uuuuuhhhh..."

I repeated the word over a dozen times, with the doctor changing the tone each time. I felt my stomach churning and I pushed the rod away from my mouth. Doctor Adonati held it firm in his hand. I was relieved when Doctor Adonati finally slid the rod out for I was about to nauseate into his hands.

"It looks like you have a cyst in your throat. We will see it better on the nasopharyngoscope."

Doctor Adonati took a cotton swab and immersed it in a reddish gelatin fluid. He wrapped the cotton swab around a hook and slipped the hook into my nostril.

"What is this for?" I asked

"The gel will numb and decongest your nostril. We'll then run a scope down your nose so that we can look inside your throat."

Doctor Adonati then left the room to allow the gel to take effect. Ten minutes later my nose became numb. Doctor Adonati came back and took me to another examination room. He pointed to a seat underneath a nasopharyngoscope and in front of a video monitor with a VCR sitting on top of it. I sat down and laid back. Doctor Adonati slid a thin filament with a light at its end down my nostril. At first I felt some pain when Doctor Adonati inserted the filament in my nostril, but the pain turned into an uncomfortable sensation as the doctor pushed the scope deeper into my nose. When the scope has gone four inches into my nose, Doctor Adonati pointed at the video screen. Then he moved the scope back and forth into my nose, searching for the tumor.

"Say aaaaahhhh..," Doctor Adonati repeated

"Aaaaahhhh."

I repeated the words for him about twenty times, with the doctor changing the tone each until he was satisfied with what he was doing.

"Excellent. I think we have a picture of all this," Doctor Adonati congratulated himself.

I was extremely relieved when Doctor Adonati removed the scope from my nose. He pushed the nasopharyngoscope out of the way and flipped a switch on the VCR. He then pointed to a small growth on this thyroid gland on the video monitor.

"How will you remove the tumor from my throat? Will it require surgery?" I asked.

"We rarely operate on a situation like this," Doctor Adonati replied. "In time the tumor will disappear. Of course you'll feel something in your throat when you swallow. It should not bother you too much. Let's go back to my office and we will have the secretary schedule another appointment for you in a month. That is all we can do for now. Is the lump bothering you?"

"I feel a tingling sensation inside my throat every now and then. The tingling causes me to cough. It also seems like my saliva is sort of gooey. It leaves a bad taste in my mouth.

"That's normal. Obviously, there is something going on inside your throat. We'll check it out again in about a month."

The nurse took my medical file from Doctor Adonati and took me back to the front of the building. In the waiting room, I wrote and handed a check to the secretary. Greatly relieved that lead was not the cause of my poor health, I climbed into my car and returned to work. The sun had appeared in the sky and the pavements were starting to dry up.

Postscript

In 1982 the City of Dallas and the Texas Air Control Board found that the air lead levels near the lead smelter exceeded the EPA's National Ambient Air Quality. The soil was sampled and was found to contain high level of lead. An analysis conducted in 1983 concluded that approximately 10 percent of children under 6 years old and living within a half mile radius of the smelter had blood lead contaminations greater than the then current standard of 30 mg/dl. Ninety percent of the children exceeded 10 mg/dl. During the same year the City of Dallas declined to renew the smelter's operating permit. In 1984 the smelter closed down. The State, City, and the Environmental Protection Agency (EPA) directed RSR Corporation, which owns the lead smelter, to undertake corrective action at the site, including installing equipment to control stack and emissions and cleaning up the residential soils within one half mile of the smelter. To expedite remedial actions at the site, which covered approximately 13.6 square miles, the EPA divided the contaminated area into five Operable Units (OU.) The private residential properties became known as OU No. 1 whereas the public residential area, owned by the Dallas Housing Authority, was referred to as OU No. 2. The slag piles and municipal landfills became known as OU No. 3, the former Smelter Facility and adjoining properties as OU No. 4, and the Battery Wrecking Facility as OU No. 5. The EPA determined that the five Operable Units presented a significant risk to public health and added the sites to the National Priorities List (NPL.) Between 1984 and 1985, RSR Corporation removed soil that exceeded approximately 1,000 ppm lead concentration in residential areas, public play areas, and day care centers. It replaced the lead-contaminated soil with clean soil and constructed a vegetative barrier in areas with low levels of contamination to keep lead from migrating. Concerns about lead contamination in the west Dallas area re-emerged in 1991 when the Texas National Resource Conservation Commission (TNRCC) received complaints from the area residents about residual slag piles and battery chips that originated from the smelter and battery wrecking facility. TRNCC consequently requested that the EPA re-evaluate the area beyond the original cleanup area. The EPA responded to the rediscovery of lead contamination by removing soil from 420 single family properties and 167 multi-family properties. In mid-1994 the Dallas Housing Authority demolished 167 multi-family buildings and initiated the removal and disposal of soil contaminated in excess of 500 ppm lead, 20 ppm arsenic, or 30 ppm cadmium. Approximately 24,000 cubic yards of contaminated soil were removed from the public housing area. In late 1994 the agency ordered the removal of 500 drums of battery acids, 55 containers of laboratory chemicals, and 1800 cubic yards of loose contaminated debris from the smelter site. Furthermore the 300ft tall smokestack, associated structures and equipment were demolished, and up to two feet of soil from the site was excavated and disposed of. In 1995, the EPA Region 6 issued Records of Decisions (RODS) on OU Nos. 1 and 2 to delete the sites from the National Priorities List. On February 28, 1996, the Deputy Regional Administrator signed the Record of Decision for OU No. 4, and on April 03, 1997, the Records of Decision was signed on OU No. 5. Finally, on September 30, 1997, the Acting Regional Administrator, Jerry Clifford, signed a Record of Decision to remedy contamination at OU No. 3. When the clean-up are completed, the property at OU No. 3 will once again be used for residential and industrial development.

PART 2: NUCLEAR WASTELAND

5 A TALE OF TWO GORILLAS

He was a humble man of modest means. He was polite, kind, caring, and above all, very concerned about the appearance of his customers' hair. Unlike most barbers, he did not like to talk when he cut his customers' hair. He let them dream their dreams while his fingers ran through their hair and his scissors clipped them off. The only time he conversed with his customers was when they begin the dialogue themselves. He was satisfied to just clip away their hair while they gazed at his artful hands in the mirror. His friends once remarked that women liked him to cut their hair because they liked the feel of his hands over their heads. However he preferred to cut men's hair because their hair needed the most attention. His female customers would go to great lengths to groom their hair. His male customers, on the other hand, were just happy to use their fingers as a comb. Whenever he saw a male client walked into his hair salon with messy and dirty hair, he scolded and slapped him for neglecting his hair. The enjoyment of his trade begins when he shampoos the customers' hair and washes away the grease. It ends when he holds the mirror behind the customer's neck for them to judge his artistry.

He was always anxious that his customers get the best of his service. Over the years, he had learned by just looking at his customers' hair what type of shampoo he should use for washing their hair. He stocked shampoos that were specifically formulated for washing oily hair and for controlling dandruff. He used regular shampoos on customers who did not need the extra manageability in their hair, and special shampoos on customers who wanted extra manageability in their hair. For men who had a hard time combing their hair, he applied a shampoo that contains a light conditioner that made combing the hair easier. For men with dull-looking hair, he used a shampoo that contains a penetrating conditioner that gave their hair a healthy-looking shine. A kind of shampoos that he used reduces tangles and flyaways in the hair; another type gives the hair a balanced cleansing without stripping off the hair. He had shampoos specially formulated for split and damaged hair, shampoos that kept no-problem hair in great condition, shampoos that protected the hair against permanent waving, and shampoos that eliminated the tugging and pulling that can split weak and wet hair. For men whose hair needed more attention than others, he used shampoos that contain aromatic resins, ointments or healing agents. For women whose hair needed the least attention, he used shampoos that gave their hair a silky feeling and an extra shine. The shampoos were all formulated with a wide variety of bases such as honey, egg, herb, lemon, wheat, alcohol, coconut oil or yogurt.

His heart ached whenever he saw a man with pattern baldness or receding hairlines walking into the hair salon. For these customers he would go to extreme length to help them grow healthy-looking hair again. Many of his customers, especially men in their early forties, had shrinking hair follicles. Whenever he combed out a lock of hair on his customer's head, the comb pulled off the hair strands, causing more hair loss. The decreasing hair growth on his customers' head worried him day and night. He knew that over the years, scientists had developed methods for transplanting hair in bald men, but the costs were so prohibitive that none of his customers was interested in the new hair transplants.

Several companies promised bald men that their hair would reappear quickly if they use their hair products. Giovanni, the barber whose hair salon is located on Greenville Avenue, grew skeptical of all these claims. He secretly set out to develop his own formula for stimulating hair growth. In his quest to find the magic potion, he stocked various kinds of chemicals which he used in his experiments. When he was not cutting his customers' hair, he mixed the chemicals in various proportions in his back office. He labeled the solution according to the ingredients used, proportions used, and the date the mixture was concocted. Then he secretly rubbed the paste on the scalp of a customer with pattern baldness or receding hairlines. During the early stages of his experiments, he tried a mixture of zinc pyrithione, citric acid and sterealkonium chloride. When the mixture did not produce the desired result, he added dicetyldimonium chloride, pantenol or polysorbate to the mixture. During the later stages, he switched to a mixture of propylparaben, methyparaben, magnesium aluminum silicate, and titanium dioxide in various combinations. When the mixture still did not produce the desired result, he tried a mixture of triethanolamine and dimethylamine, adding hydroxypropyl methycellulose and hydroxiethyl cellulose later in various proportions. When none of these chemicals worked, he started to use nioxin and minoxidil and added varying amount of vitamins, herbs, proteins, amino acids and humectants into the mixture. The results were not always what he expected.

Sometimes his customers came back with hardly any trace of hair left on their scalps. At other times they returned with a greenish smudge all over the hair. Occasionally the hair on his customers' head hardened and remained stuck up like twisted copper wires. Once a customer returned with a swarm of bees on his head. Another came back with his eyebrow hanging down his cheeks. Giovanni wanted the hair to grow on his customers' heads, but the hair was growing on other parts of their bodies instead. The mixture stimulated hair growth in his customers' nostrils, eardrums and other parts of the body, but had no effect on their scalps. Giovanni was obviously very disappointed with the result of his experiments, but he was nonetheless encouraged by the hair growth. He was hopeful that in due time he would come upon the right mixture. He was so certain that he would soon find the miracle potion that he openly talked about it to his customers. His customers were delighted at the news. They started coming to the hair salon every week instead of every month to have their hair washed and trimmed. Words soon spread around that Giovanni had discovered the magic solution to make hair grow again. People from all walks of life came to the barber shop to have their bald heads massaged with his mixture. Day in and day out, Giovanni rubbed the concoction on his customers' scalps. He then washed off the mixture and applied a paste of yogurt and eggnog on their heads. His Labrador then licked off the yogurt and eggnog from the customers' heads to complete the treatment.

On the other side of town lived a man whose head was as bald as an egg shell. He wore a toupee on his head to hide his baldness. He had been using, quite unsuccessfully, various brands of hair growth stimulants in an effort to grow his hair back. The man's name is Ugo. He was big and tall, and he was always dressed in a cream-colored business suit and black cowboy boots. Sometimes he would come to work wearing a cowboy hat. He walked with his hands held apart like a gunslinger, but his arms never moved except to check that his toupee was on his head. Ugo was secretly in love with a colleague, a woman fifteen years younger than him. He was, oh lackaday, too conscious of his baldness to declare his love to her. When Ugo heard that Giovanni had developed a concoction to stimulate hair growth on bald men, he decided to pay the barber a visit. Like thousands of other bald men who wanted to grow their hair again, Ugo hoped that Giovanni's formula would make hair grow again on his head. On a cloudy and chilly October day, Ugo left his office and drove to Giovanni's hair salon on Greenville Avenue. He walked into the barber's shop, sat down in a chair and patiently waited for his turn. One by one Giovanni's customers climbed on the barber's chair to have the concoction rubbed on their scalps. After rubbing the concoction into their scalps, Giovanni washed off the mixture from their heads and applied the yogurt and eggnog mixture. The customers then dropped down on their knees and crawled to the waiting Labrador. The Labrador licked the eggnog and yogurt from their scalps. When the Labrador stopped licking their scalps, they got up, paid Giovanni his dues and left the salon with full of hopes. Giovanni finally looked at Ugo and beckoned him to the barber's chair. The barber removed Ugo's toupee and washed his head. Then he took a paintbrush, dipped it in a bowl containing his formula and applied the concoction on Ugo's scalp. While Giovanni rubbed the mixture on his head, Ugo disclosed to the barber that he was madly in love with an attractive young woman. He timidly confessed to Giovanni that he was afraid that she would spurn him when she finds out that he is bald.

"You are not the first bald man to fall in love with a younger woman," Giovanni reassured him. "It happens all the time. My grandfather used to say that women prefer to marry bald-headed men. Do you know why?"

"Why?"

"That's because a bald man can hear his wife better. There is no hair to block the ears, you see? She never has to say: 'Honey, don't forget to take the trash out tonight' more than once to her husband."

"I think that you are right," Ugo admitted. "When I removed my hairpiece, I could clearly hear my former wife say: 'Honey, you left the toilet seat up again.'"

"When my wife tells me: 'Darling, the toilet paper must always hang down from the inside,' I cover my ears with my toupee."

"I do the same when my dad tells me that I should wear my belt with the point pointing left. Who cares whether the point of my belt points left or right?"

"It's the same thing here. When my wife asks me to separate a double-ply roll of toilet paper and make two single rolls out of it, I know that it's time to cover my ears with my toupee."

"My former mother-in-law used to nag me all the times about hanging the dental floss tapes to dry and using them again the next day. I'll go crazy without my toupee."

"A bald man has a happier marriage," Giovanni acknowledged.

"Is that so? I am concerned that my baldness will interfere with my relationship with Sophia."

"What relationship? Do you mean your sex life?"

"Yes, I am talking about my sex life."

"Turn the light off when you make love to her, or leave your toupee on your head. I don't think that your baldness will interfere with your sex life. I know that because I am bald myself. I have fathered seven beautiful children." Giovanni knocked on Ugo's crane. "It's all in your head, do you hear?" Giovanni knocked on Ugo's head again.

"Yes, I hear you all right. I once forgot to remove my hairpiece while making love to my former wife."

"What happened?" Giovanni moved his ears closer to Ugo.

"The hairpiece came loose and fell on her face. She almost suffocated. I thought that she had reached her climax."

"I know what you mean. Not too long ago, my toupee slid off while I was dining in a restaurant. It fell into my chicken soup. I did not notice that my toupee had fallen into my chicken soup. I thought that the chef forgot to pluck the feathers off the chicken. There must have been at least twenty people inside the restaurant laughing at me. You no longer have to worry about being bald forever because my new formula will make long, thick and beautiful hair grow on your head all over again. It may take a few weeks, may be a few months for your hair to grow back. Believe me; your hair will grow back. I guarantee it."

"I believe you, but if I tell Sophia now that I am bald, she may not like me anymore."

"Rubbish!" Giovanni said. "Take her out to the movies. When the lights dim out, remove your toupee and tuck it under the seat. Then kiss her."

"Oh no, I can't do that. What if she runs her fingers into my hair while I am kissing her? She will find out that I have no hair. That will be very embarrassing. Besides, without my toupee, my chrome dome will reflect the light from the big screen directly into the eyes of the person sitting behind me. This is going to make him furious and he'll beat on my head with his shoes."

"I think that the light glowing on your egghead will make you look like an angel with a halo."

"You mean to say: 'a dead angel.'"

Giovanni shrugged off his shoulders. "Have you ever seen an angel who is not dead? If you have you must have a sixth sense. Why not tell your girlfriend the truth about you hair? She may like your head better without hair. Does she ever watch Telly Savalas, the lollipop cop? He is always surrounded by beautiful women. Tell her about that lollipop cop the next time you meet her. She will then think of your bald head as a giant lollipop and will like it even more."

"I wish it was that easy," Ugo sighed. "I cannot imagine myself kneeling down in front of her, toupee in hand, and saying: 'I am a bald-headed man who is passionately in love with you.'"

"No, no," Giovanni quickly said. "That's not the way it's done in the old country. Let me show you how." The barber removed his toupee and knelt down in front of Ugo. He held the toupee close to his heart and uttered: "Ti amo."

"I might try that, but I am an old-fashioned man. I would rather say it with flowers."

Giovanni rose to his feet and put the toupee back on his head. "You just need to practice," he said. "Come on, get down on your knees and try it now."

Ugo knelt down in front of the barber and held his toupee in front of his heart. Giovanni suddenly noticed that the point of his belt pointed right. "Oh shit," he muttered. "I think I'd better put my belt on the right way otherwise the old woman will yell at me again when I get home tonight." Giovanni unbuckled his belt and his pants slipped down his legs.

"Giovanni, I love you with all my heart," Ugo said aloud. A woman holding a small boy by his hand walked into the hair salon, but quickly walked out when she heard Ugo proclaim his love to Giovanni with his pants down.

"Very good," Giovanni said. He pulled his pants up and fastened his belt the right way. "You were so convincing that I almost fainted." The barber helped Ugo back to his feet and then held his thumb and forefinger about half an inch apart in front of Ugo's eyes. "I am that close to finding the magic potion," he announced. "When I find it, the word 'baldness' will be stricken out of every books and dictionaries."

"I hope that you will find that magic potion soon." Ugo covered his head with his toupee and paid the barber his due.

"Here," Giovanni said, handing Ugo some large rubber bands. "Use these rubber bands to hold your toupee on your head when you eat your chicken soup. They will prevent your toupee from falling into the soup bowl. They work for me. You put them on like this..." Giovanni stretched a rubber band out with the fingers of his hands and slipped it under his jaw and over his toupee.

"Thank you. What do you think about those pills that make hair grow back again? Do you think I should try them?"

"I have heard that they will cause decreased libido and impotence in some men. You have to choose between being able to make love with a toupee and having plenty of hair but forgoing sex. But you don't have to worry about making that choice with my magic formula. You will be able to have plenty of hair on your head and enjoy sex too."

"I wish you would hurry up with that new product of yours."

"My formula will make real hair grow on your head, not just fuzz like what appears when you use those commercial hair growth stimulants. The stuff that you buy from the store will make your hair look like a row of dried corn plants. Besides, it is going to cost you about $50 for each application. You may have to wait six months before you can see any new hair growth. With my concoction, it's... Pouf! You will have hair growing on your head overnight. My concoction will also relieve your hair of dryness, flaking, itching or tightness. It will also restore moisture balance in your hair. You won't have to buy any hair conditioner ever."

"I appreciate your kind advice."

"My formula will remove hair growth in unwanted places and put hair where it is needed the most. You won't find any other formula in the store that can do this."

"Uuh...? Ugo exclaimed. "You mean to say that when the hair starts to grow on my head, I won't have hair under my arm pits?"

"Do you need them there?" Giovanni quickly replied. "My wife always shaves them off. Sometimes God makes mistakes too, you know."

"Are you also saying that my pubic hair will disappear once the hair starts growing on my head?"

"My wife feels that she does not need them, so she shaves them off. I am telling you that in a few weeks you will have beautiful hair on your head. Forget everything else, my friend. You love Sophia, don't you?"

"I do. I love her very much!"

"She will find you irresistible once hair starts to grow on your head. Go home and start planning for your honeymoon. Come back in one week and I will give you a second application."

Ugo became a regular customer at Giovanni's hair salon. Every week Giovanni rubbed his concoction over his head, increasing the strength of the mixture with each application. A few weeks later Ugo began to notice a few strands of hair appearing on his ear lobes. Then his face turned purple. The discoloration on his face worried him and he went back to see Giovanni. Giovanni assured him that the discoloration was merely a side effect of his magic solution and that it would wear off when the hair begins to grow on his head. A few days later Ugo's face turned dark green. He went to see Giovanni again. This time Giovanni told him that it was a good sign; a green tint around his head indicated that the mixture had indeed set into his scalp and was stimulating the hair root. Giovanni warned him that he might notice other side effects while the hair grows, but he should not worry about them. Shortly afterwards Ugo started to feel the side effects that Giovanni warned him about. While cruising along I-35, his hand jerked up and he stuck his middle finger at a motorist who abruptly cut him off. When a driver parked his car too close behind him, his hand suddenly flicked the transmission into reverse and his foot snapped down on the accelerator, sending his car crashing into the vehicle behind him. When he stood in line in a donut shop, his foot twitched and kicked the posterior of the woman who jumped the line in front of him. When he watched a film in a movie theater, his foot quivered and rammed the seats of the couple talking loudly in front of him. When the CEO of his company gave a speech on how employees should be empowered, he sprang up from his seat and pumped up his fist at him. He fluttered his tongue and wobbled his head when his supervisor gave him a 1.023997 percent raise for doing a wonderful job. He gulped, slurped and spit on a passerby's face when the latter tossed an empty beer bottle on the sidewalk. When he read in the newspaper that the CEO of a company received an annual bonus totaling eight hundred million dollars, he tore up the newspaper with his teeth and chewed on the pieces. When the service advisor at a car dealership presented him with a $1,275 bill for car repairs, he experienced spasmodic movements in his arms and punched the service advisor on his face. He lurched at pregnant women smoking, wiggled at teenagers sniffing drugs, and jounced when he heard that a criminal had walked away scotch free. Soon after the side effects appeared, Ugo started to walk unnaturally. Then his speech started to slur. He was however too excited about the hair growth on his head to pay any attention to the side effects and the change in his body posture.

Ugo woke up one morning feeling like something unusual had happened to his hair while he slept. When he ran his hand over his head, his fingers closed on a bushy pile of hair. He jumped out of bed and dashed to the bathroom. The new hair on his head had grown over one inch long. The greenish tint on his face and body had now turned black. He raised his arms above his head to stretch out, but felt a pain on his back. Ugo mused that sleeping on a worn-out mattress caused his back pain. The springs protruded through the mattress and made bumps on his bed. He had been contemplating buying a new mattress, but was too preoccupied with his baldness to go to the department store. Thinking that the new hair on his head was only a dream, Ugo pulled hard on them. The pain he felt by pulling on his hair convinced him that he was not dreaming. He screamed with joy and threw his toupee out of the window. That morning, he left his office at 10 o'clock and drove to the hair salon to show his new hair to Giovanni. He shook the barber's hand and congratulated him for developing the hair formula.

"Oh my God," Giovanni exclaimed, looking at Ugo's hands. The skin on Ugo's hand had turned black. His hands felt rough and heavy. "What happened to your hands?"

"It's probably another side effect of your hair formula," Ugo replied. "The purple and green tints on my face had totally disappeared. I am sure that my hands will return back to normal soon. Giovanni, you are a genius. Your hair formula will make you rich. Please apply for a patent for your invention now before someone else beats you to it."

"Not too soon," Giovanni cautiously advised. "Not too soon! Remember, I am still experimenting. It is wise to wait for some time and see the complete result before I tell the world about my hair formula." Giovanni frowned and looked at Ugo's hands. "I am worried about your hands," he said somberly.

"Don't worry," Ugo said. He waved off the barber's concerns and slapped him on his shoulder. Giovanni felt like someone had just hit his shoulder with a baseball bat. He wavered under the slap, but regained his composure. Ugo bid him goodbye and left the hair salon. He walked out with his body bent down in front of him.

"Ugo, what happened to your back?" Giovanni said as Ugo left the hair salon. "You are walking and jumping around like a monkey."

"It's my bed," Ugo replied. "I need to buy a new mattress."

Ugo was so thrilled with the new hair growing on his head that he went to Sophia's house in the evening to declare his love for her. He then asked her to marry him. Sophia was enchanted and dazzled by Ugo's new hairstyle. She immediately accepted.

Ugo had kept his love for Sophia a secret for some time. No one at the company where they both worked ever suspected that they were dating each other. It was rumored that Sophia was having marital problems and that she was about to divorce her husband. Her idiotic husband tried to win her back by coming to her office every day and watching her work. He befriended everyone working at the company and tried to rally them on his side to save his marriage. It was peculiar that he would spend his whole day keeping his wife company at the office. It was almost like he was keeping a close eye on her. That irritated Sophia even more and she finally gave him the pushover. About the same time, Ugo walked out on his wife of fifteen years and started to date Sophia openly. A few weeks later, Ugo divorced his wife and Sophia became estranged with her husband. Everyone at the office started to wonder if Ugo was going to propose to Sophia. The cat was finally let out of the bag when Ugo suddenly announced that he and Sophia were engaged. The stunned employees quickly collected some money to buy the couple a wedding present. The employees had noticed before that Ugo was suffering from back pain. When they asked Ugo about it, Ugo told them that the loose coils protruding from his mattress were hurting his back. Thereafter the employees secretly bought a new mattress with the money collected for his wedding present. A few days before they were married the employees gathered together to congratulate the future bride and bridegroom. They presented them with a wedding card signed by everyone who had chipped in their lunch money to purchase the mattress. Since the wedding gift was quite out of the ordinary and bulky, they had arranged for the mattress to be delivered to Ugo's home. Ugo was very thankful to the employees for their thoughtfulness. His back had started to worry him. The new mattress was just what he needed. After the wedding the couple flew to Acapulco for their honeymoon.

Giovanni was delighted that hair was finally growing on Ugo's head. He was pleased that his hair formula had finally started to work, but he was disappointed that out of the thousands of people who tried his formula, only Ugo had hair on his head. He did not understand why the formula worked on Ugo, but not on anyone else. His customers had lost faith on his formula and stopped patronizing his hair salon. Some of them were disgusted that he used them as guinea pigs for his experiments. Others could no longer tolerate the embarrassing biological changes they underwent as a result of his experiments. Some customers even talked about suing the barber for making hair grow uncontrollably inside their ears and nostrils, between their legs and out of their alimentary canals.

When Ugo and Sophia returned from their honeymoon, Ugo's neighbors noticed that he had undergone a drastic physical change. He grunted and walked like a gorilla. When they saw his long fingernails and dark face, the neighbors ran into their houses and bolted the door shut behind them. The children in his neighborhood became frightened whenever Ugo talked to them. They went into hiding the moment Ugo came out of his house. When Ugo returned to work, his colleagues were stunned by his physical transformation. They worried about his appearance and whispered unpleasant remarks about him to each other. Some of his colleagues worried more for their safety than about Ugo himself. Ugo's skin had turned dark. The skin looked thick and rough. His nose was wrinkled up and took on a peculiar shape. Everyone thought that Ugo was being transformed into a gorilla, but no one had the courage to speak to him about his metamorphosis. People these days just don't walk up to a person and say: 'Hey man, you look like a gorilla!'

One morning Ugo looked at his reflection in the bathroom mirror and gasped with horror. Overnight, his hair had grown to shoulder length. The hair was growing faster than he could have them cut. He ran his fingers down his thick beard and discovered for the first time that his jaw line had shifted. When he looked in the mirror, he saw not himself, but what looks like an ape. Sophia came into the bathroom and ran her fingers through the thick hair on his chest.

"What is the name of that Englishman who said that man evolved from apes?" he meditated aloud.

"Charles Darwin," Sophia replied.

"He was wrong in making that statement. I think it is quite the opposite."

Sophia laughed and caressed his back. "Is your back better now that you've got a new mattress?"

"I don't feel any pain in my back anymore, but I can't keep my back straight up. What's wrong with me?"

"Nothing," she whispered into his ears. "I like a man with an animal instinct."

"If the hair doesn't stop growing soon I will be that person." Sophia sniggered. Ugo looked at his arms and legs. "They are growing over my arms and my legs too."

"And on your back too," Sophia said, cuddling him.

"There is hair on my back too?" Ugo exclaimed. He turned his back to the vanity mirror and shrieked. "I think I'd better have a few words with that Italian hair stylist. I am going to kill him. No, I think I am going to lynch him."

The following day Giovanni was startled to see a gorilla dressed in a business suit and wearing a cowboy hat walked into his hair salon. A small child ran and hid behind his mother.

Giovanni looked closer at the face of the gorilla and recognized Ugo.

"What do you think you are doing, walking around dressed like a gorilla?" he sternly reprimanded Ugo. "You just frightened the hell out of that little boy. Halloween is still a few days away."

Giovanni took him to his back office and asked him to remove his shirt.

"Holy shit," Giovanni muttered. "I have never seen so much hair on a human being until now." He went back to the front of the shop and returned with his hair cutting tools. He ran his shears over Ugo's body and clipped off the hair. Ugo was furious. He demanded that the barber reversed the hair growth on his body immediately.

"You ought to be grateful that you have hair on your head," Giovanni retorted. "Do you think that Sophia would have married you if you were still wearing a toupee?"

"You are right," Ugo said apologetically. "Maybe the chemicals that you've rubbed on my scalp will wear off eventually and the hair growth will slow down. I am sorry."

"That's quite all right. I think that I might have used too much chicken droppings in my formula. These things are potent."

"You used what in your formula?"

"I used chicken droppings or maybe pigeon droppings. I can't remember now."

"You are kidding me."

"No, I am not. It is quite normal to use chicken and pigeon droppings to stimulate hair growth. The Greek physician Hippocrates rubbed pigeon droppings on his scalp every morning in order to re-grow his hair. We should let nature take its course as naturally as possible. Healthy hair growth is the result of the 'humors' of the body being in balance with each other. Have you never heard of the theory of humors? The characteristic of a person's hair is determined by the different proportions of humors in the person."

"Who said that?"

"Hippocrates said that."

"Well, he'd better be right otherwise I'll turn you into minced meat."

"King Solomon wrote that a merry heart does a lot of good to one's hair. So don't worry, be happy!"

Ugo hoped that the growth of hair would soon slow down, but he hoped in vain. The hair continued to grow wildly over his body. He became tired of going over to the hair salon to have Giovanni trim the hair back and he let the hair grow unchecked. Whenever he left the house he covered his head with his cowboy hat, wrapped his face with a ski mask and wore thick gloves to hide the hair on his hands. The hair around his body was so thick that whenever he was at home he took no trouble to hide his nudity. He paraded in front of the windows covered with nothing but his body hair. Eventually his neighbors began to see a strange animal pacing up and down in Ugo's living room. Some of the neighbors thought that Ugo had acquired a gorilla as a pet. They cautiously kept away from his house to avoid confronting the beast.

While Ugo was at home lounging around in the nude, a young male gorilla named Victorio escaped from the city zoo. The news media warned the citizens to stay indoors until the escaped gorilla is found and captured. They warned that Victorio is very dangerous and could harm small children. They asked people to report any gorilla sightings to the police. Upon hearing the news, panic struck among Ugo's neighbors. They brought their binoculars out and aimed them at Ugo's living room. They kept a watchful eye on the house for long hours. When they spotted Ugo pacing up and down in front of the window, they called each other to confirm their sightings and then called the police. The police alerted the zoo authorities and dispatched half a dozen squad cars to encircle Ugo's house. The officers sealed off all escape routes from the house. A dozen animal caretakers from the zoo accompanied the police and prepared to capture the escaped gorilla. Ugo had just returned into the living room after going to the bathroom to examine his hair. He looked outside his window and noticed the unusual police activity in front of his house. Several police cars were parked in the normally quiet cul-de-sac and a group of policemen crouched behind their patrol cars with their riffles pointed at his house. Two police sharpshooters were perched on the roof of the house facing his. He became worried at the police activity in the street and ran to the back of the house. There he saw another group of policemen, riffles in hand, jumping over his fence and taking position behind the trees and garden shed. The presence of the law enforcement officials in his back yard disturbed him and he stepped out of the house without his clothes. The crowd behind the police line grew uneasy. "Watch out!" someone shouted. "The gorilla is coming out!" The curious onlookers pointed their fingers at Ugo while the policemen raised and aimed their riffles at him. The uproar astonished Ugo and he stared in disbelief at the guns being pointed at him. A police marksman brought out a shotgun loaded with a tranquilizer dart. Ugo suddenly realized that the policemen were after him and he ran back to the house. The marksman fired the dart at Ugo as he sprang back into the doorway. Ugo felt the sharp needle in his posterior. He stiffened, clutched the dart and tried to pull it from his buttock. He stumbled back, wavered across the front yard and finally fell down on the lawn. He wrangled to get back on his feet, but the substance had started to paralyze his nervous system. He collapsed and rolled over to his side.

"Let's get the gorilla back to the zoo before he regains consciousness," a zoo official bellowed.

Assisted by the policemen, the animal caretakers loaded Ugo on a stretcher and carried him to a van. They chained him down on the van's floor, closed and locked the doors. When the van drove off, Sophia returned from the grocery store and pulled up in front of her house. Her neighbors immediately surrounded her and told her that an escaped gorilla had somehow found his way into her house.

"You are darn lucky that we spotted the animal and called the police before you got here," one of her neighbors said.

Meanwhile the real gorilla hid among the trees surrounding the zoo and avoided walking directly into the path of human beings. When darkness fell over the city, he ventured out of the wood and into the streets. He walked aimlessly from one street into another and eventually ended up on Central Expressway. The automobiles racing by him and the loud traffic noise confused and frightened him. He howled at the motorists, jumped up and down, beat his chest and chased a few cars. A motorist mistook the errant gorilla for someone dressed up in a Halloween costume and stopped to give him a ride. After all it was Halloween night and the goblins were out trick-and-treating. At first the confused Victorio was hesitant to enter the small, crowded car. The occupants were all dressed up in Halloween costumes and were on the way to a nightclub to party. The car occupants beckoned Victorio into the car, but the gorilla would not budge. Thinking that the costume of the hitchhiker was preventing him from getting in the car, the driver and his passengers came out to help the gorilla into the subcompact car. Victorio had lived in a zoo all his life. He understood that human beings sometimes behave rather peculiarly towards animals.

"Nice Halloween suit," a partygoer, dressed like Bluebeard said to the gorilla. "Why don't you come and party with us tonight, euh?"

Victorio grunted at the partygoer. He snatched his beer can and gulped its content down.

"Good for you," Bluebeard said, slapping the gorilla on his back. "You must have come straight out of a jungle book. You look like a real gorilla in that suit."

They drove Victorio to a nightclub located on Upper Greenville Avenue. When they arrived at the nightclub, they joined a long line of people waiting to be admitted. Two bouncers verified the age of the partygoers before allowing them into the discotheque. They also checked the race and nationality of the partygoers who were not whites. A doorman asked a gentleman from the Middle East to produce two picture Ids. Unable to present the two picture Ids asked of him, the gentleman from the Middle East was denied entrance to the nightclub. When the doorman saw Victorio, he pulled on his facial hair and said: "Sorry, buddy. No one with a beard is allowed into the nightclub. It's club policy." Victorio growled at the doorman. His new friends were infuriated and protested.

"Oh, come on, don't give us that bullshit. He is not Arabic. He is an American citizen. You've just turned away one man because he is from the Middle East. Are you going to turn away your own countryman?"

"It's the club's policy," the doorman stressed. "I can't let him in because he has a beard on his face."

"You guys are a bunch of racists," a white woman standing in line yelled. "You are turning him away because he is black, not because he has a beard. This is not fair."

"If the gentleman would simply go home and shave off his beard, I will let him in when he comes back," the doorman said. "I am only enforcing the club's regulations."

"Let's go find another place to party," someone said.

"All right," the doorman said. "I will make an exception for the gentleman tonight. It is Halloween night and we all want to have a good time, don't we? If the gentleman would produce two picture Ids, I will let him in."

"Nobody carries two picture Ids, you idiot," another white woman shouted. "That's just another way to deny a black man entrance to the club." The woman turned to her friends and pulled on their arms. "Come on, gals, let's go party somewhere else."

Victorio became agitated at the shoving and shouting. He growled and pounded his chest. He jostled the doorman and a couple of bouncers out of his path and walked into the club. The bouncers made no effort to stop him. The bystanders cheered.

The partygoers in the nightclub were attired as famous movie characters. They came dressed as Superman, Count Dracula, Mickey Mouse, Batman, King Kong, Donald Duck, E.T, Spock, Godzilla and Spiderman. They came made up as a clown, robed in black as a witch, clothed in white as a ghost, disguised as Matari, masked as Zorro, garbed as Samson, costumed as Wonder Woman, and stripped down as Tarzan. Victorio came to the club as himself - a real gorilla. He appeared like King Kong and mingled with the crowd as Donkey Kong. The comic characters shuffled on the dance floor, gathered along the bar, and sat around tables to drink and chat. They gawked and exchanged greetings with one another. Victorio got separated from his ride companions and wandered around, pulling and pushing everyone that stood on his way. Balloons flew around him, confetti fell on his head, and buffoons blew paper curlers at his face. A man deposited a fancy paper cone on the gorilla's head. Victorio removed the cone from his head and slammed it back on the man's face. A woman pulled on his arms and started to dance with him. He danced with her for a while. Then the woman hugged and kissed his cheeks before disappearing into the crowd. Confused by the flickering lights and the loud music, Victorio walked around in a circle. He clinched beer bottles and wine glasses from the crowd and emptied their contents into his large mouth. He caught sight of a bowl of peanuts on the bar and pushed off a patron from his stool to reach for it. After emptying the bowl of peanuts, he pounded on his chest and grunted at the bartender. The bartender removed a jar of peanuts from under the bar and filled up the bowl.

When Victorio emptied the bowl again, he jumped over the bar and seized the jar. The bartender tried to get the jar back, but Victorio pushed him away. The bartender became furious and ordered Victorio to stay on the other side of the bar. Victorio ignored him and drank beer directly from the tap. The customers crowding the bar cheered. Victorio grabbed bottles of beer from the icebox and handed them to the patrons. More customers crowded around the bar and begged for beer. The gorilla then amused himself by tossing bottles of beer to the customers. Unable to control the gorilla, the bartender called the bouncers to come to his help. Four burly bouncers jumped on Victorio, immobilized and dragged him away from the bar. They carried him to the door, but midway on the dance floor, Victorio broke loose from the bouncers. He snarled and swung his front paws at a bouncer. He plucked another bouncer by the bottom of his pants and hurled him over the bar. The other two bouncers ran for cover. At the sight of the angry gorilla, Superman fled to the powder room and Spiderman ducked behind a broom. Batman raced for cover and Wonder Woman shrieked with terror. Victorio's eyes turned fiery red. He bared his teeth and howled at the people trying to eject him from the nightclub. The crowd stood in awe and gawked at the agitated gorilla. Victorio lowered his long and heavy paws and languidly walked to the bar. He seized another jar of peanuts and a few bottles of beer and headed towards the exit. At the door he turned to the stupefied crowd, thumped on his chest and hollered. He finally left the nightclub and disappeared in the dark of the night.

The music started to blare again and the dancers quickly crowded the dance floor. The bouncers cleaned up the mess around the bar and picked up empty bottles from the floor.

"Does anyone know the man in the gorilla suit?" the nightclub Manager asked the crowd at the bar.

"He hitched a ride with us," Bluebeard ventured to say. "He hardly said a word in the car. I think he drank too much beer."

A bouncer, nursing a bloody nose, put two empty beer bottles on the bar. "You gave a ride to a gorilla and brought him here," he said. "Did you not know that a gorilla escaped from the zoo this morning?"

Bluebeard's eyes popped out. "Nah," he said, shaking his head. "I swear that he is a man disguised as a gorilla."

Seeking to avoid the human beings, Victorio loitered behind the shops surrounding the nightclub. He ventured in a dark alley to escape the glaring lights that were hurting his eyes. Tired and broken-hearted, he searched for a place to hide and rest. He walked up to a trash container and dropped his heavy mass behind it. With a dismal and tired look on his face, he leaned against the trash container to rest. He uttered a soft moan and rapped his upper trunk in defeat. Dispirited and despondent, he drowned his sorrow with beer. The gorilla's massive frame began to tip over and slide sideways.

Seconds later he fell asleep. Giovanni, fearful that he would be sued, decided to stop using his hair formula on his customers. Late that night he came to his hair salon to dispose of the chemicals he used for his concoction. Under the cover of darkness, he dumped the chemicals in the trash container behind his hair salon. Giovanni discerned a dark object lying on the ground next to the container. Thinking that it was a trash bag, he stooped down to pick it up and put it into the trash container. The bag, to his surprise, was very heavy and would not move. "I wonder what's in this trash bag?" he muttered. Unable to lift the trash bag, he left it where he found it,. He slid the dumpster cover to close it, but it would not move. Giovanni bang on the cover with his fist to free it, but it remained stuck. He gave up trying to close the trash container and walked back to his hair salon. The noise had woken the gorilla up and he became inquisitive at what the human being had left in the container. He picked out a gallon from the trash container, unscrewed the cap and drank its content. The chemical tasted like nothing he had drank before while he was incarcerated in the zoo. He retrieved another gallon, and another, and another until he had quenched his thirst. Then he dropped back to the ground to sleep.

At sunrise Giovanni returned to the dumpster site accompanied by two men from the business park's maintenance staff.

"I don't know what's in the bag," Giovanni complained to the maintenance crew. "It was too dark to see anything, but I can tell you that it was darn heavy." When they arrived at the waste container, Giovanni and the maintenance men saw a naked man sleeping next to the container. They moved closer to Victorio to examine him.

"He sure has a lot of hair on him," a maintenance worker remarked.

The chemicals that Victorio drank had caused some of his hair to fall off his body. The anthropoid ape had metamorphosed into a primitive man.

"Good grief," Giovanni cried out, "that man is Ugo, one of my customers. He looks so awful. Please help me carry him inside the hair salon."

They carried the gorilla into the hair salon and laid him down on a chair in front of a washbasin. Giovanni feared that his experiment had gone awry. He quickly ordered the maintenance men out of his hair salon less they became too inquisitive. One of the maintenance men looked fixedly at the gorilla sleeping on the chair

"That's a very strange-looking man," he muttered. "What do you intend to do with him?"

"Don't worry, I'll take good care of him," Giovanni replied. "I will call his wife and tell her that he is safe. You may leave now. I'll take care of him."

"That big hairy thing has a wife?" the first maintenance man asked.

The second maintenance man shook his head at Victorio. "She must have been very desperate when she married him."

"He will look more presentable after I wash him," Giovanni assured then.

Giovanni put on his work overall and grabbed his hair cutting tools. He trimmed back the hair on the gorilla's head and shaved off all traces of hair from the gorilla's torso, back, arms and legs. He lopped off the hair from his face, leaving just enough under his nose to form a mustache. He turned the chair around and tilted it towards the washbasin to wash the gorilla's head. After he was done washing the gorilla's head, he dried his head and wiped his face with a wet towel. Then he combed back his freshly cut hair and dabbed his cheeks with after-shave lotion. He fetched a bundle of clothes, clean socks and a pair of shoes from the back office and started to cover the gorilla up. He brushed off the loose hair from around Victorio's genitals and slid a pair of underwear on him. He slipped a vest over his head, put a shirt on him, and pulled a pair of pants over his legs. Then he socked him up and slipped a pair of shoes around his feet. Finally he tied a cravat around Victorio's neck and stepped back to admire his work. He sighed with relief when Victorio started to stir in the chair. He quickly sprayed a mist of perfume behind the gorilla's ears, around his neck and on his wrists. The scent tickled the gorilla's nose and woke him up.

"Thanks God we wear the same shoe size," Giovanni said. "Everything fits just nicely." He rubbed his hands and grinned with satisfaction. He grabbed a mirror from the table and held it in front of the gorilla's face.

"You look sharp with your new mustache," he said. The gorilla sat up on the chair and stared at his reflection in the mirror. Giovanni moved the hand-held mirror to the back of the gorilla's head. "In all my life as a hair stylist, you are probably my most unusual customer. You had so much hair on you this morning that I was afraid that my formula had transformed you into an ape." The gorilla grunted at his reflection. He took the mirror from Giovanni's hand and held it closer to his face. He pulled on the mustache and growled.

"You looked terrible before I shaved off your beard. You were a pitiful sight. For a brief moment I thought that you were an ape."

The gorilla stared at the shoes and tried to shake them off his feet. He stood up and gazed at the sleeves over his arms and the pants on his legs. When he pulled on the cravat tied around his neck, Giovanni laughed.

"The clothes are all mine," he said. "Keep them as long as you need them. You were stripped off of all your clothes when I found you. You did not even have any shoes on. It must have been quite a striptease party you went to." The gorilla moved towards Giovanni. Giovanni stepped back and raised his hands in front of him. "Don't worry, I won't mention a word of it to Sophia," he quickly said. "I have prepared an alibi for you. I will tell Sophia that you were too drunk to drive home last night, and you came over to my house to spend the night."

Giovanni slid a jacket on the gorilla's back. "I'll call a cab to take you home."

At the zoo Ugo regained consciousness and found with consternation that he was enclosed in a cage with two other gorillas. Solid iron bars separated him from the free world. He felt a pain in his posterior and rubbed the painful area with his hand to soothe the pain. The cage had an arrangement of dead tree trucks in the center, several buckets of fresh fruits and a pail of water. Caves molded out of plastic provided shelter to the gorillas whenever it rains. Water dripped from a hose hooked up to a faucet on the wall. The two gorillas in the cage were jittery of Ugo and kept away from him. Ugo wet his face from the water dripping from the hose. He bent over a bucket of fruits and reached out for a banana. The gorillas in the cage growled, jumped around him and shooed him away from the bucket of fruits. Ugo dropped the banana back into the bucket and took shelter in the grotto. When he saw visitors crowding around the cage to watch the gorillas, he suddenly realized that he was naked and cupped his hands over his private parts. The children on the other side of the cage exploded with laughter. Ugo realized with horror that the zoo officials had made a terrible mistake. They had mistaken him for Victorio, the escaped gorilla.

"I am not a gorilla," he shouted at the crowd. "It's a mistake. I am a man. I want to talk to my lawyer. PLEASE GET OUT ME OF HERE!" Ugo's speech had deteriorated to the point where no one could understand anything he said. His unintelligible words sounded like the grunting of an ape. Nonetheless the zoo visitors were amazed at his babbling. They were amazed to see a gorilla attempting to communicate to them in the English language. Ugo's loud grunting and mad gestures captivated the children. A foreign student was amused to see a gorilla that could speak English. He removed his 'Test of English as a Foreign Language' book from his backpack and tossed it at Ugo. Ugo picked up the book and threw it back at the student. The crowd burst into laughter. In desperation Ugo covered his head with his hand and retreated to the grotto. Then he thought of a way to get the visitors' attention. He approached the foreign student and gesticulated to him to give him the TOEFL book back. The student gave him the book. Ugo took the book and asked the student for a pen.

"Pen," he said. "Give me a pen to write with." He pretended to hold a pen between his thumb and index finger and moved his hand swiftly over the book.

"He wants a pen to write with," a child said. "Give him a pen."

The student held out a pen to him. Ugo took the pen and quickly scribbled a message on the cover of the book. He checked the message, gave the book and the pen back to the student, and asked him to deliver the message to his wife.

"What did the gorilla write?" someone asked.

The student scanned the message on the front cover of the book and read it aloud to the crowd. "My name is Ugo. I am a human being who used to be bald. Giovanni applied his magic formula on my head and turned me into a hairy ape. Please call my wife Sophia to come and get me out of here. Tell her that Giovanni is responsible for the mix up. Tell her that I love her."

The crowd chortled, giggled, tittered and roared. Ugo's heart sank at the laughter and the merriment. He covered and dropped his head in despair. The roar of laughter made the other gorillas in the cage anxious. They became envious of Ugo getting all the attention from the visitors. One of the gorillas unfurled the water hose and aims it at Ugo while the other gorilla turned on the water faucet. Ugo shielded himself with his arms against the jet of water and ran back to the grotto. The gorillas scrambled around and squeaked with joy at the sight of Ugo running for cover. The crowd regaled and convulsed at the unexpected show inside the gorillas' cage.

The foreign student stared in disbelief at Ugo's writing on the cover of the TOEFL practice book. He was heart-broken that a gorilla could write English better than him and saddened that apes living in America were more educated than the children in his poor, undeveloped country. He was amazed that the US government would choose to spend money to teach gorillas to read and write instead of educating inner-cities children. The student took the book to the visitor's center and explained to a man behind the service desk that a gorilla had borrowed his pen and scribbled English words on his book. The man asked him to fill out a form and to include his full address and phone number. The student did as he was told and handed the form and the TOEFL book to the man.

"You will receive a full refund for the damaged book in four to six weeks," he said. "We are very sorry that the gorilla had defaced your book."

Dr. Roselyn Goriatchev, a zoologist and fervent admirer of the Anthropologists Jane Goddall and Diane Fossey, was just returning from delivering a lecture on the apes of Central Africa. She overheard the student and was intrigued by his account of the gorilla writing on his book. She approached the zoo employee behind the service desk and asked to see the TOEFL book. The zoo employee gave her the book and told her to keep it. Dr. Goriatchev sprinted out of the visitor's center and ran after the student.

"Excuse me," she called out after him. The student stopped walking and waited for her. "Which gorilla wrote on your book?" she asked him. The student accompanied her to the gorilla's cage and pointed at Ugo.

"I knew it," she exclaimed. "I knew it had to be Victorio. He had previously shown some tendencies to read and write. I am thrilled." The bespectacled woman danced around and screamed with joy. She rushed to her office and requested that Ugo be moved immediately to a separate cage.

Throughout the day visitors came to gawk at Ugo. He begged the visitors to help him, but they tossed foods at him instead. At first they tossed peanuts at him, then popcorns and hotdog bits, and later cookies and bananas. His voice had turned coarse from begging the visitors to help him. Eventually he lost his voice and he could hardly speak. In utter despair, he dropped down near the dead tree trunk in the middle of the cage and lied down on the ground. An old woman came by his cage and threw bread morsels at him. Ugo watched helplessly as the breadcrumbs flew around him. When the crowd around the gorilla's cage thinned out, the old woman removed a large coconut from a sack and threw it at Ugo. The coconut hit him on his head. Angered at all the projectiles that were hurled at him throughout the day, he dashed to the iron bars and cussed at the woman. The old woman stared at Ugo with her mouth agape.

"Can't you read the sign?" Ugo mumbled. "DO NOT FEED THE ANIMALS! My God, do you want to kill us all?" Then he realized that he was not an animal, calmed down and smiled at the woman. "Well, thanks anyway. I can surely eat it. Thanks again, Ma'am. Have a good day."

The old lady stepped back in consternation and hurriedly left. Ugo picked up the cookies and bananas thrown to him by the visitors. He pounded the coconut on the floor to crack it open and scooped out the meat with his fingers. When the other two gorillas came forward to take his foods, he was suddenly overtaken by the instinct to survive. He jumped up and down and waved them off with loud cries. "Stay away from my food," he warned. "Stay away from my food."

At dusk when all the visitors had left the zoo, the animal caretakers climbed above his cage and hosed him down to clean him up. After he was washed down, the caretakers descended into the cage and forced him into an enclosure and closed the door shut behind him. Too tired to resist the animal caretakers and unable to communicate with them, Ugo settled down in the grotto for the night. Ugo's first day as an imprisoned gorilla, the fourth order of the Anthropoid Apes, had just ended. His newest neighbors, the gibbons, the orangutans and the chimpanzees also settled down for the night.

Ugo was transferred to a new cage the next day. Upon entering his new habitat Ugo was transfixed at the setup inside it. At first he could not believe what he saw. The cage looked more like a glass house with an unobstructed view of the zoo outside. The floor was covered with thick carpet and the furnishing included a bed, a sofa, armchairs and a floor lamp. There was also a TV set, a VCR, a HI-FI system, a personal computer and a telephone. Thick curtains and vertical blinds surrounded a door that opened to a small courtyard enclosed by a heavy metal fence. The courtyard was covered with thick wire mesh. The bathroom had a shower stall, a sink and a toilet bowl. A bookcase filled with books stood in one corner of the room. Ugo sat down at the computer desk and powered on the computer. At that moment a side door flung open and Dr. Goriatchev stepped inside the cage followed by her assistants.

"Victorio had previously learned to communicate using a keyboard with special symbols called lexigrams," Dr. Goriatchev said to her assistants. "He can understand syntax and infer meanings from words. He is the first gorilla in the zoo to pick up the English Language naturally. He is capable of proto-grammar as complex as that used by a two-year old child. I have been probing his brain to look for structures and patterns of activity that, in humans, produce language. There is absolutely no doubt in my mind that the basic cognitive substrates for language are present in the gorilla. He is very intelligent and he surprises me every day with his abilities."

"If Victorio possesses language structures and activates them when using language, wouldn't it suggest that the last ancestor of man had used these structures too?" an assistant questioned.

"I deduce from Victorio's language ability that the mountain gorillas of West Africa can adapt to our environment and quickly learn our ways. The experiment I am conducting will show that by altering a gorilla's environment, the gorilla will change its behavior and eventually choose to live the way humans live. The goal of my research is to prove that learning a new behavior is not restricted to humankind only. I believe that gradually a gorilla will speak the language of the human beings, learn a trade, seek employment and pay federal and State income taxes. Can you imagine what my research will lead to? I can envision both men and gorillas sharing a cubicle and writing computer codes together to solve complex mathematical problems. The impact on the American economy will be just tremendous. With a larger work force, the government tax revenues will increase. The increase in tax revenues will help reduce the national debt."

"Dream on," Ugo blurted.

"Pardon me?" Dr. Goriatchev said, turning to Ugo. Ugo ignored her and fiddled with the controls on the Hi-Fi system. Dr. Goriatchev shrugged her shoulders and looked at her assistants. "I have chosen Victorio to be the subject of my research because the young male gorilla had exhibited some incredible intelligence in the past. More recently he wrote a few words in American English. Several visitors to the zoo had reported that they had heard him talk in English too. A woman swore that Victorio cussed at her using a four-letter word. Now, where else in the world would anybody, man or animal, learn to use four-letter words? Isn't that amazing?" Ugo jumped from his chair and pointed to the bruise on his head.

"The old bitch hurled a coconut at my head."

"Sit down, Victorio," Dr. Goriatchev ordered him. Ugo sat back on the chair and clicked on the remote control to turn the TV set on. "Turn the TV off, Victorio. I am talking with some eminent people in the room."

"Yes, mama," Ugo replied. He clicked the TV set off and dropped on the king size bed. "Ooooh, a comfortable bed at last," he relished. He stretched his arms and legs and uttered a sigh of relief.

Dr. Goriatchev meticulously removed the TOEFL practice book from a bag and showed the gorilla's writing on the book cover to her assistants.

"This is the most significant piece of writing that man had ever come across since the Dead Sea Scrolls were found in Jordan," she said. "It is the first time that a gorilla had communicated in written English to a human being." Dr. Goriatchev's assistants crowded around the TOEFL practice book to examine Ugo's writing.

"What does the writing mean?" one of the assistants asked, puzzled at the message.

"I am puzzled too by what he wrote," another assistant confessed.

"I don't know yet, but look at how neat his handwriting is. The letters are neatly shaped and the words are evenly spaced. He spelled all the words correctly. The grammar is just faultless. His writing is a summation of the case for cleanliness, accuracy and brevity in the use of English. Nowadays you cannot find a high school student who can write as cleanly as this. Not even my boss, who has a Doctorate degree from a prestigious University, can write as well as Victorio."

"Who is Ugo?"

"My guess is that the gorilla tried to write his name, but he did not know the correct spelling of the word. So he wrote 'Ugo' instead."

"Who is Sophia?"

"I think that he is referring to Victoria, the female gorilla that the Miami zoo is loaning to us. I wonder how he knows about her. Notice the last phrase: 'Tell her that I love her.'"

"This is really amazing."

"Yes, indeed. It shows that gorillas can express their emotions and feelings in written words. I find it even more amazing that Victorio chose to write in the English language instead of Kiswahili or Bantu. I anticipate that before long the gorillas will communicate with each other on the Internet." Dr. Goriatchev removed an abacus from her bag and approached Ugo. "Victorio, Professor Strunk would be so proud of you if he were still alive today," Dr. Goriatchev said. "I brought you a present." She gave the abacus to Ugo. "Gentlemen, I am using this abacus to demonstrate that Victorio exhibits intelligent signs. Victorio, please add two to three on the abacus and show us the result."

Ugo took the abacus from Dr. Goriatchev and tossed it over his shoulder. He walked to one of her assistants and pulled out a scientific calculator from his coat pocket. The zoologists stood back in consternation.

"Does any one of you know how many reindeers Santa Claus will require at Christmas time to carry and deliver 660 million pounds of toys to 32 million homes spread across 130 million square miles?" he asked. The zoologists stared at each other and shook their heads.

Ugo rapidly punched some numbers into the calculator.

"The answer is two hundred and twenty times ten to the power of three reindeers. It means that Santa will have to visit one thousand one hundred and seventy eight homes every second on Christmas Eve in order to deliver all the toys to the children by Christmas morning." He put the calculator back in the pocket of Dr. Goriatchev's assistant and shook his shoulders. "I am a human being," he yelled at his face. "I am not a gorilla. Sophia is not a female gorilla on loan from Miami zoo. She is my wife. PLEASE GET ME OUT OF HERE!"

Dr. Goriatchev and her assistants hurried through the side door and disappeared. During the next few days Dr. Goriatchev brought Ugo all sorts of games and toys for him to play with. She took notes while Ugo played with the toys. She gave him special games to test his mental and physical abilities and to develop his hand-eye coordination. Ugo played along with the zoologist. He stunned her by solving quadratic equations, writing down quotations from Shakespeare's novels, and showing her how to program a VCR. Dr. Goriatchev was astonished by the gorilla's intelligence and awarded him a certificate for his ability to program a VCR. As the side effects of Giovanni's mixture began to dissipate, Ugo began to regain the full power of his speech.

"Something tells me that you are not an ordinary ape," Dr. Goriatchev said while she measured and noted down Ugo's physical attributes. "I will need solid evidence that you are indeed different from the other apes, otherwise I am not proving anything. All the apes in the zoo can play games, and some can even write their names. If you will talk to me in a clear, concise way and say something that I can truly understand, then I will believe that my research will be worthwhile."

Ugo looked sympathetically at her. She brought him books to read and old Tarzan movies to watch. Whenever he felt bored or lonely, she came and played chess with him. He found her work fascinating and admired her patience. He was grateful to her for putting him in an apartment and appreciated all the modern conveniences inside the apartment. Ugo bent over Dr. Goriatchev.

"You are standing in front of a naked man," he whispered. Dr. Goriatchev did not quite understand what Ugo said to her. She knelt down in front of Ugo and took measurement of his legs.

"Just give me some signs that I can work with," she muttered. "Convince me that you are not an ordinary ape."

Ugo raised his voice. "Will you be shocked to learn that you are standing in front of a naked man?" he said. Again, Dr. Goriatchev did not get the meaning of what Ugo said.

Ugo took a deep breath and shouted at the top of his voice: "Why are you measuring the size of my penis?"

Dr. Goriatchev stiffened up and stared at Ugo.

The shocked anthropologist stepped back and shook her head in amazement at the gorilla talking to her. "I want an immediate end to this farce," Ugo snapped. "My name is Ugo and I am not a gorilla. I want to go home to my wife now. I am sick of all the things that you make me do in the zoo. I am a human being, not an animal."

Dr. Goriatchev clasped her hands in front of her in ecstasy. "He is talking," she muttered. "I've finally got Victorio to talk English to me." She ran out of Ugo's apartment screaming: "Victorio has spoken to me in the English language. The ape is talking in English."

In exasperation, Ugo ran to the glass window and banged his fist on the 3" thick clear plastic wall. "I am a man, you lousy bum," he shouted after her. Dr. Goriatchev sprang out of the apery and rushed back to her office. Ugo dashed into the courtyard and looked at the surprised zoo visitors. She pointed his finger at Dr. Goriatchev. "That woman is crazy. She thinks that I am an ape. I am a human being, will you please help me?" The visitors exchanged looks at one another and smiled. Then they moved on to the other cages. "That's silly," he cried out. "I have never heard of a talking ape in my whole life." He shook the iron bars and yelled at the crowd.

"Listen to me, all of you God-loving people. You delight in torturing and inflicting pain to other creatures. It's cruel and inhuman to keep animals in cages. Animals are creatures of God and must be treated fairly. They have the right to live their lives with dignity and without being subjected to cruelty, unnecessary pain and exploitation." Intrigued, the zoo visitors moved closer to the gorilla cage and stared at Ugo. Ugo snatched a fur-lined leather jacket from a woman's hand and held it above his head.

"Each year 22 million animals, among them foxes, coyotes, otters, opossums and minks are killed by leg traps and neck snares. These devices crush the animals' limbs and induce prolonged and excruciating pain. This pelt comes from the fur of a seal. Thousands of baby seals are clubbed to death in Canada and the US just for this pelt." He threw the jacket back to the woman. The crowd jeered. Ugo moved swiftly to the other end of the cage and pulled a necklace from another visitor. "This ivory comes from the tusk of an elephant. Do you know that each year 80,000 elephants are wiped out by machine guns in Africa so that a woman can wear this thing around her neck? They call this thing jewelry, I call it murder." He threw the necklace over the crowd. The visitors clapped their hands and applauded. "Who are we to imprison and torture the less clever species? What right do we have to oppress the animals? There is no excuse for this unjustifiable prejudice against animals. We have a special duty to all animals in the same way that we care after the young, the old and the sick in our society." The crowd became silent. Ugo leaned against the railings and slumped down.

"You look ridiculous in this gorilla suit," a man said. "Your acting is deplorable. You can't fool us." Someone remarked.

"How much do they pay you to play out this monkey act?" Another man asked.

"The fate of animals is of greater importance to me than the fear of appearing ridiculous," Ugo replied.

"Come on, let's move on to another exhibit," the man said, pulling his companion along.

As he gave in to despair over his fate, Ugo felt someone's hand on his shoulder. A small girl smiled at him and said: "You forgot to tell the crowd about the male chicks at the farmhouse."

"Tell them about the male chicks at the farmhouse?" Ugo stammered back.

The girl nodded. "You look tired. I can tell them for you."

"Oh yes, please. Go ahead, sweetheart. Tell them about the chicks."

The small girl crossed her hands in front of her and looked up at the crowd. "Farmers who are in the egg business stuff male chicks in large plastic bags to suffocate them because the male chicks cannot lay eggs," she said. "They also ground the male chicks alive to make foods for other animals."

The crowd of bystanders applauded. Her mother patted her on her head and led her away. She turned to Ugo and said: "Goodbye, Sir. I really liked the show."

The real Victorio meanwhile was reunited with his wife Sophia. Well, not exactly reunited because the gorilla and the female human being were never united in the first place. The mix-up occurred because Giovanni thought that Victorio was Ugo and sent him home to Sophia. When the taxicab dropped the gorilla at Ugo's home, Sophia rushed out and helped him into their home. For a few days the confused Victorio did not utter a word to Sophia. Sophia did not question the gorilla's silence because she already knew that her husband had developed a speech problem while they spent their honeymoon in Acapulco. She was just happy that Ugo had returned home safely, particularly after a gorilla broke into her house a few days ago. Victorio, on the other hand, was tired of running away. He was glad that Sophia gave him refuge in her home and was delighted when she fed him with fatty potato chips, nachos and beer. He did not quite like the hot jalapeno peppers on the nachos because every time he ate them, he felt as if his pants were on fire. He would rush to the bathroom to dip his bottom in the commode, but then his behind would then get stuck in the toilet bowl. Sophia had to call the firemen to come and pull him out. Sophia became worried about her husband's ability to communicate effectively in English and took him to a speech therapist. The therapist recommended speech therapy to help Victorio talk normally again. Victorio met with the therapist three times a week to begin the painful and arduous process of learning to speak American English. One thing that Dr. Goriatchev was right about was that Victorio was indeed a very intelligent ape. In a very short time, the gorilla mastered the English Language and became an avid reader. He developed a keen interest in English literature and eagerly read books written by Dickens, Austen, Hemingway, Faulkner and other novelists. With Sophia's encouragement, Victorio took the TOEFL examination and passed the test with flying colors. He adapted quickly to the ways of the humans and became a law-abiding citizen. Sophia encouraged him to continue his education and pleaded with him to go to college to further his education. Victorio began to study for the SAT examination so that he could go to college and be an anthropologist like Dr. Goriatchev. When Victorio showed up for work as Ugo, he had no problem convincing everyone that he was indeed Ugo. As Dr. Goriatchev had earlier predicted, Victorio woke up every morning to commute to work and grudgingly paid federal income taxes on his income. The gorilla liked the comfort of his new life, the wide assortment of foods, and his new freedom. However, not everything he did, saw or experienced made him happy. He wept when he watched hunters shoot down elephants in old TARZAN movies. He cried when he saw chimpanzees forced to perform acrobatic feats at the circus for the enjoyment of human beings. He whimpered at the sight of small monkeys performing tricks to entertain spectators at flea markets. His heart sank when he saw bare-buttock gibbons chasing after cars to beg for food scraps. The day Victorio dreaded the most finally came when Sophia took him to the zoo. His eyes filled with tears as they strolled past the gorilla cages.

"The zoo has a new attraction," Sophia said. "A unique kind of ape had recently been discovered and is on public display in the apery. He can speak English."

Sophia took him to the stylish apery where Ugo lived. The glass house had been attracting a lot of visitors since Ugo was displayed in it. Once there, Sophia pointed at a gorilla sitting in the glass house and reading the Wall Street journal. Ugo, oblivious of the crowd, went over the DOW Jones Index and picked stocks. The stock-picking session had turned into a major attraction at the zoo and a large crowd of people had gathered to watch Ugo play the stock market. Dr. Goriatchev stood by Ugo.

"Purchase 5,000 shares of stocks from the ColorVision Company," Ugo advised Dr. Goriatchev. "Their new video game, Monkey Kong, has broken all sale record. I think that the company will announce a big profit by year's end. This will push up the price of their stocks."

"You've got it."

Dr. Goriatchev scribbled a code on a scrap piece of paper. "Oh, I want you to know that I have put in a request to establish a bank account in your name. Soon you will be able to buy stocks on behalf of the zoo. You will become the first gorilla in the world to ever hold a bank account."

"Great!"

"The bank is giving a free toaster to customers who open up a new account. I'll get you a toaster when I get back." Dr Goriatchev exited.

"And I will be the first gorilla to own a toaster," Ugo muttered.

"That's him over there," Sophia whispered. "He is the talking ape."

Ugo put the Wall Street journal down and looked outside the glass cage. He saw Sophia among the visitors and leaped up from his chair. He opened the door and ran to the iron bars separating him from Sophia.

"Sophia," he yelled. "It's me, Ugo."

"The gorilla just called my name," a stunned Sophia exclaimed. He looked at Victorio. "How does he know my name?"

"Sophia," Ugo begged, "Listen to me please! I am Ugo, your husband. GET ME OUT OF HERE."

"He sure does talk," Sophia cried out. "I have never heard an ape talk like this before." Frightened at Ugo's gestures and shouting, she clutched Victorio's arm. Ugo glanced at Victorio and became suspicious.

"Who is this man," he roared.

"This man," Sophia replied, "is my husband. Repeat after me, HUSBAND."

"He is your husband?" Ugo repeated, perplexed. "The two of you are married?"

"You have it right," she said, smiling. She turned back to Victorio and said: "He learns fast, doesn't he? What an intelligent ape! His English is perfect. It is unbelievable."

"I am your husband," Ugo screamed. "The man standing next to you is an impostor. Someone please call the police. I am Sophia's legitimate husband. That man standing next to her is an impostor." The crowd was amused by Ugo's cries. Victorio took Sophia's arms and led her away. He later came back to the apiary while Sophia visited the elephant house. He sat next to a small microphone that allowed zoo visitors to communicate with the talking ape. For a short moment he watched Ugo as he laid down in misery on a couch. He cleared his throat to draw his attention. Ugo recognized him instantly and switched the intercom system on.

"Who are you? What are you doing with my wife?"

"She gave me refuge and took care of me," Victorio said. "She is protecting me from the evil human beings who want to capture me and return me to the zoo. I am very grateful to her for that."

"Look, I don't care who you are, where you come from, and why you are running away. I want to get out of this cage. I am not a talking gorilla, do you understand? There has been a mistake. PLEASE, GET ME OUT OF HERE."

"I know that you are not a gorilla. I can smell a real ape from miles away because I have lived with them all my life."

"Then tell them. For God's sake, go tell them that I am a human being. Can't you see the inhuman conditions that I am in? Put me in a cage like an animal for the rest of my life? This is barbarous!"

"How do you think I felt when I was in your place? How do you think the gorillas in the zoo feel as they walk around in a circle from day to day?

Look at the sad chimpanzees and the teary-eyed gibbons around you. Look at the lonely Colobus monkeys and the white-faced Sakis. How do you think they feel? They are no less sensible of pain than human beings. They have nerves and organs of sensation similar to man. They feel joy and happiness and they experience physical and emotional pains. They cannot utter their cries and groans by speech like human beings. If they have the power of speech, they will all be screaming: 'GET ME OUT OF HERE.' They don't have a mattress to sleep on like you do. I did not have a television set, a telephone or a private bathroom when I was kept in a cage. All I had was the dead trunk of a tree to swing on. Look at you now! You are living like royalty. You spend your days reading the Wall Street journal and buying stocks. Soon you will have your own bank account. All they gave me was a bunch of bananas."

"You were here before?" Ugo asked, bewildered. "You were in this zoo?"

"Yes. I was kept in a cage in inhuman conditions until I decided to escape. I am now a free ape and I have learned to live like humans. I took the TOEFL examination and passed with flying colors. I overcame the problem I had with the T-sound and the hard vowels. I am now preparing to sit for the Scholastic Aptitude Test and applying for College. Every morning I wake up and go to work to earn a living. Like most people I pay federal income taxes on my earnings." Victorio moved his head to and fro. "The part about paying Federal income taxes sucks!" he told him.

"This is amazing," Ugo murmured in consternation. "Dr. Goriatchev was right. She had envisioned gorillas living and working with human beings in harmony and writing computer codes together to solve complex mathematical problems."

"I drive myself to work too."

"What kind of car do you drive?"

"Oh, it is only an old clunker with a 5-speed transmission."

"I am amazed. Sophia can never drive a car with a shift stick. It takes her forty-five minutes to just engage the clutch and drive to the grocery store which is just a few feet from our house. You are an incredible ape. Do you like driving?"

"It's a lot more fun than being in a cage and swinging on a tree."

"You are the talking ape. You ought to be inside this glass house. I am a human being and my place is to be among my fellow human beings outside. Will you please get me out of here?"

"I like my new freedom," Victorio said. "Besides, I do not wish to end up in a laboratory and to be used for various kinds of experiments by humans. Each year thousands of animals suffer and die as a result of product testing by manufacturers. They smeared them with cosmetics to test their effects on their skins. They make them eat household cleaners to see how fatal the cleaners are when swallowed by children. They shovel new untested medication down their throats and used them as dummies in automobile crashes. It offends one sense of justice that so much harm is being done to so many animals."

Victorio rose up and walked away. "Stop that man," Ugo shouted. "He is the real talking ape!" The zoo visitors crowded around the glass cage and commented on his incredible power of speech. Ugo switched off the intercom system and slumped down on the sofa, sulking and fuming with anger and frustration. The side door suddenly opened up and Dr. Goriatchev walked back into the cage accompanied by her assistants. Behind them, two animal handlers accompanied a gorilla, keeping a close eyes on her.

"Victorio," Dr. Goriatchev happily announced, "the time that we have all been waiting for has finally arrived. You won't be lonely anymore. Victoria, the female gorilla from the Miami zoo, had just arrived to keep you company." She turned to the door and beckoned an animal caretaker to bring the female gorilla inside the glass house. The caretaker ushered Victoria into the glass house. The female gorilla's eyes flickered as she laid eyes on Ugo. She grunted and sauntered towards him. Ugo jumped up from his couch and ran to the other side of the glass house.

"Don't be afraid," Dr. Goriatchev said. "Victoria is very sweet and gentle. She will make a perfect mate for you."

"Are you mating me with a female gorilla from the Miami zoo?" Ugo cried out.

"You have been alone for too long, Victorio. A little bit of love will do you some good. The world is clamoring for a new generation of talking apes. We just can't wait to see an even more intelligent breed of hairless gorillas coming into our world. The name, Dr. Roselyn Goriatchev, will appear in every magazine, book and newspaper around the world."

"You want me to make love to a female gorilla?" Ugo groaned. "I am a human being."

"You are young and strong and I know that you can do it. I see that Victoria is already delighted to have you as a mate." Victoria trudged towards Ugo. He leaped to the side door, but the caretaker shut it close before he could escape. Ugo dashed into the bathroom and slammed the door shut behind him.

Dr. Goriatchev knocked on the bathroom door. She waited a few minutes then said: "Have fun, Victorio. We are leaving now." She pulled the blinds closed and dimmed the light. The zoologists left the room and quietly sat down on a row of chairs behind a two-way mirror. Notepads and pencils in hand, they patiently waited for Ugo to come out of the bathroom and mate with Victoria.

A few minutes later Ugo crack-opened the bathroom door and peeped inside his glass house. The female gorilla was slumped on the couch and calmly waited for him to come out. Ugo boldly stepped to the glass wall and drew the blinds open to let the light in. The female gorilla became fascinated with the blinds swinging and gliding across the glass. She scrambled up and grabbed the chain to pull the blinds close. Ugo turned a dimmer switch on the wall to increase the light intensity in the apartment. The knob on the wall attracted the female gorilla's attention. She played with the knob and dimmed the light. Ugo pulled the blinds open again. The female gorilla pulled them close again. Ugo increased the light intensity. The female gorilla decreased the light intensity. The female gorilla imitated and exasperated him. In desperation, Ugo grabbed a book titled 'How to say No without hurting your partner's feelings' from the bookcase and pretended to read. The female gorilla became inquisitive at the row of books in the bookcase. She picked up a book titled 'Sex for Dummies' from the bookcase and sat down to examine the pictures inside the book.

Frustrated at the two gorillas reading in the glass house, Dr. Goriatchev and her assistants stood up and left. Over the next few days they returned to watch Ugo and the female gorilla in the glass house. They took notes, made comments and waited for them to copulate. During the course of their daily visits they observed that the female gorilla was melancholy and ate little. Dr. Goriatchev became alarmed at Victorio's weight loss and state of mind.

"The situation is very serious," Dr. Goriatchev admitted to her assistants. "The male gorilla is rejecting the female gorilla from the Miami zoo and this is affecting the female gorilla's health. I am concerned that if we do not act now, the female gorilla will become sick and die."

Dr. Goriatchev sought the opinion of the zoo veterinarians who in turn sought the advice of a team of sex therapists from a nearby hospital. The team of veterinarians, zoologists and sex therapists rushed to the glass house to observe Ugo and Victoria. Ugo stared at the computer screen while Victoria fingered through the Wall Street journal. Ugo had taught the female gorilla to pick stocks from the Dow Jones index to keep her mind off sex.

"It appears that the male gorilla is exhibiting persistent and pervasive inhibition of sexual desire," Dr. Goriatchev told the sex therapists. "This is profoundly affecting the health of the female gorilla on loan from Miami zoo."

The team of sex therapists, followed by Dr. Goriatchev and animal caretakers entered the glass house. The caretakers forced Ugo to lie down on his bed so that the therapists could examine him. Ugo fought back and tried to leave the cage. The zoo caretakers roped him and tied him down on his bed.

"Proper sexual functioning in apes," the principal sex therapist explained, "depends on the sexual motive state, effective vasocongestive arousal and orgasm. Sexual desire is a psyshosomatic process based on brain activity, sexual aspiration and motivation. When these components are desynchronized, the result is Inhibited Sexual Desire or ISD. ISD is commonly caused by boredom in the relationship, depression, psychoactive drugs, antihypertensive medication, and hormonal deficiencies. Inhibitions of sexual desire are often related to traumatic events in childhood or adolescence, the suppression of sexual fantasies or low levels of androgens. Generally a testosterone level that is less than 300 ng/dl in the male gorilla is considered a potential cause. Has Victorio ever complained of a lack in interest in sex, even in ordinary erotic situations?"

"His vocabulary of the English Language is fairly limited," Dr. Goriatchev explained. "He may not know how to communicate these feelings to us yet. But we know that he has been lonely."

"There is also the potential that Victorio is exhibiting Erectile Dysfunction," the second sex therapist said. "This is usually a sign that the gorilla is suffering from Inhibited Sexual Excitement."

"What would cause Victorio to exhibit Erectile Dysfunction?" Dr. Goriatchev inquired.

"The inability to attain or sustain an erection satisfactory for normal coitus may be primary or secondary," the principal sex therapist explained. "Primary erectile dysfunction is almost always due to intrapsychic factors. In rare cases biogenic factors, usually associated with low testosterone levels and reflecting disorders of the hypothalamic-pituary-gonadal axis, is the major cause. Intrapsychic factors include an abnormal fear of the vagina, sexual guilt, and fear of intimacy or depression."

"Erectile dysfunction may be situational, involving place, time, a particular partner, some perceived competitive defeat and damage to self-esteem," the second therapist added.

"In Victorio's case, is there something that can be done?" Dr. Goriatchev asked.

"We must first determine whether the psychic factors are primary or secondary," the principal sex therapist answered. "The inability of Victorio to have an erection under any circumstances requires that we search for organic causes. I recommend that Victorio be put under observation for nocturnal penile tumescence. The absence of erections during sleep will suggest, but does not prove, an organic basis. The gorilla can be monitored for nighttime erections in a special sleep laboratory. The number of erections, the duration of each erections, and the number of penile vasocongestion during the course of a night's sleep can be evaluated to devise a quantitative estimate of erectile capacity."

"Is there any treatment that we can administer to Victorio in the meantime?"

"I would suggest a general medical evaluation first," the second therapist said. "The evaluation should include an examination of the genitalia to look for any signs of vascular or endocrine dysfunction. Laboratory procedures could be performed to test for testosterone, hormone and prolactin levels. If physical abnormalities are found we can then use therapy to alleviate the underlying disorder. If Victorio's androgen levels are found to be low, he should be injected with testosterone every two weeks for three to four months."

"I would also recommend counseling for Victorio to alleviate secondary factors," the principal therapist added. "A specific technique is the 3-stage sensafe focus method of Masters and Johnson, involving stepwise non-genital pleasuring, genital pleasuring, and non-demanding coitus. If the counseling sessions do not bring immediate results, referral to a sex therapist should be considered."

"Gentlemen, we need to act soon before the health of the female gorilla deteriorates any further."

Life among the human beings was beginning to lose its appeal to Victorio. The gorilla was not accustomed to competing for a livelihood, and the ways of the human beings were starting to irritate him. He was tired of the traffic bottling up during his morning drive to work, and he was weary of fighting for that little bit of road on the freeway. The television programs were boring him to death, and the long weekends that he spent watching football were tearing him down. When he lived in the zoo he did not have to do a thing. Now Sophia exacted him to take the trash out before retiring for the night and hollered at him to drop the toilet seat down after urinating. She instructed him to cook dinner, wash the dishes, do his laundry and clean the house. She ordered him to run errands, take the car to the repair shop, mow the lawn, water the flowerbed and do dozens of other interminable chores. He was startled at all the strange things that the human beings had to do in order to stay alive. He was even more astounded by all the strange things that they engaged in to pass the time. He watched children aimlessly skate around the ice-skating rinks instead of doing their homework. He observed football players viciously pummeling at each other to catch a football. He noted that baseball players ferociously hurled balls and bats at each other. He disliked eating his bananas split up and covered with ice cream. He hated to eat his coconut grated and baked. He disliked eating his peanuts roasted and salted. He felt his stomach churned whenever Sophia stir-fried and seasoned his vegetables. Most of all he hated to pay Federal and State income taxes on his earnings. He began to feel nothing but envy for Ugo who did not have to work for anything. While he enjoyed studying the English Language, there were however many new words that he hated to add to his vocabulary. Words such as pedophilia, nepotism, arrogance, greed, hypocrisy, infidelity, racism, corruption, vandalism, discrimination, envy, violence, rape, murder, assault and battery; these words brought tears to his eyes and made him want to throw up. Racial profiling sickened him. The division of black and white, rich and poor, the educated and the illiterates; they often made him want to throw up. One night the gorilla got out of bed and called for a taxicab. When the cab driver arrived, he directed him to take him to the zoo. When they arrived at the zoo, he asked the driver to wait for him, jumped over the gate and walked to the apery. He made his way to Ugo's glass house, opened the door and stepped inside. Ugo woke up and stared at the night visitor. His future bride Victoria was slumped on the couch and asleep.

"Who are you and what do you want?" Ugo asked the stranger.

"I am Victorio."

Ugo sprang up on his feet and charged at the gorilla's neck. "I am going to kill you," he screamed.

Victorio restrained him. "Be calm. I am here to help you escape."

"You mean it?" Ugo asked, relaxing his hold on Victorio's neck. "You came all the way here to help me escape?"

"I am giving you the chance to return to your lice-infected and selfish world. Your world is brimming with people who have no strong sense of respect for the rights of others. I don't ever want to live in that kind of world again."

Ugo sat down on the bed. "If I understand, you want to exchange places with me?"

Victorio looked around the glass house. "It looks very comfortable here. I will have all the comfort of your world less all the painful struggles I have to put up with in order to stay alive. It's a rat race out there."

"I am glad that you've finally found out that my world is not as pretty as you had previously thought. We humans are accustomed to living with the problems that we create ourselves. It is a trait only found in human beings. You may think that we are humans, but we are more like a pack of rats."

"There is a taxicab waiting for you outside. The driver will take you back to your house. Sophia will not notice that we've swapped places." Victorio gave Ugo the keys to his house and removed his clothes.

Ugo shook his head and refused to take the keys back. "I don't want to go back to Sophia," he said.

"She loves you," Victorio emphasized.

"Who wants to love a woman who sleeps around with a gorilla?"

"Don't be silly," Victorio said. 'Gorillas don't copulate with humans. I never touched her."

"Try telling that to the female gorilla from the Miami zoo. She's been hot ever since they brought her in my cage." Ugo put on Victorio's clothes.

"What book are you reading?" Victorio asked, pointing at the book on the bed.

"A Tale of Two Cities," Ugo replied

"My favorite book indeed," Victorio added.

Ugo shook Victorio's hand and thanked him for his kindness. "I will always remember this kind gesture coming from an ape for the rest of my life," he said. "Watch out for Dr. Goriatchev," he warned. "She has asked for a medical evaluation of your genitalia and she plans to put you under observation for nocturnal penile tumescence." Ugo hugged the gorilla and hurried to the side door. "Death, thou art the guest long looked for by Giovanni," Ugo murmured as he made his way to the cab.

The moment Ugo drove off in the taxicab, Dr. Goriatchev appeared out of the dark and quietly walked to Victorio's cage. She opened a small door in the wall and deposited a bundle of Playboy and Penthouse magazines inside Victorio's apartment. Then she slipped behind the two-way mirror and sat down on a chair, notepad and pencil in hand, to observe the gorilla.

Victorio walked up to Victoria and patted her on her head. "I am home, babe. That gorilla was a fake and he is no good for you. I got rid of him." He curled up his mustache and gazed lovingly at the female gorilla. He removed a bottle of cologne from a fanny pack and sprayed the scent around his face and neck. Then he stretched out on the bed and became pensive. "I wonder what Ugo means by nocturnal penile tumescence," he pondered. He then caught sight of the magazines on the floor, shrugged the thoughts off his mind and got up to pick up a magazine.

"It is a far, far better thing that I do, than I have ever done; it is a far, far better rest that I go to, than I have ever known," he murmured.

6 THE BRINGER OF MADNESS

FBS Incorporated, a small data processing firm, fired its Comptroller and handed pink slips to another eleven employees. The company's President and Chief Executive Officer named Noah Burkel Interim Comptroller and ordered a pay freeze for all remaining employees. Three months after the downsizing and restructuring, the President gathered the employees in the lunchroom and announced that the restructured company would make a profit in the fourth quarter. When the sales of the company's software products increased, it hired two new employees to meet the new demand for its software products. The CEO then officially appointed Noah Burkel as the new Comptroller. The promotion elated Noah who had vied for the position for two years.

Noah Burkel left his office an hour earlier than usual to avoid the rush hour traffic. The traffic jam had already started to build up when he drove onto I-35. The buildup worsened as I-35 merged into I-635. The bumper-to-bumper traffic snaked and hardly moved for about half a mile. When Noah finally cleared the traffic bottleneck, he slammed on the gas pedal and drove home as fast as he could. His wife Rebekah was in the kitchen baking a cake when he arrived home. She was surprised to see her husband arriving home earlier than usual.

"You are home early today," she exclaimed. "What happened?"

"I have been promoted to Comptroller," he broke the news to her. He wrapped his arms around her and pecked her lips.

Rebekah congratulated her husband. "I am so happy for you," she jubilantly said. "You deserve to be Comptroller."

"The boss has asked me to dine with him tonight," he added.

"That's wonderful. I think that you should go."

"He wants me to bring you along."

"I cannot," Rebekah said regretfully. "I promised Dinah that I will be at her birthday party tonight. She will be upset if I don't show up. I am very sorry."

"Oh, I forgot that today is Dinah's birthday," Noah said. "The boss isn't expecting us until seven o'clock. We can leave the party at six o'clock."

"Sarah will never forgive me if I leave the party so soon," Rebekah said apologetically. "I can't do that to her."

"Then I will have to go by myself. I hope that you don't mind."

"Of course not," Rebekah assured him. "Besides, you and your boss will probably be talking about balance sheets and annual reports. You know that numbers bore me to death. I will be totally out of place there."

"I know, I know. I am sure the boss will understand. What time is the birthday party?"

"Sarah is expecting us now but I am just starting to bake the cake."

"I will shower while you carry on with your baking. Where are the kids?"

"Sarah came by earlier and took them with her," Rebekah answered.

Noah Burkel and Jonah Iffrig have known each other for many years. They both grew up in Carrollton and attended the same high school. After graduating from high school, they both went to North Texas State University to continue their education. The two friends studied Accounting and graduated during the same year. Noah met and married Rebekah while he was still a sophomore. A year after they were married Jonah met and married Sarah. The two couples stuck together after they left NTSU to begin their professional careers. They moved to a small town located twenty miles north of Dallas. They frequently organized picnics and outings together, took vacations together, and supported one another during times of hardship. Noah and Jonah were always seen working on their cars or in each other's back yards. They played baseball or went fishing together and frequently took weekend trips together without their wives and children. Noah and Rebekah conceived and raised two sons: Jeremiah who was 17 years old and Joshuah who was barely 14 years old. Jonah and Sarah, on the other hand, had only one child; a girl they had lovingly named Dinah. Dinah Iffrig turned nineteen years old on this day.

Noah had known Dinah since she was born. He remembered how he used to tease Jonah when Sarah became pregnant while they were still in their junior years at NTSU. He frequently looked after Dinah while Jonah and Sarah attended classes. He and Rebekah spent long summers watching over Dinah while Sarah and Jonah attended summer school and worked towards their Masters degrees. Noah had fond memories of the time he spent with Dinah, remembering every hour and every day that he spent with her when she was a child. When Rebekah gave birth to Joshuah, Noah diverted his attention from looking after Dinah to looking after Joshuah who needed special care.

Joshuah Burkel had acquired a congenital defect known as Chromosomal Abnormality. He had a small head, a broad and flat face, short nose and small ears, slanting eyes and a large tongue. His hands were large and his fingers curved inward. His head dropped down on one side on account of the floppy muscles in his neck. The birth defect had delayed Joshuah's mental and physical development. The boy could not talk, walk or move, and he needed constant care and attention. Being devout Christians, Noah and Rebekah Burkel strongly believed that the lord Jesus Christ would one day heal Joshuah.

The birthday party for Dinah was in full swing when Noah and Rebekah showed up at the Iffrig's house. Joshuah was strapped down to a chair in the kitchen. A small crowd sat in the living room and chatted away. Sarah and Jonah sat down on an L-shape orange couch in the family room that adjoined the kitchen, joining in the conversion now and then. At the other end of the family room Dinah joked and laughed with her college friends. The house was filled with laughter and cheers. Noah walked up to Dinah, hugged and wished her a happy birthday. Rebekah gave her a present.

"Rebekah chose the present and I had it engraved," Noah said. "It's from both of us."

Dinah opened the gift. She removed a pair of sunglasses from a box and tried them. "They are beautiful," she gasped. On one corner of the dark lenses was engraved the initial DWI. Two small diamonds shone on the frames. "The lenses are very dark. I can hardly see anything in the room."

"You are supposed to wear them outside," Rebekah said. "That's why they call them sunglasses."

"The young men in the neighborhood won't fail to notice you when you wear these sunglasses," Noah joked.

"Oh, they've noticed her already," Sarah quickly said. "Nowadays all the phone calls we receive are from her boyfriends."

Dinah took off the sunglasses. Jonah Iffrig took it off her hands to examine it. "You already got yourself a DWI and you are not even old enough to drink yet," Jonah said, his finger going over the letter DWI on the lens.

"I am of legal drinking age as of six hours ago," Dinah reminded her father. "Isn't that right, Mother?"

Sarah nodded at her. "You know," she said. "When I was a teenager, one hardly ever hears these terrifying letters, DWI. The talk in the office these days is always about who has received a ticket for driving while intoxicated? Had I known that drinking and driving would popularize the letters DWI, I would never have christened my daughter Dinah Wiersema Iffrig. I never thought about it. It must be very embarrassing for anyone these days to carry the initials DWI as an identification."

"There are definitely more cars on the road today," Dinah remarked.

"There are also more establishments for people to meet and drink," Rebekah added.

"Not to mention that there are far more opportunities for people to gather around and get drunk," Noah added laughing.

"I have an announcement to make," Rebekah quickly added. "Noah has been promoted to Comptroller. His boss has invited us out for dinner."

Sarah kissed and congratulated Noah. Jonah shook his hand and patted his back. "Well done, Noah. I am glad you got the job. Way to go, pal."

"Rebekah, I think that you should go and celebrate with your husband."

"I already told him that I dislike Accounting or anything that has to do with numbers. I think that I will stay here tonight. I never get bored when I am around you and Jonah."

"Oh, thank you. We are so glad that you could come tonight. However we don't want you to miss the opportunity to impress your husband's boss."

The conversation drifted to drinking and driving. A friend of Sarah pointed out that people driving under the influence of alcohol caused fifty percent of all road fatalities. "Do you know that more than 25,000 people had died in automobile accidents since they started keeping track of the numbers?" she said. The room became silent and everyone turned and stared at her. "Half of the fatalities are the result of drinking and driving," she added.

"I did not think that the number was so high," someone remarked, astonished at the statistics. "That's more than the number of casualties we suffered during the Vietnam War. If I recall, 46,000 US soldiers fought and died in that conflict. There must be ways to eliminate this senseless slaughter on our highways. This is a tremendous waste of human lives."

"Under the Implied Consent law," a guest said, "a driver could have his license revoked if he refuses to take a chemical test when suspected of driving under the influence. Not many people are aware of this law. I personally favor educating younger drivers on the consequences of driving and drinking before they attain the legal drinking age."

"What is this law about?" Dinah asked.

"It is called the 'Implied Consent law.' According to this law driving is a privilege, not a right. This privilege is granted to a driver when the driver has demonstrated that he is able to operate a vehicle under normal circumstances and that he can act responsibly while operating the vehicle. Under this law a driver, by virtue of being licensed to drive, consents to a chemical test if arrested for a traffic offense involving suspicion of drinking. If he refuses to take the test, his license can be revoked because he did not abide by this condition of the driving privilege. All States now have such legislation."

"I think that we need tougher laws against drunk drivers. We cannot continue to allow drunk drivers to endanger our lives and the lives of our children. Offenders should be given a jail sentence instead of just a ticket."

"Tennessee imposes a 48 hr jail sentence to first-time offenders," a guest remarked. "I think that what we need is a combination of fine, jail sentence and license suspension for all first-time offenders. Some restaurants and bars are installing barometers for their patrons to check the alcohol content in their blood. Some lawmakers are even attempting to increase the legal drinking age to twenty-one nationwide."

"Wait a minute," Dinah exclaimed. "What's all this talk about increasing the legal drinking age? If a 19-year old is allowed to marry, register for the selective services and vote, then he should be allowed to make his own decision as regard to drinking. That person cannot be told that he is too young to drink at age nineteen."

"Oh, sure," Noah said, mocking her and pointing his thumb at her. "She's just turned nineteen year old and she doesn't want to wait two more years before she can have her first drink."

Dinah pinched him and protested. "Uncle, I am old enough to drink now."

"I am in favor of raising the legal drinking age," a guest suggested. "According to some researchers, the American male is not an adult until he reaches the age of twenty-nine. His behavior remains infantile until he reaches that age. If these findings are true, then the 19-year old youth who decides that he is old enough to drink may not be making the right decision."

"I can see where this could help curtailing teenage drinking in a public establishment," Jonah added, "but I have a problem accepting it when it comes to sharing a drink at home with my buddies. Who are they to tell me what I can drink or not drink when I am at home watching football?"

"Go on, Dad, tell them."

"Because you can still get into a car and kill someone even though you are drinking at home," a guest retorted. "The point is to remove drunk drivers from our streets, make them safer for driving, and reduce accidents caused by the drunk drivers. I got rammed once in broad daylight by a pickup truck driven by a drunk driver. I could have been killed."

Dinah felt that everybody wanted to spoil her birthday party and discouraged her from drinking on her birthday. "I don't care what you all think," she snapped. "I am going out with my friends tonight to celebrate my birthday. Until some legislators come up with an acceptable solution to the problem of drunken driving, I am as of today of legal drinking age. My initials may be DWI, but don't worry, they shall never stand for drunken driving. The initials stand for Dinah Weirsema Iffrig."

"Dinah is a responsible person and I have faith in her," Sarah said. "I never dreamt that one day her initials would stand for something as terrible as drinking while intoxicated. I have many times thought about changing her first or middle name. I can imagine the stigma that her initials will cause her later.. When she signs up for computer classes later, I can imagine that the computer instructor will assign her a user id like DWI2513. Doesn't that sound awkward?"

Dinah shrugged her shoulder off. "I won't take any computer classes," she snapped.

"This is the computer age," Noah said. "It doesn't matter what you major in, you will still have to take some computer classes. You can't compete for jobs nowadays unless you are computer literate. I think that every school curriculum now requires a student to take a computer class no matter what the student majors in. When they step out of the classroom and into the business world, the new graduates will be required to work with computers some way or another."

The discussion turned to computers and the rapid advance in computer technology. While they debated the computer revolution that was sweeping the business world, Dinah withdrew to her room with her friends. Almost everyone in the room worked with a computer at the office. Paul spoke about going back to school at night to specialize in data storage and retrieval.

"This is a branch of data processing that the computer industry is not seriously looking into," he said. "I see a huge demand for data specialists a few years from now. Their job functions will be similar to the librarian in the library. They will store massive amount of data on all kinds of storage medium on behalf of the business community. People can then request the data over the telephone lines and it will be the data specialists who will be in charge of making the information available to the users quickly and inexpensively. Students, doctors, teachers, researchers and businessmen, in fact anyone who has a need for the information, can download the data to their own workstations. Just imagine this vast network of computers connected to each other by telephone lines, sharing and communicating information to whoever wants the data, anywhere and anytime. The potential for companies to exploit the possibilities in such a network is enormous."

Noah left the guests to attend to his son. He cleaned off the cake icing from his face and picked up cake crumbs from the carpet.

"It's coming," Joshuah indistinctly stammered. Noah dropped down on his knees. He lifted his son out of the chair and carried him to the living room. He called out for Rebekah. Frightened by the tone of Noah's voice, she rushed to his side. Noah laid Joshuah down on the couch.

"Hallelujah, Hallelujah," Noah intoned. "Joshuah is talking. He speaks in tongue. It's the work of our Lord, Jesus Christ."

"Praise the Lord," Rebekah whispered, clasping her hands in prayer.

"Joshuah," Noah gently asked, "who is coming? Is the Lord coming into you? Tell us, Joshuah. Speak to us."

"Praise the Lord," Rebekah repeated. Her hands shook and her body shivered. She looked imploringly into Joshuah's eyes and waited for sounds to come out of his mouth.

"Amen," Noah exclaimed. "Amen! Praise the Lord! Joshuah has finally uttered his first words. It's a miracle. Joshuah, can you tell us who is coming?"

"The pelicans, the herons and the seagulls will die," Joshuah mumbled. The words flowed out of his mouth one at a time. His eyes stared blankly at the ceiling. Rebekah wiped the drools from his mouth.

"Hallelujah," Noah shouted. Tears flowed down his cheeks. He looked up at the ceiling and gave thanks to the Lord. "The Lord has put words in Joshuah's mouth. Praise the Lord. The Lord is mighty."

"Praise the Lord," Sarah murmured. The guests stood still around them, struck in awe at the miracle unfolding in front of them. Noah's body shook. Rebekah clutched his husband's shoulders to restrain him.

"I don't want the birds to die," Joshuah gurgled. His face looked sad as if his life was flowing out of him.

"Who is going to kill the birds?" Noah asked. He held his son close to him. Rebekah caressed the hair on Joshuah's head.

"The black sea," Joshuah burbled. The fingers of his hands curled and pressed his stomach.

"Praise the Lord," Noah repeated. "He put words into Joshuah's mouth."

"The white shrimps and the blue crabs will die," Joshuah moaned. He turned his head towards his father and stared at him with imploring eyes. "Please save them from the black sea," he implored.

Noah could no longer control his emotion. He broke down and sobbed. Rebekah wiped the tears from her face and faintly whispered: "Hallelujah. Praise the Lord!" They held hands with their friends and guests and formed a circle around Joshuah. They prayed and thanked the Lord for the miracle they had just witnessed. A child had just uttered his first words, fourteen years after he was born.

The oil slick from the tanker Alvenus, grounded off the coast of Louisiana, had begun to hit the Texas coastline. Men and equipments were deployed along miles of beaches to battle the gooey oil blobs. An army of workers and volunteers placed oil containment barriers and deflection booms along the coastline to keep the oil slicks from reaching Galveston Bay. Environmentalists quickly rushed to the affected areas to assess the potential ecological and environmental damages. Black oil had already washed up on the beaches. From High Island to the Bolivar Peninsula, from East End to West Beach, the molasses-like oil blobs threatened to break through the deflection booms.

Noah lifted Joshuah into his arms. "The Lord has healing powers," he said. "He will heal Joshuah as he has promised. Praise the Lord!"

"Amen," Rebekah intoned. Drying the tears from her face, she gently reminded Noah of his dinner engagement with his boss. Noah hugged and kissed Joshuah. His son's first spoken words had overwhelmed him. He left the room and went to the bathroom to dry off his tears. When he came back, he thanked Jonah and Sarah for inviting them over to Dinah's birthday party. Jonah walked with him to the door to see him off.

The CEO showed some disappointment that Rebekah could not joined them for dinner. A hostess greeted them and ushered them to a table. They sat down and a waitress came to their table to take their orders. While waiting for their dinner, they ordered cocktails and began to discuss Noah's new job responsibilities. The CEO first told Noah that he would make a formal announcement the following day. He then began to discuss the company's finances and new direction with Noah. Half an hour later, the waitress came back with their orders. They interrupted the discussion to eat their foods. After dinner, they went through a stack of ledgers and wrote down a lot of notes. Two hours later, the two men felt satisfied of the outcome of their dinner meeting and headed for the bar to toast their new working relationship.

"Your job will not be easy," his boss warned him. "There are more than a hundred suppliers who want to be paid. We cannot pay them all at the same time and still make a profit. Go over the list of suppliers and select the suppliers who are vital to our business. Pay them the minimum amounts possible to keep them happy and let the other merchants cry their hearts out over their dues. Switch to other suppliers if you can get a better price or payment terms. You need to watch expenses closely. I want to slash the administrative overhead by one-third the current amount. Go over the accounts receivables and start getting tough on past due accounts."

After sharing a few drinks together, the CEO then bid Noah goodnight and left. Noah remained at the bar to continue savoring his promotion. He was still in shock at hearing his son's first words earlier. He did not have the slightest idea what his son was talking about, but he believed that the lord had finally healed Joshuah. He ordered more cocktails, trying one kind after another. He toasted both his success and the healing powers of the Lord with anyone sitting next to him. When the restaurant finally closed, Noah Burkel had, in one short evening, consumed more alcohol than the entire amount he drank during the year. He could hardly stand up. He bumped into tables, knocked chairs down and wandered in the kitchen while looking for the exit. The kitchen staff escorted him back into the lounge where he staggered and fell down. A restaurant employee helped him up and directed him to the door exit. A waitress offered to call a cab for him, but he insisted that he was sober and capable of driving himself home.

An eerie night greeted Noah when he stumbled out of the restaurant. A grasshopper landed on his shoulder and a pink squirrel scrambled in front of him. He brushed off the grasshopper from his shoulder and kicked at the pink squirrel. The pink squirrel scampered off and disappeared in the dark of the night. A wild turkey suddenly trotted in front of him. When the turkey gobbled at him, he raised his hands up and shooed the fowl away. Shortly

148

afterwards, the wild turkey reappeared and followed him around. The grasshopper flew back on his shoulder and the pink squirrel returned. At the sight of the pink squirrel, he hurried his steps and looked for his car. Off he went, making a few steps in one direction and losing his balance, zigzagging his way to nowhere and seeing a pink squirrel everywhere. Then he heard a roar of laughter behind him and quickly turned to the direction of the guffawing. A zombie was walking behind him. It held a rusty nail up at him and hit it with a velvet hammer. A salty dog walked alongside the zombie. It bared its teeth at Noah. Noah shuddered at the sight of the zombie and the salty dog. He hastily walked away from the apparition. A cherry hooker and a naked lady suddenly appeared from behind a car to taunt him. At the sight of the women, he panicked and ran off. Sweats dripped down from his brow. He loosened up his necktie and dropped his jacket on the ground. He stopped to wipe the sweat from his face with the palm of his hand. Just then a white elephant with an old crow perched on its back came out of the shadows and lumbered towards him. At the sight of the white elephant, he ran off in the opposite direction. The white elephant followed him. As it came closer to him, a Bengal Lancer riding a white horse emerged with a Colorado bulldog following in its heels. At the sight of the Bengal Lancer, the grasshopper, the pink squirrel and the wild turkey scattered and disappeared into the night. The zombie skittered. The white elephant came to a sudden stop and turned back. Noah shook with fear and dashed left and right. He desperately sought his car so he could flee away from all the strange creatures pursuing him in the parking lot. He uttered a sigh of relief when he finally located his car. When he walked up to it, a black Russian came out of the shadows and planted himself between him and his car. A blue flame flickered and glowed on the black Russian's hand. A purple orchid sat in the buttonhole of his shirt. Old Mr. Boston and Lord Calvert of the Imperial House of Lords stood by the black Russian. Old Mr. Boston clutched an empty bottle in his hand while Lord Calvert dangled a wristwatch in front of him.

"Welcome to the Drunk Drivers Club. Your coffin is ready for you to drive," the black Russian informed Noah.

Noah laughed. "What a joke," he blurted out at the black Russian. "You scared the hell out of me. I thought that a zombie and a white elephant were following me. I have been seeing strange animals all around the parking lot." He shook his head and fumbled in his pocket for his car keys.

"You will soon be the most cursed driver in this town," Old Mr. Boston said. "As a member of the Drunk Drivers Club, you will have the privilege to tear into the hearts of many mothers. They will curse you for killing their beloved ones. They will hunt and haunt you for the rest of your miserable life."

The keys slipped out of Noah's fingers and fell to the ground. "Damn it," he swore.

"Look around you and you will understand why you will be cursed by mothers all around America," Lord Calvert said.

Noah dropped down on his knees and hands to search for the keys. Then he saw that the parking lot was lined with coffins. A group of women wandered around the coffins looking for their sons and daughters killed by drunk drivers. He shuddered at the sight of the coffins and frantically looked for his keys so he could drive away from the coffins. The black Russian picked up the keys and handed them to him.

"Here are the keys to your coffin," the black Russian said. "The thrill of speed-driving is all yours tonight."

"You have a wicked sense of humor," Noah said. He took the keys back from the black Russian.

"The black Russian is right," Old Mr. Boston said. "You are about to drive off in your coffin."

"Drive off in my coffin?" Noah laughed. "I am not dead yet." He swayed back and forth and leaned over his car to keep himself from tipping over. "I see a car with white leather seats, but you guys see a coffin with white velvet lining. You are both drunk."

The black Russian ran his hands on the white leather seat. "This coffin is not yours but you'll soon find out who it is for."

"You are a funny man," Noah said. "What kind of joke is this, telling me that I drive a coffin?"

"It's not a joke, it's a coffin," Lord Calvert said. "Drive it like a car."

"You mean to tell me that it's a car, but I should drive it like a coffin. That's very funny." Noah laughed at Lord Calvert. He raised his hands and pointed at him. "I think that you had too much to drink tonight, Sir. You can't tell a car from a coffin." He looked at the women wandering around the lines of coffins in the parking lot. "By the way, who are all these ghostly-looking women and what are they looking for? They look like a pack of hungry wolves seeking to sink their teeth into some flesh."

"They are angry mothers looking to sink their teeth in the flesh of some drunken drivers," the black Russian said. "Too many of their loved ones have been killed by drunken drivers." Noah looked at the women meandering around the coffins and felt a chill running down his spine. He hurriedly stepped into his car.

"Hey, look," he said, pointing to the steering wheel. "This steering wheel just proves all of you wrong. Coffins don't have steering wheels." He shook a finger at the black Russian. "Ha, I knew it. You had too much to drink tonight. You had better go home now before something terrible happens to you. If I were you, I would call a cab instead of driving. Good night."

"It's a coffin, but you drive it like a car," the black Russian repeated. Old Mr. Boston and Lord Calvert of the Imperial House of Lord nodded in approval.

Noah turned to Lord Calvert. "Who are you and what are you doing here so late at night?"

"I am a Recruitment Officer for D.D.C," Old Mr. Boston replied. "We are looking for new members of our Drunk Driving Club."

"I am the Fulfillment Officer," the black Russian said. "We have a quota to meet."

"I am the Chairman of the Welcoming Committee." Lord Calvert introduced himself. "I officially welcome you to the Drunk Driving Club. We are a nationwide organization with branches in every city in the United States."

Noah moved his head to and fro. He cranked the engine to life and pressed down on the gas pedal. The car torpedoed off the parking lot and into the street.

"Coffins don't move on wheels," he shouted back to the black Russian.

The car shot over the curb, rolled onto the sidewalk and knocked over a newspaper stand. Noah steered the car back on the street and through two red lights. Minutes later he slammed on the brakes to avoid hitting the car in front of him.

"Damn it," he cursed. "It looks like everybody is driving around in a coffin tonight." He honked at the driver in front of him and stuck his head out of the window. "Hey you, what's the idea of driving a coffin around, uuh...? Are you drunk?"

Noah weaved around the car and swerved abruptly into the ramp to I-35. When he finally made it to I-35, he uttered a sigh of relief and stomped on the gas pedal. Moments later, he felt as if he was piloting a plane instead of driving a car. The vehicle elicited little concentration from him. It magically steered itself along the highway and glided like a rocket spaceship. The speedometer passed the 70 mph mark. Noah glanced in the rear view mirror and saw the Bengal Lancer riding behind him. He stepped on the gas pedal and drove faster and faster until the galloping horse disappeared from his rear view mirror. After driving for about ten minutes, he exited to highway 121 and turned into the entrance to a motor inn. He suddenly hit the brake when he realized that he had made the right turn too soon. When he reversed back into the service road, he slammed into a fire hydrant. A gush of water shot up from the fire hydrant, but he continued to back up. Then he saw the blinding lights of an oncoming car in his rearview mirror. The driver of the oncoming car honked, braked and swerved off the road to avoid hitting him. Noah hastily drove off. About a hundred yards from the motor inn, he turned right into highway 121 and headed for The Colony, an isolated suburban town north of Dallas.

Highway 121 was a narrow, undivided two-lane highway. Noah had the deserted road all to himself. Halfway between I-35 and The Colony, he crossed the lane marker and weaved into the opposite lane. The Bengal

Lancer suddenly appeared next to him on the road. The sudden reappearance of the Bengal Lancer shook him up and he quickly brought the car back to the right side of the road. Two minutes later it drifted out of his lane and back to the wrong side of the road again. Once more the white horse reappeared and forced him to stay on the right lane. After ten minutes of erratic driving, he reached The Colony and zigzagged his way to the farther end of the subdivision. A disabled car suddenly appeared in his line of vision. He slammed on his brakes and veered his car around the obstacle. He snapped a light pole that broke away from the sidewalk and flew into a small tree. Then he hit another object. The object flew into the air and is swallowed by darkness. He brought his car to a stop and came out to look at the damage on his bumper. He looked around him but did not see the object that he collided with. He shrugged off the accident, walked back to the car and drove home.

Noah staggered out of the car and wavered to the front door. He could barely stand up. He leaned against the lamp post in front of the house, unzipped his pants and relieved himself on the lawn. Without taking any trouble to fasten his belt, he opened the door to his house and kicked his shoes off. The shoes flew across the living room and landed behind the sofa. On the way to the bedroom, he stumbled on Joshuah lying across the floor.

"Joshuah," he murmured, "what are you doing up so late?"

"The pelicans cannot fly off," Joshuah stuttered. "They are encircled by the black sea."

Noah held his son's face in his hands and murmured: "Praise the Lord who hath put words in Joshuah's mouth." He lifted Joshuah in his arms. "You should be in bed," he whispered. "I'll carry you back to your room."

"Dad, is someone going to save the birds from the black sea?" Joshuah sputtered.

"Nobody will hurt the birds," Noah whispered. He kissed Joshuah and carried him back into his bedroom. Then he sneaked into his own bedroom. The clock in the living room struck two o'clock.

Noah Burkel left for work early the next day. He was too preoccupied by his new job responsibilities to think about the accident the previous night. At nine o'clock the CEO gathered the employees in the lunchroom and informed them of the company's progress towards profitability. He announced that the company had entered into an alliance with a new business partner and the marketing rep had won two new sale contracts. Finally he announced to the small group of employees Noah Burkel's promotion to Comptroller.

"Noah has been a loyal and dedicated employee," he praised. "Over the past three years he has applied himself diligently and introduced effective cost-cutting measures across all departments. He had been the driving force behind the rejuvenation of a faltering organization. Please join me in wishing him good luck in his new responsibilities."

The employees clapped their hands and congratulated Noah.

"Noah will need all the help you can give him," the CEO continued. "Reorganization always brings disruption. Noah will be adding to the disruption as he goes around looking for things to improve upon. Please give him all the help that he needs."

"Thank you all for your encouragement," Noah spoke to the employees. "I am thrilled to be offered this new opportunity, and I am very thankful to our CEO for the trust and confidence that he has placed on me. I will do the best I can."

After the meeting the employees returned to work. Noah followed the CEO to his office to discuss his new job responsibilities. An hour later, Noah emerged from the CEO's office carrying a stack of folders. On his way to his new office, he stopped by the secretary's desk to check for phone messages. The secretary handed him a small stack of phone messages. One of the phone messages was a note to call Rebekah. He went in his office and immediately called his wife.

"Dinah had an accident last night," Rebekah Burkel told her husband in a broken voice. "Jonah and Sarah got worried when she did not return home. They waited until two o'clock before calling the police."

The phone call was the nightmare that every parent in America dreaded to receive. The line became silent for a moment. "Hello?" Noah called out. Then Noah heard his wife choking up on the other end.

"The police found her car just a few blocks away from her house," Rebekah continued, sniffing back her tears. "They found her lying unconscious twenty feet away from her car." Noah stiffened up. "Thanks God she is alive. Her car broke down just a few blocks away from her house. She left the car and walked home."

"What time was it when the police found her?" Noah asked. He could feel his heart pounding in his chest.

"About two o'clock. A car hit her from behind while she was walking home. The bastard did not even stop to help her."

"Is she badly hurt?" Noah asked, his voice trembling.

"I don't know," Rebekah replied. "She has a deep gash over her head. The doctor speculated that her head hit the concrete sidewalk. He is trying to determine how severe the blow to her head is. I am off to the emergency room as soon as Joshuah's nurse comes in. I'll call you back when I find out more about her condition."

The phone went dead. Noah slowly laid down the phone and stared blankly in front of him. He closed the door to his office and buried his head in his hands. He tried to remember what happened the night before. He remembered hitting an object, but he did not know what he hit. For a long time he pondered on whether he hit Dinah Wiersema Iffrig while she walked home alone last night. He finally rose up from his desk and went to tell the

CEO about Dinah's accident. He requested permission from the CEO to visit her in the emergency room. The CEO sympathized with him and encouraged him to take the rest of the day off.

Noah called the muffler shop to check if his car was ready. He had driven it into the muffler shop the previous day to have the muffler tail pipe replaced. The service Manager at the muffler shop informed him that the work on his car was completed. Thereafter he drove to the car rental office to return the red Ford Escort that he had rented while his was being worked on. While the leasing agent checked the gas tank level and inspected the car for dents or damages, he tried to recall the accident. He remembered seeing the disabled car on the road. He recalled coming out of his car to inspect the bumper after the accident. The car leasing agent's voice interrupted his line of thought.

"Sir, would you come with me please?" the leasing agent asked.

Noah followed the leasing agent outside. The agent pointed to a large scratch mark on the front bumper. "There are scratch marks on the bumper," he said. "It appears that the car was involved in an accident." He looked at Noah and waited for him to explain the scratch marks.

"I hit a light pole last night," he admitted. Noah ran his fingers on the scratch marks. "I don't think the damage is serious."

"I will have to have the car inspected by our mechanic. The bumper may have to be straightened up and the paint touched up." Noah went back into the waiting room to wait for the technician's report. A few minutes later, the agent informed him that the bumper assembly would have to be removed and readjusted. The agent noted on the rental agreement that Noah had purchased rental insurance. He informed him that the repair expenses would be borne by the insurance company and asked Noah to sign a release. After Noah signed the release document, the agent dropped him off to the muffler shop to pick up his own car.

Dinah's car was still parked in the outer lane on the road when Noah arrived at the site of the accident. The police have surrounded the car with orange cones and yellow tapes. The damaged light post was still lying across the sidewalk. Rebekah had told him that the police found Dinah by a tree alongside the road. He walked to a nearby tree and stared at the tall grass around it. The black Russian emerged from behind the tree.

"That empty coffin in the parking lot was to have been hers," the black Russian said. Noah looked up and saw the black Russian. Old Mr. Boston and Lord Calvert of the Imperial House of Lord stood next to him. The blue flame on the black Russian's hand was snuffed out; the purple orchid had withered into a black lump. The black Russian removed the withered orchid from the buttonhole and closed his fingers on it. He opened up his fingers to let the dust fall out onto the grass where Dinah was found lying unconscious. "You hit her and she landed here," the black Russian reminded Noah.

"Your initiation to the D.D.C membership is now complete," Old Mr. Boston said. He threw an empty bottle of whisky over the crumpled-up purple orchid. "You will now be hounded by angry mothers from every part of the country. They will curse your mother and hate you to death."

"Your friends and family will avoid you," Lord Calvert added. He threw a wristwatch over the bottle. Noah bent over and picked up Dinah's wristwatch. The glass on the watch was shattered.

"Go curse your mother," the black Russian said. The black Russian's words stung Noah Burkel. He sprinted to his car and sped away.

Noah walked into the hospital with his body bent under guilt and remorse. He took the elevator to the 4th floor and looked for Dinah's room. When he found her room, he hesitated to go in for fear that he might see Dinah lying dead on a bed. The door suddenly opened and Rebekah came out.

"Noah, you are finally here," she said in a broken voice. She put her arms around his waist and rubbed her eyes dry on his shirt.

"How is she?" Noah whispered. Rebekah shook her head and squeezed him hard. Her eyes searched for answers for Dinah's accident on his face. "Don't know," she stammered. Noah quietly followed her into the room. Sarah and Jonah sat around Dinah and held her hands.

"Uncle Noah is here to see you," Sarah said.

"Uncle Noah," Dinah uttered, stretching her arms in front of her. Her eyes were covered with a bandage. Noah sat on the edge of the bed and held her in his arms. "I am right next to you, Dinah" he consoled her.

"What happened to me, Uncle Noah? Why is this happening to me?" Dinah buried her head on Noah's chest and wept.

Sarah tapped Noah gently on his shoulder and whispered into his ears. "She can't see you, Noah. She is blind."

"Blind?" Noah stammered. "Why?" He took Dinah's face into his hands and stared at the bandage over her eyes. Her warm tears streamed down her checks through the wet bandage and into his hands.

"I don't know," Sarah said, shaking her head. She sniffled and dried her eyes. Jonah placed his hands on her shoulders and comforted her. In a rage, Noah pulled off the bandage from Dinah's eyes. Her wet eyes flickered and tears dripped down her cheeks and ran down her lips.

"I can't see, Uncle Noah," Dinah sobbed. "I am blind. Why? What did I do to deserve this?"

A man in a white overall quietly entered the room followed by a nurse. He walked up to Noah and took the bandage off his hands. The nurse took Dinah from Noah's arms and laid her back on the bed. She covered her eyes with a fresh bandage.

"Who are you? What is your relationship with the patient?" the doctor asked, looking at Noah.

Noah stood up and faced the young doctor.

"I am a friend of the family," he said. "I am Dinah's godfather."

"This hospital has strict rules regarding patient visits," the doctor sternly reminded him. Noah apologized for removing the bandage from Dinah's eyes. The doctor quietly asked them to follow him in his office. Once in his office the doctor slowly walked behind his desk, removed his eyeglasses and put them in his coat pocket. He then removed a stethoscope from his neck and put it on the table. He calmly sat down behind his desk and beckoned the foursome to sit down. Jonah took Sarah's hands in his. Rebekah crossed her fingers on her thighs and gave Noah a hopeful look. Noah avoided her eyes and looked down at his feet.

"We are still doing some laboratory tests on Dinah," the doctor quietly said. "We have subjected her to a battery of x-rays. The x-rays revealed no serious damage to her major body parts. We found no broken bones and no internal injuries or bleeding. Her reflexes appear to be normal. The policeman who wrote up the accident report estimated that the car was traveling at 50 miles an hour when it snapped the light pole. The car continued forward for another ten feet before hitting Dinah. The concrete pole slowed down the vehicle which probably saved her from serious injuries or death. The car hit her below her waistline and threw her forward. She landed head-down on the concrete sidewalk and rolled over to a nearby tree. The skid marks on the road indicated that she traveled twenty feet before hitting the sidewalk. There is a big lump on the right side of her head."

"How could the driver be driving at 50 mph?" Sarah asked, perplexed. "The speed limit on that road is 30 mph."

"The driver was probably drunk," the doctor said. He stood up and pointed to the picture of a brain on the wall. "The brain is protected by the thick wall of her skull," he explained. "But despite this natural helmet, it is still susceptible to many kinds of injury. The brain can be injured even if the skull is not penetrated. Many injuries are caused by the sudden acceleration that follows a jolt or by the sudden deceleration that occurs when a moving head strikes a stationary object. The brain can be damaged at the point of impact or on the opposite side. We checked all her vital signs and tested all the basic brain functions to assess her state of consciousness and memory. We took standard x-rays to identify skull fractures and ran CT and MRI scans to evaluate possible brain injury. I am glad to say that there is no skull fracture. Since there is no skull fracture, we have ruled out Cerebral Contusions and Lacerations. The scans showed no Intracranial Hematomas either. Intracranial Hematomas are collections of blood within the brain and the skull. There is no bleeding between the meninges and the skull or from the veins around the brain. These symptoms sometimes may not be noticeable for several weeks. A brain injury may also cause damage to specific brain areas such as the cerebral cortex. Damage to the cerebral cortex usually impairs a person's ability to think, govern emotions and behave normally. It can cause malfunctions in the frontal and parietal lobes where memories of the uses and importance of familiar objects and sights are stored. These unique regions of the brain control other functions as vision, arm and leg movements. A specific disorder caused by damage to the frontal and parietal lobe is Agnosia. A person suffering from this dysfunction can see and feel objects but can't associate them with their usual role or function. I think that Dinah's lost of sight may be due to damage caused to the frontal or parietal lobes. Her brain can no longer interpret information sent by the eyes."

"Is she permanently blind?" Jonah asked.

"I think that Dinah's lost of sight is temporary," the doctor replied. "Some people suffering from Agnosia improve or recover spontaneously. Others must learn to cope with their strange disability. No specific treatment exists for this disorder. Many brain functions can be performed by more than one area and uninjured areas of the brain sometimes take over functions that were lost when another area was damaged."

"When will she regain the use of her sight?" Sarah asked nervously.

"I don't know. Dinah is young and healthy. In time she will see again."

The doctor took them back to Dinah's room. "Is that you, Uncle Noah?" she asked when she heard them walk back into the room. Her parents comforted and reassured her. The doctor told her that she would be subjected to other tests.

"Where are my sunglasses?" she asked. "The nurse said that when I leave the hospital I will have to wear dark sunglasses to protect my eyes until I can see again." She felt for her handbag around the bed and on the bedside table. Noah reached out for her handbag and looked for the sunglasses.

"It's in your handbag," Noah said. He removed the sunglasses from the handbag and put them in her hands. She ran her fingers on the initials on the lenses. "Mama, is it true that the driver who hit me was driving under the influence of alcohol?"

"The police speculated that a drunken driver hit you while you were walking home," Sarah said. "A witness reported seeing a little red car leaving the scene of the accident." Noah felt a lump in his throat and swallowed hard.

"Did they find the driver and give him a ticket for driving while intoxicated?"

"No, they did not find the driver yet." Sarah held back her tears. "They are confident that they will soon apprehend the driver."

"He ought to have my sunglasses," Dinah said bitterly. "It has the initials DWI engraved on the lens. I wasn't the one driving while intoxicated. I am Dinah Weirsema Iffrig. I am not a drunken driver. I don't want to be punished for someone else's drunken driving." She started to cry. Noah got up and walked to the window to hide his own tears. "Uncle Noah," she called out. Noah wiped his tears and walked back to the bed. He put his hands on her shoulder.

"Uncle Noah, I will not be able to see you again."

"Of course you will," Noah said.

"Why did the Lord do this to me, Uncle?"

"The Lord has healing powers. He put words into the mouth of little Joshuah. He will put light back into your eyes. In time you will see again."

"I want to see now. Why can't I see now?" Noah could not stand to see her cry again and left the room. Jonah, Sarah and Rebekah stood around Dinah and held each other's hands. They looked down and closed their eyes and gave thanks to the Lord for sparing Dinah's life. Then they prayed for the Lord to give Dinah back her sight. After the prayer Rebekah hugged Sarah and left the room. She looked for Noah and found him leaning against a window and staring outside. She put her arms around his and led him out to the parking lot.

Noah was now convinced that he caused Dinah's accident. He felt guilty of hurting her and he was full of self-reproach. The police had been driving around his neighborhood and asking the residents about a red Ford escort seen at the scene of the accident. He feared the day when the cops would come knocking on his door, handcuff him and take him to jail. He did not have the courage to tell Rebekah the truth and he refused to turn himself in. He kept the dreadful secret to himself and he slowly began to hate himself for being a coward. He wished that he could turn the clock back and return her sight back to Dinah. Every night he laid down on the bed with his eyes wide open, reflecting and relenting on the terrible thing he did to Dinah.

After the accident, Noah totally lost interest in his new job. He was melancholy, distant and irritable. He shut himself in his office most of the time and hardly did any work. He spent most of his day making and throwing paper airplanes in the air and watching them come down. He ripped pages from the ledger and rolled them into paper balls that he tossed in a basketball loop hanging over a trash can. His boss showed sympathy for him and brought in a temporary Accountant to assist him. He postponed some important projects until Noah could get a grip on himself again.

One day Noah came to work wearing a bib overall covered with paint. He carried a toolbox in one hand and a circular saw in the other. He dropped the toolbox and circular saw in his office and went back to his car. Moments later he returned with a pair of workhorses, more tools and a gallon of wood glue. Then he closed and locked the door to his office. Shortly afterwards the employees began to hear strange noise coming from his office. The CEO became very concerned at the noise coming from Noah's office, but he forbade anybody from disturbing him. Throughout the day Noah sawed and hammered away. Nobody knew what he was building behind his office door. Around noon the employees working close to his office complained to the CEO that the noise in Noah's office prevented them from doing their works. The CEO became more concerned and went to check on Noah. He knocked on his door, but Noah did not answer. The CEO pounded on the door but again he received no answer. "Noah, are you all right?" he shouted. He wrapped his fingers around the doorknob and rattled it. "Noah, please open the door." The sawing and hammering continued. The CEO rubbed his chin and returned to his office. Shortly before five o'clock, Noah emerged from the office. His hair was covered with wood dust and his hands were smeared with wood glue. He locked the door behind him and left the building. The CEO peeked out of his window and watched him drive off.

The CEO was usually the first person to arrive in the building. Upon entering his office the next day, he discovered that the leather and foam padding from his armchair had been ripped off. The white velvet cloth covering his sofa was also removed. Fearing that thieves had broken into the building the previous night, he looked for signs of a robbery around him. He checked the appearance of the desks and drawers in the other offices and noticed that all the desks and cabinet drawers were left open. Then he heard some noise coming from Noah's office and immediately went to investigate. To his surprise he found Noah sitting in a coffin in the middle of his office and gluing together two small strips of pine boards. Dismayed and shocked, the CEO screamed: "What the hell is going on here?"

Noah glued and stapled another strip of pine board to the work piece in his hands. The CEO walked into the office and stared at the little box in Noah's hands. Then he looked around the room and gasped. Noah had on the previous day sawed off his oak desk and built a coffin with the lumber pieces. He had lined the coffin with the white velvet cloth from the sofa in his boss' office and padded the bottom of the coffin with the leather from his armchair. The floor was littered with wood dust, scraps of lumber, nails, a staple gun, several boxes of staples, pieces of cloth and leather, a pair of scissors and a half-empty gallon of wood glue. The CEO was horrified to see Noah sitting in a coffin in the middle of his office. He shook his head and stared in disbelief at Noah. Noah glued and stapled another strip of pine board to the bottom of the box in his hands. His boss snatched the box away from him. "What is this?" he shouted. The CEO looked down at the floor and saw several tiny coffins lined up side by side. His eyes followed the line of coffins around the room, up one wall and over the ceiling, and down the opposite wall. He felt sick in his stomach and dropped the little coffin on top of the others. "What's happening to you, Noah?" Without looking at his boss, Noah took another strip of pine board and started to make another coffin. The CEO clenched his fingers and shook his fist in front of him. Then he looked up at the ceiling and pulled his hair. He went back in his office and slammed the door shut behind him. He took the naked armchair and flung it over his desk. He slumped down on another armchair and stared at the empty parking lot outside. A few minutes later the employees started to file into the building. When the secretary arrived for work, the CEO ordered her to bring

Noah in his office. "Noah, the CEO said in a gentle and paternal voice. What is the matter with you?"

Noah remained silent and avoided his boss' eyes.

"I know that you love Dinah very much, and I am very sorry that she had this nasty accident. I am sorry that the girl is blind as a result of her accident. If there is anything I can do for her, I will be glad to do it. If you need money to help her family with hospital bills, I can provide you with an advance. But you can't blame yourself for her accident. It's fate! We have no control over our own destiny. Have you considered taking a temporary leave of absence? Take some time off, go somewhere and get your mind off Dinah for a while. I have hired a temporary accountant to help us out. I am sure he can handle things while you are gone. I'll get your office cleaned up, get rid of that frightening coffin and get you a new desk. You need some rest, Noah. Those little coffins give me the creep."

"I cannot rest," Noah murmured. "I have made only 277 coffins. I need to make 25,000 of them."

The CEO felt as if he was struck by lightning. He almost fell off his chair. He regained his composure and stared at Noah. "But why do you want to make 25,000 coffins?" he asked Noah.

"I will make a coffin for each person killed by a drunk driver in America."

"But... I am...," the CEO stammered. Unable to come up with the right words to say, the CEO raised his hands above his head and stared at Noah. "Noah," he warned, "I am giving you another chance with this company. Take it now or else there won't be another chance for you."

"Fifty thousand people were killed by drivers driving under the influence of alcohol in this country," Noah said. He sprang up on his feet and in a heat of passion roared: "Somebody is going to have to stop this senseless slaughter on our highways."

The CEO became terrified at Noah's sudden anger. He stood up and pointed a trembling finger at Noah. "You are fired," he bellowed. "This place is not a funeral parlor. We are not in the business of making coffins and you are not going to make 25,000 coffins in my company and on company time. I have been very patient with you, and I have had enough. Get out!"

Noah left the CEO's office with guilt weighing down on him. The CEO breathed a sigh of relief and slumped down into his chair. He covered his forehead with his hands, closed his eyes, and shook his head. "I don't believe this," he murmured. "He is making fifty thousand coffins? Is he mad?" When he opened his eyes, a slip of paper on his desk caught his attention. He picked it up and read the note on it. "This pen and pencil box will serve as a reminder that 25,000 people were killed by drunken drivers in America."

"What pencil box?" The CEO exclaimed, dropping the paper slip on his desk. He opened his drawer and saw that Noah had placed all his pens and pencils in a pencil box built to look like a coffin. He picked up the pencil box and stared at it. On one side of the box were printed these words: 'Please don't drink and drive.'

"How dare he tell me when I should have a drink and when I should not drink? What does he think he is doing?" the CEO muttered. A group of employees laughing loudly outside his office interrupted his thoughts. Holding the tiny coffin in his hands, he left his office to investigate.

"You've got one too," one employee said, pointing and laughing at the little coffin in the CEO's hands. The other employees each held a little coffin containing pens and pencils in their hands.

"Get back to work," he screamed. He went back into his office and threw the little coffin against the wall. The pens and pencils flew around his office.

Dinah was released from the hospital a month later. She had still not regained her sight, but her doctors were greatly encouraged by her cheerfulness and good health. The specialists who had examined her did not find any injuries to her eyes or brain. They assured her parents that she was not in any danger. The doctors felt that it would do her good to be home with her family. Being a strong-willed girl, she quickly adapted to living and feeling her way around the house in darkness. Sarah took a temporary leave of absence from her job to care after her.

Since he was fired from his job, Noah had shut himself in an upstairs bedroom and refused to talk to anyone. He had turned the bedroom into a workshop and spent his days making the little coffins. In due time, the bedroom was filled with hundreds of the little coffins. Knowing how much he was affected by Dinah's accident, Rebekah left him alone. Jonah and Sarah got very concerned for his state of mind. They suggested that Dinah moved in the Burkel's house to keep him company. Rebekah welcomed the arrangement and set up a sleeping cot for her in the living room. Once settled in her temporary home, she spent her times listening to music and to television programs while Noah continued to build the little coffins in the bedroom upstairs. Once in a while Dinah attempted to coax Noah to come down and keep her company, but he stubbornly remained locked up in the bedroom. One morning Dinah went upstairs to talk to Noah. When he did not answer her, Dinah pushed the door opened and walked into the bedroom. She stumbled over a pile of coffins and landed on the floor. Noah helped up her and led her to a chair. He told Dinah that he had made only 1,782 coffins and asked her if she would like to help him make more of them. She agreed, only because it was the only way she could stay close to him and talk him out of his isolation. A week later the two of them had built 3,000 coffins. On the following weekend Noah loaded his car with the coffins and drove to the corner of Belt line and Preston road. Once there he stood at the road intersection and handed out the coffins to motorists stopping at traffic lights. Each time he gave out a coffin to a motorist he said: "Each of these coffins represents someone killed in a drunken driving accident. Please don't drink and drive." When he had given away all the coffins, he went back to his bedroom and built more of them. When they had built more of the coffins, Noah went and stood in front of shopping malls and grocery stores to give them out to shoppers as they walked in and out of the stores.

"Each of these coffins represents someone killed in a drunken driving accident. Please don't drink and drive," he passionately told the shoppers when he handed out the coffins.

For several weeks Noah and Dinah sat in the bedroom and built coffins. Noah cut the pine boards into small strips and Dinah glued and stapled them together. Dinah was exasperated that she was unable to talk Noah out of his madness. The only words that came out of him were: "In time you will see again" or "I wish I could turn the clock back." Noah repeated these words over and over to himself. The words so irritated her that she covered her ears with ear mufflers so that she would not hear him. One day she felt very depressed and discouraged at Noah's state of mind and left the bedroom. As she walked down the stairs she suddenly heard a loud crash and turned to the direction of the racket.

"What is it, Uncle Noah?" she yelled, alarmed at the noise.

"It's the pink squirrel," Noah answered. He had thrown a piece of lumber towards a squirrel that had suddenly appeared through the open window. The squirrel leaped off the windowsill and raced through the back yard and into the adjoining wood. Noah dashed out of the bedroom and bumped into Dinah as she was walking back into the bedroom. She hit her head on the doorframe and fell down. Without paying attention to Dinah, Noah ran down to the main floor.

"Uncle Noah, where are you going?" Dinah shouted. She got up and tottered behind him. When she reached the staircase, she tumbled down the staircase and fell head first into the family room. Noah took a shotgun from a glass cabinet and loaded it.

"I am going to shoot that pink squirrel," he said as he stepped over Dinah and ran out of the house.

"Come back, Uncle Noah. Don't leave me alone. Uncle Noah!" Dinah clutched her head and uttered a cry of pain. She ran her fingers over the right side of her head and felt a lump. "Ouch!"

Noah ran into the back yard and looked around him for the pink squirrel. He jumped over the fence and ventured into other people yards. The squirrel was nowhere to be found. His search eventually led him to a nearby park. A man jogged towards him. When the runner saw the shotgun in Noah's hand, he immediately turned around and ran in the opposite direction.

"Have you seen a pink squirrel?" Noah shouted at the lone jogger.

The jogger turned and pointed to a cluster of trees in front of him. "There are three or four gray squirrels feasting over pine nuts over there," he answered, "but no pink ones."

The runner sprinted away from Noah. He turned round and glanced at Noah.

"Leave these poor creatures alone. They are not beefsteaks."

Noah stopped people he met in the park to ask them if they had seen the pink squirrel. When they saw the shotgun in his hand, they all walked briskly away from him. After searching for the pink squirrel for half an hour, he saw a lonely man sitting down on a felled tree and drinking from a bottle. He sneaked up on him with the shotgun.

"Have you seen the pink squirrel?"

At the sight of the shotgun, the man stood up and raised his hands above his head. "You can have the bottle, but please don't kill me," the startled man begged. He gave the bottle of whisky to Noah. Noah took the bottle, thanked the man and continued his search for the pink squirrel. The man quickly grabbed his jacket and ran off. Two women, one of them pushing a baby chair walked towards him.

"Good afternoon, ladies. Have you seen Lord Calvert?" he asked the women.

"Who are you looking for?" One of the perplexed women asked.

"Lord Calvert of the Imperial House of Lords," Noah explained.

The two women stared at each other. They eyed the bottle of whisky and the shotgun in his hands and smiled. "Try calling Buckingham Palace," the other woman suggested.

Noah saw an elderly couple feeding the ducks at a pond. "Have you seen Old Mr. Boston?" he asked the elderly couple.

"He died several years ago," the elderly man replied. "Are you one of his creditors?"

Noah shook his head. "No, I am not," he replied.

"If you are not his creditor, why are you looking for him with a shotgun?" the elderly man asked.

Noah ignored the elderly man and walked on. He came upon a group of white teenagers with shaved heads loafing around. They wore earrings and combat boots, listened to loud music and drank vodka straight from the bottle. "Have you seen the black Russian?" he asked. A teenager raised a bottle of vodka in front of Noah and snuggled up to him. "What's wrong with me? Don't you like white Russians," he whispered. The earring-wearing, head-banding teenagers burst out into laughter. Noah quickly turned back. Frustrated at not finding the pink squirrel, Noah stopped and sat down on a park bench. Shortly afterwards a woman dressed in black brassieres, black knickers and black stockings and suspenders appeared on the trail. The woman wore red stiletto shoes and carried a 6ft tall Grandfather clock on her back. Her face was covered with the mask of Tunghak. One eye of the mask appeared like the dark side of the moon and the other eye looked like the bright side of the moon.

"Excuse me. Have you seen a pink squirrel?"

"Pardon me?"

"I am looking for a pink squirrel. Did you see one around here?"

"No," the woman replied, "but if you will let me have that bottle I will very likely point to you not one, but several pink squirrels." Noah agreed to let her have the bottle of whiskey. The woman paused to untie the string holding the grandfather clock on her back. After untying the clock, she slowly set it down on the ground. She took the bottle from Noah and lifted it to her mouth. "What are you looking for? A pink squirrel, you said?"

Noah's eyes were glued on the Grandfather clock. "Beautiful clock," he exclaimed. "Why are you carrying a Grandfather clock on your back?"

The woman sat down next to him. "Someone stole my wrist watch in my other life," she replied. "I just don't feel right going around without carrying a time piece. Have you seen anyone without a watch strapped around his wrist these days?"

"I understand, but a Grandfather clock...? Why not buy yourself a new watch?"

"A wrist watch divides time into hours, minutes and seconds. It guides us through the day and tells us when to eat lunch or when to stop work and go home. It helps us schedule meetings and appointments and causes everyone wearing it to rush around madly. I don't need a wristwatch because the time it displays is no longer a natural phenomenon. Too many people have left their marks on it. The Mayans recorded it, the Aztecs varied it, and the people of the Nile tampered with it. Dionysius Exiguus messed with it and Julius Caesar fooled with it. Emperor Yao dawdled with it, Pope Gregory XIII altered it and Chairman Mao adopted it. This grandfather clock, on the other hand, simply divides time between day and night. In the morning, it heralds the beginning of a new day and unlocks the light from darkness to brighten my sight. At night it draws the curtain on daylight and restores the darkness back. That is all I need to know."

The woman aroused Noah's curiosity. "Can it unlock the light bottled up in the eyes of a teenage girl?"

"If she looks up at the sky on the day of sorrow, she will see a visible flash accompanied by thunder and echo. The pap of Anu will stroke her cerebral hemisphere when the dark son of the great mother overpowers the ruler of life. Thereupon the bringer of madness will unleash her witchcraft and magic and shroud earth with a blinding light. The lost and damned souls inhabiting the moon will return to life and march among the creatures of the night to seek retribution."

"Her doctor says that in time she will see again."

"Time is of the essence. She must travel back in time while wearing a necklace graced by twelve lunar discs before she will see again. Take your cue from the Great Measurer. Why are you looking for a pink squirrel?"

"The pink squirrel will lead me to the black Russian, Old Mr. Boston and Lord Calvert. They must all be destroyed."

"I thought that I was the one who is insane," the woman said. "What are you, the Executioner or the Liberator?"

"Neither. I am the victim."

The woman took another drink from the bottle. The big hand on the face of the clock slipped over the number 12. Suddenly the clock clanged: "Bong... Bong... Bong... Bong."

"It isn't four o'clock," Noah reminded the woman, looking at his watch.

"When the cuckoo sings, it's time to harvest the cereal," the woman sang.

"It's not even twelve o'clock," Noah indicated.

"It doesn't matter. If I need to know the season, I watch the stars or the animals. Birds fly south to escape winter. The appearance of certain stars in the sky signals spring. Goats are fattest in the summer and wine tastes best during fall."

"Well, if you would take the time to reset and wind up the clock, you won't have to guess the time of the day or the season."

"I don't need the clock to unlock the light from darkness anymore," the woman replied, taking another sip from the bottle. "I can live in perpetual darkness and not fear pain." She stared at the shotgun in Noah's hands. "Can you kill pain with this thing?"

Perplexed by the woman's question, Noah looked at the shotgun, turned it over to examine it and then replied: "I guess it could be used as a pain killer. And one doesn't need a prescription from his doctor to use it."

"I'll trade you the Grandfather clock for the shotgun," the woman offered. Noah looked at the clock and replied: "That's a deal." He gave the woman the shotgun. The woman laid the shotgun on the bench and tied the Grandfather clock on Noah's back. Noah waved goodbye to the woman. Weighed down by the Grandfather clock on his back, he slowly retraced his steps back to his house. After he left, a pack of squirrels came out of hiding to resume their meals. The woman removed her stiletto shoes. She pointed the shotgun towards her left foot and pressed the trigger. The pack of squirrels scattered around and sprinted to the safety of the trees. The woman directed the shotgun towards her right foot and pressed the trigger again.

A worried Rebekah bit her fingernails and anxiously paced up and down the living room waiting for Noah to return. Dinah sat on the sofa and was silently praying for Noah's safety. Jonah sat next to her. The door suddenly opened up and Noah walked into the living room with the Grandfather clock strapped on his back. Rebekah screamed with joy at the sight of her husband. She was immensely relieved to see him safe.

"Uncle Noah, is that you?" Dinah exclaimed, standing up and extending her arms in front of her.

"I am home," Noah answered.

Dinah rushed into his arms, almost causing Noah to lose his balance with the Grandfather clock on his back.

"Oh, thank God you are safe," Dinah sighed. "I was so worried for you." Her fingers ran over Noah's face and felt for his cheeks and nose.

Jonah helped Noah unload the grandfather clock from his back. They both looked around the room for a place to put the grandfather clock.

"It will look good next to the fireplace," Rebekah suggested.

They carefully moved the Grandfather clock next to the fireplace. Noah stood back and admired the clock. The 6ft tall clock was the prettiest Grandfather clock that he had ever seen. He hugged and kissed Dinah. "I am sorry I left you alone," he said. Then he turned to Rebekah and smiled. "I am hungry. Can you please fix me something to eat please?"

It was the first time that Noah had smiled since Dinah's accident. Rebekah broke into tears at seeing her husband smile and embraced him.

After he brought home the grandfather clock, Noah never went back to building coffins again. Both Rebekah and Dinah were relieved of the change in his disposition. Together they cleared the bedroom of the little coffins and dumped them in the back yard. Rebekah asked him if it was all right for her to destroy them and Noah replied: "Go right ahead. I made my point." The whole family rejoiced. That night they built a bonfire and sat around the fire to watch the flames licking at the coffins. Through her sunglasses, Dinah perceived the souls of the dead victims of drunk-driving accidents rising out of the fire and into the sky.

"I wish you all a safe journey to Heavens," she whispered as her eyes followed the column of smoke into the sky.

The next day Noah tinkered with the Grandfather clock. When he unhooked the pendulum from the clock mechanism, a necklace fell out of the clock's bowel. The necklace was strung with twelve lunar disks. He picked up the necklace and hung it around Dinah's neck.

"This necklace will bring you luck and restore your vision," he said to her.

"I hope that you are right," Dinah said, "for I am tired of living my life in total darkness."

"I believe that in time you will see again," Noah replied.

The doorbell rang as he tinkered with the Grandfather clock. Noah shuddered. He thought that the police had finally caught up with him. His heart pounded furiously as he went to answer the door. He was greatly relieved to see that the caller was a salesman. The salesman held two little gadgets in front of him.

"Have you seen these little devices before?" he asked Noah.

Noah shook his head. "I don't think so." he replied. "What are they?"

"They are life savers," the salesman explained. "They will disable a car when they detect that the driver is drunk. These gadgets can prevent accidents and save lives." Noah looked away from the devices and closed the door. The salesman quickly stuck his foot at the door to prevent it from closing shut. "Do you know, Sir, how many people died every year in car accidents as a result of drunk driving? Just too many! I am going to ask you a little question. Do you know what a breath analyzer is?"

Noah pushed hard on the door to close it, but the salesman had his knee against it. "That's what these little devices are," he said, dangling the gadgets in front of Noah's face. "They are designed to work either outside or inside your vehicle. This one will keep you out of your vehicle when you are drunk. It analyses your breath even before you can open the door. Since you can't get into your car you can't drive it. If you can't drive it, you can't hurt anyone. The other device is a little bit more human. It will let you into your car but if the breath analyzer senses that you are over the legal limit, it will immobilize your car. This is nice when it's raining or when it's frigid outside."

"Will you please come back another time? My wife is not feeling well tonight," Noah lied. Reluctantly the salesman left. Noah closed the door and went back to work on the grandfather clock.

"Who was it?" Dinah asked. She sat in the room adjoining the family room and listened to a nature program on television. Her eyes covered by the sunglasses were focused on the TV screen. A herd of elephants streamed on the screen but Dinah could not see them. Joshuah was lying down on the sofa in the family room. His head was turned towards the Grandfather clock and his eyes were fixed on the clock's hands. Sarah and Rebekah prepared dinner in the kitchen for the two families.

"A salesman who wants to sell me some life-saving gadgets," he answered. Noah took a wet rag and cleaned the pendulum before hooking it back to the clock. Then he wiped off the dust from the cabinet and cleaned the glass door. He was eager to hear the clock tick and see the 4ft long pendulum swing. He took two steps backward to admire the clock.

"You have done a great job at refurbishing it," Jonah remarked. "I can't believe that the owner traded it for a cheap shotgun." The two friends then moved the Grandfather clock back to the wall. The hands indicated eleven o'clock. Noah checked the time on his watch.

"It is best to set the time when the moon complete its monthly cycle," Noah remarked. "My Grandfather used to tell me to turn the clock back only when the moon wanes and only if the wind blows from the North. Don't ask me why."

"That's not what my Grandfather told me," Jonah said. "There is a belief that if you turn the clock back when the moon enters its last phase, the spirits will stir about and strange creatures will appear in the night."

Noah laughed. "That's a load of bull," he said. "I don't believe in that kind of stuffs."

"Why do you wait for the moon to wane then?"

Noah laughed. "I guess it's just an excuse for me to go watch TV."

"I think so too," Jonah laughed.

Knowing that Noah and Jonah wanted to watch live coverage of sporting events on television, Dinah left the room and went to sit outside. She covered her ears with a pair of headphones to listen to her favorite music.

In her sanctuary on Lake Nemi, the divine Diana conferred with the dryads Selene and Nana to plan the Queen of Heaven's next appearance in the night sky.

"I am bored to death," Diana complained. "Let's see a new moon."

"Let play a trick on the earthlings and hide the moon from their view," Nana suggested.

"I would love to see the moon complete its cycle right at this moment," Selene wished.

"No," Diana snapped. "A full moon will require that we change the sign and degree of the lunar eclipse in the ecliptic to correspond with the sign and degree of the geodetic vertex on Earth. This will cause a solar eclipse at 19 degrees of Cancer and could result in a big disastrous earthquake in Indonesia, China or the Philippines."

"But it's too soon for a new moon," Selene protested. "A new moon will cause severe winter in the extreme Northern part of the United States with much snow and low temperatures."

"We should have a half moon then, isn't what I just said?" Nana quickly added.

"A half moon now will upset the lunar and planetary rhythms and disturb the harmony between nature and the cosmos," Diana warned. "The unbalanced states of the planets will lead to serious degeneration of animal and plant life on Earth."

The debate distracted the celestial Hecate from following the action of Noah. She suddenly appeared in front of the divinities. "Ya awl shaddup now," she screamed to the moon led. "There is a Texan down below who is turning the clock back. I need to be ready to play his life back in reverse for him."

"Seed stocks will virtually be worthless and the land will stop producing," Diana warned.

"Quiet, Please," Hecate broke in. "I need peace." The Goddess ran her finger on a row of books in the celestial library. "Burkart... Burkarth... Burkbuegler... Burke... Burkel.... Ah! Here he is, Noah Burkel." She opened the large book with the name 'Noah Burkel' on the cover and flipped back the pages. "The mortal was looking for a pink squirrel the last time. He spent some time talking with a Soothsayer in the park. He traded his gun for a Grandfather clock. Oh, my Gawd! This Texan is a moon with a dark side unseen until now. The son of a gun had been drinking. He hit his niece while driving under the influence of alcohol. As a result of the accident, the girl lost her vision. He tried to bring her sight back by making 25,000 coffins. What an idiot! Before he hit her, he was pursued by a white elephant and a bunch of other animals." Hecate put the book back on the shelf and rubbed her hands. "That should not be hard to recreate," she said. "The mortal looks repentant. He wants to turn the clock back. I think that I will help him turn the clock back."

"Can we have a blue moon now?" Selene, now beginning to show impatience to the other Goddesses, asked.

"Impossible," Nana said. "A blue moon at this time will bring famine to Central Africa causing enormous pain and suffering to a nation already exploited by white colonists. I propose that we wax the moon so that it will glow with love and unite the people."

"If ya awl don't shaddup soon," Hecate yelled to the deities, "I will exercise my magical powers and make the moon disappear into the darkness."

"How dare you tell a Roman Goddess what to do?" the vexed Diana said to Nana. "Your jurisdiction does not extend beyond the Scandinavian peninsula. You have control of the moon only where it is within the Arctic Ocean, the Norwegian Sea and the North Sea."

"Is that so?" the Norse goddess retorted. "Then let me remind you that Rome was confined to an area bounded by the Adriatic Sea in the North, the Ionian Sea in the South and the Tyrrhenian Sea in the West. You are the Roman Goddess of the moon, are you not? You have no business changing the appearance of the moon when it rotates over the Norwegian fjords."

"Wait a minute!" the shining Selene interrupted. "Are you all saying that I can only change the appearance of the moon when it appears over the Southern tip of the Balkans? I have been the Goddess of the moon longer than anyone else."

"Shaddup!" Hecate shouted to the quarreling goddesses. "If I hear any more bickering, I'll take over the control of the moon and disturb the elements. Don't underestimate my magical powers."

"Oh, just ignore her," Diana whispered to the other divinities. "She thinks that she is the Governor of Texas. By Jove, her English is goddamn awful. I wish someone would stick a silver foot into her mouth." The muses Khonsu and Artemis stopped by and tried to appease the goddesses.

"The moon has no territorial boundaries," Artemis said to the three divinities. "No country can claim the moon as its territory."

"That's right," the dryad Khonsu said.

"Who has control over the appearance of the moon then?" Nana asked.

"The Americans do," Selene sadly answered. "The ozone pollution emitted by their automobiles and the smokestack pollution discharged into the atmosphere had drastically changed the moon's albedo. The pollutant breaks the light waves in other colors. Instead of a white, silver or blue moon, the Earthlings can only see an ugly yellowish-beige moon. To hide the effect of the smog on the moon, they are calling up Christo."

"What can he do?

"They are sending the artist Christo up to wrap the moon with a 5,000 miles long banner painted with stars and stripes." Selene explained.

"I think we need to send the Moirai to the White House," the incensed Nana said. "Will someone send an email to Ishtar and ask her advice? Enough is enough. It's time for us to wrestle control of the moon back from the Americans."

"I've had it with you!" Hecate screeched. "I have heard enough of your squabbling!" The self-appointed Governor of Texas descended in the Gridiron of the Lunatics and exposed her bare buttocks to the moonbeam. The moon blinked and waned from bright to dark.

The moon suddenly turning dark brought Noah to the window. "I was not expecting to see a dark moon tonight," he exclaimed, surprised at the dark moon. "I guess I can turn the clock back now." He rushed to the Grandfather clock and swung the pendulum. He then moved the big hand 360 degrees backward. The Grandfather clock struck ten o'clock.

After her whimsical mooning, Hecate swung a rope above her head and screamed: "Yee Ha!" She caught the moon and drew it down from the sky and cut a hole on its dark side to set free the dead souls. The black Russian, Old Mr. Boston and Lord Calvert of the Imperial House of Lords stepped on the road of smoke and headed to Noah's backyard. A zombie, a cherry hooker and a naked lady followed in their footsteps. Moments later the creatures of the moon came out of the shadow to greet the dead souls. Intoning ritual laments of "Go, Cowboys, go, go, go!" Hecate transformed the creatures of the moon. The oxen became a white elephant, the hare turned into a pink squirrel, and the nightjar was transformed into a grasshopper. Hecate changed the wolf, the black cat and the bat into a salty dog, a wild turkey and an old crow. The reanimated souls and creatures headed for Noah's back yard. Finally, to complete her sorcery, Hecate cut out a hole from the moon's bright side and set free the light. The heavens clapped with thunder and the sky turned into a stage of sinuous and angled lights that blinked and flashed. Then the welkin opened up and a deluge poured out.

Dinah jumped up at the thunder and echo. She ventured into the back yard and opened up her hands to catch the rainwater. Lightning struck the statue of the goddess Anu perched on a column. Her breast broke loose and fell on her head. She fell to the ground and clutched her temple. She heard a loud thunderclap. When she looked up towards the sky, she saw a streak of light flickering in the distance. She got up and looked around her.

"Ma, look! There is a white elephant in the back yard," she yelled. Noah and Jonah glanced at each other. They shrugged their shoulders and smiled. "She is not moody, that's a good sign," Jonah said. Noah turned the large hand backward again 360 degrees. The grandfather clock struck nine o'clock.

"Stay out of the rain and get inside," her mother shouted at her.

The goddess Diana, angry at Hecate for transforming the creatures of the moon, flew into a rage. "I will teach the crone a lesson," she threatened. Thereupon Diana took on another of her many fascinating guises and became Diana Transformis. She metamorphosed into a white hippogypian, a Colorado bulldog and a Bengal Lancer all at the same time. The Bengal Lancer followed by the Colorado bulldog galloped on the road of fire towards Noah's backyard and charged at the white elephant. At the sight of the Bengal Lancer, the white elephant stampeded and stepped over the grasshopper and pink squirrel, crushing them to death. The Bengal Lancer caught up with the white elephant and shoved his lance behind its ear. It fell to the ground crushing to death the old crow and the wild turkey.

"Mom," Dinah screamed at the women in the kitchen, "the Bengal Lancer just killed the white elephant."

Unaware that Dinah was outside the house Jonah asked: "What movie is she watching?"

"I have no idea," Noah replied, looking perplexed. He turned the big hand backward again 360 degrees. The grandfather clock struck eight o'clock.

"Watch out for the zombie," they heard Dinah yelled at the Bengal Lancer. The zombie hurled the rusty nail and the velvet hammer towards the Bengal Lancer. He ducked at the projectiles and charged at the Zombie. The unarmed zombie tried to flee. The Bengal Lancer dismounted and ran after him. He drew out his saber and knocked him down to the ground. The zombie begged for mercy.

"Kill him, kill him," Dinah exhorted the Bengal Lancer. The Bengal Lancer pierced the zombie's heart with the saber. The Colorado bulldog then engaged the salty dog in a fierce fight. It sank its teeth into the salty dog's neck and swung it to and fro like a puppet. The salty dog struggled to escape the powerful jaw of the Colorado bulldog. After a short moment, the salty dog gave up the struggle and ceased to move. The Colorado bulldog dragged the salty dog a few feet before finally releasing its grip on it. The salty dog fell on the grass and never moved again.

"Mom, the zombie is dead," they heard Dinah say.

"Must be quite a movie she is watching," Noah said, smiling at Jonah. "I am amazed that she can imagine things by just listening to the audio track." Noah turned the big hand backward again 360 degrees. The grandfather clock struck seven o'clock.

"The black Russian is fleeing," Dinah shouted. Noah shuddered at hearing her referring to the black Russian. He rushed to the adjoining room. Jonah followed him with a perplexed look on his face. Dinah suddenly walked back into the room from the back yard and leaped into Noah's arms. "Lord Calvert and Old Mr. Boston are retreating. We won, we won," she screeched.

Sarah rushed into the room and watched Dinah screaming with excitement. "Who won what?"

Jonah stared at the TV set. "Who is retreating?"

"The evil and wicked Lord Calvert," Dinah replied.

"What are you talking about?"

"Lord Calvert of the Imperial House of Lords," She replied. She threw away her sunglasses and looked around her. "Mom, I can see again," she squealed. She flung into her mother's arms and clutched her mother tightly. Rebekah crossed her fingers and gave thanks to the Lord.

"Praise the Lord," she murmured. "The mighty Lord had put light back into Dinah's eyes. The Lord is great!"

"Hallelujah," Noah intoned.

Dinah looked around her and saw her watch sitting in a bowl on a table. She left her mother's arms and picked up the watch.

"Here is my watch," she said, strapping it around her wrist. "I thought I have lost it."

The grandfather clock struck six o'clock. Noah looked at Jonah and then went back to the other room. Joshuah stood on a chair in front of the grandfather clock. He turned and looked at his father.

"I have turned the clock back for you, Dad," he blurted out.

"Praise the Lord," Noah said. "The Lord has healing powers. The Lord is great!" He lifted his son into his arms and hugged him. He turned to Rebekah and announced: "Joshuah walked over from his chair to the Grandfather clock on his own." Tears rolled down his face.

"Amen," Rebekah murmured. He clasped her husband's arms and wept.

"The beaches are under the black sea, Dad," Joshuah stammered.

"I know, son," he replied. "The Lord is watching over us. He will not let his creatures die under the black sea. Praise the Lord." The two families formed a circle and held each other's hands. They prayed and gave thanks to the Lord for giving Dinah back her sight and giving Joshuah the ability to use his legs and fingers.

***

Two days later, Noah and Jonah met in a restaurant for dinner. The events of the past few weeks had worn both men out. Noah had earlier attended a job interview and he was confident that he would soon be offered a job. He was eager to return to work and forget about the accident. They sat in the dining room and waited for the waitress to come to their table. A poster of Lord Calvert of the Imperial House of Lords hung over the bar. Another poster showed Old Mr. Boston advertising a whiskey brand. The bartender poured a shot of Wild Turkey whiskey for a business traveler sitting at another table. A patron ordered a glass of Old Crow whiskey on the rock.

"You know something about this black Russian?" Jonah asked.

"I met him once," Noah timidly replied. "He almost destroyed my life and the lives of the people I love."

"What about that Bengal Lancer?"

"He is my guardian angel," Noah answered, smiling. "He watched over me and over Dinah. He saved our lives. He steered me safely home the night I was drunk. We were both lucky."

"I see," Jonah murmured.

A slender waitress walked up to their table and asked if they would like to order cocktails.

"We have two specials on cocktails tonight," she announced. "Order one cocktail at regular price and get another one free. You may choose from the following cocktails: Pink Squirrel, Grasshopper, Cherry Hooker, Naked Lady, White Elephant or Salty Dog."

"I'll just have a glass of milk," Noah said. The waitress wrote down his order.

"Or you may order a cocktail for only 99 cents," the waitress continued. "You may choose from the following cocktails: Zombie, Rusty Nail, Velvet Hammer, Blue Flame or Purple Orchid."

"No thanks; I'll have a glass of milk too," Jonah said.

The waitress wrote down the order and left. "Excuse me, Miss," the customer sitting at the next table called out to the waitress. "What do they mix in a Black Russian cocktail?"

"Vodka with coffee liqueur mixed over ice cubes in a pre-chilled old-fashioned glass. Would you like me to order you one?"

"It sounds good. I'll have one please," the customer replied.

"Good choice," the waitress replied. She wrote down the customer's order. "Are you celebrating something tonight?"

"Yes," the guest replied. "I have been promoted to Project Manager."

"Congratulations. I wish you well in your new position."

The waitress walked to another customer requesting her attention. Noah shook his head and smiled. "Never again," he whispered to Jonah.

7 ARCHERNAR THE CLOWN

The year of the Chicken

For forty days and forty nights it rained nuclear bombs over North America. Bombers strafed the gloomy skies day and night to drop their deadly cargoes. There were no soldiers landing and capturing cities, no hand-to-hand combats, and no tank battles. The warring superpowers relied heavily and solely on bombers, missiles and nuclear-powered submarines to annihilate each other. They looked to the successive nuclear blasts and the resulting fire and radiation to overpower each other. They dropped nuclear bombs upon each other until they ran out of nuclear bombs. They fired ICBM missiles at each other until there were no more ICBM missiles to fire. They sent waves after waves of bombers into each other's air space until all the planes were blown out of the sky. Laser-guided nuclear bombs blasted away oil refineries, ripped apart ICBM silos and ruptured nuclear power plants. The bombs, ranging from 15 megaton to 100 megaton each blew up military and economic targets, destroyed major military leadership installations and demolished political leadership centers. The emergency operation centers in coastal cities were leveled off, forcing millions of Americans to flee their homes. Inland, the overpressures created by the blasts toppled down entire cities, burning and burying millions of civilians. When the protracted nuclear war finally came to a close, no nation could claim victory. The 400,000 megatons of nuclear bombs that fell over North America had reduced its cities into a swath of burning rubble. Miles upon miles of highways were obliterated and millions of acres of forests were blighted. In just 40 days, the nuclear blasts and the intense radiation that ensured killed a hundred and seventy million Americans. The collapsing buildings and the resulting fires killed millions more. Many inhabitants died from their untreated wounds,

174

skin burns, terminal radiation sickness, and a lack of medical care, poor sanitation and starvation. The hospitals, unable to provide care to everyone, handed patients with terminal radiation diseases morphine so that they could end their miseries. Many survivors, finding neither comfort nor remedy, became their own butchers and executed themselves. Major outbreaks of typhus and cholera followed and claimed millions more lives. Order gave way to chaos as survivors of the nuclear attack left the burning cities and sought shelter in small towns. The radioactive fallout contaminated the lakes, rivers and streams. It decimated large herds of cattle and thousands of wild animals. The plants and the trees died. Without foods, the few animals that escaped the bombs perished altogether. Furthermore the radioactive particles released into the stratosphere damaged the ozone layer, exposing cultivated areas of land to ultraviolet rays. The UV rays in turn burned whatever crops remained after the nuclear attack. Without the life support system needed to keep them alive and healthy, many surviving Americans fortunate enough to have the means took to the sky. They climbed into their Toyota and Honda spacecrafts and sped to other habitable planets in the galaxy, leaving behind them a ravaged and inhospitable Earth. The unfortunate survivors who stayed behind fought the famine and the turmoil that ensured. They battled diseases, scarce food supply, the polluted water and the bitter cold. They fought over food morsels in hand-to-hand combats. They killed each other in order to keep the human race alive. When they could not procure foods for themselves and their families, they killed and ate their pets. Those who did not have domestic animals resorted to cannibalism and secretly ate their children.

Order came back very slowly. New leaders emerged to lead the people and organize them to better fare for themselves. Without the means to rebuild the cities, the survivors built underground concrete bunkers for shelter around the perimeter of the ruined cities. Whole new communities sprouted around the concrete bunkers. Americans learned once again to look to each other for help and support. They learned how to boil their water before drinking it, how to cook their meat before consuming it, and how to grow vegetables and raise domestic animals. They banded together to put out fires, clear the rubble and rebuild their houses, the schools, the hospitals and the churches. Despite acquiring new survival skills, they could not forget the devastation caused by the nuclear war. They lived in constant fear of a new wave of nuclear bombs dropping over their heads. They became resentful of one another, despiteful of their own relatives, and fearful of their own children. They no longer trusted and listened to anyone and they started to lose interest in raising cattle and growing vegetables. They no longer cared about drinking clean water and breathing clean air. Due to lack of proper health care, they became more vulnerable to the energies released by the nuclear rubbles. Without the proper mean to care after themselves, their organism slowly deteriorated. In time they became mutants.

After the nuclear war, the United States government diverted all available resources to rebuilding the weapon factories and building bigger and deadlier war machines. All able-bodied men and women were conscripted to work in the weapon factories. The government ordered the American people to turn in all durable properties to assist in the war effort. It confiscated the personal properties of anyone who refused to surrender them. Anyone who refused to cooperate in the war effort was sent to work in labor camps. The new Congress passed a new law banning the use of gas and charcoal grills for cooking hamburgers. People caught operating a charcoal or gas grill and cooking or eating hamburgers were arrested and sent to the labor camps. Federal troops ransacked and burned down hamburger Universities and arrested all students who were majoring in Hamburgerology. Citizens who held degrees in Hamburgerology were persecuted and forced to go into hiding. To escape the persecution, thousands of Hamburgerologists escaped to South America and Asia.

The economy remained in total disarray due to the lack of energy and raw material. The oil refineries, electrical power plants and factories remained idle. The damaged communication systems remained shut down except during emergency government broadcast. The oppressive condition as well as the rationing of food, clothing and medical supplies made the people anxious. They were weary of the destruction that wars bring with them, and they worried that there would be another nuclear attack on their country. They became dissatisfied with their government and lost faith in their leaders. Afraid that war would break out once again and destroy everything once more, they stopped the rebuilding process and drifted towards self-extermination. The rapid deterioration in the population's health caused the mutation rate to increase further. Alarmed at the rapid rate of mutation taking place everywhere in the country, the new Congress issued masks to the mutants to hide their deformed faces. To distinguish the races of the mutants, whose complexions had taken on the color of death, masks of different colors were distributed to the population. White masks were issued to the white population, black to Africans, brown to Hispanics, and yellow to Asians. Mutants of mixed races were handed white masks and asked to paint them a combination of colors representing their races. The mutants became weary of the phylogenic grouping of the people. They defied the government policy of racial division by painting ideograms on the white masks to express love, peace and nuclear disarmament. They painted teardrops on the masks and wore them to bemoan the extinction of the human race and the parturition of the new, inhuman race. In addition to the masks that symbolized the citizen's races, the government also distributed to the mutants different masks for wearing on different occasions. It claimed that the new masks would make the mutants appear more receptive to the humans who had not transmutated. Comedians were ordered to wear funny masks when they performed their acts. Young couple had to wear love masks during courtship, whereas teachers were ordered to wear knowledge masks when teaching. There were special masks for wearing at political rallies, dinner parties, company picnics, and wedding ceremonies. There were masks of death, guilt and dishonor; of exoneration, hope and gratitude. There were also masks of amazement, disbelief and stupor. Some masks symbolized hate, racism or egotism. Others expressed courage, disgrace or arrogance. They signified virginity, sympathy, hostility, stability, tenacity, villainy or even culpability. They typified pain, sorrow or boredom, or connoted corruption or trustworthiness. In issuing these masks to the mutants, the government hoped that they would reverse the genetic drift and mutation and cause the mutants to develop new adaptations and become new species. The government strongly believed that the masks would cause the assemblage of behavioral and physical characteristics of the mutants to be replaced by new forms bearing new traits. Alas! As has been done by generations before them, the mutants frequently covered their faces with masks of good faith while performing illegal and somber acts onto others. Masks signifying love or courtship were much in demand as mutants used them to forget the horrors of the nuclear war. The most popular masks were the Jack and Jackie facemasks. Some mutants refused to wear government-issued facemasks. Instead they draped themselves in white robes and covered their heads with conical hats. These mutants also developed the peculiar habits of collecting wooden crosses from church ruins and used them as firewood at night to warm themselves. At first they gathered in the woods to indulge in this peculiar pastime. Later they spread out and invaded neighboring towns where they planted their crosses on the private front lawns of some particular mutants and set them alight before leaving.

The government also realized that the mutants would perish without foods. Previous efforts by farmers to cultivate the land had failed because the soil was too contaminated. Since there was not sufficient livestock available to feed everybody, government workers recovered and processed the carcass of animals killed by the atomic blasts to feed the hungry population. The animal carcass was irradiated by gamma rays to kill harmful organisms. The processed foods were then taken down to underground bunkers, packaged in polyethylene bags and stockpiled in underground warehouses. The plastic food packages were then labeled with nutritional information and then distributed to the mutants. The irradiated food however was not well received by the mutants. After eating the irradiated foods, they covered their faces with their masks of anger to mistreat their children. The mutants blamed the children for the war and the shortage of foods. They blamed them for the outbreak of the nuclear war and for their mutation. In short, they blamed the children for everything that had happened to them. The children were frequently beaten and abandoned in fields. Left on their own, many of the abandoned children starved to death. From the nuclear rubble, a new kind of world emerged in which small children were battered, persecuted, abused and sometimes killed. It was in that kind of world that Xivana and Xalex grew up.

Xivana and Xalex were shortened representation for X-Ivana and X-Alex. The new Congress had decreed that all children born during and after the nuclear war be named differently to distinguish them from the children born before the nuclear war. All babies born in North America after the nuclear war must have their first names begin with a vowel and hyphenated with the letter 'X.' Since the hyphenated names were hard to pronounce, the frustrated parents dropped the hyphen from the names of their children. The naming system was born out of an ancient custom of segregating the races in the United States of America. People who were not white had their race hyphenated with the name of the new country they were settling in. In the old method of segregating the races, the citizens whose ancestry emanated from Asia were branded as Asian-Americans to associate them with the country from which they descended. The secret list of names were kept in a vault at the Immigration and Naturalization Service and closely guarded. It contained more than a thousand names used for segregating new non-white immigrants from white Americans. The names ranged from Akrotirian-American to Zakynthosian-American.

Xivana and Xalex were born in the town of Lubbock, Texas. Although they were spared the horrors of the war, they could still see the devastation everywhere around them. The cities of Dallas, Forth-Worth, Austin and Houston were all reduced to mangled steels and shattered concrete. The Texas prairies looked like the scarred surface of Mars with rings of fires still burning on them. The mutation was less profound in the country, but food and fresh water were still scarce. The people depended heavily on irradiated foods to stay alive. The two children had never seen fresh vegetables and fruits. At dinnertime, they listened with wide opened eyes as their parents talked about the old 'Land of plenty.' They were amazed to hear that once upon a time in America, fresh fruits and vegetables were plentiful and cheap. They were also surprised to learn that before the war, fast-food restaurants served hamburgers made with real beef in Lubbock. In the bunkers and hideaways, they heard the people talked incessantly about the beloved and delectable hamburger. The hamburger, once the national food of America, had now totally disappeared from the dinner tables. Sometimes they heard them talk about a funny man who once lived in America and who made children laugh.

A long, long time ago, before it rained nuclear bombs over North America, a group of people began to plan for the day when their country would come under a nuclear attack. The group consisted of wealthy citizens from New Mexico, Arizona, Texas and Utah. They knew that a nuclear attack of massive proportion against America would kill millions of people and obliterate their beloved land. The group sought to create an underground city that would withstand consecutive nuclear blasts and keep out the radiation fallout. The city that they envisioned building would have its own life-support system that would permit a small population to live and strive without having to rely on the outside world. Convinced that building and living in such an enclosed world was possible, they scouted the country for the ideal place to build their underground city. They found the perfect site for their underground city in a remote corner of southeast New Mexico: the Carlsbad Caverns. The caverns, which were made up of 81 caves, lied underneath 46,000 acres of desert land. It contained huge subterranean chambers, long corridors and narrow passages. Native Americans once used this underground universe as communal villages.

The survivalist group bought the Carlsbad Caverns from the Federal government. During that time, the government had closed down all the National parks and diverted public money towards military expansion. It eagerly sold the caverns to the private group in order to generate cash and accelerate the building and deployment of nuclear space stations. After acquiring the Carlsbad Caverns, the group gathered together a team of engineers and scientists to design and build their underground city. The engineers created different climates in the caves and introduced various specimens of plants, animals, insects and marine life. They built a barnyard in one cave for raising animals and constructed a farm in another for growing crops. In another cave they built an indoor village for their families to live in. It took the engineers and scientists four years to build the underground city. When it was finally completed, the survivalists moved into the caves with their friends and families. They carried with them generators, heat lamps, genetically-engineered plant seeds, livestock, computers, tools, medicines and clothing. Once everyone had gathered inside the caves, they closed the doors behind them forever. The underground city eventually became known as the Carlsbad Colony. People ridiculed the colonists when they built the underground city. They expected them to come out of the caves when they ran out of foods or when they get tired of living like prehistoric beings. Years passed by but the inhabitants of the Carlsbad Caverns never came out. The 500 men, women and children who moved into the caves with great fanfare were never seen again. Eventually people thought that they had all died in the caverns. The story of the Carlsbad Colony became a legend that was narrated time and time again by countless generations of Americans to their children and grandchildren. By the time the nuclear war that ravaged and laid waste the once mighty United States of America started, only a few people could remember the Carlsbad Colonists. The nuclear bombs that rocked North America however left the Colony unscathed. While the population outside struggled, underwent mutation and died, the Carlsbad Colonists lived on. Soon after the nuclear war, rumors began to circulate that the people living in the Carlsbad Caverns had survived the nuclear holocaust. Mutants scavenging for foods in the Chihuahuan Desert and in the rugged canyons of the Guadeloupe Mountain reported seeing people leaving the Carlsbad Caverns. They told tales of small people with guns patrolling the areas around the caverns. They told stories of yet another group of people running away from the caverns, hotly pursued by the armed guards. The guards mercilessly killed the people and left their bodies to rot among the pinion and ponderosa pines. They witnessed starving and desperate children escaping from their own world and taking refuge inside the caves. The mutants also learnt from the people who escaped from the caves that fresh vegetable and meat were abundant in the caves. Amidst all the fantastic and amazing tales that were told of the Carlsbad Colonists was one story that fascinated children the most. Inside the caves lived a clown who had the ability to make children laugh. He was known for rescuing runaway children and giving them refuge inside the caves. The mutants called him Archernar the clown. The stories of Archernar the clown withstood the test of time and became legends.

The rumors that the Carlsbad Colonists had survived the nuclear war spread across Texas like wildfire and reached Xivana and Xalex in Lubbock. Sitting amidst the ruins of their demolished farmhouse, they looked at pictures of plants and animals and daydreamed about Archernar. The picture books were salvaged out of a schoolhouse. The elders had since a long time ago given up rebuilding the schools because there were no teachers in the town to teach the children. Unable to attend school, the children spent their days and nights looking at picture books. They were captivated by the flora and fauna in the picture books and they longed to see real flowers and animals. They had never seen a butterfly, came close to a tortoise, or hugged a dog. They wished that they could hear a bird sing, watch a fish swim in the river or chase a squirrel into the wood. Their grandparents told them that the animals in the picture books once lived in North America, but the nuclear bombs had wiped most of them off the face of their country.

"Did you hear Dad talk about the funny man again last night?" Xivana asked her little brother.

"He is just a clown," her brother replied. "I heard Grandpa say so."

"I want to meet him," Xivana said dreamily. "I heard that he could make children laugh. It is so sad around here. Nobody laughs anymore."

"He no longer lives in America," Xalex hastily said. "He left the country after the nuclear war because he could not make anyone laugh anymore. That's why we have those comedians to make us laugh now. Dad said that the comedians are not funny. They cover their faces with funny masks provided by the government in order to make people laugh."

"I have been wondering about that 'hamburger' thing that mom frequently talks about. She said that everyone used to have hamburgers for lunch before the nuclear war."

"It must be something very nice to eat," Xalex answered. "They must have had a lot of nice things a long time ago. Why can't Mom cook a hamburger?"

"You have to have fresh beef in order to make a hamburger," Xivana said. "Besides, cooking a hamburger on an open fire is a crime punishable by death. Federal troops are everywhere. They will shoot anyone cooking a hamburger at sight. I am tired of eating dried beef sticks and taking vitamin pills. I wish I could have a hamburger for lunch. It sounds delicious."

Xalex closed his eyes and smacked his tongue. "Me too," he said.

"The mutants traveling from New Mexico said that the Carlsbad colonists eat hamburgers for lunch," Xivana said.

"That's just an old legend," Xalex said, mocking his sister. "I don't believe it."

Xivana flipped the pages of her picture book and pointed at a large animal with long horns. "The mutants even said that the colonists raise Texas longhorns in the caves," she added. Xalex pulled the picture book away from his sister and gazed at the picture of a Texas longhorn.

"I don't believe it," Xalex said. He threw the picture book back to her sister. "All the Texas longhorns were killed by the nuclear bombs. We are being fed their carcasses by the government."

"There are rumors going around that Archernar lives in the cave," she continued. "He must be the funny man that grandma constantly talks about."

Xalex lifted his head from his picture book and stared at his sister. "You are lying," he said.

"No, I am not," his sister answered. "It's true. Some mutants have seen him playing with children in the caves. They say that the children in the caves have hamburgers for lunch every day." Xivana rose to her feet and went to look through a window with broken glasses around the frame. "He must be a very nice man and he must be very wealthy to own and raise cattle in the caves."

"If it is true, why doesn't he come out of the caves? The nuclear war has been over for many years now. Why does he continue to live in the caves?"

"I don't know," Xivana replied. "Maybe he could not make anyone laugh anymore. I once heard Dad say that the clown had left America because the nuclear war is no laughing matter." She looked at the hole in the ceiling above her head. "Maybe Archernar feels that the nuclear bombs will never reach them in the caves."

"I don't believe you," Xalex said. He returned to the stack of picture books, picked one book out and opened it. He eyed the picture of an animal standing on top of a cliff. "Look," he said, laughing. "this deer has a small beard." Xivana looked at what her brother was laughing at.

"It's a mountain goat, silly. Archernar raises goats in the caves too. Let's go look for him," she suddenly said.

"Are you serious?" her brother asked, dropping the picture book.

Xivana turned and faced him. "I am curious," she said. "I want to go to the Carlsbad Caverns."

"It's too far away, sis. We will never get there," Xalex said.

She rushed to one end of the wall and pulled out a road atlas from under a pile of books. With trembling hands, she turned the pages until she found the map for New Mexico. Her finger followed a thick red line from the Texas/New Mexico state line to Carlsbad.

"It's only about a hundred miles from the Texas/New Mexico border," she said. Xalex knelt down next to her and stared at the road map.

"How far is the State line from Lubbock?"

"It is about seventy-five miles."

"That's about one-hundred and seventy-five miles from Lubbock," Xalex said, disappointed. "We'll never make it. It's just too far away. Forget it." He opened another picture book and turned the pages.

"We'll take Dad's dune buggy. It might take us four, may be five hours, but we can do it."

"You want to run away from home, don't you?" Xalex asked.

Thousands of children across the country were running away from their devastated homes to escape their angry and confused parents. The nuclear war had made all children unimportant, unwanted and a burden to their parents to care after. The famished citizens would rather have foods than children. They fed their children last and only after they have satisfied their own hunger first. Left on their own, many children ran away to the countryside. They scavenged for foods in the woods and looked to other humans to take them into their homes and feed them. More often than not, they found desolation and death in the blighted landscape. Many of the children tried to reach the Carlsbad caves, but most of them perished in the harsh lunar-like countryside. Their flesh rotted. Their corpses decayed and returned back into the earth. The bones eventually crumbled and returned to the earth too. The mutants hoped that someday, out of the bones buried in the ground a new life would emerge again. Government workers often confused the little corpses for animal carcasses and picked them up to be irradiated and distributed to the mutants as food. Xivana thought that it would be wonderful for her and her brother to live in a land where children are loved and treated with respect. She was fascinated by the rumors that a clown who loves children lived in the Carlsbad Caverns. She envisioned the caverns full of happy children eating hamburgers every day. She imagined the depth of the caverns filled with animals grazing on green pastures, drinking water from a limpid stream, and running around lush plants. She pictured flocks of birds flying around the caves, conjured up images of beautiful butterflies swirling around plants and flowers, and envisaged endless fields of tulips and daffodils. For several days, Xivana dreamed about meeting

Archernar. Every night she was tempted to leave Lubbock and go to the Carlsbad Caverns to join the clown. Finally, when their parents left them alone to attend the union of two mutants at the town square, Xivana told her little brother that she had decided to run away from home. Xalex became terrified.

"We'll never get there," he insisted. "It's just too far away."

"If I follow the old highway 62 west, it will take me directly to Carlsbad," she said.

"The bombs had destroyed all the roads," Xalex said. "You'll get lost and then die." Xalex swung his arms around his sister's neck. "Please, don't go, sis," he implored. "I don't want you to die. The nuclear war had killed too many people already. There are no more children in the town with whom I can play with. If you die, I will be alone."

"No, I won't die," Xivana assured her little brother. "I am strong and I am going to find Archernar in the Carlsbad Caverns. You can come along with me."

Xalex's little arms held his sister tightly. "I am not strong like you. I will die. Then the government workers will pick my body up and feed me to the mutants."

"I'll watch over you," Xivana comforted him. "I won't let anyone hurt you."

"Does this clown whom you are talking about feed the children with hamburgers?" Xalex asked.

"Yes," Xivana replied. "He makes the hamburgers with fresh beef."

Xalex smiled and wiped the tears in his eyes. "All right then. I'll go with you."

They gathered together some clothes and threw them in their backpacks. They filled another sack with irradiated foods and clean drinking water. Then they waited silently in their underground shelter for the night to settle down. Their parents had left behind their dune buggy. The vehicle was fitted with fat tires which made it ideal for driving on rough terrain. The dune buggy enabled their parents to cross the crater-filled countryside and hunt for foods in the woods. When darkness finally engulfed the town, the children emerged from their underground bunker. They ran to the dune buggy and quickly drove off into the night, leaving behind them their burned and scarred neighborhood.

Along the way Xivana had trouble finding the road and staying on it. The road was filled with bomb craters that slowed her down and forced her to take long detours. Xalex was frightened by the pitch-dark countryside. He kept seeing ghouls around him. The ghouls seemed to reach out to him and seize him. "Let's go back," he constantly begged his sister. Xivana kept on driving. Once in a while the headlights illuminated a band of mutants scavenging for food and fuel. The road became rougher and rougher as they drove farther and farther from Lubbock. After driving for about an hour, the dune buggy slid down a bomb crater and came to an abrupt stop at the bottom. The engine sputtered and then died.

"It's creepy in here," Xalex said, trembling with fear. "Please, let's go back home."

"It's all right," Xivana consoled him. "You are being a coward. I don't believe in ghosts." She turned the ignition key, but the engine would not come back to life. She tried starting the engine a few more times before finally giving up. "We'll spend the night in the crater and resume our journey in the morning."

"I am scared," Xalex said. "I want to go home." He moved closer to his sister and clasped her arms.

"You are being silly," she said. "There is nothing to be afraid of. We are safe inside the crater."

A light appeared in the dark sky. The tiny round ball of white light, looking like a small bulb, moved slowly towards them. It suddenly dipped and changed course. The light was then followed by a second light, and then by a third light. A few seconds later the lights evaporated. Other lights appeared, then bobbed and bounced above them. Terrified at the appearance of the lights, Xalex pointed at the sky.

"It's a squadron of bombers," he shouted. "They are dropping bombs again." He opened the door and ran out of the vehicle to seek shelter in the crater, but found none. He ran around the bottom of the crater until Xivana caught up with him and brought him back to the buggy.

"It's only the Marfa Lights," she explained. "They are not bombs. It is a natural phenomenon."

The two children sat down inside the vehicle and watched the light show in the dark sky. The lights sometimes appeared in a pale yellow or soft red color. Sometimes they appeared in blue or green. They moved about laterally then burst and disappeared.

"Pouf," Xalex said, pointing to the tiny stars in the dark sky. "There goes another one. And another one..."

They watched the aerial light display for about thirty minutes before falling asleep.

The next morning they woke up and saw a coyote on the edge of the crater watching them. They scrambled out of the vehicle and the coyote ran off. The crater was littered with the fragments of the bomb that formed it. At the top of the crater they saw a road sign indicating that they were on the outskirts of Hobbs city. The two children ran down into the crater and got back into their vehicle. Xivana started the engine. It roared back to life and filled the air with the smell of gasoline vapor. She shifted the vehicle to a lower gear and pressed down on the gas pedal. The light and nimble vehicle slowly began to ascend the crater, kicking a cloud of dust behind it. When she got the vehicle back on firm road, Xivana shifted the gear back to standard four-wheel drive and resumed her journey to Carlsbad. The nuclear war had left a horrible scar on the Texas prairies. The moon-like landscape was lined with downed planes and bombshells. The land was littered with pieces of thermoplastics, titanium and kryptonite. Radioactive vapors bellowed from nearby craters and amidst the charred ruins of burnt farmhouses. Xivana maneuvered the vehicle around large holes, charred vehicles and unexploded miniaturized warheads. She drove past the mangled remains of a stealth bomber and two raptor fighters. Every now and then she passed by a crippled Blackbird, a downed Osprey or an abandoned Hornet. After two hours of driving around craters, bombs and debris, they finally reached the ruined city of Carlsbad. The city resembled a war zone and was surrounded by fallout shelters and concrete bunkers. Scorched remains dotted the landscape where buildings once stood. Helicopters buzzed overhead. Large crowd of listless mutants sat atop mounds of crumbled concrete and molten metals, waiting for life to emerge from death. A few pickup trucks carrying furniture and mattresses roared through the rubble-strewn streets. Long lines of people with their faces covered with government-issued masks stood by food centers with crumbling walls and damaged roofs. A band of children with knotted rags and dirty bandages covering their heads sat on a pile of bricks and begged for foods. Dust and the smell of decomposing bodies still hung heavy in the air. Not far away, a group of brave men and women held signs above their heads. They walked in a circle to protest the nuclear war. One sign read: "Thank You, Shakharov! It could have been worse." Another sign read: "Hiroshima, we now feel your pain and sufferings."

They drove through the city without stopping. When they reached White City they found no one there. Xivana stopped the vehicle so that they could rest and eat. They ate the synthetic food from the plastic bags and drank water from their canteens.

"I hope this is the last time I eat this horrible food," she said as she bit on an irradiated meat morsel.

"Will we have fresh hamburgers soon?" Xalex asked as he chewed on the tasteless meat.

"We are about seven miles away from the Carlsbad caverns," she said. She glanced through the windscreen in front of her and saw an old man sitting next to an unexploded W88 miniaturized warhead.

"Look! There is someone over there," Xalex exclaimed.

"Yes, I saw him."

"What is he doing?"

"I don't know," Xivana replied. "Let's find out." she climbed out of the dune buggy and ran to the old man. "Hello," she called out. "Where is everybody?"

"Everyone left the city a long time ago," the man replied.

"Did they abandon the city because of the nuclear war?" she asked.

"No, they left long before the nuclear war started," the old man answered. "Strange people wearing scary masks came down from the Guadeloupe Mountains during the nights and ransacked the grocery stores and the food pantries of private homes. They stole all the foods they could carry with them before disappearing back into the mountains. The residents got tired of the nightly raids. They were fearful that ancient spirits were still haunting the ground and abandoned the city."

"Why are you still here?"

"A Mescalero Apache never runs away. The spirits of my ancestors are with me." The old man stood up and wailed a melancholy chant. He then circled the bomb and broke into a war dance.

"You can't stay here," Xivana pleaded with him. "You will die of starvation. Come with us. We are going to the Carlsbad Caverns to live with Archernar. He will protect us and give us food. What is your name?"

The old man stopped his war dance and stared at them. He slowly shook his head. "I am Gorgonio. The rest of my people had left these mountains a long time ago. Please don't go into those caves," he warned. "The people who inhabit these caves eat little children."

Xalex screeched and hid behind his sister. "You are lying," Xivana shouted. "You are telling us lies to frighten us and discourage us from seeing Archernar. Archernar loves children. He will never allow children to be eaten." She broke into tears and flung herself against the old man and pounded him with her fists. "You are lying, you are lying," she yelled at him. She ran to the dune buggy.

"Wait," the old man called out. "Keep away from the Carlsbad caverns. Go back home now before it is too late." Xivana cranked up the engine and drove off in tears. The old Apache Indian shook his head. He ran after the dune buggy and jumped on board. Xivana drove into the canyon leading to the Carlsbad Caverns. A few minutes later the earth shook. Xivana looked into the rear view mirror and saw a red and yellow fireball mushrooming behind them. She kicked down on the brake and brought the vehicle to a stop.

"My God," she shrieked, "the bomb exploded." She covered her mouth with her hands. She climbed out of their vehicle and stared at the ball of fire. Xalex clung to her. She covered her face and turned her eyes away from the ball of fire. Gorgonio put his arms around them as if to protect them from the pieces of metals flung high into the air.

"I no longer want to eat a hamburger," Xalex said. "let's go home. I am scared."

"I am glad that you came with us," Xivana said, looking at Gorgonio.

"It makes no difference," Gorgonio replied. "No one can escape the radiation."

"The Carlsbad Colonists escaped the nuclear radiation," Xalex remarked.

Despite her brother's fear, Xivana continued to drive into the canyon. They were silent and fearful. Xivana was too upset about the old man's lies to say anything. Xalex was petrified that Archernar would devour them once they enter the caves. The canyon road winds through a beautiful desert scenery. This part of the countryside was untouched and unaffected by the nuclear blasts. Inside the canyon, they found lechuguillas, ocotillo and cholla plants, some of them in bloom. Desert willows, hackberry bushes, juniper and clusters of sparse desert grass lined the road.

"We are approaching the caverns entrance," Xivana said. Xalex's face turned grim.

"Do we have to go inside the caves?" he fearfully asked. "Why don't we just turn around and go home?"

"I am curious to see what's inside the caves. I have heard many different stories about the inhabitants of the caves. I want to see for myself if there is any truth to the stories."

"Gorgonio said that Archernar eat small children," Xalex reminded his sister, his voice trembling. "There is a monster living in the caves. I don't want to go inside the caves. I don't want a hamburger anymore."

"He lied. There is no monster in the caves."

Gorgogio looked down. "My people never tell lies," he protested.

Xivana stopped and parked the dune buggy under some Douglas fir trees. She came out of the vehicle and beckoned her brother out. He held tightly to the car seat bottom. "I am not going," he said.

"Oh, you are being a coward again. You can stay here if you want, but I am going in." Xalex jumped out of the vehicle and joined her sister. "I don't want to stay here by myself," he said.

As they descended the road leading to the cave's entrance, they heard voices coming from the hills overlooking the cavern. The voices frightened them and they quickly hid behind some trees. Xalex clutched his sister tightly. A group of boys dressed in uniforms and carrying AK47 assault rifles emerged from the ponderosa pines. They pulled a man covered with a white laboratory coat by a noose tied around his neck. His hands were tied behind his back and he limped from a gunshot wound in his leg. The boy soldiers hopped back onto the asphalt road and marched to the cave. They walked down a stairway leading to a heavy steel door. Midway down the stairway the captive man swiftly slammed his hip into the boy soldier holding the noose and butted his head against the boy soldier behind him. The boy soldiers tumbled, bumped into their comrades and fell down the steps. The prisoner then bolted up the steps and ran for the hills.

"Shoot him," a boy soldier ordered. The fallen boy soldier got back on his feet and recovered his assault rifle. His comrades scrambled back to the top of the steps and fired a volley towards the runaway prisoner. The prisoner tottered but continued on to the hills. He reached the top and dashed for freedom through the ponderosa pines. The boy soldiers sprinted over the steps and pursued him. Xivana and Xalex waited for the boy soldiers to return. Moments later several shots rang out from the hills. Birds fluttered and flew into the sky. A raccoon behind them darted left and right, then leaped behind a fir tree.

Xivana sprang up and ran towards the shot. Gorgonio quickly leaped behind her and restrained her.

"Let me go," she cried. "They are shooting at the man." Gorgonio brought her back behind the trees, out of sight of the boy soldiers.

"They'll kill you too. Please wait until they depart."

The boy soldiers emerged back from the pines and returned to the cave.

"I want to go home," Xalex said, pulling on her sister's arms. "I am afraid."

Confused and speechless, Xivana took her brother's hand and ran towards the spot where the prisoner had disappeared. She looked amidst the pines for the escaped man hoping that he would still be alive. She found him lying face down amidst the pinion pines. His hands were still tied behind his back. His body was riddled with bullets and his white laboratory coat was stained with blood. Xivana knelt down by him and tried to turn him over. The man opened his eyes and turned his face towards her. His face was covered with pine needles.

"Who are the people who shot you?" she asked the dying man.

The man moved his head to and fro. "Go away, please go away," he pleaded. "Don't enter these caves." Xivana opened her canteen and poured water into his mouth and wet his face.

"What's going on inside the caves?"

The man closed his eyes. His head fell back and his body stiffened. Xivana shook him up.

"Please," she cried. "Tell us what's in these caves." The man could no longer hear her. He was dead.

In deep shock, they walked back to their dune buggy. They were disoriented and terrified by what they just saw. For a few minutes they sat motionless and speechless under the trees. Xivana started to doubt the story of a clown who lives in a cave and loves children. She was not sure anymore if she wanted to enter the caves and meet him. She now believed that the stories about young soldiers chasing and killing people were true. Suddenly they heard someone laugh. When they looked at the direction of the laughter, they saw a strange figure emerging from behind the Douglas fir trees and walking towards them. The two children shrieked. Xalex ran to the dune buggy and hid his face under the dashboard. Gorgonio hid behind a bush.

"It's the Carlsbad monster that eats small children," he yelled. "Hurry, run into the forest, sis."

The stranger was dressed in tatters and silly clothes. He wore oversized shoes that looked like the wide ends of an oar. His face was painted in shades of green and blue, and his nose was round and large. Two large solid red circles adorned his cheeks. His lips were painted white. Tiny stars twinkled on his cheeks and around his eyes. A fluffy wig in hues of green, red and yellow adorned his head.

"I am Archernar," the stranger introduced himself. The clown pointed at Xalex hiding inside the dune buggy and roared with laughter. "You need not be afraid of me, my children. I am here to rescue you from the cruelty of your world and from the abuse and molestation of grownups. Fear me not! I am here to protect you."

"You are Archernar, the clown who loves children?" Xivana stammered.

"In bones and in flesh," the clown answered. He opened up his arms to the children. Xivana hesitated for a short moment and then ran into Archernar's arms. The clown hugged her and patted her back.

"Oh, I am so glad we found you, Archernar," she sobbed. "I was beginning to doubt that you ever existed." Xivana wiped off her tears of joys and looked towards his brother in the dune buggy. "Come out and meet Archernar," she called out to Xalex.

Xalex opened the door and cautiously stepped down from the vehicle. He had never seen a clown before. His grandfather once told him that clowns lived in America before the nuclear war. They entertained children in eating establishments that they referred to as hamburger joints. He had often heard his grandma called his grandpa a junk-food lover, but he had never seen or tasted junks food. Archernar beckoned Xalex to join him.

"Are you the Carlsbad monster?" Xalex timidly asked the clown.

Archernar laughed. The clown suddenly looked grave and stepped back from the two children. He bent his knees and curled his body forward. He spread his fingers out so that they appeared like the claws of an animal, swung his body to and fro, and moved clumsily towards a ponderosa pine. Then he opened his mouth and roared. He stretched, jammed, hopped and tore at the pine needles with his teeth. Xalex exploded into a fit of laughter. "You look like a dinosaur," he said to the clown. Archernar wiped the pine needles from his face, straightened up, spread and flapped his arms. He ran round and round, flapping his arms and jumping into the air. The children crowed with delight as the clown jumped up and fell down back to earth. "He is trying to fly," Xalex said, chuckling at the clown's silly antics. They roared with laughter at the clown's back flips, tumbles and swoops. Archernar then turned towards them, stooped down, and pointed the two index fingers of his hands in front of his head to simulate a pair of horns. His feet slowly scratched the ground back and forth, back and forth. "He is pretending to be a Texas longhorn," Xalex remarked. Without warning the clown charged at them, first at Xivana, then at Xalex. They giggled and howled each time the clown charged at them. When his fingers grazed the children's back, they shrieked and ran faster to escape the longhorn. Xalex dropped and rolled on the ground, chortling and cackling. Archernar butted him with his head. He tickled Xalex until he became short of breath and stopped laughing. The clown stopped tickling him and dropped to the ground. He lied on his back and waited for the children to catch their breath.

"Come with me to the caves," he motioned to the children. "You must be hungry after your journey."

He rose up and took the two children by their hands. Xivana stiffened up when the clown took her hand.

"A group of people just killed a man," she said. "Why was the man killed, and who are the people who killed him?"

"The man who was killed is a hamburglar," Archernar explained. "The guards merely intended to catch him and bring him back inside the cave. They did not intend to kill him, but he ran away. He was punished for his act. There is nothing to be afraid of. The guards will not harm you. They are in the caves solely to protect other children."

"There are guards who watch over children in the caves?" Xivana asked, perplexed.

"We have laws in our underground city to protect children. The guards were only enforcing the laws."

"What is a hamburglar?" Xalex asked.

"Someone who steals hamburgers from children," Archernar replied. "It is a misdemeanor in our underground city for grownups to steal hamburgers from the children."

"Do you really serve hamburgers made with fresh beef in the caves?" Xalex asked, his eyes shining with delight.

"Yes," Archernar replied. "We serve them on a fresh sesame bun with fresh lettuce and tomatoes, pickles and onions. We cover the hamburger with a slice of fresh Cheddar cheese too. We also coat the inside of the bun with tomato sauce and mustard. We make them just like they used to make them before the nuclear war."

"Wow," Xalex exclaimed.

"I have heard that the inhabitants of the caves raise Texas longhorns too. Is it true?"

"We have a few Texas longhorns in the caves," Archernar replied. "Come with me and you will discover for yourselves all the wonders inside the caves." In their excitement the children forgot about their fears, the Mescalero Apache's warning, and the dying man's last words. Archernar took them by their hands and lead them down the steps to the cave entrance. Xivana looked around her for Gorgonio.

"Where is Gorgonio?" She asked while searching the thick bushes.

"He ran away when the clown appeared," Xalex explained.

Hidden behind the thick bush, Gorgonio watched with a sad heart as the clown led the two children to the caves.

The TV cameras hidden inside the walls of the caves relayed their presence to the security crew working at the caves' command center. The steel door sealing the entrance to the cave clicked open and they stepped into an airtight chamber. The airtight door immediately swung shut behind them to seal it tight. They walked up to an inner airlock door at the other end of the airtight chamber. It swung open to allow them to enter the caves and instantly closed shut when they had cleared the steel frame. Archernar directed the two children to step over a soil-bed reactor just outside the airlock chamber. He pressed a button on the wall. A fan roared to life and sucked the air around their feet. The two children felt the cold air swirling around their legs.

"What is it?" Xivana asked Archernar.

"It's a machine for sucking up the dirty air that we are carrying into the caves. The air is cleaned before it is released back into the cave atmosphere. The microbes in the soil absorb any life-threatening elements from the dirty air." Xalex looked at his feet and stepped out of the soil. "Don't be afraid," Archernar said, holding him back. "The microbes won't eat you up. Clean air is essential to our survival in the caves." A few seconds later the fan came to a stop. They stepped out of the soil-bed reactor and descended into the caves. Dozens of TV monitors and electronic sensors lined the walls. Some TV monitors showed graphs and numbers. Others showed people walking around the caves, wading in rice paddies, or harvesting fruits and vegetables. The electronic monitors and the numbers on the TV screens aroused the children's curiosities.

"What are these things on the wall?" Xalex asked, pointing to a sensor on the wall.

"It's an oxygen sensor," Archernar explained. "The sensors closely monitor our environment and help us keep our life-support system in balance. There are hundreds of them located in strategic places around the caves. They measure oxygen and carbon dioxide levels as well as the temperature and humidity. The numbers you see on the screens tell us how healthy our environment is. The sensors warn us if the levels are too high or too low. They prompt the technicians working in the analytical laboratory to make the necessary corrections. Without the sensors the atmosphere inside the cave could suddenly deteriorate and jeopardize our health."

They reached a long corridor that descended steeply into the caves. On the left side of the corridor was a heavy glass door. The children pressed their faces onto the glass to peek inside.

"It's all peaceful in the bat cave," Archernar told them. "The bats sleep during the day, but in the evening they leave the cave to hunt for foods. There used to be a million bats in the caves," Archernar said. "The population had been reduced to less than a quarter of a million. We control their coming and going and we keep them confined in the bat caves for our own safety."

"A quarter of a million bats," Xivana repeated. Archernar took their hands and steered them down the corridor.

"They produce some of the fertilizers we use to grow vegetables," Archernar explained. "Bat dung, which we call guano, is a very rich natural fertilizer."

"Why did the bat population decline?" Xivana asked.

"That was a long time ago. In a moment, you will see the children's playground."

They rode an elevator to the bottom of the cave. When the elevator came to a stop, they climbed into a small vehicle resembling a golf cart to continue their journey to the Big Room. They drove through the Temple of the Sun and past the Totem Poles. The children marveled at the walls of delicate aragonite crystals, ridges of flowstone deposits, columns of massive stalactites and stalagmites, and jutting rock formations. They were stunned by the enormous variety of structures and shapes in the caves. They were overwhelmed by the wonderland of delicate sculptures looking like waterfalls, curtains, organ pipes and gigantic columns. When the cart arrived in the Big Room, they found dozens of children playing around under its 255ft ceiling.

"This is the children's playground," Archernar said, as he stepped out of the cave vehicle. "We are 700ft below ground."

"There is a children's playground inside the cave!" Xivana exclaimed. Archernar nodded and pointed at the children around him.

The playground was filled with the laughter of the small children. Young girls jumped ropes, toddlers played in sandboxes and boys swung on trapeze bars. Children slid down a slide, spun around on a merry-go-round, climbed on a jungle gym, or balanced on a seesaw. The cathedral-like room echoed with the laughter and chatter of the children.

"The playground is part of the children's quarters," Archernar said. "This is where the children play, eat and sleep. It has its own little restaurant where the children can request food at any time of the day."

"Can they have hamburgers at any time of the day?" Xalex asked.

"The children are well taken care of in our underground city," Archernar replied. He pointed to a two-story structure along the walls of the Big Room. "They have their own individual room. The rooms have individual showers and toilets, a comfortable bed, books and all sorts of games." Archernar lead them to a picnic table in the playground. "You two must be very tired and very hungry," he said. "If you would sit down and wait for me I will bring you back something to eat."

"Can we go play?" Xalex asked.

"Yes, you can. You will enjoy the food even more after playing."

Xalex leaped over a row of sandboxes and vaulted into a swing. He swung back and forth forcefully and tried to touch the cathedral ceilings with his toes. When the swing came to a stop, he somersaulted onto a platform and glided down a serpentine chute. He then ran to a rope hanging down from the tall ceiling. He wriggled and twisted his way up the dangling rope. After climbing about 10ft he loosened his grip and let himself slide down. When his feet touched the sand below him he released the rope, blew on his hands and rubbed them together. A spare tire at the other end of the playground caught his attention. He ran towards the tire and climbed inside the center. He set the tire into motion by leaning across it and letting it run in a circle. Then he raised his feet up and let the tire swing back to its original resting position. When the tire stopped spinning, he ran to a seesaw and sat at one end. Xivana sat on the other end and they jolted each other up and down in the air until their faces were red from laughing. Xalex quickly dismounted from the seesaw when his feet touched the ground again, sending his sister reeling on her back. He laughed at her as she rolled in the sand. Xivana chased him to a domed jungle gym. When she started to climb up behind him, he hopped his way onto a trapeze bar.

"Be careful," Xivana shouted as he struggled to maintain his grip on the bar. His legs kicked the air in front of him as he advanced along the bar. Suddenly his hands lost their grip on the horizontal bars and he fell to the ground. Xivana hurried down the jungle gym and went to help his brother.

"I am fine," Xalex said, brushing the sand off his knees. A girl standing by a swing caught Xalex's attention. The smell of the food she ate wet their appetite and they walked over to the girl. Their eyes remained fixed on her hands.

"What are you eating?" Xalex asked.

"A cheeseburger," the little girl answered. "You are dumb."

"A cheeseburger," Xalex exclaimed. He heard the word 'cheeseburger' for the first time in his life. "Archernar said that the children are fed hamburgers in the caves. What is a cheeseburger?"

"Just a hamburger with cheese on it," the girl replied. "That's why it is called a cheeseburger. You are very stupid. Where do you come from?"

"We ran away from Lubbock," Xivana replied. "Is the cheeseburger made with fresh beef?"

"What is fresh beef?" the puzzled girl asked. "The cook makes the hamburger with ground beef. I don't know of any other kind."

"Did you run away from home too?" Xalex asked.

"No, I did not. I have lived in the caves all my life." Xivana noticed that the girl's skin was pale. She pondered that she was a cave dweller. Just then Archernar walked back to the playground with a tray laden with foods. He put the tray on a picnic table and hollered at the children to join him. They rushed over to the table and stopped to stare at the foods on the tray.

"What are these?" Xivana asked the clown.

"Freshly-made hamburgers," the clown replied.

Xivana stared at a plate full of French fries next to a cheeseburger. Archernar took the plate from the tray and laid it in front of her.

"Sit down, my children," he beckoned. "Enjoy a cheeseburger with French fries and a thick strawberry milkshake."

"French fries...?" Xalex asked. "What are French Fries?"

"Fried potato sticks. We deep-fried them in pure corn oil until they are golden brown and crisp. We used only Idaho potatoes that are organically grown in our own farmland in the caves." Xivana and Xalex sat down at the table. Xivana took a small bundle of the potato sticks and put them into her mouth."

"They taste better with tomato ketchup," Archernar said, pushing a little cup filled with a red sauce towards Xivana. He took a potato stick and dipped it in the red sauce. "Like this," he said, putting the potato stick into his mouth. Xivana dipped a potato stick in the ketchup and put it in her mouth.

"Ummh... I have never had anything that tastes so good," she said as she chewed on the fried potato. Xalex took a cheeseburger from his tray and slowly lifted the bun to his mouth. He stopped and stared at the green pickled slice hanging on its side. He removed the top bun and pulled out the slice of pickles from underneath the beef patty and held it in front of his eyes.

"That's pickled cucumber," Archernar said. "We put pickles and onions on every cheeseburger that we make in the caves. We grow our own cucumbers and onions in the caves too."

Xalex put the slice of pickles into his mouth. "It tastes very good," he said. They took their glasses and stared at the pink and thick liquid in them. "The milkshakes are made with goat milk and fresh ice cream," Archernar said. "The strawberries are hand-picked in the farmland every morning,"

Xalex put the half empty glass of milkshake down in front of him. His lips were covered with the milk foam. "How do you grow potatoes inside the caves?" he asked.

"And how can you survive in the caves for so long?" Xivana questioned.

"Our underground city is like a giant airtight greenhouse," Archernar explained. "In this greenhouse there is a number of living things which works together to keep us alive. The plants, animals, bacteria, microbes, water and even the soil interact with one another to create the food and oxygen necessary to sustain life. The plants and the animals play an important part in maintaining the balance of life inside the caves. They work day and night so that we may live. The ants, for example, break apart dead plants to eat them. When they do that, they recycle precious nutrients back to the soil and make room for new plants to grow again. Dead plants and animals are constantly being recycled. Animals release doses of carbon dioxide when they exert themselves. The plants then absorb the buildup of carbon dioxide and release oxygen back into the atmosphere. Everything in the caves is used up. Old elements are absorbed and changed into new elements without going to waste. This steady cycle of change keeps everything in balance and forms the basis for our life-support system."

"But where are the plants and the animals?" Xalex asked. "I only see children in the caves."

"That's because you are inside the human habitat. The caves are divided into several zones and the human habitat is just one of them. There are other villages inside the caves where people live and sleep. The plants and the animals are located deep down inside the caves where their environments are constantly being monitored. Tomorrow I will show you the animals and the plants, but now I will take you both to Dr. Yucca's office. Dr. Yucca is in charge of monitoring the health of the colony. He will give both of you a medical check."

Archernar stood up and took the two children by their hands. They crossed the playground and walked to the row of apartments on the other side. They entered the medical clinic located at the far end of the complex. A nurse in her fifties welcomed them.

"You must be new residents," the nurse said. She extended her arms to them. "Welcome." Xivana and Xalex rushed to her and cuddled up against her. "Did you eat lunch?" the nurse asked them.

"Yes," Xalex replied. "We had a cheeseburger, French fries and a strawberry milkshake."

"Good," the nurse said, smiling. "Dr. Yucca will see you in a moment. She took them into Dr. Yucca's office. Xivana looked over her shoulder at Archernar. The clown smiled at her to reassure her.

"I'll be in the waiting room," he reassured her.

Dr. Yucca gave the two children a routine health check. He weighed the children, checked their pulse rates and blood pressures, and measured their body temperatures. He examined their eyes, ears and throats. He checked their reflexes and took urine and blood samples for chemical tests. Thirty minutes later, Dr. Yucca returned to the waiting room with the two children.

"They are as fit as a fiddle," Dr. Yucca said. "They are somewhat skinny for their ages."

"That's not a problem," Archernar quickly said. "They will soon gain weight on a steady diet of cheeseburgers and French fries."

The nurse came back and gave them each a chocolate-covered candy apple. She then hugged and kissed them goodbye. Archernar thanked Dr. Yucca and lead the children out of the medical clinic.

"The President had been informed of your arrival," Archernar said as he walked up to the cave vehicle. "Although he is very busy dealing with matters of utmost importance, he wishes to personally welcome you to our underground city."

"There is a President living in the caves?" Xivana asked, astonished.

"Does he rule the people in this caves?"

"Yes. The President is always worried for the children. Our very complex underground society demands a lot from him and he is always over-extending himself." Archernar traveled to the King's Palace where the President awaited the children to welcome them. Two boy soldiers with their AK47 riffles strapped over their shoulders stood guard at the palace. They saluted Archernar and the children and then opened the door to let them into the King's Palace. The room was filled with beautiful crystal formation. The President sat on a chair surrounded by his captains and superintendents. He stood up to welcome Xivana and Xalex.

"So, you are the two children who ran away from Lubbock," he said, pointing the children to a row of empty chairs placed in a semi-circle in the room. The new arrivals went and sat down on the chairs. "Did Washington, D.C survive the nuclear war?" the President asked.

"No, Mr. President," Xivana sadly replied. "The Capitol had been reduced to rubbles of concrete and steel. Millions of people were killed by the nuclear blasts and by the radiation fallout. The nuclear war had caused enormous destruction and economic disruption in North America."

"That's what I was afraid of," the President said, "War is such a terrible thing, but I am glad that we played no part in the destruction of our fatherland." The captains nodded their approvals. "Our forefathers used to talk a lot about the Land-O-Lakes. Is it as beautiful as they describe it?"

"The Land-O-lakes is now called the Land-O-Ice, Mr. President."

"Of course, North America must now be a frigid land. Did the Land of Lincoln escape the nuclear bombs?"

"No, Mr. President. The Land of Lincoln is now being remembered as the Land that Time Forgot."

"This is unfortunate but please rest assured. You will both be safe in our land."

"It certainly looks like a very safe place. What do you call this place?"

"The Land of the Big Mac," The President replied with a grin. "I am sure the Native Americans have a new name for the devastated North American continent, don't you think?"

"They do," Archernar replied. "They now call it the Land of the Giant Mushroom Clouds."

"That's appropriate. Did the children eat lunch yet?"

"Yes, Mr. President."

"We had a cheeseburger, French fries and a strawberry milkshake for lunch," Xalex said.

"Was the beef patty cooked to our rigid specifications and was the hamburger made according to our unique recipe?"

"I personally checked the food myself before taking them to the children."

"The beef was fresh and juicy," Xalex said.

"I am glad to hear it," The President said, smiling.

"We've eaten nothing like it before," Xivana said. "All we ever ate in Lubbock was irradiated meat. The new Congress had outlawed hamburgers in North America. All Hamburgerologists had gone underground to escape persecution. Some of them are being incarcerated on Alcatraz and forced to grow broccoli and spinach."

"The children said that the guards torment the Hamburgerologists by ramming the dark green sprouts and leaves down their throats," Archernar added.

"That is a terrible punishment, to be forced-fed broccoli and spinach! How about the French fries? Did the chef use pure corn oil to fry them in?"

Archernar nodded. "He did," he replied. The President smiled at Xivana.

"I think that they will make good citizens," the President remarked. "Remember, my children, that in the Land of the Big Mac, the children do not spell potato with an 'e.'"

"And in our world," Archernar added, "the children do not go past to the back; they go forward to tomorrow."

"It's only the politicians who go past to the back!" the President said, bursting into a loud laughter.

"Dr. Yucca gave them both a good bill of health," Archernar informed the President. "They do not show any sign of infections nor do they carry any disease that will jeopardize the health of the colony."

"Good," the President said. He turned to Xivana. "Did you run away from the ugliness and ravages of the nuclear war? Or did you run away from home because of something else?"

"I was afraid for our safety, Mr. President," Xivana answered. "There was no one we could trust anymore. The children in North America are forever subjected to physical and sexual abuse. We feared that the same people we turned to for guidance would molest us. These people shield themselves behind God and the church to perform perfidious acts on children. They claim to protect us, but instead take advantage of our weaknesses to molest us. They dress in frocks to appear saintly and to hide their devious minds and behavior. Thousands of children suffered rape, molestation and other abuse by priest in their parishes"

"And in boarding schools and orphanages," Xalex added.

"I was afraid that this might be the case. No grownup will harm you in our underground city." The President turned back to Archernar. "Please take the children for a grand tour of our great underground city tomorrow."

"Yes, Mr. President."

"Archernar will take good care of you," the President assured the children, getting up from his chair. "Are there any questions you would like to ask me?"

197

"Where are all the men and women?" Xivana asked.

She looked at the President's Aids around her. They all looked very young.

"The men and women live in other villages spread out in the caves," the President replied. "When you tour the caves tomorrow, you will see them working in the farmland and in the wilderness zones." The President waved them off. Archernar signaled to them that it was time to leave.

"Archernar," the President called.

"Yes, Mr. President." Archernar replied.

"Before you go, could you please make us laugh? The subject of the nuclear war in North America has made us all sad."

Archernar bowed to the President's wish. The clown performed Act #37, imitating a White House official grinning with pleasure as he listened to a private conversation behind a closed door. The President and his captains burst into a strident laughter. Then the clown performed Act #38, mimicking a White House official knocking his head on the door frame of an airplane. He tumbled and fell head over heel down the steps. Two of the captains fell to the ground, giggling and clutching their stomachs. Next, the clown performed Act #39, impersonating a White House official sowing the seeds of human rights, but reaping peanuts instead. The President fell back on a chair, squawking with merriment. In Act #40, Archernar pretended to be a White House official falling asleep in the VIP stand. He tipped over and fell over spectators below. Xivana and Xalex rolled to the ground, chuckling and kicking. When Archernar performed Act #42, portraying a White House official sitting at his desk with a female White House employee under his desk, the children rolled on their sides. They clutched their bellies and exploded with laughter. In Act #43, the White House Official picked up some spinach from a wheelbarrow and ate them. He immediately threw up the spinach and pretended to be sick, but no one laughed. The President and his captains had fallen asleep on the floor. In their sleep, the boy President and his captains looked like little angels. Archernar lifted The President into his arms and placed him on his bed. He then carried the other captains one by one to the Papoose Room and gently put them in their beds. She returned to the King's Palace and carried Xivana and Xalex to the cave vehicle. The boy soldiers stood to attention as he drove them back to the Children's Village in the Big Room. When he arrived at their apartment, they were deeply asleep in the cave vehicle. Archernar gently carried them to their room and laid them down on their beds. He covered them with a blanket, closed the door, and withdrew to the Queen's Chamber.

Four hours later, the two children woke up and found two trays of food on a table. In each of the trays they found freshly baked bread and a bowl of bean soup. A larger bowl contained a fresh garden salad with diced tomatoes and cucumbers. Their main meals consisted of grilled salmon fillets smothered with a lemon pepper sauce with baked potatoes topped with sour cream and parsley and stir-fried vegetables. A medley of fruit salads served as dessert. They feasted on the succulent foods and finished off the meals with the fruit salads. After eating their dinner they inspected their apartment. They found in one corner of the room an ultra clean bathroom complete with a toilet and a shower tub. An aerator sat by the toilet bowl. Next to the bathroom sink they found two bags, each containing a toothbrush, toothpaste, towels, some chocolate bars and a flashlight. Bath towels and clean clothes hung in the bathroom for their use. They fought over who would take a bath first. Xivana gave up the fight and let Xalex take his bath first. After bathing they went outside the apartment. The playground was deserted and the lights were dimmed out. The children were asleep in their own rooms. They walked around the playground for a short while and then returned to the apartment. A pair of moths flew around the light under the porch. They heard the faint sound of cicadas chirping and frogs croaking. Back in their room they browsed through some books left by their bedsides. Shortly afterwards they dozed off and fell asleep again. They woke up the next day to find that someone had brought in their breakfasts while they were asleep. Their breakfast consisted of wheat porridge mixed with slices of watermelons and bananas, toasts spread with peach jam, and fresh orange juice. Xivana drew open the curtain and saw that the playground was already filled with children. They quickly ate their breakfast and ran out to join them.

The President conducted official business away in the Slaughter Canyon cave. It was connected to the Carlsbad cavern by an eight-mile long subterranean tunnel. He met with his captains once a week in the Monarch Room to discuss problems that had surfaced in their closed environment. During the weekly meeting, the captains and the superintendents overseeing their respective areas briefed him on the situation in the caves. Archernar was the President's personal advisor and was present for the meeting. The meeting started off with the children playing with their toys. Archernar brought into the Monarch Room several boxes full of plastic toys - revolvers, machine guns, airplanes, tanks and battleships. The children divided into two opposing groups and played war games. They turned the tables and chairs on their sides to hide behind them and take shot at each other. Soon, the Monarch Room was filled with the rattling of the toy guns. The children feigned being hit by the bullets and dropped on the ground clutching imaginary wounds. The President picked up two airplanes, each about a foot long, and circled the planes above his head. He accompanied the gestures with sounds of "boom bang." A boy fired his machine gun at the planes. "Rat ta ta ta, rat ta ta ta," the gun rattled. The President climbed on a chair and shouted: "Boom, bang, boom." The boy threw his gun into the air and pretended that the bombs hit him. One by one the children fell down on the ground and feigned that they were dead. The war game ended with the President standing up on a table and proclaiming victory. Archernar went around the room and picked up the toys. He put them back into their boxes and returned the boxes to the closet. The children slowly rose up from playing dead and rearranged the chairs around the table. They sat down to begin their briefing.

Seven captains and four superintendents were present in the Monarch Room to brief the President. Captains San Isidro, San Antonio, San Saba and San Elizario managed the farmland, the barnyard, the marine ecosystems and the terrestrial ecosystems respectively. The waste recycling systems were under the management of Captain San Pedro, whereas the tissue cultures laboratory was under the supervision of captain San Angelo. Captain San Benito managed the technical systems as well as the computer and communications systems. Captains San Marcos and San Patricio were the food production superintendent and the Human Resources superintendent respectively. Superintendent San Jacinto looked after the colony's energy need while the welfare and health of the cave inhabitants were monitored closely by Superintendent San Diego.

"I won the war again," the President jubilantly announced.

"I shot both your planes down this time," captain San Marcos said joyfully. "I blew them off the sky."

"My bombers dropped 20 megaton of TNT over you guys," the President protested. "None of you could have survived that. Well, maybe I'll get a faster and bigger plane next time to match your bigger guns. Archernar, could you have two new planes built for me? Have them loaded with ICBM missiles fitted with nuclear warheads."

"Yes, Mr. President."

"Your clowning yesterday was very entertaining, but you missed Act #41. Why?"

"Mr. President, the baseball bat that I used to perform Act #41 had finally broken into two pieces. I did not have another one that I could use to punish the drug dealer from Central America."

The President and his captains roared with laughter. "Have mercy on the General," the President said. When they stopped laughing, the President looked around the table and said: "Who wants to start this morning?" There was silence in the room. The President stared at Captain San Patricio. "How about going first today, Captain San Patricio? Give us an update on the colony's population."

Captain San Patricio cleared his voice. "In the last month, the size of the colony has gone from 189 inhabitants to 205," he solemnly said. "We had rescued from the outside world thirty-three children. At the same time we have lost fourteen men and three women. A group of twenty-six prisoners attempted to escape from Spider cave through a secret passageway. We captured and brought back alive nine of them. Six of them got away. The rest were killed by the guards."

"The guards had killed eleven more men and women since our last meeting, is that right?" the President asked.

"It was necessary, Mr. President."

"What is the effect of this loss of lives on the Colony's survival?"

"The eleven men and women lost were previously assigned to the machine room and the workshop. Other prisoners were shuffled around to pick up the slack in these departments. Obviously this will impact greatly on the equipment repair turnaround time, which in turn would affect food production. As of last month the colony was made up of thirty-six male prisoners, fifty-three female prisoners and one hundred and sixteen children. Of the thirty-three runaway children that arrived last month, seventeen are males. All the boys are strong and healthy. In a few years they can begin their apprenticeship in the various shops. The girls are still weak and sickly. I haven't decided how we will utilize them yet. As it stands now, before Archernar brought in Xivana and Xalex, the children population is divided into sixty-six girls and fifty boys. The elite Presidential guard is now composed of thirty-five boys and ten girls. This leaves a civilian population of seventy-one children. Five of the civilian girls are expecting. The earliest delivery is scheduled for next month. Dr. Yucca confirmed that all the five pregnancies are advancing normally and the expectant mothers are in good health."

"What is the breakdown of our labor force?"

Captain San Patricio shuffled through some papers in front of him. "The working force now stands at eighty-nine prisoners. No children are currently assigned to hard labor. Our biggest labor pool is concentrated in the farmland, the waste recycling system and the technical systems. We expect to harvest an abundant rice crop this summer. Consequently I have allocated thirty prisoners to work on the farmland. Our machines are very old and are prone to frequent breakdowns. Fifteen technicians and maintenance workers are rotated around the clock to care for the equipments. The Savannah is now dormant and does not need constant attention. All in all I have fifteen men and women rotating between the desert, the Savannah, the rainforest, the marsh, and the ocean ecosystems."

The President nodded his head in approval. "What is new with the ocean ecosystems?" he asked, looking at Captain San Saba.

"The outbreak of fire worms in the ocean ecosystems is now under control, Mr. President," Captain San Saba answered. "It took a major effort from every one of us, including the children, to remove the prickly worms from the ocean. The coral reefs are healthy again. The mammoth operation yielded several hundred pounds of worms which were fed to the chicken."

"Let's give Captain San Saba a hand for his efforts," the President said, clapping his hands. The other captains clapped their hands and congratulated Captain San Saba for his success in controlling the outbreak of fire worms.

"The mechanical algae scrubbers," Captain San Saba continued, "had to be cleaned more often because the snail population was almost decimated by the Spanish lobsters. With fewer snails around to graze on the algae, the algae accumulated and created an imbalance in the ocean environment. We have now reduced the lobster population in the ocean. The nutrients in the ocean were thoroughly analyzed. The results indicated that the ocean is much healthier now. The level of nutrients and organic sediment in the marshes are very high. Consequently we are having an unusually large population of oysters, mussels and clams. The ocean ecosystems are as healthy as they can get."

"Good," the President said. He looked at Captain San Elizario. "Anything new to report on the terrestrial ecosystems?" he asked the captain.

"After two years of poor yield, the banana trees are expected to yield a bountiful harvest," Captain San Elizario gleefully announced. "We also expect to harvest large crops of mangoes and papayas. The rainforest is swarming with new life. The frogs, the earthworms and the snakes are all showing signs of good health. The insectaries are buzzing with millions of new insects."

"Is there anything else?"

"The rainforest is blooming with orchids and bromeliads. In the Savannah the termites have been very active tearing up the old grass. The humidity level in the desert is somewhat higher than normal, but the desert plants are highly adaptable. In about two weeks the eastern part of the desert ecosystems will receive its first rain. The yellow-footed tortoises have been laying and burying large quantities of eggs. All the signs indicate that the terrestrial ecosystems are in good health."

"Good work, Captain San Elizario. Captain San Benito, how are the equipments holding up?"

"Not very good, Mr. President," Captain San Benito replied, shaking his head. "The equipments have been in use for a very long time. One hundred seventy of the original 300 pumps are no longer usable. They have been repaired time and time again and are now mainly used for parts. Of the 125 air handlers, only 60 are operating around the clock. The others are in the shop waiting for repair. The composting machines are no longer adequate for the amount of waste the ecosystems are generating. We need new composting machines, but the machine shop cannot make them fast enough. The nutrient skimmers are constantly breaking down. To maintain a clean and healthy ocean for the marine life to thrive we will need to have all the 150 nutrient skimmers and algae-scrubbers running twenty-four hours a day, seven days a week. Right now the scrubbers are operating below sixty percent capacity. We have detected very small amounts of bacteria in the condensation chambers. The bacteria were contaminating our drinking water. So far we haven't had any major problems with the wave-generators. They've been faithfully making waves in the ocean. The diving equipments are still usable, but we are running dangerously low on lubricants. Our computers are old and slow. If we had faster computers we could respond to problems quicker. We are also running out of disk storage space. Two hundred gigabytes of new computer data are generated each day. At this rate we will need to acquire new computers soon."

"The colony's Founding Fathers were adamant that total self-reliance in the caves will be the rule," the President said. "We have to make do with what we've got. Archernar, what do you think?"

"We have already broken all the rules written by the Founding Fathers, Mr. President," Archernar replied. "We raided the grocery stores and the kitchen of private homes in White City and Carlsbad when we had a food shortage. We invaded government warehouses in Albuquerque when we needed critical parts for our machines. We defied the Founding Fathers' orders when we stole Texas Longhorns from neighboring ranchers. We brought them inside the caves so that we can have hamburgers for lunch which were forbidden by the Founding Fathers. We sent a secret team to Seattle to steal 100 copies of the latest version of the Windows Operating System. We sneaked into a large computer manufacturing facility in Austin and brought back 100 new Pentium servers. We are now bringing into the caves children from the outside world to boost up our manpower. I think that our mission has failed. We can no longer be self-sufficient and sustain the colony in the years to come. Sooner or later we will have to admit defeat, leave the caves, and join the outside world."

"Archernar, did you forget that the recent nuclear war had devastated most of the North American continent?" the President sternly reminded the clown. "Our tightly sealed colony escaped the deadly radiation from the nuclear bombs. What will we expect to find in the nuclear wasteland outside if we were to abandon the caves now?"

"I am afraid that we will not find much," Archernar admitted. "We have reached the end of our journey and we can no longer remain isolated. We can all perish here or start a new life outside. What will happen to the children when all the prisoners escape, die of old age, or are murdered by the Presidential guards? The children do not have the technical skills needed to carry on the legacy of the Founding Fathers. Without the solid infrastructure of men, machines, plants and animals, the marine and terrestrial ecosystems will not flourish. The plants will wither and die. The animals will starve to death. What will the children eat when food production come to a complete stop?"

"Let me remind you that since I became President, the children had all been well fed and well taken care of," the President said. "I re-introduced the beloved hamburger to the children's diet after it was banned by the Founding Fathers. Don't anyone in this room forget how the grownups treated the children before the revolution. The children were mistreated, abused and molested by the men. If anyone wants to know how bad it was then, let him take a long walk around the Boneyard. It's full of the bones of the small children who were slaughtered by the colonists during the Great Famine. How can anyone in this room ever forgive the colonists for resorting to cannibalism in order to stay alive?"

The captains and the superintendents nodded in approval. "Long live the revolution," Captain San Pedro said.

"Long live Ultraviolet," Captain San Angelo said.

"You stopped the madness and saved the children," Archernar pointed out, "but let us not repeat the mistakes of the Founding Fathers. We should come to reason and plan for evacuating the caves now. We should abandon the caves and save the rest of our people. Many years ago, 500 colonists moved into this cave. More than 350 of them perished during the early years of their struggles. Please let's take the rest of our people out and end this madness."

"The colony will stay underground," the President strongly affirmed.

"Mr. President, I urge you..."

"That's enough, Archernar," the President interrupted the clown. "Captain San Isidro, do you have anything new to report on the farmland?"

"We have added five new garden plots to the farmland," captain San Isidro answered. "We can now rotate three crops on each of the 100 garden plots on the farmland. The rice seedlings were meticulously examined for nematodes and other water-borne bacteria, but none were found. Earlier in the month the oxygen level around the farmland suddenly dropped down to 14.89% and remained low for 23 days. The farm workers complained of dizziness and had to be evacuated. A few workers required hospitalization. Food production waned as a result of the low oxygen level and the interruption in the work flow."

"Why was the oxygen level drop not caught in time and rectified immediately?" the President asked.

"The oxygen sensors around the farmland are in need of repair," Captain San Angelo quickly said. "I suspect that the farm workers sabotaged the sensors."

"Have all the oxygen sensors checked and replaced immediately," the President ordered. "Find out who are behind the sabotage and have their food ration cut in half. Captain San Angelo, dispatch a team to the farmland to investigate the drop in oxygen level."

"Yes, Mr. President," Captain San Angelo replied. "I suspect that the soil in the farmland may be responsible for the low level of oxygen. The high concentration of organic material is probably absorbing the oxygen from the atmosphere."

"Have a random sample of the crops analyzed to check for their carbon and oxygen ratio. Is it possible that the oxygen is being trapped by the concrete walls that were recently erected in the farmland?"

"It's possible. I'll have a piece of concrete from the wall analyzed for oxygen content immediately."

"Captain San Pedro, has the problem with holding tank #16 resolved yet?"

"No, Mr. President, but we are working on it."

"What's holding up the work on the tank?"

"I don't have enough people to work on it full-time. The 3,000-gallon tank has to be emptied, removed and carried to the workshop. Six of the Prisoners who work in the repair workshop were killed."

"I know that," the President snapped. "Could you run a bypass line from holding tank #15 to holding tank #17?"

"We can try doing that but overflowing might occur. The farmland is directly in the path of the sewer line and the waste overflow may contaminate the soil."

The President sighed. He looked at Captain San Antonio. "Do you have any good news from the barnyard, Captain San Antonio?"

"As a matter of fact, I do," Captain San Antonio gleefully replied. "I am pleased to announce that two calves were born to the herd of Texas Longhorns this morning. We now have a cattle head count of 13."

"Hurrah," the President cheered. "Let's all have a double cheeseburger for lunch today. Archernar, will you please see to it that the double cheeseburgers are delivered to the Green Lake Room?"

"Yes, Mr. President."

"Instead of milkshakes, let's have rice beer and pear wine. This calls for a real celebration."

The other captains and superintendents cheered the President's decision and banged on the tables to express their approvals. "We want a jumbo order of French Fries too," they screamed at the clown.

"I'll see to it that you get them," Archernar promised.

"Where were we?" the President asked. "Is there anything else going on in the barnyard?"

Captain San Antonio hesitated. "We lost over a thousand chickens to the Avian Influenza," he dejectedly announced. "The virus was discovered in the cells of the infected chicken last week."

"I thought only the pigs were infected by this particular virulent strain," the President said. "Did we not kill all the infected pigs last year?"

"Yes, we did, Mr. President. The chicken and the pigs live in close proximity to each other. It is quite possible that the chicken were infected by the pigs."

"Superintendent San Diego, give us a quick medical report on the health of the colony."

"The overall health of the population is excellent, Mr. President. Everyone's cholesterol level is extraordinarily low as a result of eating fresh and uncontaminated foods, breathing a biologically cleansed air and drinking pure spring water. Blood pressures among the population are very low, but the lack of fluoride in the spring water has accelerated the tooth decay process in some children. Dr. Yucca reported an increase in the number of cavities found in the children's teeth. Up to now no harmful gases from the outside world had flowed into the caves. A 13-year-old girl was struck with flu symptoms and was hospitalized. She later died of viral pneumonia. The child suddenly got sick with a unique flu strain called H5N1. There are five other children in the medical clinic who show symptoms of viral illness, but they show no sign of developing influenza. Dr. Yucca randomly tested some of the children and discovered antibodies to the virus in their blood stream. The presence of the antibodies indicated that some children have developed resistance to the virus."

"Did the dead girl contract Avian Influenza from eating the chicken?" Archernar asked.

"I don't know," Superintendent San Diego replied.

"How did the flu virus jumped from sick chicken to humans?"

"I don't know."

"Has the bird flu mixed with human genes? Will it spread from person to person?"

"I don't know. Dr. Yucca prepared the medical report. He is in a better position to answer that question."

"Mr. President, the Avian Influenza is a threat to all of us in the caves. We have no natural immunity to it; an epidemic will wipe the entire colony out. The medical clinic is not equipped to deal for the outbreak of chicken Ebola."

"Archernar, the avian virus only infects birds," the President rigorously asserted. "It cannot be transmitted to humans."

"What else would have caused the girl to die? According to Superintendent San Diego, no harmful gasses flowed into the caves from the outside world. How could the girl die if she only ate uncontaminated foods? I am very concerned that the flu virus will be transmitted to the other children."

"Let's move on," the President snapped. "Superintendent San Jacinto, everybody is nervous about our power source. What can you tell us to enlighten us?"

"Mr. President," Archernar protested, "If the other children had contracted the avian virus it means that no one in the caves is immune to it."

"Carry on Superintendent San Jancinto," the President continued.

"I am afraid I don't have any enlightening news to report, Mr. President," Superintendent San Jacinto said gloomily. "I have grave concerns about the ability of the power plants to function indefinitely. The power plants are old and are prone to frequent breakdowns. Of the 20 gas-powered generators we currently have, only 9 are operating at maximum efficiency. We are also running out of replacement bulbs for the hydroponic lights. All plant and animal life will cease on the day the lights go out in the caves."

"Can't we manufacture the light bulbs in the glass factory?"

"We are out of silica, and there is no known source of silica inside the caves. We cannot extract sufficient argon gas in the enclosed atmosphere for use in the manufacture of light bulbs."

"We'll address this problem on our next meeting," the President said. "Superintendent San Marcos, what was our food production last month?"

"We produced 30,000lb of foods last month, Mr. President. The foods are composed of 4,000lb of fresh meat, 5,000lb of fruits, 9,000lb of vegetables and 12,000lb of grains. The grains consist mostly of beans, wheat and sorghum. The hens laid 100 dozen eggs and the goats produced 500 gallons of milks. Twenty tons of fodder was collected for the domestic animals and forty tons of wastes were converted into compost. The supply of food is adequate for now, but I am afraid that we will not be able to produce enough foods to feed everyone in the months to come. The number of prisoners working the land continues to decline. Since January fifty prisoners escaped or were killed by the guards."

"I know that," the President snapped.

"Well... euhh, the decline in the adult population will affect our ability to produce adequate foods in the near future. We have more children in the caves. "

"The meeting is over," the President abruptly announced, standing up. "You may all leave the Monarch Room except Archernar." The captains and the superintendents gathered their notepads and filed out of the room. Archernar remained seated. The President waited for the last captain to exit, and then faced Archernar.

"Ultraviolet, please listen to me," Archernar implored. "Let's take everybody out before the caves become our tomb."

"This is the third time that you have humiliated me in front of my captains. I have had enough." Ultraviolet walked to a large credenza and opened a drawer. He took out a whip and returned to the table.

"Too many of us had died in these caves," Archernar pleaded. "We must save the rest of our people. We will all die if we don't leave now." Ultraviolet unfurled the whipcord with a jerk of his wrist. His eyes burnt with hate and his hands trembled. He flicked the thong to his side and ferociously flogged Archernar. The clown shrieked with pain and fell on the floor. The whip whistled as it cut through the air and slashed at the clown's back. Archernar covered his head and sobbed.

"Ultraviolet, stop it," he screamed.

"I should send you to the rice paddies and let you work to death," Ultraviolet said. "You deserve no better than die with the other prisoners."

"Please, stop it," Archernar implored.

Ultraviolet threw the thong aside and left the Monarch Room. Archernar broke down and started to sob. A short moment later he wiped the tears off his painted face and stood up. Like a mother picking up after her son's mess, he picked up the whip and put it back in the credenza. He painfully walked to the door and opened it wide. The Presidential guard rushed to his aid as he tottered out of the Monarch Room, but Archernar waved him back. He climbed in the cave vehicle and drove to the Queen's chamber.

Upon entering the Queen's Chamber, Violet removed her hairpiece and dropped down on a chair in front of a mirror. Her long golden hair unfurled and covered her teary eyes. She carefully removed her garb and turned her back to the mirror to examine the whip marks. The pale skin on her back was scarred with long bluish lines. She ran her fingers over the whip marks and sobbed. The tears mixed with the makeup and turned her face into a kaleidoscope of colorful crystals. She wept silently for a few minutes. She suddenly remembered that Xivana and Xalex were waiting for the clown. She wiped her tears and went to the bathroom to wash the colors off her face. She returned and applied fresh makeup on her pale face. Then she put on a goofy shirt and covered her head with a silly hat. The fresh makeup and the clown's attire once again turned Violet into Archernar, the beloved clown.

"Are we going to see the animals today?" Xivana asked when the clown came to meet them in the playground.

Without saying a word, Archernar took Xivana by her hand and walked to a statue of Ultraviolet in the center of the playground. The clown caressed the limestone face of the boy and wiped off the dirt from his forehead.

"He is very young to be President," Xivana remarked.

"Ultraviolet is only thirteen years old," Archernar said. "He led the rebellion against the grownups when they mistreated the children during the Great Famine. He had vowed to protect the children from the grownups and care after them for the rest of his life. He also vowed to give refuge to all the runaway children from the outside world."

"We have eaten so many foods since we arrive. How could you have a famine in the caves?"

"The first colonists were faced with tremendous obstacles during the early years. They struggled against frequent machine failures and low food production. Then a locust plague destroyed all the crops. All the animals became sick and died. In order to stay alive, the colonists ate the bats. During the winter months, the bats left the caves and flew south. Without foods the colonists turned into beasts and fought among themselves for foods."

"What did they eat when the bats left the caves?' Xalex asked.

"They ate their own children," Archernar replied.

Xivana shrieked and covered her mouth. "Gorgonio had told us the truth."

"I told you so." Xalex squeezed her sister's arms.

"Don't be afraid," Archernar assured them. "Ultraviolet and his friends got hold of the weapons cache and took control of the caves. He proclaimed himself President and renamed the colony the Land of the Big Mac."

"Are you sure that no one will eat us? Xalex asked, trembling with fear.

"You are safe with me," Archernar assured him. "No one will harm you."

"Where are we going today?"

"We will descend to 2,000ft below ground," Archernar replied.

"Won't the spirits of the Mescalero Apache warriors become upset at this intrusion?"

"Since the dawn of mankind, humans and spirits have lived together in harmony. We share our water and air with the spirits of the Mescalero warriors. We had fought dozen of wars with Native Americans, but had never engaged their spirits in battle. We are at peace with their spirits. They will not harm us." Archernar took the two children by their hands and led them to the cave vehicle. He drove back into the subterranean tunnel connecting the Carlsbad cave with the Slaughter cave. About half way through the tunnel, he drove into a dark passageway guarded by the Presidential guards. They boarded an elevator built into the solid limestone wall and descended deeper into the caves.

"There are more caves underneath than anybody can ever imagine," Archernar said. "We are going down into what is possibly the largest cave in the world. It has an area covering 650 acres. Inside the cave, you will see the plants and the animals that you have been hearing about."

"But how can you grow anything in the caves?" Xalex asked. "There is no sunlight."

"We use sodium lights to grow the plants. There is an abundant supply of underground spring water and natural gas inside the caves. We use the water and the natural gas to generate electricity which in turn provides the light necessary to support plant life."

The elevator came to a stop and the children walked into a world that they thought never existed. The large cave was swarming with plant and animal life. They saw orchids, bromeliads, ferns and vines on an artificial mountaintop. Below the mountain they saw banana trees, Panama hat plants and ginger shrubs. They caught a glimpse of Cana plants waving gently under a breeze amidst bamboo clumps and Ceiba trees.

"The cave is divided into five zones," Archernar explained. "There are a rainforest, a savannah, a marshland, a desert and an ocean. Electronic sensors and computers control the climate in each zone. The rainforest receives moisture all year round. The moisture keeps the soil soggy for the plants and shrubs to grow. The temperature in the rainforest is maintained between 55 and 95 degrees Fahrenheit."

Xivana and Xalex gazed speechless at the verdant vegetation in front of them. Large frogs leaped around them, snakes darted from cover to cover and snails moved slowly in their paths. They left the rainforest zone and stepped on the grassland of the savannah. They stopped at a mound to watch an army of ants breaking down a pile of leaves. Half way into the savannah they stopped to climb an acacia tree festooned with passion fruit vines. They climbed down the tree when they saw a yellow-footed tortoise and ran after it to examine it. They sat astride the tortoise and let it carry them around. A pair of galagos came down from a nearby tree to watch them with curiosity.

"The savannah stream has its own system of recycled water," Archernar explained. "When rain is needed in the savannah, the computers turn on the pumps and sprinklers."

"I can feel the breeze," Xivana said. "Where is it coming from?"

"The breeze is made by giant wind-making machines," Archernar explained.

They left the savannah and ventured into the marsh zone. The children watched oysters, crabs and mussels darting and swimming about in the slow-moving water. Xalex ran after a frog that leaped out of the marsh. He tried to catch the frog, but to his disappointment it sprung into the dense tangle of mangrove roots and disappeared.

"Are there alligators in the marsh?" Xivana asked.

"No," Archernar replied. "Animals, reptiles or mammals that are dangerous to people are not raised in the caves."

The two children felt a sudden rise in the temperature as they crossed into the desert ecosystems. Xalex was puzzled at the sight of a huge carrot hanging upside down with giant toothpicks stuck to it.

"What is that?" he asked.

"That's a Boojum tree," Archernar answered. "They thrive in the desert. In the summer the temperature in the desert zone can reach 110 degrees Fahrenheit. The desert receives rain only during certain part of the year. The desert climate is all controlled by computers."

The children trod on Bermuda grass and wound their way through a variety of cactus plants. They stopped to pick flowers from desert plants and smell the sage bushes. On the other side of the sage bushes, Xivana saw a pile of rusted and twisted metals clustered together. Next to the pile was a posted sign with the words 'Sea of Invisibility' printed on it. Curious, Xivana walked up the piles of rusty metals followed by Xalex and Archernar.

"What are these?" Xivana asked, surprised to see the machines. She was not expected to see these machines inside the caves.

"They are the lunar landers from the Apollo Moon Landing Mission," Archernar replied.

"My grandma used to tell us stories about the moon landing. Why are they here?" Xivana questioned, looking perplexed. "They should be in a museum. That is where they belong. They were used to ferry Americans for the first moon landing."

Archernar laughed. He grabbed Xivana by her hand and pulled her away from the wrecks. At the end of the desert ecosystems they came upon the ocean zone. Waves rolled along the ocean surface and splashed on a sandy beach.

"Look at the waves," Xalex exclaimed. "How do you make waves?"

"The waves are made by machines," Archernar replied. "We try to create an ocean that is as natural as possible."

"Are there any fish in the ocean?"

"There are all kinds of fish in the ocean."

The children took their shoes off and ran to the beach. They waded in the shallow water and picked seashells.

"Can we go for a swim?" Xivana asked Archernar.

"Yes you may, but please don't go too far."

They took their clothes off and dived into the warm water. The swarm of butterfly fish and sea urchins swimming beneath the ocean dazzled the children. They swam around the coral reefs and tried to catch pork fish and clownfish with their hands. While the children swam in the ocean, Archernar climbed on top of a sand ridge and sat under a palm tree. He took a logbook and a pen out of the picnic basket, opened the logbook and recorded the day's events. He then put the logbook back in the picnic basket, closed his eyes and waited for the children to return from swimming. A few minutes later the happy children dashed out of the ocean and ran towards him. He took a towel and dried them.

"Can we go to the barnyard now?" Xalex asked. "I want to see the animals."

"There has been an outbreak of influenza among the chicken," Archernar regretfully said. "It's not safe for humans to go near the animals at this time. I am very sorry."

"Oh," Xalex moaned with disappointment. "I can't see the goats and the Texas Longhorns?"

"I am afraid not, but I have planned something else instead. Tonight you will dine with me in the Queen's Chamber."

"We will dine in the Queen's Chamber?" Xivana exclaimed. "But, children are not allowed in the Queen's Chamber!"

"The guards will make an exception tonight. But first we'll visit the orchard and pick up some fresh fruits."

They took the elevator and returned to the tunnel. Spider cave was divided into several plots of land on which grew potatoes, tomatoes, onions and cucumbers. The children filled their bags with ripe, red tomatoes and big onions. They watched a group of men and women harvest a crop of cucumbers and pick peanuts from the roots of peanut greens. They later stopped at a barn and watched workers pickle cucumbers and bottle mustard and tomato sauces.

"There are more than 150 crops being grown in the caves at various time during the year," Archernar said. "Everything that we grow is used up. For instance the peanuts are pressed into oil or made into peanut butter. The greens are fed to the domestic animals at the barnyard. Crops that cannot be consumed are turned into compost for nourishing the soil."

"Do the workers have a home to go to at night," Xivana asked.

"The men and women live in Spider cave," Archernar replied. He pointed to a tall concrete structure at the end of the cave. "At night they sleep behind those walls."

"The building looks like a prison," Xivana remarked.

"I am afraid it is," Archernar sadly said. "These men and women are prisoners in their own land. They toiled on the plantation fields so that the children can live." A group of prisoners carrying picks and shovels appeared from behind a tomato field. Xivana saw that their feet were chained to each other. The prisoners passed by them. One of the men looked up and stared at Xivana. Then he leaped towards her. "Leave the cave before it becomes your tomb," he shouted. He tripped on the chain and fell down. A guard rushed to him and kicked him. The guard butted the prisoner with his riffle and forced him back towards the other prisoners. Xivana cowered behind Archernar.

"Are they hambuglars?" Xalex asked.

"Why are they in chain?" Xivana asked.

"They are chained to each other to prevent them from leaving the caves," Archernar explained. "If they run away, there won't be anyone left to look after the plantation fields and the animals. The plants and the animals will then die. Without foods the children will die of starvation."

"They are being treated like animals," Xivana said. The two children silently followed Archernar back to the cave vehicle.

"Is there anything else you want to ask me or wish to see?" Archernar asked. The two children sadly shook their heads. "I want to go home," Xivana said. "The people outside are free even though the nuclear war had destroyed their homes. They don't have chains around their ankles and they can go anywhere they want to."

Archernar smiled. "We'll return to the Carlsbad cave. You can spend the rest of the day playing and having fun in the playground or looking around the cave if you wish. I will send for you at dusk." The two children quietly nodded their heads.

Xivana and Xalex spent the rest of the day walking around the Big Room. They showed no interest in playing and they were no longer excited about living in the caves. They wished that they had never left Lubbock. Suddenly they became fearful that they would not be able to leave the caves. They had witnessed the guards kill a prisoner. They knew that if they attempt to escape the guards would kill them too. At nightfall two Presidential guards came by their apartment to drive them to the Queen's Chamber.

They reluctantly threw their knapsacks over their shoulders and followed the guards. When they entered the Queen's Chamber they were greeted by a woman with long golden hair and dressed in a long, flowing robe. Frightened at the sight of the woman, they stepped back to the door.

"Who are you," Xivana asked.

"My name is Violet," the woman answered.

"Where is Archernar," Xalex asked, looking around the chamber. "What have you done to the clown?"

The woman smiled. "Without the clown's apparel, I am Violet," she said. She then pointed to a pile of clothes lying on a chair next to a dressing table.

"You are a woman," Xivana exclaimed. She smiled and ran into Violet's arms. "Oh, I thought that you were a man."

Xalex ran and hugged her. "You fooled us. You had us believed that you were a man."

"Have you never seen a female clown before?"

Xivana was puzzled by Violet's question. "I don't know," she answered. "I have never seen a clown without make-up. How will I know if the clown is a man or a woman?"

"A clown without makeup isn't a clown," Violet said. "The funny clown is neither a man nor a woman."

"The world would be a happier place to live if there were more clowns like you to make us laugh," Xivana said. They heard a knock on the door. The door opened up and a guard walked in the room pushing a cart laden with foods.

"Your dinner is here, Ma'am," the guard said. He placed the foods on a table and departed. The children stared at the sumptuous meals in front of them and forgot their fears. Their dinner consisted of roasted chicken with plum stuffing, grilled Portobello mushrooms, scalloped potatoes and banana bread. They accompanied their dinner with freshly squeezed fruit juices. They had succulent truffles for dessert. After dinner the children climbed on a sofa and admired the limestone deposits on the walls and ceiling.

"How come you don't live with the other grownups in Spider Cave?" Xivana asked Violet as she cleaned the dinner table.

"I was appointed the cave's jester and spared the hard labor," Violet explained. "My job is to entertain the children."

"Are there any school in the caves?" Xalex asked.

"Ultraviolet closed down the school after the revolution," Violet answered. "He does not believe that children should have to learn anything."

"Why?"

"Ultraviolet thinks that once the children are taught to read and write, the next thing they want to do is to tinker with nature and build nuclear bombs. The world will be a safer place if nobody knows about nuclear physics. Without the knowledge of nuclear fusion, nobody can build atomic bombs."

"I don't want to live in a cave and live like a slave until I am carried to my grave," Xivana lamented.

"You don't have to," Violet said.

Xivana suddenly became sad. "We can't leave the caves," she said. "If we do the guards will capture us and bring us back. We are prisoners." Violet took the tray of empty plates to the door. She opened the door and handed them to the guards outside. "Why are the guards outside the Queen's Chamber? Are you a prisoner too?"

"Yes," Violet answered, sitting next to the children on the sofa. She put her arms around Xivana. "Ultraviolet wants to make sure that I do not leave the caves."

"Why?"

"The Carlsbad Colony is ruled by children led by Ultraviolet. All grownups in the caves are prisoners. Those who attempt to escape are brought back or killed."

"I knew it," Xivana said. "We are prisoners too."

"Not if you leave the caves now," Violet said.

"How can we leave the caves? There are guards everywhere."

Violet closed her eyes and took a deep breath. She drew the two children closer to her and squeezed them.

"Get your knapsacks," she ordered. "You stand a better chance to escape if you leave under the cover of darkness."

"I am afraid of the dark. Can we wait till daybreak?" Xalex said.

"No, you should leave now. It's dark enough for you to leave the caves without being seen." Xivana and Xalex jumped up from the sofa and grabbed their knapsacks. Then, in despair, Xivana threw the knapsack back on the sofa. "The guards standing outside have guns. They will shoot us," she said.

"There is a secret passageway that no one but me knows about. We will use it to leave the caves. The guards won't even know that we had left the room."

"Where is the secret passageway?" Xivana whispered.

Violet changed into her clown's garb and put her wig back on her head. She took a picnic basket filled with foods and vegetables and walked to a tall cabinet at one corner of the chamber. She moved the cabinet to one side and pulled back a slab of limestone, revealing a narrow and dark opening.

"Get your flashlights ready," she advised the children. "It's very dark inside the passageway. Stay close to me and don't make any noise. Point your lights towards the ground and don't look at the light directly while you are inside the passageway. It's so dark inside that looking at the light may cause you to become blind." Violet handed sunglasses and hard hats to the children. She slipped another pair of sunglasses over her nose and covered her head with a hard hat. "The sunglasses will protect your eyes and the hats will shield your heads from falling limestone pieces."

The children covered their heads with the hard hats and followed her inside the dark passageway. It was so quiet inside the passageway that they could hear themselves breathe. Midway into the tunnel the passageway narrowed. Violet became stuck trying to squeeze through the narrow opening.

"I have gone fatter since the last time I used the passageway," she revealed as she heaved through the opening. The children pushed her through the cramped opening with all their might. Pieces of limestone fell from the ceiling and the walls around them.

"Push harder," Violet whispered. "I am almost on the other side." The children pushed harder and they suddenly fell on top of Violet on the other side of the passageway. Ten minutes later they emerged into a long corridor. Violet stopped at an oxygen sensor on the wall.

"Listen carefully," she said. "When I open the door the air coming inside the cave will cause the oxygen level to rise. The oxygen sensor will sound an alarm and the technicians at the control room will pinpoint the location of the airflow on their computer screen. The guards will then be sent to investigate." Violet removed a can of shaving cream from her picnic basket and sprayed the shaving cream over the oxygen sensor. "The shaving cream will temporarily delay the sensor from activating the alarm. This will give you time to run out and hide behind the Douglas fir trees on the other side of the caves. I will use another door to divert the guards and lead them away from you. Wait until all is quiet again and then head for Fort Stanton. To get to Fort Stanton you will take highway 285 North from Carlsbad. When you get to Roswell take highway 380 West and continue driving until you reach the Fort. The journey will take you about two hours. It'll take longer if you have to drive around any obstacles. Your dune buggy is exactly where you left it."

"Come with us," Xivana pleaded.

Archernar gave Xivana the picnic basket. "There is a set of logbooks in the basket. When you reach Fort Stanton ask to see the commander of the Fort and give him the logbooks. Tell him that there are 160 men, women and children held captive in the Carlsbad Caverns by an army of gun-toting kids. Tell him that an epidemic of Avian Influenza is threatening to kill everyone." She embraced the children and kissed them goodbye.

"Please come with us," the children begged. "We are not leaving unless you come along too."

"I can't leave Ultraviolet behind. He needs me. Be careful."

She pulled open the door latch and pushed the door wide open. She looked out in the darkness and waited a few seconds, then beckoned the children to run. "Hurry," she whispered. Xivana and Xalex dashed out and ran to the trees. Violet closed the door and hurried to the opposite side of the corridor. She threw the can of shaving cream into a crack in the wall. Halfway through the corridor, she turned into a tunnel and scurried towards another door. She flew the door wide open and stepped out into the night. The air rushed into the caves and created an overpressure. Seconds later the sirens wailed.

"Gorgonio," Xivana screamed as a shadowy figure came from behind the trees to help them. "Thanks God."

Gorgonio led them away from the caves. They hid behind the trees when they heard the guards rushing out of the cave and barking out orders at each other. The guards scattered around and looked for escaped prisoners. After a few minutes the two children heard several shots rang out in the night. They trembled and closed their eyes. They clasped their hands and held them in prayer in front of them. Another shot rang out followed by a long silence. Then they heard the guards return to the caves. When the night fell silent again, they jumped out of their hiding place and ran to the dune buggy. Gorgonio sat at the wheel and drove off in the dune buggy with the children still shaking with fear.

"The guards have killed Archernar," Xalex moaned.

"The guards can only kill men and women," Xivana said, comforting her brother. "They cannot kill a clown for the clown is neither a man nor a woman. Archernar will live on forever. Let's hurry up before the guards return."

Rumors spread to Lubbock the following day that aliens were hiding in the Carlsbad Caverns and preparing to attack North America. People were accustomed to seeing airplanes and starships flying in the skies. Counter-insurgency aircrafts routinely circled above their devastated cities and low-range tactical fighters frequently patrolled the skies. Every day people expect bombs to rain over their heads all over again. The news that a group of aliens was invading North America took them by complete surprise. They gathered around their television sets with apprehension to watch an emergency government broadcast. The news shocked and terrified them.

"Authorities at Fort Stanton, New Mexico, had detained two children who said that they met and talked with aliens from outer space. After questioning the two children were returned to their parents in Lubbock. The children told authorities that the alien invaders held them captive in the Carlsbad Caverns for three days. They had been missing since Sunday and it was believed that they ran away because they feared that their parents would abuse them. Early this morning the children suddenly appeared at Fort Stanton carrying three sacks containing a variety of unidentified objects. The bizarre objects which looked like soft cosmic rocks were flown to the National Space Control Board in Virginia for analysis. The children said that the aliens fed them with the strange objects. They referred to the variety of the odd objects as lettuces, onions, tomatoes and potatoes. Authorities were intrigued by the strange names given to the objects and speculated that the names may be a part of the vocabulary of the aliens with whom the children had contact with. The NSCB scientists are particularly attracted to one of the specimens, a soft round piece of matter consisting of several layers of green leaves. The children called the green matter a lettuce head, but the NSCB scientists think that the green round matter may hold the clue to the earth's origin. The scientists discovered several bulbous rock specimens inside the sacks and speculated that the large round matter are anti-aircraft rocket shells. The children on the other hand insisted that the objects are jumbo yellow onions grown inside the caves. They denied that the aliens are stockpiling anti-aircraft rocket shells in preparation for a massive attack on North America. When the scientists sliced the bulbous matter, it released an acrid volatile oil that brought tears to their eyes. Humankind as we know had stopped shedding tears since the last nuclear war in which there were no victors but only losers. The discovery that the onion could make human beings weep is giving hope to humanity that someday the plant can be mass-cultivated on earth. The scientists are hopeful that the oil from the plants may be used to make men weep when they look at the lingering ravages of the nuclear war. Another specimen that is captivating the minds of the scientists is something the children called tomatoes. Enclosed within the thick red crust are several tiny particles bound together by a jelly-like substance. There was an unconfirmed report that one of the scientists accidentally squirted the jelly-like substance on the face of another scientist. The incident caused the other scientists standing around to laugh, an emotional reaction never seen on the faces of people since the nuclear war. This discovery led the Scientists to believe that it can someday be used to make mutants laugh again. Another specimen that the children brought back from the caves looks very similar to a rock discovered not too long ago in an Idaho field. The scientists were astonished that the rock specimen had similar properties to their own rock that they had named the Idaho potato. Particularly interesting among the rock specimens is a curious-looking specimen that the children called a cheeseburger. The NSCB scientists were horrified to learn that the aliens fed cheeseburgers to the captive humans inside the caves. They found that the cheeseburger consisted of several layers of other matter not currently found on Earth, among them the cucumber. The top crown is covered with seeds whereas the inner core is a round piece of dark substance that the children referred to as a hamburger. They said that the hamburger was made from fresh beef. We have an unconfirmed report that one of the NSCB scientists ate the beef without telling anyone. When one scientist discovered that the beef was missing, she panicked and scurried around the laboratory asking everyone: "Where is the beef?" That piece of matter is covered with yet another thick layer of yellow substance which the children named Cheddar cheese. The scientists argued that the new substance is the melted ore of pure gold. In New Mexico the announcement that the yellow substance is the ore of pure gold set off a mad gold rush to the Guadeloupe Mountains. Not since the California gold rush of 1849 has this nation seen such a rush by people to find gold. An interesting powder that was found on the two children is something the children called pepper. The powder causes everybody near it to sneeze. The scientists believe that this strange powder can someday be used to force priests to come out of the closets, confess their crimes, and bless the souls of the 170 million Americans who perished in the nuclear holocaust."

After the emergency broadcast, people covered their faces with their masks of stupor and anger. They stared at the ground and murmured: "Holy Plutonium!" Then they grabbed their guns and organized search parties to hunt down the aliens. They fanned out in small groups to search the storm sewers, canals, ditches, bomb craters, underground bunkers and caves. When they did not find any alien, they returned to their bunkers to vent their frustrations and anger on their children. In a dark bunker on the outskirts of Lubbock, a frustrated and angry man covered his face with the mask of depravity. He walked into Xivana's room and kicked her brother out of the bunker. He then stood in front of the petrified girl, unbuckled his belt and pulled it out of his trousers. Xivana wrapped her tiny arms around her shoulders and moved back to the wall.

"Please, Dad, don't ...," she begged.

Terrified, Xivana covered her face. Xalex hid and wept under a table.

A succession of explosions in the city center drowned the poor little girl's voice. The sky became obscured by the smoke and dust fanned out over the city. Up in the Yellowstone Mountains, the few remaining buffaloes still alive gathered on the grassless mounds to graze. It was the year of the buffalo, but the destitute and hapless animals had hardly anything to eat. Groups of mutants wandered about aimlessly, but one man among them seemed to be looking for something. He was Gorgonio and he was looking for Xivana and Xalex so he could take them back to the mountains.

PART 3: A PLEDGE FOR A BETTER WORLD

8 THE WATERHOLE

Sam Goodman, a retired fireman, left his house after dinner and went for his customary walk around the neighborhood. He greeted a neighbor working in his front yard and smiled at a group of children riding their bikes. The children greeted him with a cheerful: "Hi, Uncle Sam." Goodman stepped around a pool of water on the sidewalk and dodged the spray of water from a lawn sprinkler. A woman moving a birdbath to a new location suddenly and fearfully looked up at him. He smiled at her to appease her fear and she timidly smiled back and resumed her yard work. Goodman walked along rows of parked cars for four blocks without meeting anyone else. A few cars, their door mirrors momentarily reflecting back the sunlight, drove past him. When he arrived at the waterhole, he saw a young girl whom he had never met before. She was tall, poorly dressed and appeared to be in her early teens.

"Young lady," Goodman warned, "be careful! The waterhole is very deep. I don't think anyone knows for certain how deep it is."

The girl ignored his warning and stared at the bottom of the waterhole.

"Did you drop something in the waterhole?" Goodman ventured to ask the girl. The girl's eyes remained transfixed in the waterhole. Goodman moved closer to her. "Do you need any help?" he softly asked.

"Mind your own business," the girl replied. She threw her head back and swept her hair from her face. Goodman saw her badly bruised face and swollen eye.

"New kid in the block, I presume," Goodman said. "My name is Sam. The kids in the neighborhood call me Uncle Sam. What is your name?"

"Leave me alone," the girl snapped at Goodman.

"Are you looking for something in the waterhole?"

"Go away," she said. "I haven't lost anything. I am meditating."

"Ha!" Goodman exclaimed. "You have lost your good manners in the waterhole." Goodman looked inside the waterhole. At first he could see only the murky water. "Miss, you are in big trouble. Unless someone comes to your rescue and give you your manners back, you will not make it through life. Manners are what maketh a man. Oh, excuse me! I should really say 'manners maketh a person.' In a nation plagued with lawsuits, one should avoid saying any gender-specific words."

"You can spare me all that bullshit," the girl responded.

Goodman looked down the waterhole. "It won't be easy to fish out your good manners in all that filth."

Looking deep down inside the waterhole, Goodman saw broken marriages, racial disharmony, corruption, injustice and lost battles; a forgotten war and a badly mauled economy; drug addicts, pimps and immoral do-gooders; youths drawn into the downward spiral of drugs and teenage pregnancies; broken hearts swollen with the muddy water; and middle-income families sinking under the weight of government taxes. He saw piles of memories drifting amidst lost words and lost cultures. Broken promises sat atop rotten political platforms. Bald tires and rusty automobile parts were scattered everywhere. Drums filled with chemical pollutants decorated the edges of the waterhole. Goodman had little hope that the girl's good manners would survive amidst the effluent. People from around the country came to the waterhole to dump their problems in it. In time it became known as America's wastebasket. Goodman once fought in Vietnam, but despite living amidst the atrocities, the killing and the destruction, he had deep respect for the jungle. Whenever he was not fighting, he let his eyes feast on the beautiful sights around him. In contrast, the waterhole in his own backyard hurt him more than the 12in bamboo spikes that pierced through his boots when he crossed the Mekong river. Somehow he had managed to stay alive. When he was discharged, he came to live by the waterhole. Other soldiers were fortunate that they never had to come back and live anywhere close to the waterhole.

"It is not too late to get your good manners back again. You are still young. Let me look at your face." Goodman held the girl's chin and grimaced at her swollen eye. "Who did this to you?"

The girl pushed Goodman's hand from her face. "Leave me alone," she screamed.

"Calm down. I am not going to hurt you. Who hit you?"

"Nobody did. Get away from me. You are weird. Don't come near me again or else I'll scream."

"You are our hope and our future. You must be saved. I will see to it that you don't get sucked into the waterhole. What is your name?"

"I have many names," the girl replied.

"We all have a name. What does your mother call you?"

"Whatever she feels like calling me."

"Like what?" Goodman asked.

"She calls me a brat. Sometimes she calls me a pig-faced bitch."

"Doesn't she ever call you by your real name?"

"I don't have one," the girl replied. "My mother calls me 'Ugly.' She says she can't stand to look at me. Sometimes she calls me 'Stupid.' This morning she calls me 'Jackass.' I don't know what name I will be called by tomorrow. My name changes as frequently as her temperament."

"That's not nice of your mother to call you names like that," Goodman said. "If you don't have a name, I'll give you one. Let me see. How would you like to be called Penny?"

"I don't care. It makes no difference. Tomorrow I will be called by another name."

"My lucky day," Goodman said. "Someone throws a penny away and I get to pick it out and make a wish."

Penny's eyes brightened up. She stared at Goodman. "Will you make a wish for me?" she asked.

"I wish that America would take care of its children better," Goodman said.

"Why?" Penny asked, disappointed. "I wish for new clothes." Penny held the bottom of her dress and raised it up for Goodman to see. "Mom wears expensive designer clothes. I have been wearing the same dress year after year. Life stinks!"

"There you go again," Goodman sighed. "Come with me; we'll find you some good manners."

"You can't fool me. Good manners can't be bought in America. They can only be acquired in Europe, and only if you are a member of the royal family. You can buy me some new clothes instead."

"All right, let find you some good clothes to wear. Maybe the new clothes will bring the good manners out of you." Penny smiled and moved closer to Goodman. He sought his hands and squeezed them. "You are a funny man," she grinned.

"Let me look at your eyes." Goodman touched Penny's swollen eyes. The girl uttered a painful cry.

"It hurts," she moaned.

"Who did this to you?" Goodman inquired.

"Nobody," Penny replied, looking down. "I slipped on the stairway and fell down on my face. It's nobody's fault but me. I should have been more careful."

"Humm..."

"It was nobody's fault, I swear."

They quietly walked towards the cluster of homes in the subdivision. Penny held Goodman's hand firmly. She looked down and kicked at the soda cans and plastic bottles in her path. Her shoes showed signs of wear at the front. The sun dipped lower behind the trees and the sunlight flickered momentarily through the branches. Then the light ceased to filter through the trees and the sun turned into a reddish ball. It plunged behind the trees and disappeared from sight. They walked upon a yard sale sign along the street. A man sat under the porch and waited for passers-by to purchase their wares. A woman picked up things from the ground and took them back inside the garage.

"Can we take a look?" Penny asked. "Maybe they have some used clothes that I can use. I don't mind wearing used clothes as long as they don't have any holes in them. Please!"

"It looks like the sale is over. The woman is packing up. We can look if you like," Goodman replied. The woman came back from the garage. The man did not move.

Goodman walked to a table in the driveway and inspected the guns, grenades and knives spread out on a table. Sitting next to the assortment of weapons were a number of small packets containing various substances. Goodman recognized them all: cocaine, marijuana, heroin, black tar, crack, and others less known drugs. He dipped his hand into a jar and removed a fistful of Ecstasy pills. He examined and sniffed the synthetic drugs before dropping them back into the jar. Various sexual devices, syringes, whips, handcuffs, surgical clamps and tubing sat on another table. Under the table were several gallons of mercury, lithium nitrate, benzene, chloroform and sulfuric acid.

"If you don't find what you need here, let me know," the man said with a wink. "I can get almost anything through another source."

"Where do all these things come from?" Goodman asked.

"From the waterhole," the man replied.

A corpse at the end of the driveway attracted Goodman's attention. "Who is the woman?" he asked, pointing at the corpse.

"We pulled her out of the waterhole this morning," the woman replied. "I think she jumped in the waterhole to search for the ending to her life. Evidently it did not take her long to find it." Goodman stared at a row of plastic bottles next to the corpse.

"What about the blood?" he asked.

"Government surplus," the man replied. "Price support sucks and free enterprise kills, but you have to choose one or the other."

"Right," Goodman told the man. He walked to a box containing shoes of various sizes and color. He picked up a shoe and looked at the label.

"Made in China," the woman said. Goodman dropped the shoe back into the box. He looked into a wheelbarrow filled with bric-a-bracs. He spotted a toilet seat and picked it up to examine it. "You can have the toilet seat for three hundred dollars," the woman said.

"What? I can buy a toilet seat at a home improvement center for ten dollars."

"This one is bomb-proof. It was once used by a big brass at the Pentagon. He paid six hundred and forty dollars to acquire it."

Goodman glanced disappointingly at the other items displayed. "We won't find any clothes for you here," he said, looking at Penny. These stuffs are for courting Death. Let's go somewhere else."

"She is still going to end up in the waterhole, with or without clothes," the woman sarcastically said. "I may just have what the young girl needs. Something that is far better than clothing."

"The girl's clothes are worn out. She needs something decent to wear," Goodman explained.

"Clothes are not going to save her from the waterhole. Why not buy her a gun?" the man proposed. He got up from the chair and walked to the table. He picked up a huge revolver and showed it to Goodman. "This one has been fired only once. It's $20."

"Fired once or killed once?" Goodman asked.

"It doesn't matter," the man replied. "A gentleman once owned this gun. He could not buy happiness with all the money he had, so he bought the gun instead. He killed his unfaithful wife with it, called the cops and gave himself up."

"What happened to him?" Goodman asked, looking at the man.

"He disappeared after he was released on bond," the man replied. "His body was later found in the waterhole, along with many others like him. Some people say that he merely multiplied in the waterhole."

"If I were you, I wouldn't go near the goldfish in that waterhole," the woman whispered to Goodman. "There are rumors going around that the goldfish in that waterhole has electronic devices planted behind their ears."

"What?" Goodman exclaimed, staring in disbelief at the couple. "Who would do such a thing to a goldfish?"

"I heard that a CIA agent planted the electronic device in the goldfish to record the sound they make during mating," the woman replied. Goodman took the revolver from the man.

"Goldfish have ears?" Penny asked in disbelief.

"They do now," replied the woman. She went to the table and came back with a packet of chewing gums and a lottery ticket.

"I found the lottery ticket on the dead woman's body," she said. "Her number must have come up. A veteran who saw action in Vietnam had previously chewed the chewing gum. He was taken prisoner by the Vietcong who kept him in a bamboo cage. He chewed gum during his captivity. His captors were weary of looking at him chewing gum and set him free. When he came back home, he went to every schools and libraries in the country to scrape off the stuck gums from underneath the desks and tables. He stood in front of malls and supermarkets and stopped people to check their shoes. When he found sticky gum on the soles of their shoes, he scraped them off. Some people said that he used a spittoon to catch the gums that passersby spit out in the subway and on the sidewalks. Within two years he had collected hundreds of tons of the chewing gums. Then he carefully repackaged the gums and sold them back to the government. He told the government that the gums would save American lives in Vietnam. Fooled them bureaucrats, didn't he? They are twenty dollars a pack of 10 chewing gum. The handgun is included."

"Where did you find the chewing gums?" Goodman asked.

"Joe found them in an Army surplus store."

"I can't read the numbers or the date on the lottery ticket. It's worthless," Penny exclaimed.

"Honey, your number had already come up and you lost," the woman said.

Penny turned to Goodman and stared at him inquisitively.

"This gentleman found you by the waterhole, didn't he?" the woman asked. "What were you doing by the waterhole?"

Penny looked down and muttered: "My number came up."

"You lost everything the day you were born," the woman continued. "Go look inside the waterhole. It's full of losers like you. Matter of fact, you owe me $187,000 for telling you about the goldfish."

"Don't be too harsh on the girl," Goodman said. "We don't care for the gun, but we'll buy a packet of chewing gums."

"Sorry," the woman replied. "You can't have the chewing gums without buying the gun."

"I don't have a use for the handgun."

"The law requires that guns be equipped with child safety devices to prevent accidental discharge. I must sell the chewing gums with the handgun so that you can jam the firing mechanism with them. It's to protect the user from accidentally firing the gun and killing young innocent children. Throw the gun away if you only need the chewing gums."

"What kind of law is that?"

"I call it a stupid law. Gun control laws will not reduce the number of children killed each year by unintentional firing, but I am required to sell the trigger locks with the guns. I know that the children will merely remove and chew the gums. Would you believe that here in America guns kill 7,200 children each year? What makes it so sad is the guns belong to the children's parents. Where else in the world will parents sign their own children's death sentence?" Goodman took the handgun and chewing gums from the woman. "Is the handgun loaded?"

"Of course it is loaded! What use is a handgun if it is not loaded? The gun is also useless if you have to hide the bullets in another room."

"What about the corpse?" he said, pointing to the body on the driveway. Goodman gave the handgun to Penny while he fumbled in his pocket for his billfold. He pulled out a $20 bill and handed it to the woman.

"It will get recycled back into the waterhole," the woman said as she pocketed the $20 bill. "There are people who are in the business of trading the body parts of homeless people. Do you know that trading body parts is a thriving business? I can easily get $990 for the woman's brain. Here, let me give you my business card." The woman slipped a business card into Goodman's hand. Goodman held it close to his face to read it. "Fresh fetal tissues harvested and shipped anywhere," he read.

As it was getting darker, the man picked the items from the table and moved them into the garage. Clutching the revolver, Penny silently followed Goodman. Goodman removed the wrapping from the chewing gums. "Life stinks, isn't?" People get robbed and killed all the times. The government levies an estate tax on the dead person's estate. We pay taxes in life or in death."

"Mr. Goodman." Penny said. "May I have a chewing gum?"

"When a large number of people die, the government collects less income tax revenue," Goodman continued. "So the government taxes the dead person's estate in order to make up for the lost revenues. When a person robs and kills a person, the government suffers two revenue losses. First it loses the income tax revenue that the robber would have paid if he had earned the money honestly. Second, the estate tax that the dead man would have paid on his estate is reduced by the theft that took place before his death. The government is turning a blind eye to the trading of body parts because the dead has no voice. I think the corpse in the driveway is the man's mother-in-law."

"Mr. Goodman, may I have a chewing gum please?"

Goodman gave Penny a stick of chewing gum. She smiled at him. It was the first time that Goodman saw her smile. "Thank you very much," she said. "I promise you that from now on I will be a good girl."

"See?" Goodman exclaimed. "I told you that we were going to find your good manners back." Goodman wrapped his arm around Penny. "Stay away from that stinking waterhole."

"I will, Mr. Goodman. I promise."

A matronly woman walked with her dog on the other side of the road. A man walking in the opposite direction stopped to chat with her. He pointed west and she pointed east. The dog jumped up and barked towards the north. The pair stopped talking and stared at the dog. They exchanged glances, laughed and both pointed to the north. A car zoomed by and hid the threesome from Goodman's view. Further down the road a trailer had left the road and plunged into a ditch. The rear doors of the trailer read: 'follow the leader.' Another trailer, its long bed loaded with boxes of Japanese electronics goods, drove by a billboard exhorting Americans to buy goods made in America. Penny pulled the stick of chewing gum from the wrapper and put it in her mouth. The gum was as hard as steel and she took it out of her mouth.

"This gum looks like a sheet of hard metal," she muttered.

"Let me see," Goodman said. Penny handed him the stick of chewing gum. "We've been had. It is not chewing gum."

"What is it?" Penny asked.

"An ID tag," Goodman replied. "Sometimes they call it a dog tag. They hang them around the neck of the soldiers shipped to Vietnam so that the government can keep count of how many had died in the fighting. The poor soul had no chance." Goodman handed the ID tag back to Penny.

"Is the owner of this ID tag dead then?" Penny asked.

"If he wasn't killed in Vietnam, the waterhole had probably claimed him."

"Can we talk about something else, Mr. Goodman?" Penny asked. "The waterhole scares me."

Goodman drew Penny close to him and squeezed her shoulder. "You are right, Penny," he said. "You know, I am beginning to like you." Penny smiled. They walked silently side by side. A few minutes later Goodman broke the silence. "What were you doing by the waterhole, Penny?" he asked.

"I was thinking about running away from home," Penny answered.

"You are too young to run away," Goodman advised. "Besides, what's a little girl like you going to do when faced against the world alone? Promise me that you won't do such a thing."

"I promise," Penny said. "Mr. Goodman, you should meet my parents. Won't you come and visit us some day?" she asked.

"Sure," Goodman replied. "I will be delighted to meet your parents."

Dusk had fallen over the town. The streetlights came on all at once. One of the lights flickered on and off before finally burning out. A few cars turned on their headlights as they turned into a dark street. A cat, covered with camouflage paint emerged from the shadow of a house. Its long bayonets protruded at the corner of its mouth and pointed east and west. It furtively crossed the street, tiptoed across a lawn and leaped over a fence.

"What are we to become without manners?" Goodman pondered aloud.

"I don't know," Penny replied. "Maybe we will all become extinct like the dinosaurs. How will I pay back the woman the $187,000 that I owe her for telling me about the goldfish?"

"Without his manners, the man is a beast," Goodman mused. "He becomes just another animal. An alley cat! He hides from other animals during the day and scouts for foods at night. Don't worry about the money. The taxpayers will pay her back."

"I am very fond of animals, Mr. Goodman," Penny said. "When I grow up I want to be a veterinarian."

"He turns lawless and violent. He kills others to assert his dominion."

"What is your favorite animal?" Penny asked. "I want to live on a farm and raise horses. Do you like horses, Mr. Goodman?"

"I like horses very much," Goodman replied. "I prefer them to humans."

Darkness had now engulfed everything around them. The muggers started to file out into the streets. Soon petty thieves, rapists and complete street gangs came out to join them. They restlessly paced up and down the street looking for opportunities. A mugger approached Goodman. Goodman took the gun from Penny and pointed it at the mugger.

"I have a gun," Goodman said to the would-be attacker. "Back off!" At the sight of the gun, the mugger walked away. Goodman handed the gun back to Penny. "Someone said that power comes from the barrel of a gun. I think that he meant to say 'powder' instead of 'power.' Or maybe the journalist who reported it inadvertently dropped the letter 'd' from powder. What do you think?"

"I am scared, Mr. Goodman. Take me home, please," Penny implored.

At the end of the street a long line of restless opportunists stood waiting in front of a white house. The line had been getting longer each night. As Goodman walked past the line, an impatient man jumped the line. He walked up to the white house and threw a brick into a window. The glass panes shattered with a loud crash. The man then climbed into the window and disappeared in the white house. A few minutes later he emerged from the white house with several pieces of jewelry and a bag filled with cash.

"That man just broke into the white house," Penny exclaimed. "Look, he stole a few things from the white house."

"It is happening every day," Goodman said. "There is nothing we can do."

"Aren't we going to call the police? This is robbery."

"Pretend that it did not happen," Goodman answered. "Pretend that you did not see anything."

"Are we going to let him get away?"

"The man just collected his unemployment benefits," Goodman explained. "He is using an unconventional method. We can't blame the man for wanting to eat and feed his children."

"When I grow up I want to be a Police Officer, Mr. Goodman," Penny said. "Then I will catch all the thieves and put them behind bars for good."

"Stick to caring after animals, Penny," Goodman advised. "There aren't enough cells to keep the criminals locked in. There is a criminal born every minute, and the job of keeping criminals behind bars is never finished." Goodman looked at his watch. "It's getting late. We'd better hurry up or else your parents will start worrying about you."

They hurried their paces. A few minutes later they came upon a house situated at a crossroads. The sides of the house were painted with red and orange flames. From a distance, the house appeared to be on fire. The gaping mouth of a demon was painted on the front door.

"This is where I live," Penny said, pointing at the house.

As they approached the house Goodman saw a low marble wall fashioned after the Vietnam War Memorial in the front yard. The contour of a child's shoe is etched on the headstone. An edging constructed of several handguns joined together by a chain surrounded the shrine. Suddenly the mouth of the demon opened up and coughed out an ogre. The face of the ogre was covered with mud.

"What's the devil," Goodman exclaimed at the sight of the woman.

"It's my mom," Penny said. "She covers her face every night with mud to clean the pores."

Goodman sighed with relief. "I thought that it was a monster."

"The mud actually turns her into a monster," Penny added.

"Here you are," the woman yelled at Penny. "Where the devil have you been all day?" The mud cake on her face cracked and blood oozed out of the cracks.

"Mr. Goodman took me to a garage sale," Penny explained. "See, Mom, he bought me a pack of chewing gums, but they are not real chewing gums. The Pentagon used them to keep count of the number of soldiers who were killed in Vietnam."

"Get in that house right now," the woman screamed. The mud cake on her face fractured and dropped to her feet. "Your father had been looking for you." The woman slapped Penny's head repeatedly. She shrieked and ran into the mouth of the demon.

"Please don't punish the child." Goodman begged. "It is true, Ma'am. I took Penny for a walk in the neighborhood. We stopped and rummaged through stuffs at a garage sale. That's where we picked up the chewing gums."

"Who gives you the right to take my daughter to a garage sale?" the woman asked.

"Ma'am, there is no need to get upset. We went for a stroll around the neighborhood to get acquainted. We met at the waterhole."

"Never mind," the woman said. She waved Goodman off and walked back in the house.

"It isn't nice of you to punish her like that," Goodman shouted after her. "It was I who suggested that we go look for clothes at a garage sale. I am the one to be blamed. I am the one to be punished, not her." Goodman took the pack of chewing gums from his pocket and showed it to the woman. "Here are the gums that I bought for her. Would you please give them to her?"

The woman took the chewing gums and held them up towards the streetlight. "Where do they come from?" she asked, puzzled by the chewing gums. "A man in uniform gave me one of these when my brother did not come home for Christmas. Are our boys still being killed?"

"Yes, Ma'am, but the killing field is right here in our own cities."

"I'll be damned."

"One of the chewing gums belonged to a P.O.W. When he was captured by the Vietcong, he amused his captors by chewing the gum from dawn to dusk. His captors could not stand looking at him chewing the gum, so they set him free."

A stout bearded man with his hair agog walked out of the mouth of the demon. He held a can of beer in his hand and a lighted cigarette in the other. He wore a black t-shirt with short sleeve over a pair of tattered blue jeans. A crown of barley covered his head and a scythe hung on his belt. The tip of the blade was smeared with blood. The blood dripping from the scythe had turned one of his shoes blood red. "Vietnam?" he echoed back. "I've been there. I was once a P.O.W myself."

"Oh, sure," the woman said, eyeing her husband with contempt. The Vietcong set your body free, but still hold your mind and your soul captive. You shouldn't have bothered to bring your carcass back to the States. What good is it to me now?" The woman gave him the pack of chewing gums. "Maybe you know the guys who used to chew on these gums." She disappeared into the mouth of the demon. The man pulled out a gum stick and read the number on it. "Well, I'll be damned!" he exclaimed. "This dog tag used to belong to my fighting buddy Jeffrey." Goodman saw him smile. "Thanks for bringing me back his dog tag."

"No sweat," Goodman said. He glanced at the marble wall. "Did he die in Vietnam?" Goodman asked. The man did not answer. He walked back to the house and was swallowed up by the demon.

"Maybe he died or maybe he didn't," Goodman murmured. He turned back and headed for his home. "Then again," he muttered, "maybe we all drowned in the waterhole while he continues to live his life in the jungle."

On his way to the waterhole the next day, a dog with a machine gun strapped on its back ran out from behind a house and barked at him. Goodman stopped and stared at the dog. The dog suddenly stopped barking. It turned back with its tail between its legs and its head hanging close to the ground. "You lurched at me with the fury of 46,000 soldiers, but you stopped and turned back when I look at you in the face," Goodman said to the dog. "Your retreat symbolizes our country's shame." A sprinkler bedewed the lawn in the front yard of a house. An older woman, sitting on a garden stool with low legs, pulled weeds from her well-manicured lawn. Goodman headed for the waterhole. He found Penny standing and staring blankly at the murky water.

A five-legged frog emerged from the waterhole and hopped on a rock.

"Penny," Goodman said. "You promised me that you would stay away from the waterhole." Then he heard her sobbing. "Is something wrong?" he asked. Goodman saw the slash on her upper lip. The blood has coagulated at one corner of her mouth.

The frog lifted its fifth leg and saluted the US flag on a flag pole.

"Did your mother do this to you?"

Penny threw her arms around Goodman's neck. He wrapped his arms around her and comforted her.

"Dad went into one of his fits last night and punched me. He does that every time he talks about Vietnam." Penny ran her arms over her cheeks to dry out the tears. "He said that his country had betrayed him and Jeffrey."

"It is alright," Goodman repeated. "Please don't cry."

Penny took out the revolver Goodman bought her at the garage sale. "Mr. Goodman," she said," You may have the gun back." She handed the gun and the pack of chewing gums to Goodman.

"Oh my God, I completely forgot about the gun. Thank you."

Penny smiled faintly. "Mr. Goodman, I won't be going home anymore."

"Where will you go?" Goodman asked. He stood up and took Penny's hand in his. They walked together along the bank of the waterhole. He looked down into the waterhole and suddenly saw Penny's reflection in the murky water. "Oh, no," he murmured, shaking his head at Penny's reflection in the murky water.

Penny looked down the waterhole. "What's in the waterhole, Mr. Goodman?" she asked. Not far away from them, a duck with a six-pack plastic loop around its neck swam around followed by its ducklings. Nearby a truck dumped dioxin-tainted waste oil in a basin.

"There are moral goods and moral wrongs, rebellion and aggression. That's just some of the things that I see. It's only the tip of the iceberg, Penny. Some other things, like corruption, domestic violence and drug abuse are down there too, but nobody pays attention to them anymore. They are so common nowadays that they don't cause a stir in anybody." At that moment a young man walked to the waterhole and bent over to drink the water. "He is now one of them," Goodman said. "Pretty soon he will have it flowing in his veins and he will be convoluted on the floor of his dingy apartment. Another life just wasted."

Penny picked up a dirty penny half-buried under the soil and jumped with joy. She rubbed the dirt off the copper coin. "I picked up a penny," she said.

"These coins are useless nowadays," Goodman said. "All they do is to create clutter in our pockets and desk drawers. They are only good for filling up empty jars in kitchen cabinets and adorning water fountains in shopping malls."

Penny started to cry. "It means that I am a dirty and useless girl, unwanted and unloved," she sobbed. "Is that why you call me Penny?"

"No," protested Goodman. "I always see pennies lying on the floor when I go to a restaurant, the grocery store, or the mall. Our government is not interested in saving pennies, but I am. Last night I picked up the largest and brightest penny ever. I think that it was minted in 1971."

"That was the year when I was born. I will bring you a lot of luck."

A snake slithered through the murky water.

"That snake looks peculiar," Penny remarked, pointing at two elongated lumps on the snake. "It has arms, isn't that weird? Did you see that, Mr. Goodman?"

"Yes," Goodman replied. "I see some other things too."

"What?" Penny asked.

The snake quietly cut through the water and swam towards the five-legged frog.

"Dead fish," Goodman replied. He laughed. Penny chuckled. Goodman threw the gun into the waterhole. "Thou shall kill no more," Goodman said.

"It's no use, Mr. Goodman. It will just get recycled. There are a lot more guns in the country than there are people. They just keep making them." Penny clung to Goodman. Together they slowly walked away from the waterhole.

A two-headed alligator surfaced near the five-legged frog.

"Mr. Goodman," Penny asked, "what will happen to me? Am I going to drown in the waterhole?"

They heard water splashing behind them and quickly turned around to look. The two-headed alligator shot up from the murky water. The jaws on the left head of the alligator snapped close on the five-legged frog, while the teeth of the other pair of jaws tore at the winged snake. At the gruesome sight Penny fainted. Mr. Goodman quickly caught her in his arms. He lifted her up and carried her back to town.

9 DOUG KROUSSE

Shortly after midnight the phone rang in Herman LaSalle's bedroom. His friends and relatives rarely called him at night, but the Computer Operators frequently woke him up at all hours of the night to report problems at the data center. Herman reached for the telephone in the dark. He immediately recognized the voice of Jose Vergano, the Lead Operator. He sounded out of breath and terrified.

"Herman," Jose said, panting and gasping for breath. "You had better come over here quickly."

Herman sat up on his bed and turned on the light. He was accustomed to being called when a production job fails or when the computer goes down. He usually managed to solve the problems over the telephone. Sometimes he had to go to the data center to help the computer operators resolve the problem.

"Calm down, Jose," Herman urged in a sleepy voice and with his eyes closed. He resigned himself to hearing Jose say that another job did not complete successfully or the computer went down or the power went out or the third shift operator did not arrive for work. "What is the problem this time?" he asked.

"I had to leave the computer room because I was afraid he was going to shoot me," Jose said, speaking in his strong Puerto Rican accent. "I am calling from a pay phone across the street." Jose sounded very frightened.

Herman's eyes popped open. "What did you say?" he asked. "What are you talking about?"

"Doug came to work carrying his hunting rifle with him," Jose said. "He had this funny look on his face again and I was scared to death. I ran out of the computer room and went to a pay phone to call you. I am not going back to work again."

"What riffle?" Herman asked, still unsure about what Jose was telling him.

"I am telling you the truth," Jose exclaimed. "I don't want to go back to the computer room. I mean it! This guy has gone crazy. I don't want to work with him anymore. I am resigning now and I am going home."

"Wait a minute, you can't leave now," Herman quickly said. Jose was an indispensable employee. He was a conscientious Computer Operator, never missed a day, and always showed up for work on time. He was his best employee and Herman did not want to lose him. "Where are you?"

"I am calling from the convenience store at the street corner," Jose replied. "I was too scared to use the phone in the computer room. Doug walked in the computer room with his riffle and started looking behind the tape drives. He said that he is looking for communists."

"Okay, slow down," Herman pleaded. He got out of his bed and unbuttoned his pajama shirt. He felt that he needed to go to the data center to sort things out.

"I am telling you," Jose forcefully said, "that this guy has gone mad. I was going to call the police, but I decided to call you first."

"You did the right thing, Jose." Herman threw the pajama on the bed and reached for his pants. "Have you called anyone else?"

"No. I don't know who else I should call. I thought about calling Bill."

Herman sighed. "Well, don't call Bill," he advised. "I am coming over to the data center right away. You can wait for me at the convenience store. Don't try to do anything, do you understand?"

"I am not going back to the computer room."

"Good. I'll be there in about half an hour." Herman returned the telephone on the nightstand. He slid into his faded and tattered blue jean and put on an old crumpled shirt. He slipped into his tennis shoes, grabbed his car keys, and climbed into his car. He drove as fast as he could. As he sped along the dark highway, he envisioned the spectacle of the computer room littered with the dead bodies of the computer operators working under his supervision. He wished he had listened to Bill Oberwinder a few weeks ago when he suggested that he terminates Doug. As he drove to the data center, his mind relived the time when Doug was hired for the first time to work at the data center.

He went back to college

Doug Krousse briefly worked under Herman's supervision in the summer of 1979. Herman recalled that Doug was nineteen years old when he was hired as a Data Controller. At the time that Doug was hired, Herman was the 2nd shift Data Control Supervisor. The Vice-President of Operations, Bill Oberwinder, a retired Air Force Lieutenant, interviewed and hired Doug in the summer. He assigned him to work on the second shift. Doug, Herman recalled, was a very quiet, shy and polite person. He was tall and solidly built. Herman personally trained him to operate the Wang terminals in the Data Control room. Doug learned his new job very fast and completed all the work assigned to him on time and without errors. He never complained of being overloaded with work. He was a cheerful, dedicated, likable and dependable employee. He was always respectful of his peers and his Supervisor. All the other employees, particularly the computer programmers, took a liking for him. At the end of the summer Doug left the data center to return to college. Herman was saddened when he left, but he respected the young man's desire to continue his education.

He was hired back

The following year the second shift Computer Operator left. Herman had always wanted to move into computer operations. When Bill offered him the position he gladly accepted. He spent two weeks with another Computer Operator to learn how to run the IBM mainframe computer and monitor the nightly batch jobs. After his initial training he moved to the third shift to perform his new duties. The graveyard shift was not as hectic as the second shift where eighty percent of all production jobs were processed. On the third shift Herman could horn up his newly acquired skills without being subjected to the work pressure on the second shift. His good performance as a Computer Operator eventually earned him the Lead Computer Operator job on the second shift. His chance for promotion came in early 1981. When the Computer Operator working on the graveyard shift called in sick, the Operations Supervisor filled in for him. The next day Bill Oberwinder walked into the computer room and found the Operations Supervisor spread out on the floor. An empty bottle of wine and a half-full bottle of Jack Daniels were lying next to him. Bill helped him get back on his feet and to his car. Later that day, when the Operations Supervisor reported to work Bill fired him for drinking while at work. Bill then offered the vacant position to Herman. Herman remembered the sad look on Bill's face when he offered him the job. Bill had great confidence on Herman's abilities, but he was heart-broken to have to fire the Operations Supervisor. The next day Herman moved to the day shift to assume his new role. The third shift Computer Operator was moved down to the second shift to take his place. A new Computer Operator was needed to work on the third shift. Impressed by his previous work performance during the summer, Bill called Doug Krousse and offered him the job. Doug accepted and returned to work under Herman's supervision. Herman could not ask for a better employee to handle the workload on the third shift. Doug was very dependable and he performed his new duties conscientiously. When one of the second shift Computer Operators resigned, Herman moved Doug to the second shift and adjusted his salary accordingly to compensate him for the extra workload. Jose Vergano was then hired to work on the third shift. Despite the heavier workload and the hectic pace on the second shift, Doug proved himself again. He diligently handled the extra workload and proved to be a valuable employee. He comfortably and successfully performed all his new work assignments.

Doug's promotion coincided with the data center's financial problems. The data center provided data processing services to a number of clients spread across the United States and Canada. The number of clients however had been decreasing each month. Inexpensive midrange computers and the need for Business Managers to have information quickly prompted many clients to acquire their own information systems. With a dwindling customer base, the company saw its revenues dropped considerably. The alarming rate at which the clients terminated their service contracts and the consequent lost in revenues forced Bill to look into every possible ways to trim back the costs of operating the data center. First Bill sold the IBM mainframe computer and leased a compatible machine from IPL, a lesser-known computer vendor. The sale of the old IBM computer generated much needed cash. In addition the new computer saved the data center $2,500 per month in maintenance fees. The new computer was installed over the weekend to minimize disruption to the daily workflow. After the initial bugs in the new computer were ironed out, the nightly batch processing resumed. Bill then ordered the removal of three disk storage devices and had them shipped back to the vendors. He exchanged an advanced punch card reader with a separate controller for a basic card reader with a built-in controller. He reduced the number of disk storage packs on lease from seventy to thirty packs and re-negotiated the maintenance contracts on all the computer peripherals. The new measures saved the company another $2,000 per month. The reduction in disk storage capacity did not allow for extra disk packs to be readily available when a storage device crashes.

He could not handle the pressure

The new computer took longer to process the raw data and the new printers took longer to print the clients' reports. Despite the slower processing and printing speed, the deadline for completing the batch processing remained unchanged. The heaviest workload was on the second shift and Doug began to feel the pressure mounting on him. When data had been collected during the afternoon, they were turned over to Doug for batch processing. After processing the raw data, the clients' reports were then printed on two fast line printers. The reports consisted of Packing Slips, Route Trip Sheets, Pickup Instructions, Record Cards, Error Listings, Sales Adjustments, and Summary Reports. The various reports were then taken to the mailroom. Carlos then separated, decollated, folded and boxed up the reports for shipping. Purolator picked up the first shipment of boxes at 8.00 P.M. Federal Express arrived at 9.00 P.M. to pick up the second shipment of boxes. At 10.30 P.M., Carlos loaded the remaining boxes in the company van and dropped them off at a US postal service facility and other airline terminals. Doug was responsible for printing all the reports by 8.30 P.M. each night so that they could be boxed and shipped on time. However hardware problems cropped up every now and then and delayed the shipments. It was absolutely necessary for the clients to receive their trip sheets and pickup instructions the next day. These instructions were vital to the truck drivers when they make their delivery and pickup trips. Without the delivery and pickup sheets, the truck drivers could not perform their jobs.

Late during the year Bill decided to eliminate one printer from the computer room. Until then Doug printed all the reports on two high-speed impact printers on lease from Storage Technology, Inc. The first printer was rated at 1500 lines per second; the second at 3000 lines per second. The faster printer was the newest, state-of-the-art printer, but it was also more expensive to lease and maintain. The two printers were vital to the computer operations. It was not unusual for all the reports to be printed by 7:30 P.M. when both printers are running. No shipment would be possible unless the printers print all the reports first. Despite Herman's thought to the contrary, Bill believed that all the reports could be printed on time using one printer only. He asserted that it had become too costly for the data center to have two printers do the work of one printer. Herman argued that the second printer would be an insurance against the failure of the first printer, but Bill said that keeping a second printer was not economically sound. Bill argued that he could save the company an additional $1,300 a month by using one printer only. To prove that Doug could get by with only one printer, Bill ordered the faster printer powered down for two weeks. The result of the shutdown indicated that one printer could print all the reports before the deadlines for shipping. However, in making his assessment, Bill ignored such considerations as late data transmissions, power outages, and unexpected CPU downtime. Other problems with the disk controllers and disk packs could also affect production, not to mention that the printer itself could fail too. Air conditioning failures and operator's fatigue were two other factors that could delay the printing of the reports. The reports were printed on four customized forms and multi-part computer stock paper. Consequently the printer had to be cycled several times in order to print all the reports. Each time a special form was used to print a report, the printer had to be paused, the forms changed, and the carriage control loop reloaded. This simple functions added time to the time it took to print all the reports. Herman had previously worked as a Computer Operator, and he understood how tiresome changing computer forms on the printer could be. Doug was not as agile as Herman. His size limited his ability around the printer. With two printers running, Doug could spread the printer load without tiring himself.

Satisfied that one printer could do the work of two printers without affecting the shipping deadlines, Bill arranged for the STC technicians to remove the faster printer from the computer room. Doug became worried that he would not be able to make the shipping deadlines. Herman explained to Doug that it was Bill's decision to remove the printer and he could not convince him otherwise. After the second printer was removed, Herman stayed late a few nights to help Doug cope with the new working situation. On the nights when Doug fell behind with his work, Herman came in and helped him catch up. In due time Doug started to feel the pressure of turning out the reports on time. His attitude changed and he was no longer the same, cheerful employee he once was. He rushed madly around the printer to print the reports for Carlos to box up. Doug particularly appeared overwhelmed when he had to work around the printer. Sweat constantly dripped over his forefront. His smile disappeared forever from his face. Shortly after the printer was removed, the customer assistance department was inundated with calls from customers complaining that they did not receive their trip sheets and reports. The number of complaints grew larger day after day. Every morning the Account Representative frantically sought alternate shipping methods to get the computer reports shipped to the clients. Herman made frequent trips to the airport to drop the boxes so that the customers would receive them on the same day. Something always seemed to go wrong on Doug's shift. Carlos Ramon was the first employee to show concerns about the change in Doug's behavior.

He solved the riddle of the Messiah

"I don't know what's wrong with Doug," Carlos frequently complained. "He wanders around a lot during his shift. He is not doing his work as he was supposed to and I had to keep reminding him which reports to print out first. He is printing out reports that he was not supposed to print until later at night. Every night he leaves the printer idle and paces up and down the hallway. He seems to forget that I have shipping deadlines to make."

Carlos was a neat worker, but he always complained about someone not doing his work. He was scornful that Doug was promoted before him.

Herman frequently waved off his comments as retaliatory and derogatory. A few days later Carlos brought up the subject of Doug's behavior again.

"Doug is acting up again," Carlos noted. "I don't like the look on his face when he looks at me. I am looking for another job. He paced up and down the hallway last night, mumbling to himself for close to an hour. He must have walked up and down the hallway about fifty times. He seems to go to the restroom all the times. I don't think it's normal for anyone to go to the restroom fifty times in an hour."

"Was he really going to the restroom?" Herman asked. "Maybe he was just going to the lunch room and getting a can of soda."

"It seems that way," Carlos replied. "I don't know for what other reason he would be going to the restroom so many times unless he is not behaving normally. I carry a pocketknife with me just in case. The other night Jose saw him standing on the shipping dock and staring at the sky. He was outside staring at the sky for so long that Jose got worried for him and went out to check on him. Did Jose tell you what Doug told him?"

"No."

"Doug told Jose that he had finally solved the riddle of the Messiah."

"What's the riddle of the Messiah," Herman asked, perplexed.

"I don't know," Carlos replied. "Ask Jose when he comes in. He heard him say that. One night Doug came in looking very worried and asked us if we have seen his eggs."

"He lost his eggs?"

"Yeah, that's what he said. Then he went everywhere in the building looking for his eggs. Most of the time we don't know what he is saying."

"Do you think that Doug is using drugs?"

"I can't tell by just looking at him," Carlos replied. "Last week he showed me his left arm and pointed to a red dot on his vein. He said: 'See what this man did to me?' I had no idea what he was talking about. One night he returned from his break and asked us if we have seen his pickup truck. He did not remember where he parked it. We all went out to the parking lot to look for his pickup truck, but it was not there. We drove around as far as I-35, but we still could not locate his truck."

"Where was the truck?"

"We later found his truck on the other side of the street with the engine running."

Jose Vergano and Damon Page, another operator working on the third shift, also noticed Doug's strange behavior.

"I think Doug is going through some mental state change," Damon said. "He needs to see a psychiatrist. Carlos and I went along with him to a nightclub one night after work. After drinking two bottles of beer, he started saying things that didn't make sense at all. He sounded weird. He had this strange look in his eyes. I am terrified whenever I see that look in his eyes."

"Are you two suggesting that Doug has a mental problem?"

"I know he's sick up there," Carlos said, pointing at the right side of his head. "A few years ago my sister-in-law behaved exactly like Doug. We had to call the police and had her taken to Terrell Hospital. The doctors there told us that she was crazy and kept her in the hospital for a psychiatric evaluation. They locked her up in that hospital for two years."

The story of Carlos' sister reminded Herman of his own encounter with a mentally ill person a few years ago. He was moonlighting in a restaurant while attending college and worked with a waiter whose name was Mustafa. Mustafa was a Turkish Cypriot who spoke and understood English, but most of the time spoke Greek to the Greek Cypriot waiters. It was unusual for a Turkish Cypriot to get along with Greek Cypriots, even more unusual that he would speak their language. Mustafa was very friendly with the diners who patronized the restaurant especially women and children. On his days off, he stayed home and watched the Charlie's Angels television series. He became very fond of the female characters in the show and constantly talked about them in the restaurant. Eventually the other waiters nicknamed him 'Charlie.' Mustafa liked to refer to her young female acquaintances as Charlie's angels. On many occasions Herman noticed that Mustafa talked and laughed to himself when he was alone. Herman did not understand what he said and he could not make out whether he talked in English, Turkish or Greek. Mustafa suddenly became rude to customers and frequently got into fights with the other waiters. It became impossible to talk to him about anything. The other waiters became concerned for his well being, but there was little they could do. They left him alone whenever he mumbled to himself. Finally when he started arguing with the Jewish restaurant owner, the owner fired him. After he was fired he returned to the restaurant and shouted vociferation at everyone. On two occasions he walked into the restaurant, grabbed a handful of bills from the cash register and ran off. He claimed that the owner did not pay him when he fired him. On another occasion he returned with a butcher knife and threatened to kill the Greek Cypriot restaurant Manager. The restaurant owner called the police. Mustafa was arrested and confined to a mental hospital for psychiatric evaluation.

Based on his subordinates' accounts, Herman hypothesized that Doug might be suffering from a similar brain malfunction. Doug exhibited the same behavior as Mustafa did just before he was fired. The employees who worked closest to Doug had observed the change in his mental state and openly talked about it. Something, perhaps the pressure placed on him by his job responsibilities, was causing Doug to crack up. Herman could not fire Doug on account of what he had heard. His job demanded that he used his interpersonal skills whenever there was trouble between his subordinates. He was however not qualified to analyze and take action on Doug's behavior. He speculated that drugs and alcohol might cause Doug's problem. He had no proof that Doug was drinking or using drugs while at work. The other employees were worried for their safety, but Herman did not know how to appease their fear.

"I no longer talk to him," Jose told him. "I tell him once to do this or that and if he doesn't want to do it, I leave him alone."

"He's not being of any help on the shift," Carlos frequently remarked. "I can't get him to print the reports that need to go out first."

Something bothered him

Despite all the cost-cutting measures, the data center continued to lose money. Because of the reduced amount of processing, there was no longer a need for two Computer Operators on each shift. Bill ordered him to terminate three employees. Bill also felt that there had been too many complaints about late shipments and missing reports since Doug began working on the second shift. He rescheduled Doug to work from noon to eight o'clock. In making the schedule change, Bill intended to relieve Doug from the pressure on the second shift, but Doug's mental state did not show any improvements. The other employees working with him continued to complain about him. One evening Herman walked into the computer room unannounced. It was almost 10 o'clock when he arrived at the data center. He found Doug loitering around in the computer room. From the hallway, Herman saw Doug standing by the glass door separating the computer room and the mailroom. Doug crossed his hands behind his back and stared fixedly at the computer room floor. Unaware that he was being watched by Herman, he walked over to the data transmission room and stared at the video display screen. Jose and Carlos stood at a safe distance from Doug in the mailroom and watched Doug's movements with trepidation. When Doug went into the mailroom they hurriedly retreated to the computer room. Suddenly Doug hit the doors separating the mailroom from the computer room with his arm. The doors flung open and swung back and forth on its two-way hinges. Herman stepped into the computer room and confronted Doug. "What do you think you are doing?" Herman shouted. Doug turned and stared in bewilderment at Herman. He seemed awaken from a trance. He was astonished to see Herman at the data center at night.

"I am sorry," Doug apologized. "I did not mean to do that."

"Why did you do it?"

"I was thinking about someone," Doug replied.

"Have you been drinking?"

Doug's mood suddenly changed. He shook his head left to right and smiled. "It's up to you to find out," he said musically.

"Go home," Herman told him. "Jose can handle the shift by himself. Your shift ended at eight o'clock. Why are you still here?"

"I am leaving now," he replied. He paced up and down the computer room and then stopped at a stack of boxes. The boxes contained various kinds of computer forms. He leaned against the boxes and crossed his left foot on his right. He then ran his fingers over the sole of his left shoe.

"What are you doing now?" Herman asked him.

"Something is bothering me," he said. "I am trying to get it off." Herman looked at his shoe but found nothing on the sole. Yet Doug appeared to be pulling something off it. Doug's action reminded Herman of someone pulling chewing gum stuck on the sole of his shoes.

"I think you should go home and get some sleep," Herman advised him. "Tomorrow we'll begin month end processing. It'll be a very busy day."

"I prefer to work on the third shift," Doug said.

"You would rather work on the third shift?"

Doug smiled and shook his head. "It's up to you to find out," he sang melodiously.

Herman asked him once more to go home. Doug's mood suddenly changed and he stared at the computer floor without saying anything. Then, without warning, he hit the mailroom door again and bolted out of the computer room. He ran out of the back door and drove off into the night. Jose and Carlos were relieved that Doug had finally left. Trembling with fear they gathered around Herman.

"What got to him?" Herman asked, still puzzled at Doug's behavior.

"He does that every night," Carlos replied. "First he paces around in the computer room. Then all of a sudden he says that he had forgotten something and he hastily runs outside. Just like tonight. An hour later he comes back and does the same thing again."

"I followed him out last night," Jose said, "He ran to his truck and drove off like a madman."

Herman raised his hands up in defeat and shrugged his shoulders. "I don't know what to tell you," he told his two employees. "I don't understand why he behaves like that." The front door opened and Damon, the third shift data controller walked in and joined them in the computer room. He was not scheduled to start his shift until eleven o'clock, but he had been so worried for his own safety that he came to work an hour earlier to ascertain that Doug had left. They heard the back door in the mailroom opened up. Shortly afterwards Doug walked back into the computer room. Jose and Carlos stepped back and kept at a safe distance from him. Damon moved and stood behind Herman.

"You are still here?" Herman asked, surprised by the sudden reappearance of Doug.

"I came back to check that everything is all right," he said.

"Everything is running smoothly tonight," Herman assured him. "You can go home now."

Doug stood still and stared at everyone. Then he went to check the terminals in the transmission room. Jose stayed close to the main console and Carlos retreated to the lunchroom. Damon kept a watchful eye on Doug. Doug suddenly broke into his anxiety attack once more. He slammed his arm into the door and bolted out of the mailroom. Herman rushed to the back door and saw him jump into his pickup truck and drive away.

"I always see him with this weird look on his face when I come to work," Damon angrily said. "If I find him here when I come to work I will turn back and go home," he warned Herman. "I can't do my work with somebody like him around me. He gives me the creep when he stares at me. I feel threatened by him. My life is more important to me than this job. Doug is cracking up. I don't know what he'll do next."

Carlos came back from hiding in the lunchroom. "Damon is right. You have to do something about Doug."

Jose stood by with his fingers crossed in front of him. "I just leave him alone," he said in resignation. "I don't even talk to him anymore. What is happening to him? He used to be such a nice guy?"

"I don't know what I can do or should do," Herman said in desperation. "I'll talk to him tomorrow when he comes in. I'll try to find out what's bugging him."

He lived with his parents

The pattern of Doug's behavior was the same each day. He would come to work at noon, looking fresh and healthy and normal. By night time his mood changed. Instead of going home at the end of his shift, he hanged around the computer room. Damon had complained that Doug frequently walked into the building at odd hours of the night. This bothered Herman because Doug should not be at work at night unless he was scheduled to work. When Doug came to work the next day Herman summoned him into his office. Doug walked into his office holding a pen in his hand. He looked pale and nervous.

"Doug," Herman said. "I have received a lot of complaints about you during the past few weeks. I am told that you have been behaving erratically. Are you feeling sick or tired? Is there something I can do to help you out?"

"I am all right," Doug said. He rattled his pen nervously on the arm of the chair.

"Carlos said that you are not printing the reports early enough for him to box and ship out. Some customers had complained that you took their calls, but did not collect their data."

"There is only one printer now," Doug explained. "I can't print all the reports on time. Since the second printer was removed it has been very hard for me to print all the reports on time. I need another printer to do my job."

"We did some tests prior to removing the second printer and we know that we can make the deadlines working with just one printer."

"I am nervous every night," Doug continued. "I worry that I will fall behind and not make all the shipping deadlines. Missing the shipping deadlines makes me very nervous."

"You can't be blamed if the computer goes down and prevent you from finishing your job. There is nothing one can do if the computer goes belly up. Bill won't hold you accountable for that sort of things."

"Bill will fire me if I don't make the shipping deadlines."

"You are working for me," Herman assured him. "Bill cannot fire you unless I tell him so. I heard that your mother had you evaluated by a psychiatrist. Is there any truth in that rumor?"

Doug turned white like a sheet and ran his hand over his forefront. "That was quite a while ago," he replied. "I got an 'F' in three subjects at school. My mother thought that there was something wrong with my mind."

"When did that happen?"

"I don't remember."

"Was that before you started working for us?"

"It might have been last year. Yes, I think it was last year."

"What did the psychiatrist say?"

"He said that my mind is all right."

"Do you remember the psychiatrist's name?"

"I think it was Jones."

Herman jotted down the name of the psychiatrist on his notepad. "Do you remember his first name?"

"No, I don't."

"After you left last night your father called and asked if you were still at work. I told him that you had left the data center at around 11 o'clock. When I got home, I called your mother to make sure that you got home safely. She said that you were still not home. Where were you?"

"I was driving around," Doug said. "I did not want to go home."

"You were driving around town at midnight? What time did you get home then?"

"I don't recall."

"Two o'clock?"

"I don't know."

"Three o'clock?"

"I think that it was about five o'clock when I got home."

"You were driving around town until five o'clock in the morning? Why? Were you not concerned that your parents might be worried for you? You should call them and let them know whenever you are going to be late."

"I don't like to bother them," Doug said. "I feel guilty that I am still living with my parents. I try not to spend too much time at home."

"If it bothers you so much to live with your parents, why don't you move out into your own apartment?" Herman suggested. "It would seem a logical thing for you to do if you don't like to hang around your parents."

"I am afraid to move out of my parents' house and rent an apartment," Doug said. "If the data center shut down, I will be out of work."

"You won't be the only one, Doug," Herman said. "All of us will be without a job. That does not mean that we have to stop breathing. We'll just have to go out and find another job when we get laid off. There are lots of jobs around and I don't think you'll have any problems finding a new job. I am in the same boat as you are. Besides it will be several months before a decision is made about shutting down the data center. Even if the decision is made to close down the data center, we will still have to convert the remaining customers to their own systems. I figure that we'll be employed for another six months. Stop worrying about being laid off and focus on doing a good job. I have moved you to the afternoon shift because there isn't a lot of work between noon and four o'clock. You have less work assigned to you now."

"The telephone drives me crazy," Doug complained.

"Would you rather not answer the phone? I thought it was the easiest part of the job."

"I don't like to answer the telephone."

"I'll have to talk to Bill about that. I heard that you go to the restroom frequently during your shift. Is something wrong?"

"I was thirsty," Doug replied. "I went to get some water."

"Do you recall seeing me here last night?"

"Yes."

"You slammed your arm into the mailroom door a couple of times. Why did you do that?"

"I was thinking about my parents at the time."

"I am very concerned for your well being, Doug. You could have hurt yourself when you hit that door. Are you taking any drugs?"

"No."

"Can you handle your new working hours?"

"I prefer to work on the third shift. My mind won't get too tired since there isn't much to do at night."

"I'll have to talk to Bill first. Would you like to take some time off?"

"I'd like to. I haven't been able to sleep much since the second printer was removed. My mind is very tired."

"Take Monday and Tuesday off," Herman advised him. "I will ask Bill if I can move you back to the third shift. Are you sure you want to work on the third shift? Not too long ago you said that you were tired of working on the graveyard shift."

"I think working on the third shift is better for me. My mind is very tired."

He was such a nice employee

Later that afternoon Herman talked to Bill about Doug's strange behavior. "I don't understand," Bill exclaimed. "He did a wonderful job when he was working in the Data Control room. He always did what he was told to do and he did not cause any trouble for anyone. I can't believe that this is happening to him."

"Things may have changed a bit since then," Herman said. "That was three years ago."

Bill smiled. "People just don't change like that," he remarked. "Maybe Doug cannot handle the pressure on the second shift. You are right, Herman. We have to do something."

"We have already made some changes," Herman reminded Bill. "I moved him away from the second shift where the workload is heaviest and scheduled him to work at noon so he could go home at eight o'clock."

"Is his new work hour helping?"

Herman shook his head. "I am still hearing a lot of complaints from the other employees. Doug now wants to work on the third shift."

"How is Damon handling the third shift?" Bill asked.

"No better than when he was working on the first shift," Herman replied. "I am ready to let him go anytime. I am running out of patience with him. There have been a couple of complaints about him reporting to work intoxicated. He had constantly been tardy particularly on Friday nights. One night he did not show up for work and did not notify anyone. The number of incomplete data transmissions has increased since he started working on the third shift. I gave him several warnings, but they don't seem to serve any purpose."

"Did you put them down in writing?"

"They have all been recorded and added to his file," Herman assured Bill.

"Was Damon fully trained before you moved him to the third shift?"

"He is mainly doing what he used to do on the day shift," Herman answered. "I think Damon is working at another job during the day. He was working as a cook at Dillard's before we hired him. He may have gone back to that job. I think that his job at Dillard's is the reason why he wanted to work on the third shift."

"Is he sleeping on the job?"

"I don't know."

"Do you think that he's drinking on the job?"

"I don't know, but both Jose and Carlos said that Damon frequently comes to work intoxicated."

"I think we have done everything we can to accommodate Damon. Let him go whenever you are ready. I still don't understand what is wrong with Doug. He was such a nice employee. Is he using drugs?"

"I don't know. I know that he drinks beer. I don't know if his behavior is linked in any way to drugs or alcohol. I don't know if he is mentally ill or not. He said that the psychiatrist who evaluated him told him that he is all right, but I don't even know if Doug told me the truth or not. I really don't know, Bill. How do we prevent Doug from turning violent or carrying out hostile acts against other employees? Are Managers supposed to analyze an employee's behavior and report their behavior to their families or spouses? Should Managers be trained to recognize trouble signs and look for unusual behavior in employees?"

"No." Bill smiled. "That's not our job."

"Perhaps we should profile employees when they are hired to identify those who are prone to violence."

"Let's concentrate on doing our jobs. I think you are getting worried for nothing."

"I can relieve him of some of the work pressure. He may be on the brink of a mental breakdown. Jose said that if I terminate him, he would come back and shoot at everybody."

Bill laughed. "Doug is not going to shoot at anybody," he said. "Jose is just being funny."

"Jose was very serious when he made that statement. He is already looking for another job. He is my best employee and I don't want to lose him. Perhaps we should talk to Doug's mother. She may be able to tell us something about his recent behavior."

"I think I may just do that." Bill scribbled a reminder to himself to call Doug's mother. "Will Damon agree to work on the second shift?"

"I have not asked him yet."

Damon would not switch shift with Doug which was what Herman had expected. He suspected that Damon initially requested to be moved to the third shift so that he could go to sleep when he completes his tasks. Herman did not have sufficient reason to terminate him so that he could move Doug to the third shift. Doug continued to perform poorly on his job. It took him longer to understand a work instruction, continued to miss shipping deadlines, and frequently left the computer room unattended for long period of times. He constantly paced up and down the hallway and terrified the other employees by his bizarre behavior. His conversations with them were becoming more and more frightening and confusing, and he often talked in circles. One night he powered down the computer in the middle of the nightly batch processing for no apparent reason. Jose was furious. It took him an hour to recover the lost data and catch up with the batch processing. As a result of the unscheduled shutdown, all shipments were delayed. At the end of the month, Herman scheduled Doug to work until midnight to help Jose with the extra workload, but they were still unable to complete the month end processing before the end of the shift. At midnight they turned the shift over to Damon when he came in. Damon called Herman and complained that Doug had left too much work for him to complete. Herman came in to assist Damon to complete the month end processing before the next morning. When Herman arrived at the data center Damon left the computer room. When he did not returned after an hour Herman went to look for him. He found him asleep in the lunchroom and fired him on the spot.

He fired the anti-matter weapon

The following day Herman moved Doug to the third shift. The move however did nothing to change his bizarre mood. His work performance on the third shift took a downturn for the worse. Customers called every morning to complain that they did not receive their data transmission. The first shift Data Controller found that many tapes were not transmitted to the customers during the night. There was also a drastic increase in the number of incomplete data transmissions. Doug did not reset and restart the incomplete transmissions when they occurred. The incomplete transmissions had to be restarted the next morning which tied up the data terminals. The first shift Data Controller also complained that Doug did not stay long enough to brief her before leaving his post. He ran out of the building as soon as she walked into the room. Other employees began to complain that Doug stared at them for long periods of time. When Bill came to work early one morning, he was blasted away by loud music coming from the company's intercom system. He went to the transmission room to investigate and found Doug dressed in a hunter's vest. He sat in total darkness and watched the data flowing on the terminal screen. Dark sunglasses covered his eyes. Disturbed by what he saw, Bill met with Herman later that morning to express his concerns about Doug's bizarre behavior. His behavior was impacting the employees' morale. He was also unhappy that the number of customer complaints had shot up since Doug started to work on the third shift.

Tired of all the complaints about Doug, Herman made a surprise visit to the data center at 3 o'clock in the morning. The lights in the building were all turned off. Doug had moved an armchair from an office to the Data Control room. He sat in an armchair in the dark and watched the data racing across the terminal screen. His eyes were covered with a pair of dark sunglasses. The green phosphorescent data from the screen glowed in the dark.

"Why are the lights turned off?" Herman asked.

Without moving his gaze from the video screen Doug calmly said: "The eagle has landed." He was hypnotized by the data flowing across the screen.

"What?" Herman asked, stepping closer to the terminal screen.

"It was in Aladdin Castle, the war in Vietnam. We won. Danang massacre! I was there. Fire the anti-matter weapon to complete the kaleidoscope pattern. Who flew in the unknown soldier's pattern?"

Herman suddenly realized that Doug was talking nonsense and became frightened. "I don't know what you are saying," he stammered. "I came by to see if everything is all right." He looked at the stacks of tapes waiting to be transmitted to the customers' data terminals. These tapes, Herman thought, should have already been transmitted.

"Take me to the artificial moon. Catch her in the eye. Secure all M1 tank assembly. I smell the blood of a Chinese karate monkey wrench," Doug continued.

"Do you mind if I turn the lights on?" Herman asked.

"Go ahead, but remember that it was I who built the Taj Mahal. It was not John Mahal."

"How did you do that?" Herman switched the lights on in the transmission room.

"We are gone," Doug said, looking and smiling at Herman. He waved his hand at him and said: "Goodbye, Texas Instrument calculators." He suddenly turned solemn and stared at the terminal screen. "The immortal Babe Ruth; they will never sink the goddamn ass. The Telstar fires the laser canon. Fire the anti-matter weapon above your head."

Herman put his hand on Doug's shoulder. "Doug, are you all right?"

"Don't steal from me," he warned.

"How can you work in the dark? Why aren't you sending out those tapes? Are the data terminals out?" Four data terminals were shut down.

"Tell Nugent to turn up the volume on his guitar," Doug said.

"What?"

"He is at the Tutankhamen boot camp at the NWSA. The Milky Way Space Administration is no Communist. Did you know that? Open fire with the anti-matter weapon; it's solar-powered. Coordinate: Rod Stewart Beach. I cannot get a date because of the Russians and the communists. They are both made in the USA."

Herman was taken aback by Doug's mood.

"Do not enter the Western Hemisphere without response time," Doug continued.

Herman turned down the volume on the radio.

"Turn it up, turn it up. I am the usher, boo boo." Doug looked at his wrist. "What's my pulse rate?"

"How the hell will I know?" Herman replied.

"What is my blood pressure?"

"I don't know."

"Who killed Jimmy Cricket?"

"I don't know. Who is he?"

"He is match 51, Woody. A power ball champ! We call him Spike."

"Have you been drinking?" Herman looked around him for a beer can or bottle."

"Drinking? Pabst Blue Ribbon, vintage 1909. I love the taste." He stood up from the armchair and walked down the hallway. "Just whistle if you need me, merchant marine! Don't forget to fire the laser canon. It's brand new."

Herman watched him walk to the water fountain at the end of the hallway. He filled his mug with water and came back. "Where is my paycheck?" he asked.

"You got paid last week," Herman reminded him. Herman picked up the transmission log and read the entries.

"I can't believe that he thinks that he is a tractor beam. He ought to add the rest of the color spectrum and not rescue any survivors." He drank some water and then put the mug on the shelf above the table. He dashed to the computer room and loaded a tape on the tape drive. Herman followed him into the computer room with the transmission log in his hand.

"I am Marco Polo. Where is my cup?"

"You left your cup in the transmission room."

"Tell them to build a pyramid. Tell them that I will be back in the year 200 million B.C." He ran back to the transmission room with a tape, laid the tape on the table and hurried to the water fountain. He filled up the mug with water again and came back. "What did Tyrannosaurus Rex tell you?"

Herman stared at Doug with his eyes wide opened.

"Feed the lion from Judah's tribe a cheeseburger if it roars. Let the lizard eat a communist." Doug returned to the computer room and unwound a tape from the tape drive. He pulled the write ring from the tape and threw it in a box. "Feed the fish, feed the fish, it's not a guppy."

Herman remained silent and watched him. He tried to make sense out of the strange words flowing out of his mouth. Jose and Carlos were right. Doug was indeed talking nonsense. Or perhaps Doug thought that he was talking to someone else, not Herman.

"From the halls of Montezuma to the shores of Tripoli, we can fight our country's battles on land, sea and air," Doug continued.

"I believe we can," Herman said.

"I think Patrick Henry Strange stole the space marines' silver tea set and hot coffee." Herman looked at the computer room log and job run schedule. "Are you looking for a land mine made in the USA?" Herman ignored him and continued to read the log.

"Read to yourself and not too loud please."

Doug went back into the transmission room and mounted the new tape on the tape drive above the Wang terminal. He picked up the telephone and dialed the customer's data terminal to initiate the data transmission.

"Can you hear me, Sam Houston? Like I said, let him eat a communist." He hanged up the phone and stared at Herman.

"Let's rework the Bay of Pigs," he solemnly asked. "We can now fire the laser canon."

He removed a can of tobacco from his back pocket. The can had left a circle on the faded blue jean. He opened the can, took a pinch of tobacco and rubbed it between his lower lip and gum.

"This is one heck of a moat. The giant iguanas like it when they chew on Havana Tobacco. What?"

"I did not say anything," Herman said.

"He likes it in Tucson, Arizona. It's the laser canon testing area. Did you test a nuclear device there?"

"No, I did not."

"It fires before you hit the detonator. They sell them at the Army and Navy stores. Maybe we can get our tax dollars back."

Herman was overcome by a sense of helplessness.

"Apollo 12 is securely assembled and ready to fly into the negative infinity." Doug pointed to the data flowing on the terminal screen. "That's me landing over there. There is a communist tank commander behind these rocks."

"How can you be at two places at the same time?"

"I increased my negative response time." Herman was amazed at his answer. Doug suddenly pushed him back. "Get me the secret service quickly," he said in a panic. "I think that he shot at John F. Kennedy. Ask him what happened in the early sixties on Motor Street."

"Who shot JFK?"

"He shot himself, ha, ha, ha. It's not JFK or RFK."

Doug exploded into a mad laughter. "Don't bury him in Washington D.C unless he wants to shoot himself again. He is the holiest man on the planet."

"Who is the holiest man on the planet?"

"Tell them to do negative response time exercises in the morning to push up the world record. Lady, I know! I hope nobody ever hurts anyone at a Milky Way Space Administration facility."

Herman thought that Doug was referring to the National Aeronautics and Space Administration.

"Last night I went into Fidel Castro's bedroom and put the lights out for him," Doug continued. "I told him to have a nice day but I wish I haven't said that." His mood changed from excitement to sadness.

"Too late now," Herman said sarcastically.

"I am Yogi Bear and there isn't a ranger in the park. I don't have to play baseball in order to make a living. It's my hope that no one gets hurt on his day off. The Telstar just fired a laser canon. Have a nice day."

The transmission ended abnormally and the terminal beeped. The beeps irritated him. "Beep, beep, beep, you trash," he yelled at the terminal. "Don't slow me down. That was one heck of a company picnic."

Doug went back to the computer room to turn the lights off. He came back and switched off the light in the transmission room and increased the volume on his radio. He mounted another tape on the tape drive and initiated another transmission. When the data started to zip across the screen, he dashed to the water fountain again. He came back with his mug filled with water, slumped down on the armchair and watched the data flowing across the screen. All of a sudden he was locked up in his own world and became oblivious of Herman's presence around him. Herman had seen enough of Doug's dark side. He quietly left the data center and went home.

He was jailed for a traffic violation

Herman met with Bill the following day and told him that he was very concerned about Doug's behavior. He recounted his meeting with Doug and expressed concerns that Doug might cause damage to the computer or the customer databases. The damage in turn would hurt the company's business. He gravely informed Bill that Doug might do harm to himself.

"I don't understand," Bill lamented. "He has always been a nice employee. Do you remember the time when he was working for us one summer? He did a superb job then. He never missed a day, and he was always on time. He was one of the best employees working in the shipping room. I have always like him."

"I think Doug is mentally ill," Herman said. "He is delusional and he suffers from severe anxiety. He is unable to separate facts from fiction. I really think that he needs to undergo a psychiatric evaluation before he gets out of control. I don't know too much about mental illnesses, but I can tell you that his behavior last night was bizarre. The things he talked about frighten me. I am not the only one to have heard him talk like that. Carlos, Jose, Damon... They all said the same things. The day shift employees are telling me the same things again. We have to do something about Doug. I am afraid that if we don't act now, some of our employees will leave the company."

"You are right again, Herman. We have to do something about Doug. He could knock us out of business if he tampers with the computer system. I don't have any objection if you terminate him now although I was not planning on terminating any more employees. On the other hand it would not be fair to bring in another person to take his place and then lay him off three months later. We are losing customers at the rate of ten per month. We may have to eliminate the third shift altogether."

"Have you talked to his mother yet?"

"I haven't," Bill admitted. He smiled and then turned solemn. "I did not call her because I don't know what to tell her. What would you tell her?"

"I wouldn't know what to tell her myself," Herman answered.

"Do you think that Doug is suffering from dementia?"

"The other employees think so. I'll run an ad this weekend."

"I am leaving for my vacation tomorrow. Let put off advertising for a new replacement for Doug until I come back."

While Bill was on vacation Doug ran into trouble with the law. He could not produce his automobile insurance papers when he was stopped for a moving violation. The police officer ran a check on him and discovered that he did not pay a prior speeding ticket. He arrested and took him to the county jail. Doug later called Carlos to tell him that he could not come to work. When Herman was informed that Doug was arrested for a traffic violation, he called the county jail to inquire about him. The county clerk informed him that Doug would have to pay a prior fine of $282 before he could be released. Herman then called Doug's parents. His father picked up the phone but hung up when Herman told him that Doug was in jail. Herman covered for Doug that night. At daybreak he called his parents again but constantly received a busy signal. Later during the day he called Doug's parents again and finally got hold of his mother.

"I don't have that kind of money," she said when Herman told her about her son's previous traffic violation. "Nobody has that kind of money handy. He'll just have to languish in jail until I can find the money." She then hung up. Herman had spent the night covering for Doug. He was tired and he was eager to go home and sleep. Before he went home, he called Doug at the county jail. Doug sounded scared and desperate. He pleaded Herman to come and get him out of jail.

"If you would get me out of jail now I promise you that I'll get you out when you are in jail," he proposed.

Herman refrained from laughing. "You should call your mother," he told him.

"I have called my parents several times already but they are not home. I don't want to call them again."

"I just talked to your mother. She said that she is rounding up the money and will get you out soon."

"You should not call my parents. I don't want them to know that I am in jail."

"They already knew when I called them. The police must have informed them."

"I have money in the bank. I'll pay you back after you get me out."

"You mother said that she would have you released soon. She may already be on the way to the county jail. Call her and talk to her. Call me back if she does not help you."

As Herman left for home, the Production Scheduler walked up to him. She told him that Doug was on the phone and wanted to speak to him. Herman went back to his office and picked the telephone up. Doug once again pleaded with him to have him released from jail.

"Did you call your mother?" he asked Doug in a weary voice.

"She is not home," Doug replied. Herman knew that Doug did not call his mother.

"I'll see what I can do for you. I'll call you back."

Herman went to talk to the Vice-President of Finance to ask him to pay Doug's fine.

"Do you think it's our responsibility to get him out of trouble?" the company officer sternly asked him.

Herman wished he had never gone to him for help. "No, I don't think so," he admitted. "But his parents don't seem to care. This young man has a problem. How can we all be so insensitive to his problems?"

"Did you call his parents?"

"Yes, Sir. I did, but, like I said, they don't seem to care."

"Call them again," the Vice-President advised. "If you can't get hold of his parents, let me know." Unable to keep his eyes opened any longer, Herman went home without calling Doug back.

The next day around ten in the morning, Doug's mother called him and informed him that she was on the way to the county jail.

"Mrs. Krousse," Herman said before she hung up. "Doug has been behaving strangely lately. Is there something that you can tell us about his mood change?"

"We have noticed it too," she admitted. "I don't know what to do."

"He said things that don't make any sense to anyone. Do you understand what I mean?"

"I know exactly what you mean," Mrs. Krousse answered. "He talks like that at home too. What do you think is wrong with him?"

"I think that he may be..." Herman hesitated.

"Don't be embarrassed to tell me. We already know that he is not right."

"I think that he may be sick."

"I think so too but I don't know what to do. Why has he been moved to the third shift?"

"He asked to be moved to the third shift. We thought that the late night shift would be better for him. There isn't a lot of work for him to do on that shift."

"I wish I know what to do," she said in despair. "If there is something else you want to ask me please don't be afraid to call me." She hung up. Herman was relieved that she would soon have Doug released from jail. He was also relieved that he did not have to work again that night. He looked forward to a restful night. Unfortunately for Herman, he did not have the restful night that he had longed for. Jose interrupted his sleep around midnight to inform him that Doug brought his riffle with him to work.

He hunted for communists

Herman arrived at the data center forty minutes after he left his house. There were no lights in the hallway. When he walked up to the front door Jose came out of the shadows to meet him. He shook like a leaf.

"Don't go in there," he implored him. "He has a rifle and he is hunting for communists. He might mistake you for a communist and kill you. I think that it is better to call the police."

"Doug isn't going to shoot me," Herman assured him. Herman unlocked the front door and walked into the dark building. Jose stayed outside.

"Be careful," Jose shouted at him. "This guy has gone crazy."

Herman flipped the hallway lights on and walked to the transmission room. He saw Doug's head amidst an array of red, green, yellow and white lights. Without hesitation he opened the door to the computer room and felt for the light switches on the wall. He turned on the lights. Doug stood behind a stack of boxes of computer paper. He pointed his rifle at the computer.

"Don't make a lot of noise," Doug whispered to him.

"What is it, Doug?" Herman sternly asked, looking towards the computer. "What are you doing with this riffle?" He spoke loudly to intimidate Doug and remind him that he was in charge. Doug suddenly looked like he was being scolded for missing a shipping deadline. Jose had finally gotten enough courage to follow Herman inside the building. From the hallway he watched the two men in the computer room.

"Someone is trying to screw up the computer," Doug said.

"Is that why you brought your riffle with you to work? Are you trying to scare him off?"

"He is giving me a hard time."

"I see. Why not bring in the SWAT team and let them deal with him?"

"I can handle him. He is a communist."

"You can't kill a communist with a hunting riffle," Herman pointed out. He tried to get the riffle from him. Doug jerked it away from him.

"What do you suggest that I use?"

"You will need anti-matter bullets."

Doug looked disappointed. He stared at his riffle. "I don't have any," he said.

"Give me that laser canon," Herman said, again trying to take the riffle away from him. Once again, Doug jerked it away from him. "Do you mind if I look around?"

"Go ahead," Doug said. Herman pretended to search the computer room.

"There is no one here except you and me," he said.

"I saw someone hiding inside the computer."

"Do you mind if I look inside the computer?"

"Go right ahead," Doug said.

Herman removed the front panel of the computer and pretended to peek inside. He swung open another panel to reveal a wall of memory boards. He found a crumpled brown lunch bag and two hard-boiled eggs at the base of the computer. He picked up the eggs and the lunch bag. He looked into the bag and found stale popcorns in it. Herman closed the door and screwed the panel back onto the computer.

"There is nobody inside the computer," he said.

"I swear that I saw a communist inside the computer."

"If there is a communist inside the computer then we'll have to use anti-matter bullets to get him out. Unload your riffle and load these anti-matter bullets instead." Herman dipped his hand in the brown bag and handed Doug a handful of popcorns.

Doug stared at the popcorns in Herman's hands. "This is not going to work," he said.

"How do you know they won't work?"

"I can try them if you want me to, but I don't think they'll work."

"Unload your riffle, merchant marine, and load the anti-matter bullets now," Herman snapped back at him. "That's an order!"

Doug stood to attention. "Yes, Sir."

"On the double," Herman ordered.

"Yes, Sir," Herman handed him the brown bag of popcorns. Doug took the bag and looked inside. His hands shook as he took a few popcorns out of the bag. "I am telling you that this is not going to work."

"Give me the laser canon and let me try."

"Go right ahead," Doug said, handing Herman the riffle. Herman took the rifle from Doug's hands and quickly locked it inside a tape cabinet. "Go home," he told Doug. "You look tired. Take the night off and get some sleep."

"You really mean it?"

"Yes, I mean it. I will ask Jose to cover up for you tonight."

"You know, honestly, I haven't been able to sleep at all these last few days. I was really concerned about the communist inside the computer."

"Jose and I will take care of him. You have done everything you could."

"It's just like the phone lines in the transmission room, you know," Doug continued. "Each time I dialed the customer's number, I get the impression that someone is trying to stop me from doing my job."

"Must be another communist hiding inside the telephone lines; we'll take care of him too."

"I want my riffle back." Doug tried to open the tape cabinet.

"I need it just in case that communist sticks his head out of the computer. You don't mind, do you?"

"I sure don't," he said. "I really appreciate it." Doug then left through the back door.

When Bill returned from his vacation, he authorized Herman to look for a replacement for Doug. Fifteen applicants responded to the ad and sent Bill their resumes, but Bill was still reluctant to replace Doug. Herman interviewed five of the applicants and recommended a suitable applicant to Bill. He waited a few days for Bill to give him the go-ahead to hire Doug's replacement. After a week went by, he gave up hope that Bill was intent in replacing Doug at all. A week after the incident, Doug moved out of his parents' home and into his own apartment. Then, on Labor Day, his father died of a heart attack. When he returned to work after his father's funeral, Doug was seen dancing around in the computer room.

"His father's death will probably do him a lot of good," Bill said to Herman when they met in his office to plan the orderly shutting down of the data center. "On the other hand, the loss of his father could also make him worse." Two weeks later Herman asked Jose how he felt about Doug's behavior. Jose smiled and replied: "He is very calm and don't talk much rubbish now. He looks one hundred percent better! You must come out one of these nights and see him dance. He dances every night in the computer room while he works."

Puzzled at Jose's request, Herman asked: "Why?"

"He is very happy. He dances around the printer while he is waiting for the reports to print. He closes his eyes and smiles when he waltzes around. I have never seen him so happy."

10 LESSONS IN LOVE ECONOMICS

The recession that hit the United States in 1982 drove many Northerners to seek employment in the economic fortress of the Southwest. The newcomers were mostly from the industrial and farming States of Michigan, Ohio, Iowa and Idaho. Unemployed farmers and automobile workers drove south to Texas in large numbers, and many of them settled in the Dallas metropolis. Among the new arrivals were three women who left their homes in Iowa to seek greener cornfields in Texas. They left behind them the men who made their lives miserable in order to start a new life. They were driven to the south by the prospect of landing new jobs, making new friends, and finding new husbands. When they arrived in Dallas, they were impressed by the modern office buildings and bewildered at how clean the city was. They were amazed to see so many construction cranes on the city's outskirts and surprised at the vast expanses of virgin land between office towers. The three Iowans liked what they saw and decided to make Dallas their new home. The women, like the New Yorkers and the Michiganites who migrated to the city, chose to stay close to each other. They moved into an apartment complex south of the Lyndon Baines Johnson freeway. After they had secured a roof over their heads, they began to put the pieces of their lives back together.

Esther was the oldest of the three women. She brought with her two children: a 16yr old boy and a 12yr old girl. Her husband kicked her in the stomach when she was two months pregnant with a third child. She eventually had a miscarriage. After the incident, she decided to strike it on her own. Against her parents' wish, she divorced her husband and moved into a home for battered women. There she met Vivian and Elizabeth. Vivian was a divorced mother of three girls and Elizabeth was the unwed mother of a small girl. Before taking refuge in the home for battered women, Vivian was beaten, harassed and stalked by her former husband. Just one day after she filed for divorce, he forced himself into her apartment and slammed her face against the bedroom wall. Then he forced her to have sex with him. Her nose required reconstruction. Ever since then, she had suffered from post traumatic stress syndrome. When she left the hospital, she sought refuge in a women's shelter. Elizabeth, the youngest of the three women, was the unwed mother of a four-year old girl. Her former boyfriend pushed her out of a moving car while they argued about a babysitter for her daughter. In addition to sustaining injuries to her head, the fall broke her right arm. The three women were unemployed. The recession made it more difficult for them to find a job. They did not find it pleasant to live in a home for abused women. They believed that Texas may have a lot more to offer to them than Iowa. When Esther announced to her two new friends that she would move to Dallas, Vivian and Elizabeth decided to go along with her. Vivian was living in constant fear of her husband and sought to distance herself from him. Elizabeth saw the move to Dallas as an opportunity to get away for good from her former boyfriend.

During their second week job hunting, Esther found a job as a Bank Teller with a Savings and Loans bank. Vivian landed a job as an Assistant Manager with a store selling party supplies. She was at first baffled by the concept of a store selling just merchandises for partying. She doubted that the store would be around for a long time, but nevertheless accepted the job offer. Her debts were getting larger each day, and she could not afford to wait for the right job to come along. She soon discovered that the people in the city partied every night. The city's *nouveau riche* crowd was not afraid to flaunt their newly acquired wealth. They spent huge sum of money on foods, liquor, paper plates, paper cups and napkins. They lavishly entertained their families, friends and business partners, and spent huge amounts of money on foods and alcoholic beverages. The large crowd of customers patronizing her store every day convinced her that her job would be secure for some time. Elizabeth was the only woman with some college education. While staying in Des Moines, she took some marketing classes and briefly worked in sales with a farm equipment company. She found a job as a Marketing Secretary with a small printing company conveniently situated within walking distance of the apartment complex. Since she did not own a car, finding a job close to her apartment saved her the trouble and expense of taking the bus or the subway.

The three women gradually settled down in their new environment. They had successfully taken care of two problems newcomers to Dallas were normally faced with: finding shelter and getting a job. The women soon discovered that the cost of living in Dallas was much higher than in Des Moines. They found it difficult to make ends meet on their meager salaries. After paying the rents and buying the groceries, they had little money left for spending on entertainment or luxuries. They hardly had any money to buy their children new clothes or toys. They realized that they would not be able to live a comfortable life without additional financial support from men. It was also time for them to attend to matters of the hearts. Despite not having much money, they agreed to meet in a nearby bar after work to unwind and talk about their plans.

Bar Nuevo was a quaint little nightclub not far from where the three women lived. The club offered the women a quiet atmosphere to relax, unwind, and enjoy a few drinks. It was not so big as to attract a large crowd, and not so expensive as to deter customers from coming in. A pitcher of Margarita was $5.00 during Happy Hour and some decent foods were provided for free. The menu items were reasonable should a customer wish to order dinner. It was the ideal place for the three women to meet as they could drink all the Margaritas they want without spending a fortune. They could enjoy the evening eating, drinking, and chatting without being harassed by men.

The bar was just a few minutes' drive from their apartment. On the following Friday, Esther picked her two friends after work and drove to the bar. There were few customers inside the bar which suited the women perfectly as they did not like men to chat them up. They sat at a table away from the crowd and ordered two pitchers of Margarita. While waiting for the Margarita, they went to the food bar and brought back plates laden with pizza, nachos, tacos, and corn chips. When the waitress brought the pitchers of Margaritas, they poured out the drinks into their glasses and wasted no time in eating and drinking. Esther raised her glass to her friends and toasted their successful move from Des Moines to Dallas.

"We made it, girls. Let us hope for the best!"

"For the best," Vivian and Elizabeth repeated.

"Thank God, we all have a job," Esther congratulated herself.

"And a roof over our head too," Vivian added

"I don't have a car yet," Elizabeth reminded them

"I still need some furniture," Vivian said. "But there is no hurry. Does anyone know where the Goodwill store is located around here? I could use a dresser and perhaps a chest of drawers."

"Let go find it tomorrow. I am sure the apartment Manager can tell us where to find it." Esther advised.

The women went on to talk about their new jobs, the people they met in the workplace, and some new places of interest. A man stood up from the bar and went to the jukebox. He dropped a few coins in the machine and punched a few buttons. When the music started, he walked up to Esther.

"May I have the honor please?"

Esther turned her head and smiled at the man. "No, thanks," she politely declined.

The man thanked her and went to another table. Elizabeth pinched Esther on her arm. "Why did you turn him down?" she whispered.

"Too young for me," Esther replied. "I figured that he is 25 years old."

"What is wrong with that?' Elizabeth asked.

"I have set new rules for myself when dating men," Esther told her. "I will only date a man who is over thirty years old because he is more likely to have money to spend on me."

"How do you know he's got no money to spend on you?" Vivian said.

Esther turned and gave a long look at the young man. "I don't know', but he is too young for me to date."

"What other kinds of men do you plan to exclude when dating," Elizabeth asked, puzzled at Esther's comment about the man being too young to date.

"I will avoid dating a man who had just graduated from college. He may have an impressive degree in Genetic Engineering, but his wallet is usually thin. Guys like that also have over $20,000 in student loans that they will have to repay back. I will not support a man on my salary while he uses his money to pay back the government loans. A new college graduate also likes to shine and show off his new status. He drives a sports car to impress people. I gather that after paying his new car note and whatever he owes the government, he wouldn't have anything left to spend on me. So I will avoid dating these kinds of men. When I was staying in the home for battered women, I had some reservations about starting a new relationship with a man. I have now decided that I will date a man who can provide me with material things rather than flowers and dreams. Flowers will wither and die away after a few days. I can't eat them. The next time somebody asks me what I would like for my birthday, I will ask for 100lb of rib eye steaks. I have two grown-up kids to feed, and they eat like ten lions."

"You could ask for a bottle of perfume instead of roses," Esther suggested.

"I don't want perfume either. I would rather have one gallon of barbecue sauce or ketchup. My kids love them."

"You want a bottle of ketchup for your birthday present?" The two women giggled. They ordered more drinks and made another trip to the buffet table.

"So, what kinds of men should we be looking for?" Vivian asked.

"We should look for an economically sound partner," Esther replied. "Someone who can provide us with the material things we need to be comfortable in life. I have experienced love in my younger days. Just like they say, love is blind. I fell for a man who was all muscles, but no brain. I was attracted to his motorcycle more than his body. He spent more time with his motorcycle than with my kids and me. I don't want to be swept off my feet by someone who has nothing to give but himself. I don't want to date a man with children either. I don't care about whether he is single, married or divorced as long as he can provide for me. A man in his thirties is more likely the type of man that I will look for. He would already have paid off his automobile loan and he would more likely have money to spend on my children and me. I don't care what he does for a living and what kind of car he drives as long as he has a fat wallet."

"Divorced men are not necessarily better off financially," Elizabeth remarked.

"True," Esther replied. "I will definitely avoid dating a man who is still going through a divorce. When I said 'divorced,' I meant someone who had already been through a divorce. People marry for love, but divorce because of money. I will obtain a credit report on a man first before I will date him. That way I'll know if he is financially sound to date me."

"I don't mind dating any man as long as he is not a spouse beater," Vivian said.

"My second rule for dating a man," Esther continued, "is not to stick around the same guy for too long. One to two years is the most time I will spend with my new man. I have decided that I don't want to marry again. What's the point of marrying if two years later you have to go through a divorce? I have been through a divorce once, and I don't ever want to go through one again. When you go through a divorce, your life momentarily stops. You can't sleep, eat or do anything until it's all over. By the time it's over, you are deeply in debt. You owe money to your lawyer, the banks, your mother, and all your friends. I think a year is long enough for my man and me to get what we want from each other. Besides, after six months, he probably would not have any money left to continue our relationship. Don't let your emotions dictate whom you will date. Instead, let your choice of a man be the mean to fulfill your material needs. You should seek a man not for love alone, but for what he can provide you and your children to survive in this concrete jungle."

Her companions were silent. Esther sipped her margarita and checked the pitcher on the table.

"Just remember that we are women living in a society controlled by men," Esther continued. "I don't earn half of what they make, but I still have to pay the rent and feed my children, purchase school supplies, and pay the doctor's bills. I can't afford to pay for these things on my salary alone. Unless I choose a man who can economically benefit me and my children, I will have to live on food stamps."

"I think that it's cruel to turn emotions and feelings into a profitable arrangement," Vivian remarked.

"I don't think that I can love a man just for his money," Elizabeth added.

"You will change your mind when you find out about your needs," Esther said. "I have two teenage children to look after. I cannot do it on my paycheck alone. Neither can you. I don't want to hurt anyone. I just want to find a man who can provide me with the things that my children and I need. Life is full of inequalities and unfairness. How do you think I feel when my ex husband doesn't send me the child support money? He was ordered by the court to provide me with child support when we divorced, but I have yet to receive a dime from him. I don't think he feels sorry for my kids and me. Men are selfish. They are all hypocrites and heartless. Don't feel sorry for them."

"You are being vindictive," Elizabeth pointed out

"I am only fighting back. I have been through a lot. I just want a better life for myself and my children." She munched on a strip of pizza and sipped margarita. "The events of the last few months had drawn all the energy out of me. Right now I feel the need to go on vacation."

Her friends laughed. "Now, where are you going to get the money to pay for a vacation?" Vivian asked.

"You just started a new job," Elizabeth said. "You don't have any vacation time due."

"Last night I wrote down my immediate needs on a piece of paper," Esther replied. She fumbled in her handbag and removed a note and opened it. "First, I would like to take a vacation. I will lose my sanity if I don't take some time off soon. After I come back from vacation, I would like to replace my old clunker with a newer car. I cannot afford to have the old one fixed up anymore."

"Wait! Stop for a moment," Vivian said, raising her hand in front of Esther's face. She was amused at her friend's candid revelation. "How can you afford a new car on your salary?"

"I can't," Esther confessed, "but I will rely on my love economics to help me attain my goals."

"Love economics?" Elizabeth exclaimed. "What is that?"

"I've written down some rules for dating men. I call them the Economics of falling in love. If I follow these rules, I will attain my goals. After I get my new car, I'll take care of my kids' needs. They need new clothes and new toys. I would also like to get them a new computer." Esther folded the piece of paper and put it back in her handbag. "I will tape this note on the bathroom mirror to remind me of my goals."

"For Heaven's sake," Vivian cried out. "Did you inherit a fortune from a wealthy uncle?"

Esther shook her head. "I wish I had a rich uncle," she said. "I will feel more secure."

"You want to go on vacation, buy a new car for yourself, and get a new computer for the kids! Wow! How are you going to buy that new computer?" Vivian asked.

"I don't know yet," Esther calmly said. "I'll worry about that after I have my vacation. One thing at a time! Right now, I would like to take a vacation."

"What does that mean, the economics of falling in love?" Elizabeth asked.

"It is my idea of how I should have a relationship with a man."

"I never studied Economics in College," Vivian admitted.

"I passed by a travel agency on the way to the grocery store the other day. I peeped through the glass wall and I saw a handsome man sitting inside. He will take me to Hawaii."

"You must be kidding. You already have a date?" Vivian asked.

"No, but I will have one soon. Love has four seasons. In the summer time, love is about walking barefooted on sandy white beaches, lying down on the beach, and sipping highballs. The travel agent does not know it yet, but he will soon experience summertime love with me."

Every day during the lunch hour, motorists jammed the stretch of Harry Hines Boulevard between Stemmons freeway and Walnut Hill Lane to watch the prostitutes parading alongside the road. Sometimes the motorists pulled up alongside the prostitutes and chatted with them. Sometimes they picked them up and drove off to a love motel. On some days the boulevard was lined up with so many prostitutes that they caused traffic jams all the way to Walnut Hill Lane. The prostitutes taunted the motorists by raising their skirts and showing off their legs. Many of them gathered in front of the porn shops along the boulevard to solicit the men going in or coming out of the porn shops. When competition for men near the porn shops became intense, the prostitutes fanned out to adjoining streets. Some of them got so daring that they solicited customers at the junction of Harry Hines Boulevard and Walnut Hill Lane. When the lights turned red, they boldly walked to the cars stopped at the lights to tease the drivers. The traffic buildup along the boulevard got so bad that someone joked about building a whorehouse with a drive-thru window in order to ease up the bottleneck. Soon after, rumors spread among the small business community that an entrepreneur planned to build a whorehouse with a see-thru window. However, some office workers maintained that they had heard that a whorehouse with a slip-thru back door would be built in the new whorehouses to accommodate the company executives who picked up prostitutes during the lunch hour.

From his office in the small business park on Walnut Hill Lane, Aaron watched a prostitute wave at motorists. A few minutes later, a motorist pulled up and drove off with her. Aaron sighed and looked at his watch. It was close to noon. He got up from his desk, hanged a 'CLOSED' sign on the door and left for lunch. Like many of the men working in the area, he ate his lunch while cruising the boulevard and watching the prostitutes. Aaron had spent so much of his lunch times eating burritos and watching prostitutes while cruising the boulevard that all his shirts and pants showed stains of taco sauce.

Esther came to the travel agency just as Aaron was closing up. The timid travel agent asked her to come back later. Not to be daunted, she followed him to his car. When Aaron removed his car keys from his pocket, Esther took a chain out of her handbag and approached him.

"Excuse me," she apologized. "You dropped this chain."

She dangled a chain in front of him. A small disk with illegible marks on each side hanged on the chain.

"It isn't mine," Aaron said, examining the chain. "One of our customers must have dropped it."

"It does not have a name on it," Esther acknowledged.

"No, but there are etchings on both sides of the disc," Aaron pointed out, turning the disc in his hands. Intrigued, he examined the markings on the disc. "The etchings look like hieroglyphic symbols."

"They could be clues to a word puzzle," Esther suggested.

"You may be right," Aaron said. He spun the disc by a flip of his finger. "Look. The symbols appear like words when the disc is spun."

"I think I know what it is," Esther said with excitement. "I used to have one like it when I was a kid. Blow on the disc and let it spin. You will then be able to read the message on the disc."

The disc came to a stop, but Aaron gently blew on it to set it back in motion. "You are right. I can read the message now. *'I love you,'*" he said, reading the conjoined message on the disc.

Esther feigned disappointment. "You don't really mean it, do you? After all, I hardly know you."

Aaron laughed. "Here," he said, good-humoredly. "Keep it. After all, you are the one who found it. I would not know whom it belongs to. Dozens of people walked in and out of the travel agency every day. I don't think it's worth anything."

"I cannot accept it," she said, looking embarrassed. "This is a token of love. You should give it to your wife, not to a stranger."

"I don't have a wife," Aaron said.

"Or give it to your girlfriend."

"I don't have a girlfriend either. I'll hang it on the door when I get back from my lunch break. Maybe someone will recognize and claim it."

"Thank you. I am sorry I wasted your time." She walked back to her car. Aaron noted the out-of-state license plate on her car.

"Are you from Iowa?" Aaron asked.

"Yes," Esther said. "I have only been in town for a few weeks. Are you from Iowa too?"

"No, but I have an uncle who lives in Cedar Rapids. Welcome to Big D."

The old rundown warehouse at the end of Restaurant Row was recently converted into a restaurant and entertainment complex. The entertainment area extended to the rear of the restaurant and was lined with pool tables, pinball, poker and slot machines. The place was swarming with people. While they waited for a table to be available, Aaron took Esther to the video arcade and showed her the pinball machines. She was dazzled by the flashing lights, charmed by the cacophony of ringing bells, and mesmerized by the crowd of cheerful people. Aaron ordered drinks for both of them. He tried his luck at the poker machine, then gave Esther some game coins and watched her fish dolls from a glass casing. Whenever she clawed a small doll out of the box, she jumped up and screamed with joy at winning the one-dollar doll. Later they went to a clobber machine to try their physical strengths. Aaron clobbered the heads of the chipmunks with a large rubber mallet as the heads popped out of their holes. When his time ran out, Esther took the mallet and pummeled on the ugly little heads with all her might.

"You have outscored me," Aaron exclaimed at the end of the game. "Where do you get your strength from?"

"I closed my eyes and thought about all the years that my ex-husband had battered me. I felt like I was clobbering him for all the hurt that he had caused me."

"People come here every day to unwind and release their anger and frustration," Aaron said. "I feel much better when I return back to work."

"It's a fun place to be," Esther acknowledged.

"The US postal service should provide a facility like this for their employees to unwind after work. This will stop the postal workers from shooting at their fellow workers."

"It sounds like a good idea," Esther said. "Happy people don't shoot at each other."

The hostess announced through the loudspeaker that their table was ready. They made their way amidst a constant stream of people and returned to the restaurant at the front of the building. The hostess escorted them to their table and handed each of them a menu. For starters, they ordered Buffalo wings and frog legs. For their main meals, Aaron ordered a Chicken salad pie with water chestnut. Esther ordered a 22 oz steak. They sipped wine while they waited for their meals. Aaron took the chain out of his pocket and fiddled with it.

"What do you think I should do with this chain?" he asked.

"It's probably looking for a nice woman who can speak its language," she replied.

"Then I don't have to look any further." Aaron unlocked the chain and hung it around Esther's neck.

"I am flattered," she whispered. The waitress came back with their appetizers. She placed the plate of Buffalo wings in front of Aaron and the plate of frog legs in front of Esther. Esther took a frog leg from her plate and nipped at it. "If the Creator had put more men like you in my path, I wouldn't have to spend my life kissing frogs in order to find my handsome prince."

Esther and Aaron started to meet more often. During the evenings Aaron took her to the fine dining establishments around town and to musical shows. On weekends they went to the movies, visited the zoo museums, and attended craft shows. They discovered that they lived in the same apartment complex and used the same laundry facility. Whenever Aaron did his laundry, he stopped by Esther's apartment and picked up her basket of dirty laundry. He washed, dried and folded her clothes while waiting for his own clothes to dry. Then he carried the basket of clothes to her apartment and entertained her children. The children enjoyed having him around the apartment. He frequently added some toys and candies to the sacks of groceries he brought for Esther. Aaron spent so much of his time in Esther's apartment that Esther eventually asked him to stay over. Little by little, Aaron brought his personal items in her apartment and spent the weekends there. Then one day Aaron suggested that they were both wasting money leasing two apartment units. They could both save money if they were to share one apartment instead. Esther liked the idea. Aaron surrendered his unit when his lease expired and moved into her apartment. Esther was relieved that she had finally found someone to look after her and her kids. Aaron paid the rent and all the utility bills. He was also a fine cook, enjoyed sharing the housework with her, and was generous to her children. He was like a father to them. He helped them with their homework and constantly surprised them with small gifts. One Saturday, while Aaron was in the laundry room, Esther noticed Aaron's checkbook lying on the dresser. Out of curiosity, she opened the checkbook to look at the checking account balance. She blinked and rolled her eyes at the account balance. She decided then that the time was ripe for her to take a vacation.

When the women met again at Bar Nuevo the following Friday, Vivian and Elizabeth were eager to hear about Esther's relationship with Aaron.

"How is Aaron treating you?" Vivian asked.

"Oh, he is so sweet," she replied. "He is paying all the bills, what else could I ask?"

"When is that cute travel agent of yours going to take you to Hawaii?" Elizabeth asked.

"I am working on it," Esther assured them. "We've been together for only two months. How are you girls doing? Caught any big fish yet?"

"We are trying," Vivian replied. "A few guys asked us out, but we figured that they do not conform to the rules that you have set up for dating men. I turned down a date because the guy drove a brand new BMW automobile. Before I turned him down, I looked at his back pocket. It seems that his wallet was pretty flat. I figured that he was spending half his paycheck on the car payment."

"A gentleman from the middle east calls her every night," Elizabeth said. "He would like her to occupy a prominent place in his harem in Kuwait. He will have two servants to attend to her needs."

"Oh...?" Esther exclaimed.

"What's a harem?" Vivian asked. "He made it sound like it's a fun place for a woman to be in. He said that he will pay all the expenses of flying me there. "

"Oh, sure," Esther quickly added. "Drop him. You'll be better off living with a spouse beater in America. At least you can divorce him when things don't work out."

"You sound like my mom," Vivian said, looking crestfallen.

"Just follow my advice and you won't regret it," Esther said. "Let me pass on to you what I have put together on my Economics of falling in love. Lesson one: you must avoid dating men who drive flashy cars. These men usually don't have any money left after paying their car notes. Lesson two: You should date an older man because he is more likely to shower you with gifts. He is also more likely to be faithful to you. A younger man will always look at other women. Lesson three: you should avoid dating a man who has children from a previous marriage. He could be paying child support to his ex wife. Lesson four: you should never move in your boyfriend's apartment. Instead, you should have him move into your apartment."

"Why?" Elizabeth asked, puzzled at lesson four.

"It's a lot easier to get rid of your boyfriend when you are on your own turf. Having your own apartment when you break up a relationship also means that you don't have to look for another apartment again. Besides, an Apartment Manager doesn't look favorably on a single or divorced woman looking to rent an apartment from him. Here is Lesson five: once your boyfriend moves into your apartment, close the trap door. Get him to pay the rent and the utility bills, and have him help you with the housework. Just think of all the extra money you will have left over to spend on other things. You can spend the extra money on new clothes or new shoes. You'll have many more happy hours like this one." Esther looked at the bottom of the pitcher and waved at the waitress.

"Is Aaron paying the rent?" Vivian asked.

"You bet he is, otherwise I'll cut him off."

"Cut him off of what?" Vivian asked, puzzled.

"Sex," Esther replied. "That's what every man wants from women, isn't? Aaron isn't going to get it from me unless he does what I ask him to do. If you have something that a man wants, use it as your weapon."

"Aren't you afraid that he will leave you?" Elizabeth said.

"I doubt that he wants to spend his lunch hour watching prostitutes." Esther replied.

"What is lesson six?"

Esther licked the salt from the rim of her glass before sipping the margarita. "I am still working on that one," she answered. "I'll tell you more next time we meet."

The summer abruptly came to an end and Esther's children returned to school. It was a propitious time for Esther to start planning for the vacation that she longed for. When Aaron came home from work one evening, she suggested that they dine at a garden restaurant.

"What's a garden restaurant?" Aaron asked her.

Esther explained that the restaurant was decorated to look like the Garden of Eden. The hostess parades half-naked around the tables and places apples on the customers' tables while they wait for their meals. If the male customer picks up an apple and bites into it, he is banished from the restaurant. Aaron was intrigued.

"I have never heard of such a place," he said. Aaron's curiosity was aroused. He had spent most of his working life watching the prostitutes flaunting along Harry Hines Boulevard. He knew nothing else about the city other than the porn shops and the areas where the prostitutes hung around. He was stunned that he had missed out on other aspects of the city life. Esther called the garden restaurant and reserved a table for them.

They drove to the garden restaurant on the appointed evening. A hostess escorted them to the garden room where they sat at a table surrounded by trees and plants. Aaron stared at the plants around him. He looked up and gazed at the small lights twinkling on the dark ceiling. A feeling of joy overtook him.

"I have never been in the forest," he mumbled. "I have lived in a concrete jungle all my life."

"Many years ago," Esther said, "the people in North America cut down the forests and used the timber to build houses for shelter. When the trees started disappearing from the North American continent, they felt guilty of destroying part of the ecosystem. So they started growing back the trees inside the buildings. The trees are no longer free to sway with the wind. They have become prisoners in the free man's world."

"This is not fair," Aaron moaned. "The trees ought to be free like the birds." Aaron stood up and shouted: "Death to the first parents of the human race!"

A naked woman walked out from behind a tree. A small maple leaf covered the nipple of her right breast and a larger maple leaf covered the upper part of her legs. Her long hair was combed to the left and flowed down her shoulder, covering her other breast. A live snake was curled around her neck and around her waist. She carried a basket of apples and walked from table to table. She walked to their table and smiled at them. Aaron gawked at the naked hostess standing in front of him. His eyes bugged out and his jaws dropped. The woman took an apple from her basket and slammed it into his mouth.

"Welcome to the Garden of Eden," she said. "Eat the forbidden fruit and be expelled."

When the hostess walked away, Aaron removed the apple from his mouth and laughed with joy. On the balcony above them, two naked men dropped dried leaves and tossed apples to the customers below. A few leaves landed on Aaron and on their table. Aaron swept away the fallen leaves from his head and from the table. Esther caught an apple and placed it in front of Aaron.

"Eat the forbidden fruit," she said. She held the apple in front of his mouth. Not wanting to be banished from the garden restaurant, she brushed it aside.

"I love the forests," Aaron asserted. "It's so romantic to be in the woods. The people from the West Indies placed their foods on banana leaves and eat with their hands."

"It will not be appropriate for you to eat your foods on banana leaves dressed in black tie and tuxedo," Esther said.

"There ought to be a dining establishment strictly for nudists," Aaron said. He waved at a waitress. "Ma'am, may I have my dinner served on banana leaves?"

"I am sorry, Sir," the hostess replied, "We are out of banana leaves tonight."

"I'll have it on a plate then." Aaron gazed at the ceiling above him. "I love rainbows," he said. "But the painted rainbow on the ceiling makes me look unreal."

"The best place to look at rainbows is Hawaii," Esther said in a soft voice. "You can see rainbows in Hawaii almost every day. The Hawaiian sky is so mysterious at night."

"Are they real rainbows? Not like this painted rainbow above us?" Aaron pointed at the ceiling.

"Natural rainbows," Esther replied. "They are just like the colorful rainbows that appeared over London when Richard of York gained battle in vain. In Hawaii they sprout each time the Hawaiian Sun God sprays the islands with liquid sunshine to clear off the air pollution. The rainbows appear so low above the skyline that you can reach out and touch them."

"I have never seen a rainbow in Dallas. Each time a rainbow appears in the sky, someone starts to build a new office tower. The new building rises up so fast that it completely obscures the rainbow from my sight." Aaron rose up and clenched his fist. "Death to the male descendants of the first parents," he yelled. The naked hostess came back and stuck an apple into his mouth. Aaron removed the apple and set it on the table. Apples adorned the tables around them. The diners saved them for the last show on Earth.

"When you touch the tail of a rainbow in Hawaii, you will put an end to world hunger," Esther said.

"I often dream of wiping out hunger from the face of the world," Aaron confessed. "Look at these apples on the tables; they could be used to feed hungry people. Instead, they are all going to be thrown away later."

"You can have a shot at it in Hawaii," Esther said. "The rainbows in Hawaii are real and not made of neon lights. They won't make you look unreal either. When you gaze at the rainbows there, your heart will burn with romance and love. They will arouse your true feelings and you won't have to fake anything when you return to the mainland."

"I won't have to lie when I give my boss his annual review?"

"You can see the rainbows all day long. At night the Hula girls will step down the clouds and embrace you."

"Is it true?" Aaron wondered. He was mesmerized by the images of Hawaii painted to him by Esther.

"You can open the sky and unravel its mysteries."

"Let's go to Hawaii," Aaron exclaimed. He stood up and pumped up his fists and shouted: "Long live the female descendants of the first parents." Aaron took an apple and hurled it at the two naked men on the balcony. The apple hit one man on the head and he fell down on a table below. A woman gazed at the pair of buttocks on her plate and screamed. The other naked male employee fired an apple back at him. The diners started to pitch apples at each other. The apples exploded into pieces as they hit the diners, landed on furniture or crashed on the walls. Pieces of apples struck a woman dressed in a satin gown. She screeched at the stain on her dress and ran to the powder room. Shortly afterwards, she returned stark naked and joined in the apple-throwing fiesta. She seized the basket of apples from the hostess and hurled the apples at every one close to her. The men undid their neckties and shirts and slipped out of their trousers. The women stepped out of their clothes and tucked them under the tables to protect them from the apple juice. Within a few minutes, the garden room was filled with the laughter of the naked diners chasing and throwing apples at each other. A volley of apples flew at Aaron and Esther. They covered their heads and ducked at the apples.

"Will someone please save the last descendants of the first parents?" the hostess cried. She tore at her hair in despair and darted left and right among the diners. The maple leaves had fallen off from her breast and from the top of her legs. Apple juice dripped down from her breasts and ran into her belly button. The snake slid down her body and disappeared into the kitchen. Aaron and Esther quickly exited the restaurant before the last show on Earth ended.

The DFW airport terminals bristled with passengers in a hurry. Aaron and Esther dragged behind them their suitcases as they made their way to the departing terminal. They were on their way to catch the American Airline flight number 580 to Hawaii. They arrived at the terminal an hour earlier than the departure time and spent the time reading the Dallas Morning News. After a while they put the paper down and daydreamed about the sun, the sandy beaches, the mountains, the foods, the flora and fauna. A group of vacationers standing in front of them talked about their last vacation in Greece. Some passengers looked for empty seats around them. When they found none, they squatted on the floor. Finally, after waiting what seemed like an eternity, the airline employees opened the door leading to the airplane docked nearby. The first class passengers boarded first. Then the passengers who had tickets to the rear seats followed in their heels. The passengers with the middle seat tickets boarded next. Finally, the passengers with the front seat tickets tagged along. The air hostess swung the airplane door shut behind the last passenger. Twenty minutes later the plane was airborne. Esther was finally on her way to accomplishing her first of her three goals.

During the flight to Honolulu, the flight attendants entertained the passengers with quizzes and games. The passengers were asked to estimate the altitude at which the plane was flying, the distance between Dallas and Honolulu, and the arrival time to certain points along the flight path. Aaron did not like to work on anything that involved numbers. He chose to watch movies instead. Esther drank margaritas and savored her victory and success.

After an eight-hour flight across the Pacific Ocean, the plane landed at Honolulu airport. Esther and Aaron picked up their luggage and joined the other passengers to board the bus that would take them to their hotel. Two young native Hawaiians dressed in traditional clothes greeted them before they boarded the bus. The greeters hanged lei garlands on the vacationers' necks, hugged and kissed them on their cheeks. A young woman greeted the men while a young man greeted the women. Aaron did not notice that the two lines were segregated by gender. He followed Esther and patiently stood in line behind the other women. When he reached the front of the line, he flung at the male greeter and smothered him with kisses. The stunned greeter broke free from him and coiled back. He hid behind a potted palm tree and pointed to the woman greeter. When the greeting ceremony was over, they boarded the bus and were driven to their hotel along Waikiki beach. After unpacking and changing into lighter clothing, they set out to explore the island.

They were captivated by the island's botanical splendor. They drove along lust tropical rainforest and winding mountains to do their sightseeing. When they were tired of driving, they stopped and laid down on the white sandy beaches to soak in the sun. Later in the evening, they went to a restaurant to eat dinner. After dinner, they went to walk along the sandy beach and mixed with the crowds. When they could no longer keep their eyes open, they went back to their hotel. The next day they drove along the coast and stopped at a few places to sightsee. They visited Waimena Falls Park and watched a young native woman execute the ancient Kahiko dance. They gawked at divers leaping in the lagoon from the cliff above the falls and watched tourists swimming and canoeing across the lagoon. They gasped at the giant hibiscus plant while hiking along the nature trails around the park. They drove to Manao and wandered in Paradise Park to admire the fauna and flora. They went to an amphitheater to watch cockatoos perform acrobatic feats. They spent three days just visiting these places. On the fourth day they sojourned at Sea Life Park and snorkeled at Kahana Bay. On the fifth day they drove along the coast and climbed up to the Pali Lookout Point to admire the scenery. Later in the evening, they went on a ship cruise along the western shoreline on a ship. While strolling on the upper deck, Aaron reached out to touch the tail of a rainbow. A sudden wave rolled towards the ship and lifted it up momentarily. The ship rocked dangerously for a while. When the giant wave had flattened out, the ship came down with a roar. A dozen of panicked vacationers rushed to Aaron. They clobbered, punched and kicked him. Esther tried to protect him from the angry passengers.

"I only want to wipe out world hunger from the face of the world," he explained to the crowd of panic-stricken vacationers.

On the last day in Hawaii, they visited the U.S.S Arizona Memorial. Aaron looked below the sea and saw the ghosts of American marines and Japanese airmen singing songs of hope and love to each other. When he returned back to the hotel, he was troubled by what he saw and heard. He and Esther sat silently on the balcony and watched the mysterious sky above them. They waited for it to open up and reveal its secrets. Finally a gang of Polynesian warriors came out of the clouds and descended on the island. They broke into a spirited and spectacular dance routine, crying and moaning the lost of their cultures to the outside civilization. At the end of the dance, the angry warriors stuck out their tongues, cursed them and threw their spears at them. They angrily demanded that they go back to their decadent ways on the mainland.

After returning to Dallas, Esther met her friends at Bar Nuevo to flaunt her new suntan. Her two friends turned red with envy when she showed them her vacation snapshots. While all her friends gasped at the vacation snapshots, she took her list of goals out of her handbag and calmly crossed out the first item on the list.

"My first goal has been met," she said, her eyes gleaming with satisfaction. "I am happier and more relaxed now."

"It looks like you and Aaron had a wonderful time together," Vivian said. "Did he propose?"

"Not yet, "she replied. "Anyway, I need to get a new car before winter arrives. I think the engine will fall out any time soon. I have been driving this clunker since David was born."

"We want to hear more about your vacation in Hawaii," Elizabeth said.

"I had a great time. I feel re-energized. Follow my advice. Take a vacation as soon as you find the guy who can take you there. Life is too short. Don't just sit around and wait for the perfect guy to come along and sweep you off your feet. There is no such thing as the perfect lover. He only lives within the pages of a romantic novel."

"We are still looking," Vivian said. "When you get tired of Aaron, let us know. We could use a man like him."

"He is a wonderful man," Esther admitted, "but he would not buy me a new car."

"Oh, come on. Don't be so hard on him. You just came back from an expensive vacation," Elizabeth said. "Give him some time."

"I don't want to wait till next year to get my new car. I want it now."

"How will you pay for it? Did you save enough money for the down payment?"

"No. I will have to follow my own rules on love economics. I promised to tell you about Lesson #6. Lesson six is: exploit the resources of your man to derive the maximum benefit from the relationship."

"This love economics thing sounds very complicated," Vivian said. "A relationship between a man and a woman is already complex. Now you are adding more complexities to it."

"It's really not that complicated. You just have to know who to date and how to plan. Write your goals on a piece of paper like I do."

"How do we do that?"

"Do what?"

"Exploit his resources."

"You have just seen a real life example. Aaron is a travel agent. I have exploited his position at the travel agency for my own benefit."

"You could have used your credit cards."

"I would still have to pay for the charges sooner or later. Since Aaron is a travel agent, he was able to find the cheapest vacation package for us. As an employee at the travel agency, he also got a discount on the vacation package. Aaron paid for the vacation for the two of us. He even paid for all the entertainment and the foods. I did not spend a penny."

"I think that you are going a little bit over your head about this love economics," Elizabeth said.

"Aaron can be useful to both of you," Esther said. "The rest is up to you." Vivian and Elizabeth glanced at each other with a surprised look in their eyes.

Later that night Esther complained to Aaron that she felt pain in her uterus. The next day she called in sick and asked Aaron to drive her to her doctor. At the doctor's office, she told Aaron that she would take a cab home after the visit with the doctor. As soon as Aaron drove off to work, Esther went to a nearby pay phone and called a cab. When the cab arrived, she directed the cab driver to take her back to her apartment. She spent the morning lounging around the apartment, and then went shopping. When Aaron came back from work in the evening, she feigned pain and told Aaron in a weak voice that her doctor wanted her to stay off sex for three months. To show him how serious she was, she told Aaron that they would have to sleep separately. Thereafter Aaron spent his nights sleeping on the sofa alone. After a few days he became very miserable at the sleeping arrangement. Tired of spending his nights alone, he went to the porn shops and spent the evenings flipping through the pages of pornographic magazines. Esther encouraged him to go out with her friends. Soon Aaron started to date Vivian. Vivian felt sorry for him and kept him company often. They went to the movies and stayed out late. One night Esther confronted Aaron about his love escapades with Vivian. She accused him of betraying her trust and dating her best friend. Aaron got so sick of her accusations that he left Esther and moved into Vivian's apartment.

The following day, Esther called her boss and told him that she would be late for work. She then drove to an automobile dealership on Preston Road in North Dallas and stopped her car in the middle of the road in front of the car dealership. She turned on the emergency lights and raised the hood. Then she walked into the showroom.

"Good Morning, Ma'am," the car salesman greeted her. He had a big smile on his face. "Having car trouble?"

"Yes, unfortunately," Esther replied. "But first I would like to find the asshole who owns the white car parked on the sidewalk." She pointed to a white car parked on the sidewalk in front of the showroom. The car salesman exclaimed: "That's my car. There aren't many parking spaces around the lot. It's all right for employees to park on the sidewalk."

"Bullshit! You are parked right in the path of that elderly man," she scolded the car salesman. The car salesman looked outside and saw an elderly man standing in front of his car. The old man appeared lost and confused. He hesitated and looked around him.

"Why doesn't he walk around my car?" the salesman said, perplexed. "There is plenty of room to walk around the car."

"You can go outside and tell him that," Esther said, "but I don't think it's the proper way to handle this situation. "I think that you should move your car so that the old man can continue his morning walk."

"Yes, Ma'am," the salesman answered.

The salesman drove his car to the rear of the dealership and the elderly man resumed his walk.

"I am really sorry about that," the salesman apologized to Esther when he came back into the showroom. "We really ought to give way to older people all the times, whether they are driving or walking. What can I do for you?"

"I have been thinking of trading my clunker for a new car," Esther said, "but after looking at the sticker price, I don't think I can afford a new car."

At that moment a pickup truck slammed into her car. The hood fell down with a crash and pieces of glasses flew off the taillights. The stunned driver stepped out of his pickup and went to examine the car he just hit. Esther's car was dragged 20 ft from where she left it.

"Oh, shit!" she cussed. "There goes my daily transportation."

"Now you really need a new car," the salesman said, grinning. The receptionist in the showroom called the police. Esther dashed out to her mangled car followed by the salesman.

"Is this pile of junks yours, Ma'am?" the stunned pickup driver asked, running his hand over his head.

"That was my car before you hit it. Look at what you did to my car?"

"Well, Ma'am, the car suddenly appeared in front of me. I don't know where it came from. I thought it was a flying saucer. Then I felt the soft hand of an Angel on my face. When I woke up I saw this pile of junks right in the middle of the road."

Esther raised her hand and slapped the man across his face. "Do you feel like you've just been touched by an Angel?"

The man brought his hand to his cheek and murmured, "No, Ma'am. I feel like my mother just slapped me for telling her a lie."

Esther walked around the car and examined the damage. The salesman inspected the hood. "The driver of the pickup truck must have been asleep at the wheel," she murmured to the salesman. "How much can you give me for it?"

"Not much now. What year is it?"

"I had it for so long that I don't remember. It is older than my son David."

"And how old is David?" the salesman asked.

"Sixteen."

"I can't believe that anyone would still be driving a 16 year old car."

"If you were a poor, single mother with two teenage children, you would be driving a car like that too. How much can I get for it?"

"Nothing," the salesman said. "You probably have to pay somebody to tow it away for you. I may have just the car for you. While the two of you exchange information about the accident, I will go and check my car inventory. We can talk about it when you are finished. The police should be here any minute. Do you have insurance coverage for your car?"

"I don't," Esther replied. "Let's hope that the asshole has auto insurance."

A few minutes later a police car arrived. Esther gave the police officer her account of the accident. Then the pickup driver explained what happened. Meanwhile the salesman summoned the tow truck driver to tow Esther's car to the service area. When the police officer finished writing up his report, Esther went back into the showroom. The car accident had come at an inopportune moment; it left her with little room for bargaining. She was nevertheless determined to buy a new car. The salesman walked with her to the new car lot and showed her several late model cars. He handed Esther the keys to a shining white car and asked her to take it for a test drive. Esther liked the car, but she balked at taking it for a test drive when she saw the price on the window sticker. She asked to be shown some older cars, found one that she liked, and returned back in the showroom to negotiate the final price and the financing plan. The salesman described to her three financing plans that she can choose to finance her car.

"Plan S is a Simple financing plan" he said. "You put down 20 percent and finance the balance for 48 months. Your monthly payment will be $179.09 per month. Plan E is just an extended version of plan S. The payments are stretched over 60 months. If you opt for plan E, your monthly payment will be about $153. With the Xtra plan, you can use a lower down payment. If your credit is good, you can even finance the full price of the car. Of course your monthly payment will be higher, but you won't have to come up with a large down payment. Say you put down 5% and finance the car for 60 months. In this case your monthly payment will be $181.80."

"I don't have much money for the down payment," Esther said. "How much is my car worth?"

"You are in luck today," the salesman said. "We are running a special promotion this month. The dealership will pay you $500 for your trade-in no matter what shape it's in. It is just like the ad on the TV. You drive it in, push it in, or have it towed in."

"$500 is not much," Esther said, shrugging her shoulders.

"Lady, you won't get a hundred dollars for your car now."

"I know, you've told me that already. What else can you do for me?"

"Well, I am sure I can work something out."

"You are a gentleman and a crook," she said.

The salesman grinned. "I like that." He opened his desk drawer and removed a set of car keys and handed them to Esther. "I am sure you need something to drive in the meantime," he said. "My car is the white car that you asked me to move earlier. I will take care of your clunker for you."

"And what are you going to drive in the meantime?" she asked him.

"I can drive a car provided to me by the dealership," he answered. "I like cars. I also like to work on them. I have three other cars at home. That's why I am in the car business. Which part of Iowa are you from?"

"How do you know I am from Iowa?" Esther asked.

"From the license plate on your car obviously, unless you are driving a stolen car."

"Do I look like a thief?"

"I never thought about it. Do you like Cajun foods?"

"I have never eaten Cajun foods. Do you trust me with your car?"

"Don't worry, lady. We are also in the car repossession business. The repo man will find you wherever you go. You'll probably never set your eyes on him, but you'll know he came by."

"I have no intention of going anywhere. Where do you go for Cajun foods around here?"

"I know just the right place. What's your name?"

The new man in Esther's life was named Daniel. She dated him regularly after their first meeting in the car showroom. Daniel was a transplant from New Orleans. He had lived in Dallas for about four years. The domestic car dealership he worked for in New Orleans laid him off when the American consumers opted for the small, gasoline-efficient Japanese automobiles. He was a single man, had never been married, and lived in an apartment in North Dallas. He liked to cruise along Belt line road in his 1962 black corvette that he had rebuilt from the ground up. Esther loved to ride in the car whenever Daniel took the car for a Sunday drive along Preston road. The wind whipping her face gave her new energy with which to face life's adversities. She liked Daniel because he did not play games with him. He was genuinely trying to help her when he temporarily gave her his car to use. He was very sincere with her and offered to help her in any way he could. Esther was moved by his kindness and interest in her. After eating dinner at a Cajun restaurant he drove her back to her apartment and walked with her to her door. Before he left, he handed her the hundred dollars that he received from the auto salvage company that purchased her car. Esther was moved to tears. She thanked him and kissed him goodnight.

A few weeks later Daniel moved into Esther's apartment. Like Aaron, Daniel did not have a lot of furniture to move. He liked the simple things in life and avoided buying things that were not useful to him. He avoided the purchase of real estate property and large furniture that would have tied him down to just one place. Living a simple life without material things allowed him to move to other cities easily when the economy turns sour. He drove a car provided to him by the dealership and he had the option to purchase new or used cars at huge discount. He resold the cars to his friends and families for a small profit. Occasionally he would go to car auctions across the country to bid on inexpensive cars that he later resold for a profit. He regularly scanned the newspapers and automobile magazines to look for old cars that he could fix up and resell. A week after he met Esther, he drove her to a car auction and bid for a car on her behalf. He bought her a five-year old car in excellent condition and with low mileage. Daniel had the car's internals checked out by the mechanic at the dealership. Esther finally had her car. Her friends turned green with envy when she showed them her new car.

The DM transplants, as the Des Moines ladies became known at the apartment complex, continued to meet at Bar Nuevo on Friday evenings. They shared news of their new lives with each other, drank margaritas, laughed, and often cried when they talked about the things that they missed in their hometown. They missed the cornfields, the smell of the dried cornhusks, the farms, the grain elevators, the crisp air and the uncluttered country roads. They criticized the cranes sprouting up all around Dallas, the traffic jams, and the higher cost of living. They were appalled by the high rate of divorce in the city, the killings that went on at night in the inner city, and the insensitivity of the powerful and wealthy. Sometimes they talked about getting married, going back to DM and settling down to a quiet life without material things.

Aaron and Vivian went to spend the Thanksgiving holidays in Jamaica. It was the first time that Vivian had left US soil to vacation in another country. They stayed in a hotel perched on a cliff in Negril on the West coast. The sights of the poor people living in ramshackle huts covered with tin roofs made her realized how fortunate she was living in the United States. Every day, from dawn to dusk the local people welcomed them to Jamaica and tried to sell them some souvenirs. The local people relentlessly pursued them to lease bicycles, motorcycles or automobiles from them. They pursued them on the beaches to sell crafts and souvenirs to them. Hotel employees tried pushing drugs to them on the hotel grounds. While they cruised along the coastline, a catamaran with naked men and women on the decks sailed by them. After the close encounters with the nude sunbathers, Vivian vowed never to go back to Jamaica again.

Soon after they returned from Jamaica, Aaron and Vivian broke up. Aaron then took an interest in the younger, more attractive Elizabeth. Esther had gotten tired of Daniel and had the apartment management evict him from her apartment. With nowhere to go, Daniel moved in with Vivian who was beginning to appreciate Esther's love economics.

Esther was starting to feel guilty for neglecting her two children. They have been wearing the same clothes since they arrived in Dallas. Christmas was just a few days away and she wanted to buy Christmas presents for herself, her kids, her friends and her families back in DM. She did not have much money to buy gifts, so she began to look for someone who could help her achieve her final goal.

On the day after Thanksgiving, Esther went to a store that was situated on the other side of the highway. She ambled in the toys aisles and gawked at the price of the toys. She contemplated using her credit cards to make her purchases when a stranger suddenly interrupted her train of thoughts.

"Excuse me, Ma'am," the stranger said. "You dropped this chain." The stranger dangled a chain in front of her. On the chain was a small disc with hieroglyphic symbols on both sides. Esther recognized the chain, but she was not in the mood to play the love game.

"I used to play this game myself," she said. "Don't you have any new trick for chatting up a woman?"

The stranger closed his fingers on the chain and dropped his arms down his side. "Definitely not my luck today," he said in resignation. He looked down and walked away.

"You look like an interesting guy. Do you always look for dates in a department store?"

"Only around Christmas," he replied.

Intrigued, Esther stepped closer to the man.

"Why Christmas?" she asked him.

The stranger shook his head and his hands at her.

"Oh, no," he stammered. "There is no problem. I am sorry I interrupted your shopping." The stranger quickly left the store.

Esther bit her lips. She felt sorry that she had frightened the stranger off.

After looking at several computers and video games and checking their price tags, Esther decided to put off her purchase. When she walked back to her car she noticed the stranger who tried to befriend her earlier sitting in his car. His window was rolled down and he held the steering wheel in both his hands. He stared blankly in front of him. Esther walked to the car and leaned over the window.

"Excuse me, sir," she said. "You dropped this chain in the store." She dangled a chain in front of him. On the chain was a small disc with hieroglyphic symbols on both sides. The man was jolted out of his meditation. He stared at the chain and felt his pocket.

"It can't be," he blurted out in confusion. He removed a chain from his pocket and showed it to Esther. "See? I still have it. I don't know who that one belongs to."

"I am sorry I was rude to you earlier," Esther said. She put the chain back in her handbag.

"It's yours?" the man asked, surprised.

Esther smiled and nodded. "I am going across the street to eat lunch. Would you like to come along?"

Inside the restaurant the stranger introduced himself to Esther as Amos. He was the Department Manager in the toys section. He was off work that day, but came to the store to chat up female customers. Every year he became very lonely and depressed around the holiday seasons. He had no family and no friends and he dated no one. To relieve himself from his loneliness and his depression, he looked for divorced women with children so that he could shower their children with gifts. He did not care whether the women like him or not as long as he could play with their children. He did not mind if the women were dating other men as long as he could bring toys for their kids. He did not give a hoot if the women did not love him as long as he could shower some love on their children.

"I ran away from home when I was 15 years old," Amos told Esther. "My father was always beating my mother and my other brothers and sisters. I was afraid that he would beat me too. He would lose control real easy. I thought running away is the only way to put an end to all the miseries. I have not seen my father or my mother since I ran away from home. I don't even know where they live or if they are still alive. I have not seen or heard from my brothers and sisters for nine years."

"Have you tried to make contact with them?"

Amos shook his head. "I am afraid that I will uncover something unpleasant if I try to locate them," he said. His voice took on a tone of reverence. "Sometimes it is better to leave things alone. What you don't know can't hurt you. I have been lucky so far. When I was a kid, I met a nice man who helped me out at a time when I needed it the most. He cared after me as if I was his own son and gave me sound advice."

"You are indeed very lucky. There are people with devious minds out there who prey on runaway kids like you. Many of the runaway children end up in houses of debauchery."

"The world we live in is not a good place to raise children," Amos said. "There are thousands of children around the world who will spend Christmas without toys. It's a shame that some of them are born to and raised by selfish and callous parents. I get really angry when I see an adult mistreat a child. I am surrounded by toys every day. I know that there are some kids who just won't get any toys this Christmas."

"You can get involved and make some children happy this Christmas."

Amos' face lit up. "How?" he asked.

When Esther returned to her apartment, she requested permission from the Apartment Manager to organize a toys-for-tots drive in the apartment complex. The Manager thought that it was a wonderful idea and consented. They placed receptacles in the apartment office, the laundry areas and the recreation room. They prepared flyers announcing the programs and posted them next to the mailboxes. The DM ladies asked their boyfriends to place bins at key locations in their workplaces to collect toys. Amos told his coworkers about the toy drive. They were very supportive and very enthusiastic of the program, and they eagerly helped him collect toys for the children. Esther spent her spare time with Amos collecting toys from the residents in the neighborhood and from various organizations. When she went with Amos to retrieve toys from his apartment, she was stunned to see his apartment filled with toys.

"Good Heavens," she exclaimed. "Where do all these toys come from?"

Amos' eyes turned misty. He blinked his eyes to clear the mist off. "I bought the toys to give them to children," he said. "People thought that I was a child molester and they forbid their children from accepting the toys. Some people even called the police and tried to have me arrested. I was beaten once when I handed out candies to kids in a playground. I was reprimanded when I hugged a child in a store and I was prohibited from touching or hugging children in the store anymore."

The response to the toys drive was extraordinary. They had collected more toys than they had expected. They distributed the toys to the children living in their apartment complex as well as to the children living in neighboring apartment communities. They took truckloads of leftover toys to the Salvation Army depot, the United Way and various church groups. Amos had finally given away all the toys that were cluttering his apartment. He was glad that he brought some joy to hundreds of children on Christmas day. He gave Esther's children a new computer and new clothes. Esther was extremely happy that she met Amos at the department store. It was the merriest Christmas she ever had in her life. She fell in love with him while they collected toys for the children. On Christmas Day Amos took the children to the movies. When they came back from the movie theater, Amos cooked them a wonderful Christmas dinner.

Soon after the New Year holidays, Amos moved into Esther's apartment. Vivian and Aaron had split up. Elizabeth now understood the love economics preached by Esther. She wholeheartedly opened up her apartment to Aaron and his wallet. Aaron was forever grateful to Elizabeth for giving him a place to stay and, at the first opportunity, took her on a cruise to the Bahamas. Daniel, having been expelled from Esther's apartment moved in with Vivian.

During the remainder of winter, the DM ladies were inactive and stayed inside their apartments with their male companions. When spring finally sprung up, they were dismayed to find moth holes in their clothes. They each woke up to a closet full of worn-out and out-of-fashion clothes and shoes. They dragged their boyfriends to shopping malls where they scampered from store to store trying out the new spring dress collection while their boyfriends looked on. The three women had never been so happy in their lives. For a while they enjoyed their lives to their fullest. They went out shopping often, took weekend trips frequently, dine out in expensive restaurants, and worry less about their future. Then, without warning, the economic downturn in the North caught up with them in Dallas. An out-of-state financial institution acquired the S&L Bank where Esther worked. The new owner merged all the check processing operations at their data processing headquarters in Indianapolis and handed pink slips to hundreds of employees. Esther's position was eliminated and she was laid off. The party warehouse where Vivian worked saw a big decline in its sales and the store released some employees. Vivian's working hours were cut back to twenty hours a week. Eventually the store closed down and all the employees were terminated. Elizabeth's marketing job was phased out when her employer sold the company. The economic outlook in Houston was as bleak as in Dallas, but the mammoth drop in Real Estate values there was enticing a different breed of carpet baggers to that city. The DM transplants heard that in Houston there were oil magnates and Real Estate barons waiting to be picked up. They heard that the Real Estate barons in Houston lived in big mansions with live-in housekeepers. They were starting to feel tired of living in their cramped apartments, and they now wished for a bigger home in which to raise their children. Without jobs and money in a city that was no longer kind to them, the three women decided to move to Houston to seek a better life for themselves and their children. They disposed of all furniture collected during the last year and kept only personal items and clothing. They bade farewell to their new friends at the apartment complex and at the office. They hugged and kissed their boyfriends and thanked them for their helps, promising them that they will write or call them after they arrive in Houston. Then they loaded their cars with their children and their belongings for the drive to Houston. Elizabeth still did not have a car and rode in the front seat with Esther. She stifled back her tears as they left Dallas and began the trek south to greener cornfields. They hoped that in the greener cornfields they would at last find the ever-elusive Methuselah. He would give them love, warmth and comfort, and bring a happy ending to their stories.

"Life is unfair," Elizabeth moaned.

"There is still one important lesson in love economics to be learned," Esther told her.

"What?" Elizabeth asked, drying her tears.

"It is Lesson seven: do not follow your heart. Follow a man's wallet."

After the DM ladies left for Houston, Aaron went back to cruising Harry Hines Boulevard and patronizing porn shops. He frequently saw Daniel in the porn shops looking at sex novelties or flipping through the pages of pornographic magazines. Occasionally he caught sight of Amos slipping into the peeping booths. At first the three men would not speak to each another. One afternoon Aaron walked into a topless bar after work to escape his loneliness. He purchased a pitcher of beer and a couple of sandwiches and sat in the front row to watch the topless dancers perform their acts. As he unfurled a roll of one dollar bills to tip the topless dancers, he saw Daniel and Amos sitting at the opposite end of the stage. They each held a bundle of dollar bills in their hands. Daniel and Amos saw him too. Aaron was slightly embarrassed, but a topless dancer stood in front of him and obstructed them from his view. The topless dancer moved back and forth in front of the customers. She squeezed and stroked her huge breasts to draw attention to their size. She came around and stood in front of Aaron, dancing, wriggling and blowing kisses at him. At the other end of the stage, Daniel suddenly shouted to the topless dancer "Give him a face rub." The topless dancer knelt down and spread her thighs out in front of Aaron. Aaron took a dollar note from the bundle of bills and slipped it into the dancer's skimpy underwear. He moved his face closer to the topless dancer's bosom. She leaned over him and rubbed her breasts over his checks. She massaged his cheeks with her breasts, and then slapped his face with them. Weighed down by her pendulous breasts, the dancer tipped over the stage and fell on Aaron. Daniel and Amos rushed over to help them. When the dancer regained her composure, she hugged and kissed Aaron and stammered an apology to him. Then she gave him another face rub and climbed back on the stage to continue her act. Aaron suddenly noticed the necktie that Daniel wore.

"You are wearing my necktie," Aaron said.

Daniel lifted the tie in his hand and stared at it. "Esther gave it to me for Christmas," he said timidly.

"I thought I had lost it," Aaron said. "I guess I must have left it at her apartment after I moved out." Then Daniel noticed the shirt that Amos was wearing.

"Hey, that's my shirt that you are wearing," he pointed out to Amos.

"Is it?" Amos said. "It was a gift from Vivian for Christmas. I did not know that it was yours." Then Amos noticed Aaron's pants. "You are wearing my pants," he pointed out.

"Oh no," Aaron said. "What an embarrassing mix up! You can have your trousers back. It looks like you are wearing my pants too."

The three men removed their neckties, unbuttoned their shirts and slipped out of their trousers. The spectators in the topless bar were amused by the sight of the three men undressing and exhorted them on. Then someone shouted: "Get on the stage!" They climbed on the stage and took their clothes off and passed them to each other. The spectators clapped and cheered. The trio bowed to the spectators and waved their pants and shirts to them. Two bouncers suddenly appeared and climbed on the stage. They lead the three men down the stage and ushered them to a side door. As they were being expelled from the bar, a slip of paper fell off of the pair of trousers in Aaron's hand. Aaron picked up the piece of paper and read the message on it. It was a note on love economics that Esther wrote to herself.

Lesson #8
You can save money on Christmas gifts
if you take something from your boyfriend
and use them later
as Christmas gifts for your new boyfriend

11 THE VAGRANT ON HER DOORSTEPS

He perceived the single women he met as self-centered individuals who were only interested in their careers and in the pursuit of material things. He felt that they were all prejudiced against divorced men and that they were not interested in dating him. For months he waited for a chance encounter with a woman with whom he would build a long-term, meaningful relationship. Alas! He waited in vain. More than two years had passed by since his wife left him. The specter of going through life without love and companionship frightened him. Loneliness began to gnaw at his mind. His male colleagues no longer socialized with him because he was an unmarried man. His closest friends, who were married and had children, deserted him because they felt out of place in the company of an unwed man without a female friend. The single women at the office found him boring and unattractive; they repeatedly turned him down for dates. They chose instead to be in the company of the men higher up above him in the company hierarchy. He was a simpleton, did not earn the salary of a company executive, and did not drive a flashy car. He could not afford to take the women out to fancy restaurants on his modest earnings. His colleagues drove the latest sport cars, lunched at full-service restaurants, and spent the evenings in bars drinking, eating and socializing. He ate lunch at fast foods restaurants, drove a clunker, and ate TV dinners alone in his modest one-bedroom apartment. There were in the metropolitan area close to 120,000 eligible single women. Yet he felt that no one wanted him as a friend, a companion or a lover. Since his wife left him for another man, seventeen women had spurned him down. He stopped counting when the number reached twenty-five. Women of all nationalities turned him down for dates. They thought that he was not tall enough, not macho enough, and not wealthy enough. Worse of all, he did not have sex appeal. A colleague dealt him a terrible blow one day when he confided to him that he had dated and slept with more than a hundred women over a period of three years. He was heartbroken that his colleague, a handsome tall man from Eastern Europe, could date so many women while he had difficulties dating just one woman. He slowly began to hate himself for his inability to befriend a woman and started to think that there was something wrong with him. He thought about ending his life several times. In sheer desperation, he turned to a new form of dating: answering personal ads in local newspapers and singles' magazines. He was not looking to date a hundred women like his colleague. He just wanted to find a good woman.

With renewed hopes, he began to browse through the personal ads in the Sunday papers. He circled the ads from the women with attributes and characteristics similar to his own and then narrowed down the choices to four or five women. Then he composed eloquent letters to the women. He clipped out the personal ads and saved them so that he could remember which personal ads he answered. A week went by after he had mailed the first batch of six letters, but he received no reply. He waited another week, and still no reply. Every night he sat by the phone and waited for someone who read his personal ad to call him, but no one called. He concluded that the women he wrote to did not find anything particularly interesting about him. After waiting for two weeks, he crossed out the ads from the newspaper clippings so that he would not write to the same advertiser again. Then he scrutinized the personal ads in the next Sunday paper, circled another five ads from single women looking for men and wrote to them. He thought that perhaps he did not include enough details about himself in his previous letters, so he wrote lengthy letters the second time. He told the women about his occupation, his hobbies, and his likes and dislikes. He wrote that he likes to jog and bike, enjoys taking long walks in the woods and loves to watch movies. He wrote that he is a much disciplined person, keeps a clean house, loves to cook, and is very fond of children. He also wrote that he does not drink, smoke or use drugs. He also told them that he hopes that someday he would marry and have children. He mailed the letters and waited for the replies to come in. When he came home from work each day, he eagerly checked his mailbox and patiently waited by the phone. One more week went by, then two, and finally three weeks passed by him, but still no one replied to his letters or called him. He waited for another three weeks before finally throwing away the newspaper clippings. On the following Sunday, he started again with a new batch of personal ads.

He was getting bored perusing the singles ads in the newspapers and magazines, but nevertheless he kept on trying. Week after week, he picked out a few women from the Sunday paper and wrote letters to them. But none of the letters generated a response. He reviewed and edited the contents of his letters, rearranged the words around, and removed entire paragraphs that he thought might not be of interest to the women. He added some punch lines or wrote a funny joke here and there in the letters to capture their interests, but nothing worked. Despite the utter despair, the rejection and the cost of replying to the personal ads, he continued to hope that a woman would eventually take interest in him. One of his friends, a married man with two teenage boys, occasionally came by his apartment to give him moral support and friendly advice.

"The statistics indicate that you are compatible with nine other persons," his friend told him during one of his visits. He thought that his friend was mocking him, but nevertheless quietly listened to him. "Assuming a 50-50 distribution," his friend continued, "five of the nine compatible partners are men and the other four are women. For you, my good friend, this brings the number to just four or five compatible female partners. Unfortunately, the four compatible female partners may be living anywhere in the country. To make your search for a suitable partner more difficult, only a small section of the singles population use the personal ads to look for a partner. That makes it even more difficult for someone like you to meet that right woman. Don't forget that women are choosy too. If you wish for a good-looking woman, there is no reason why a woman should not wish for a handsome man. There is no law that says that a woman must like you. She is entitled to choose for herself, and she may not like you."

His friend's comments were not very encouraging. He could be half right and half wrong, or he could be a hundred percent right. He thought that he was not attractive to women and therefore he should not look for a beautiful woman.

"Perhaps I should advertise for an ugly woman," he suggested. "My ad will read: 'Ugly man seeks ugly woman for long term relationship.'"

His friend laughed. "I am saying that you must not give up. Keep trying."

He had never considered himself an attractive man. He did not think that he was very ugly. He was not very smart, but his boss told him that he was a conscientious worker. He owned a small condo and he had a good job. He had difficulties finding dates when he was still in high school. He never had the look that women look for in a man. He was not handsome, big, tall or athletic. But while his physical attributes were lacking, God gave him a different kind of gift. He was a very caring person. He discovered sadly enough that women don't like to date ugly or short men. When it comes to courtship, he just did not have the physical attributes to compete with his fellow American men.

Despite his shortcomings, he continued to respond to the personal ads from single women. His friend had earlier suggested that he advertised for a female companion in the paper too instead of just replying to personal ads. He resisted the idea at first because he thought it ridiculous for a man to advertise for love in the newspapers. He felt a little bit ashamed of having to place a personal ad in the paper to look for love. His letters, however, were not eliciting any responses, so he decided to give it a try. He started writing a personal ad, but he tore it up before finishing it and without reading it. He rewrote the ad, tore it up and rewrote it again. He wrote the short note about himself twelve times, each time crumpling up the note and tossing it in the trash can. He was embarrassed whenever he read about himself. He doubted that his ad would attract any woman's attention. He thought that no matter how beautiful or witty his letters were, no one would respond to them. After two hours of writing and tearing up his profile, he finally took a completed profile and placed it in an envelope without reading it again. He was weary of playing the love game and losing every time. He was beginning to lose hope that he would ever marry.

"I possess neither intelligence nor beauty," he sadly wrote in his diary. "I am a man doomed to live my life in solitude. What a tragic fate! Without love and companionship, what is a man to become? Can he go through life without touching another human being? Can he face to live life without holding a woman's hand? Can he bear to sit down at a table and eat his meals alone? Can he lie on a bed and go to sleep without kissing a woman good night? Can he bear to live in a world in which no words are heard or uttered? Will he live happily if his eyes never drop a tear? Will he miss the warmth of a female body close to him? I cannot see myself living such a life. I would rather die now than face living alone. I would rather be infected with the AIDS virus and die a slow death than be healthy and spend the rest of my life alone. I prefer Death to loneliness. Death, the Liberator, will free me from the humiliation of rejection."

Every night he checked the mailbox with trepidation. When he found an empty mailbox, he lingered around it and searched the ground underneath the mailbox, hoping that perhaps the mailman had dropped his letters. In the evening he sat by the telephone and waited for a woman to call him. He waited and waited. Three more weeks went by, and still no responses to his personal ads.

"What does a woman look for in a man?" he added to the pages of his diary. "Does money buy love? If money buys love, then I'll have to do without it for I have barely enough money to pay my bills. I have spent many long nights secretly studying the personal ads from single women. I now think that I have finally understood their needs. Women have very complex needs. It seems to me that they all want a man with fat lips, beard, mustache and strong arms. They all want a man who is big, tall, rugged and outdoorsy. They also want a man with class who is into sports, movies and dancing. They want a man who is mature, honest, sincere, sensuous and passionate. They wish for a man who is stimulating, strong, confident, independent, creative and witty. They desire men who are humorous, responsible, romantic, positive, open-minded, stable, devoted, sophisticated, sexy and handsome. They want men who are spontaneous, charismatic, adventurous, unencumbered, gainfully employed, attractive, caring and affectionate. They hankered for men who are captivating, charming, optimistic and wealthy; good-hearted and generous; men who are respectable, degreed, energetic and hardworking. They want to travel and attend symphonies. They want to drink champagne, sample brunches, hike along trails, walk along sandy beaches, climb mountains and ski the Alps. They want a playmate, a roommate, an inmate, a classmate, a paper mate, a rubber mate, a soul mate and a comfort mate. They all want to have a good time with their mates, no matter what kind. Some women prefer to date men with olive skin, whereas others only want to date palefaces. A few women wrote that they want men to add pizzazz to their lives and sweep them off their feet. Others forbid anyone less than six feet tall to lay eyes on them and request that anyone weighing less than 200 pounds not to write to or call them. They all make use of secret codes, such as ISO SDWCM to communicate their secret desires. The more sophisticated women want to climb up a Mayan Temple and give their former boyfriends or husbands up for sacrifice. They like to curl up in front of the fireplace, dine in restaurants, and eat by candlelight. Most of the women wish to date a Christian, a Jewish or a Catholic man. None of them want to date a monk, a Buddhist or a communist. Many of them disclose that they derive sheer enjoyment when they kill a fish. They don't like to play games and they want a man who will take them to Kokomo. They seek men who resemble Tom Cruise, Clint Eastwood, Robert Redford, Pierce Brossman or Bruce Willis. They want a man whose head resembles a chocolate-covered candy apple. They warn that befriending them may result in fatal attraction and may eventually lead to death by marriage. They all unanimously want to tie a leash around their man's neck and take him to antique shops, garage sales, flea markets, art galleries and shopping malls. Some women even confessed that they want to live the remainder of their lives making love in coffee shops with the man of their dream. Some will only date police officers, fire fighters, military officers or college professors. A few women wish to be electrified into starting a complex relationship with someone well versed in bio-chemistry."

"How can I be everything that a woman wants in a man?" he wrote. "How will I ever be able to give a woman all the things that she wants? There can never be a perfect match between a woman and a man. I don't think there is such a thing as true love. I think that it only exists in Shakespeare's mind. Oh Lord, why is love so complicated? It is so much easier for me to understand Einstein's theory of relativity than trying to understand the complex needs of a woman."

He possessed none of the characteristics that the women listed in their personal ads. He was short and thin, knew nothing about biochemistry and possessed no experience in electrifying women. He had never eaten his dinner by candlelight and he was too gentle to kill a fish. He was not a military officer, he had no facial hair, and he had never been to Kokomo. He didn't know what the women expect to find in that dusty, industrial town in Central Indiana. Dispirited, he began to study the personal ads from men who were seeking women. He hoped that the personal ads from the men would give him a clue on how to write a good personal ad that would attract the women's attention.

"I have come to believe that I have none of the qualities that will make me attractive to women," he sadly noted down in his diary. "So last night I starting to read the men's ads hoping that I may learn something from the lonely men who are seeking women through personal ads. I found that they are all athletic, cultured and charismatic. They describe themselves as being introspective, non-fanatical, conservative, sensitive, enthusiastic and vibrant. They all claim to be respectful, thoughtful and decent people. They assert that they are selective, magnaminous, eclectic and shindigish."

He concluded that while the men wanted a beautiful and intelligent woman, the women, on the other hand, looked for fun, excitement and good times. Armed with this new information about women, he went over the personal ads once more and selected the ads from women that were more likely to generate a response. To avoid any further disappointment, he made his letters brief. He no longer cared whether the women he wrote to would reply to him or not. Weeks after weeks he read through the personal ads and wrote letters. He wrote 127 letters over a period of six months, but no one replied back. Finally, just when he was about to give up, he found a solitary letter in the mailbox. The letter came from a woman whose personal ad he responded to. He hurried back into the apartment and opened the envelope with trembling hands. He pulled out a letter and two small photographs from the envelope. He glanced at the two pictures before reading the letter. The first photograph showed a white woman holding a small baby. The woman was thin, had long red hair, and wore large eyeglasses. In the second photograph, the same woman wore a pair of blue jeans and sat alone on a long sofa. Her hair was shorter in the second picture.

"At long last a woman has answered my letter," he later wrote in his diary. "I gather from her red hair that she is a temperamental person and it worries me that we may not be compatible. She did not say in her letter if she smokes or not, but I figure that if she avoided the subject, then she must be a smoker. Nevertheless I'll wait a week or two before calling her. I gather that she will probably want me to go to the flea market with her. I hate going to flea markets or Art & Crafts shows, but if she asks, then I will go. In any case I think that it will be more fun to be at the flea market with a stranger than sitting home alone."

Two weeks later he called the woman and asked her for a date. She agreed to meet him. On the appointed date he drove over to her house to take her out to dinner. A Volkswagen Beetle, with signs of 'JESUS LOVES YOU' plastered on the rear bumper and on the rear window, was parked in front of her house. He parked his car behind the Volkswagen and walked up to the house. The door was open. The living room was engulfed in darkness. He glanced through the screen door and inside the house. Seeing no one in the room, he rang the doorbell and waited. A woman emerged from the dark living room and stood by the screen door. It was so dark in the living room that he could not see her face. He wasn't sure if she was the woman he was meeting. The woman opened up the screen door and told him in a melancholy voice that she was not ready. She asked him to wait outside. Ten minutes later, she emerged from the dark living room holding a carrier with a baby in it.

"I hope that you don't mind," she said almost apologetically in a low voice. "I can't afford a babysitter."

"No, I don't mind," he replied. He offered to help her carry the baby to his car, but she declined. They walked to his car without saying another word to each other. She silently strapped the baby carrier on the rear seat and then stepped into the front passenger seat.

"Is it a sports car?" she asked him. In the semi darkness, she had mistaken his old car for a fancy sports car.

"No, it is not," he replied. "I can't afford to drive a sports car." They drove to a restaurant nearby. They hardly said a word to each other along the way. She constantly looked back to the back seat to check on her baby.

"Are you familiar with this area?" he asked her when they reached the restaurant.

"I used to live in an apartment about two blocks away from the restaurant," she replied. "My roommate and I come here often. She visits the medical clinic in the plaza. Our dentist has his office around here too. There are all kinds of shops around here. When the weather is warm, I bring Amy here for a stroll."

They sat at a table close to the door. They both felt uncomfortable meeting on a blind date and for a few minutes remained silent. They sat facing each other, but she avoided looking at him directly. They were two lonely people meeting for the first time and looking for love and companionship. They were both discomfited that they had to go through the personal ads in order to find each other. A couple stopped by their table to admire her baby.

"Isn't she cute?" the diner said to her male companion.

Her companion's mouth was agape with admiration for the pretty baby. His eyes were glued on the little baby's face. He was so fascinated by the stunningly beautiful baby that he stood transfixed at their table without saying a word.

A few minutes later another couple walked by them. They too stood frozen in admiration at seeing the baby.

"What a beautiful baby," the second diner murmured.

Her date thanked the woman and covered her baby with a small blanket. She moved the carrier from the top of the table to the seat corner. The waitress came by their table and took their orders.

"I enjoy reading your letters very much," she finally said. "I get the feeling from reading your letters that you are a man of my own temperament. I also detected some cynicism and even some anger in your letters."

"I feel some bitterness," he admitted. "You are right. When things do not go well, I have a tendency to get angry."

"I thought I was bitter myself," she confessed, "but despite swimming in all that bitterness, I still find a great deal of hope and optimism. You appear to be bravely refraining from drowning. I think you are very capable of abstract thoughts."

He smiled. "Do you still want my autograph?"

She laughed. "Yes," she answered, "but it must be signed in blood on the inside cover of my bible. I won that bible in a drawing held by a Christian Insurance Company who wanted to sell me a life insurance policy."

"I saw the bumper stickers on your car. I assume that it's your car. Is religion important to you?"

"I am a Christian mother," she replied. "Someone slashed the tire on my car yesterday. I had to buy a new tire. This is the second time that they've done this to me. I think that there is a crazy person living in my neighborhood. That person does not like the religious stickers on my car." The food server came back with the drinks they had ordered.

"The signs on your car draw attention to a lot of people. I am sorry about your tire."

"I was raised a Catholic when I was a young girl, but I spent many years ignoring God. Every now and then I'll attend a religious meeting just to investigate a religious fad. I recently started to attend services at a Baptist church not too far away from my house. The church where I worship is too far away from my apartment."

"I don't understand how any woman can love a man who hit her?" he said, referring to the first line of her personal ad.

"I drew the first line of my personal ad from a well-known poem. It gives me something to work on when I start approaching the end of my rope, which happens from time to time."

"I could not stop laughing when I read that you like blowing bubbles. I thought that only kids blow bubbles."

"When was the last time you blew a bubble?" She gave a quick look at her baby who was sleeping soundly. "How do you know that you don't like blowing bubbles?"

"Maybe I'll try it someday."

He took a sip from his glass. A roach landed on the table. It meandered around the table, looking for scraps of foods. She shrieked at the sight of the insect. He swept the roach off the table with the back of his hands and it landed on her seat. She jerked her body away from it, knocking the carrier and jolting the baby awake. The roach spread its wings and dived under the table. She rocked the baby back to sleep. "I hate roaches," she screeched.

"Oh, they are just inoffensive bugs created by God with a purpose," he said, laughing at her fear. "They won't hurt anyone. When we kill roaches we destroy a part of the ecosystem. Too many roaches are being decimated by humankind. They will soon start a revolution in Texas if we don't stop exterminating them."

"Good heavens," she protested, "I already know about the roaches' assault on single and unmarried women. I disagree with you on their usefulness. They are at the bottom of the ecological system. All they do is cause havoc with single and unmarried women. They have infiltrated every bathroom and kitchen in Texas, and they are now working on the entire continental United States. It seems that they have built up immunities to most common methods of extermination. I have seen quite a few of them with wings. This is the ultimate last straw. As soon as they figure out what those wings are for, we might just as well kiss the human race goodbye." She took a sip from her glass. "The battle against the roaches is on. I bought some boric acid yesterday. Now I have to figure out how to spread it around the house so that the children won't be in danger of coming in contact with it."

The food server came back and spread their foods in front of them. The baby opened her eyes, stretched her tiny arms and yawned. She smiled and said: "Hello." The baby stared at the light over the table and then closed her eyes. The waitress asked them if they wanted more drinks. She gave the waitress an empty baby bottle and asked her to fill it up with lukewarm water. He asked the waitress to refill his glass with iced tea.

"What do you like to give?" he asked her as he picked up a slice of garlic bread.

"Give?" she asked, puzzled. "What do you mean?"

"The second line of your personal ad read that you like to give," he explained. "I wondered how a single mother raising a baby all by herself can have anything left to give."

She remembered the personal ad that she wrote and smiled. "You have hit the nail right on the head," she said. "Being a single mother, I do have difficulties making ends meet. I am usually not on the giving end, but I try to give whenever I can unless I lose my temper. I have been losing my temper quite a lot lately. My roommate and I helped another single mother not too long ago. We looked after her baby while she worked at two new jobs and we loaned her some money to pay her bills. While we were at work ,she looted my wardrobe, stole our money, and carried off our baby foods. She did not pay us back what she owed us after she got paid. I got fed up with her and threw her out of the apartment. I will give a great deal of rope, but when someone reaches the end it, that's it. It snaps! I can really be mean when the safety and well being of my own child is at stake." Her baby made a sudden move. She quickly dropped her fork and rocked the baby carrier.

"Your personal ad raises many questions in my mind," he said, as he chewed on his steak.

"You can't get a lot said in just fifty words," she objected. "I find it hard to believe that anyone would advertise in a singles' magazine if they were simply looking for a casual friend. I am looking for a permanent relationship. I was married in 1977. My husband and I stayed together for about three months. We divorced five years later. We did not divorce sooner because neither one of us had a reason to finalize the divorce. In case you are wondering, I was not married to Amy's father. I was trying to help someone, but somehow managed to get emotionally involved. I thought that it was not possible for me to bear children and, lo and behold! What a wonderful surprise I got. I am extremely happy with Amy. She is now seven months old. Her father is a 20-year old juvenile delinquent who had just been released from jail. He has no intention of taking responsibility for his own baby. I doubt that he would ever be capable of taking care of her. Amy is not old enough yet to know whether she has a father or not. I know what it is like to grow up without a father in the house. The ideal situation is to have one around. I hope that I will eventually find a father for her. This is the reason why I placed a personal ad in the paper. I heard someone on the radio proposing the idea that people who want to divorce their spouses should have to go through the entire ceremony again. They should send out invitations to all the people who attended their wedding, take back their vows, give back the wedding gifts, throw rice back at the people, etc., etc. It sounds like a promising idea to me. It's kind of running a movie projector backward."

The waitress came back with the baby bottle. She took the bottle and squirted a few drops on the back of her hand to feel the water temperature. The waitress asked them if they needed anything else. She answered her in the negative. The waitress stared at the baby and said: "She is so beautiful."

"Where did you meet him? I mean, Amy's father." He washed down the food in his mouth with the iced tea and took another mouthful of the steak.

"I came home one night and found a vagrant lying on my doorsteps," she answered. "He was drunk. I took him into my apartment and let him spend the night in my living room. When he woke up the next day, he told me that he did not have a family and had no place to go to. He said that he did not have any money and did not work. So I took him in my apartment." She paused and mashed the baked potato on her plate with her fork. She had eaten her vegetable, but the steak was barely touched. "There again," she sadly said. "I thought I was only helping him."

He glanced at her baby and said: "He must be a very handsome man."

"He is a very beautiful man," she said, staring down on her plate.

"Why did you not marry him?"

"I did not marry him because he was not ready to marry anyone. He still is not ready to marry anyone to this day. He is incapable of caring for himself. I don't even know where he is now. Even if I know where he is, I doubt that any effort on my part to obtain child support for Amy would do any good because he can't even support himself. For all I know, he may end up in jail again. Change comes slowly, and it is a long, hard process. It had been that way for me. It's like taking two steps forwards and falling backward three steps. All his life he tried to get other people to do everything for him. He is not a kid anymore. The world is telling him to stand on his own two feet. I hope he learns how to do it. For me it has always been a choice between life and death, and that does not make the process easier."

She lifted the glass to her lips and drank the iced water. He looked at her baby and wondered what her father would think when he sees her. The waitress came back and asked them if they wanted to order deserts. He encouraged her to have desert, but she declined.

"I really enjoyed reading the poems that you sent me," he told her.

"I started writing poetry when I was young," she said. "Like my father, my dream was once to write the great American novel. That has not been my dream for quite some time now. Writing for me takes a great deal of time and concentration. I have had very little time to spare since Amy was born."

"Do you live by yourself now?"

"My roommate and I had recently moved in with a young family. Where we used to live, the Apartment Manager would not allow my roommate to babysit, which is her only source of income for the time being. We are all having a difficult time getting adjusted at the new house because it is very crowded and tense. The owner of the house has a two years old daughter and his wife is six months pregnant. They are having their own problems and I am not used to having a man around me. But things are beginning to settle a little bit at a time. I think that the two of us will be able to manage for a while there. I drive a little wind-up toy. The car payment is $70 a month. I think the car will hold out until I finish paying for it next year. What do you do with your spare time?"

"I like woodworking, but the tools are very expensive. I am making a bookshelf. I like to hang wallpapers. I also enjoy photography. When I was young, I collected postage stamps. After a while, I grew tired of it."

"I appreciate and enjoy good photography, but I don't know anything about it. I enjoy nature, but I have not done much in the way of yard work. I never cared much about going to school when I was younger. I always had problems with learning, but I somehow managed to get an education. I believe that the day we stop learning will be the day we die. If someone says to me that he does not enjoy learning, I would think that he does not enjoy life either. I don't know anything about putting up wallpapers. Is that a hobby or what? It seems to me that this is something that someone will do as a vocation although I don't think that I will enjoy such a vocation myself. I guess I will never know till I try it first. What are you looking for in a woman?"

"Nothing special, just plain honesty," he answered. "I don't like hypocrites. I especially don't like women who lie and cheat on their husbands. I abhor people with false pretensions. I have zero tolerance for lazy people."

"I would definitely think that there is something wrong with you if you like to be in the company of hypocrites. There are truly some live ones out there, but we are sometimes guilty of making poor judgment. I think that a lot of times we misunderstand each other. I don't believe that people intentionally set out to deceive one another. Sometimes it is hard for me to convince myself otherwise. There are all kinds of people in this world. You are one of them and I am one of them. We spend a lot of time trampling one another, but I think we all want to be needed and loved."

"Where are you from?"

"I am from Philadelphia. I have lived in Dallas for two years. I worked for a while as a waitress. It was hard work and I did not like it. After a few months I went back to my previous occupation. I am a school teacher. This is something that I enjoy doing. I like Dallas very much. Sometimes I missed Philadelphia. I missed my family and my old friends. My father and my stepmother live in Louisville. It is not too far for me to visit them from here."

She took the baby from the carrier and held her in her arms. Another couple walked by and admired the baby. He thought that she looks much better than in the photographs. She dipped a napkin in the glass of water and wiped the baby's mouth. Her eyeglasses were hanging down on her nose. She pushed them back towards her eyes.

"My eyeglasses are too big for me," she said. "I need to have my eyes examined again because I have some problems with my eyes. I would like to get another pair of eyeglasses."

"It must be hard for you to hold a full time job and care after your baby too."

"I live from day to day and I put my faith in God's hands. At the moment I am not sure anymore what my plans are, other than to raise Amy the best I can. I would love more than anything else to be able to live out in the country or by a lake some day. I don't care very much for the city. My ultimate goal is to be happy with whatever I am doing and wherever I am. I am very happy with Amy, but I also feel that there is another kind of relationship missing in my life."

He put his elbows on the table and laid his chin in the cup of his hand. He watched her put her baby back in the carrier.

"You wrote that you don't like hot-tempered women. I am sometimes extremely temperamental. I can also be very moody. I don't make it a practice to yell unless I am provoked. I don't believe that yelling accomplishes anything positive. I especially don't believe in raising my voice in public for any reason unless there is a fire. I have seen mothers yelling at their children for spilling a glass of milk. I have also watched people getting angry with others for spilling a cup of coffee on the sofa."

"You share a small house with two other women, one man and three small children. One of the women is pregnant. Your roommate babysits in the same house. I think that I will go crazy too if I live in that house."

"You are right. If I were not surrounded by people bickering all the times about money, I will probably be happier. If the people in my living environment were mutually supportive, I will not have a temper. Last night my roommate and my landlady went out to the store and left me alone to watch the children. At first, one child was fussy. Then the other child wanted a bottle. The oldest child was emptying a large box of crayons on my bed and taking the crayon box apart. She tried to put the crayons back into the box, but instead dumped the crayons all over my bed. After a while she got crayon markings all over the bed sheet. I got a little upset and threw the crayon box across the room. Her father was taking a nap and he did not have to watch her." She choked on her last word and stifled back her tears. She turned to look at her baby to hide her tears from him. Her baby was peacefully sleeping.

"If I were you I would have asked the husband to look after his own daughter."

"He felt that he was entitled to his rest after coming back from work. I hope that I have not frightened you with my admission of guilt."

"These things happen."

"I got thrown out into the cold world at an early age and told to make it one way or another. I spent a good part of my life blaming others, particularly my parents, for all my problems and my inability to cope. I finally realized that my mother would never change. She will never be the mother I wanted her to be and no matter how hard I tried, she probably never will."

Tears ran down her cheeks. She lowered her head and wiped her eyes.

"Do you want another drink?" he asked, looking for the waitress.

"No, I still have water in my glass," she replied. She took a sip from the glass. She quietly and lovingly gazed at her baby.

"I finally realized that the only one I could change was me. It was up to me whether my life was spent in misery or happiness. I can never go home to a loving father when I am overwhelmed or just needed to feel loved. I realize that I have a whole life ahead of me even if I shall die tomorrow. I particularly feel the necessity of it right now as I have been under a lot of stress lately." She covered her face and sobbed. He saw her tears dripping through her fingers and lowered his head. He was at a loss for words. She lifted her face and wiped the tears from her face. "I am sorry. I hope that I have not put you off with my whining."

"Life can be very cruel," he said. "But we have to go on."

"I want to thank you for not calling me right away after you received my letter. A misplaced word can easily put an end to a beautiful beginning. Too often people are in a big hurry. They want what they want right now. That usually succeeds in destroying a relationship before it even had a chance to get started."

"Did someone else respond to your personal ad?"

"I received three letters before yours. The first letter was only fit for the garbage. The writer of the second letter had previously written to my roommate. He wrote in his letter that he had never made love to a woman. I put that letter in the trash can too. The third respondent had previously dated my roommate and she was not interested in meeting him again. I threw his letter in the garbage can too. I thought that you were rather insolent yourself."

The waitress came back with the check. He paid for the meals and left her a generous tip.

"Do you have any regret replying to my letter?"

"No. I enjoy reading your letters tremendously."

"You have a beautiful baby," he said. "Every diner in the restaurant stopped to look at her. I had the feeling that the last couple who stopped to adore your baby wanted to hold her in their arms."

She removed the baby from the baby carrier and held her in her arms. "Last night I carried her outside so she could feel the wind on her face. Then I let her stare at the trees and the branches dancing in the wind. That makes it all worthwhile. God had given me a gift and a task to fulfill."

He took a $20 bill from his wallet and slipped it in Amy's fingers. "I will never understand why people steal baby foods from their own friends."

"Thank you very much," she said, taken aback by his generosity. "I will not be too proud to use it. Before I had Amy, I was extremely reluctant to ask anyone for help. But after I had her I realize that we will never survive if I did not know how to accept help from other people. After Amy was born, a woman brought me frozen foods which I could just warm up. At first I hesitated to take the foods, but she insisted that I take them. The frozen foods kept me going during the first few weeks. I would never have been able to cook meals for myself as I had one arm around Amy twenty-four hours a day. It still makes me uneasy to accept help from other people. I prefer to be as self sufficient as I possibly can."

"Better times will come to you someday," he predicted.

"I have been aware of that for a while now. Whenever we are enduring some sort of hardship, something comes along at the last hour. I believe that God places circumstances and people in our paths and then he leaves it up to us to make the best use of them." She dug out a packet of cigarettes from her handbag. "There is something that I have to tell you," she said, as she took a cigarette from the pack and lighted it. She brought the cigarette to her lips and deeply inhaled on it.

"You don't have to tell me anything if you don't want to," he quickly said.

"I want to tell you now and get it over it with," she said, puffing the smoke into the air above her.

"Is this so important that you have to tell me now?"

"It is something that you should know."

"All right, but remember that I was not the one who asked to know."

"I know. I want you to know that I am a heavy smoker. I go through three packs a day."

He smiled. "You are so honest."

"I know that smoking is bad for me, but I cannot stop. I tried very hard before to give it up, but I just can't. Smoking helps me to relax. I was dying for a cigarette all the time I was talking to you, but I manage to control my urge to smoke until now. I could not suppress my craving for a cigarette any longer."

"Thank you for telling me," he said.

"I was smoking six packs a day not too long ago. I have managed to cut my smoking down to three packs a day. I was a nervous wreck then."

"You won't find many non smokers nowadays. For some people, smoking is almost like eating a sandwich or having a drink," he said.

"I want you to know first before you make a commitment."

He did not want her to feel guilty about her smoking addiction and changed the conversation to another subject. "What makes you decide to run a personal ad?" he asked.

"I had no choice. What else could I have done? It was so embarrassing for me to pick up a copy of the singles' magazine in the grocery store. I felt that everybody was watching me. After I removed a copy from the magazine rack, I hid it inside another magazine so that no one sees me with it." She laughed at her own revelation. "If you are still interested, we could go to the flea market this weekend. My roommate will probably want to come along too. Call me and let me know if you would like to do that. I must go home now and feed Amy."

They left the restaurant and walked back to his car. He helped her fasten the baby carrier to the rear seat and then drove her home. When they arrived to her house she somberly removed Amy from the back seat. The street was very dark and he walked with her to the front porch. Without saying a word she disappeared into the dark house.

When he returned home he sat down at his desk and opened his diary. "I have spent many nights studying the personal ads from single women so I could understand how to win their hearts," he noted down. "I think that I have wasted my time. From now on I shall wait until darkness fall upon the city and then find myself a clean porch and lay in wait for the lady of the house to come home. I will pretend to have no home to go to, no money and no job. She will open up her door and her heart to me and let me into her apartment. Oh my, I can think of a dozen nice things that she will give me once I am inside her apartment. Things like foods, warm clothes, spending money, and a roof upon my head. This beats writing hundreds of letters and waiting for months for a reply. What a fool I have been all this time, wasting my energy and my hard-earned money in bars and singles clubs and answering personal ads. The vagrant on her doorstep knew what he was doing. I believe that he must be quietly sleeping on a porch in another part of the city, calmly waiting for the lady of the house to come home. I have a great deal to learn from this vagrant. He must be the greatest lover of all times. There is still hope for lonely people like myself."

12 FINDING CHEIKO

The sun rises on the side facing the apartment bedroom window. On sunny days, it bathes the window curtains with a bright yellow light, and the radiant sunlight brightens the small bedroom. The living room, in contrast, is always dark. The balcony on the second floor is directly above the patio area which is enclosed by a 6ft fence. The balcony as well as the apartment unit on the opposite side blocked the sunlight, thus causing the sitting room to be always dark when Keiji returns home.

When Keiji came home from school, he turned on the light and the TV set in the living room. Then he went in the kitchen and opened the fridge to check for leftovers. The small kitchen was next to the living room by the door. A window let the daylight in and there was no need for the light to be turned on. There was nothing left from the previous night in the fridge, so he decided to cook chicken teriyaki. Cooking dinner was a simple affair. He rarely spent a lot of time in food preparation and cooking. To save cooking time, he cut the meat into small pieces. He separated and wrapped the meat pieces into individual portions. He then froze the single servings of meat until he is ready to cook them. Before going to class in the morning, he removed the meat from the freezer so that the meat would be unfrozen when he returned home. There was no more steamed rice left from the previous night either. He scooped up 2 cupfuls of rice and poured them into the rice cooker. After starting the rice cooker, he cooked the chicken in a frying pan. When the chicken pieces were cooked, he smothered them Teriyaki sauce.

The steamed rice was ready in fifteen minutes. Keiji filled a plate with the steamed rice and then covered the rice with the Chicken Teriyaki. He poured milk in a glass and took the milk and his dinner plate to the living room. He sat in front of the television to watch the evening news while he ate his dinner. After dinner, he turned off the TV and played some Japanese music.

Then he turned off the lights, laid down on the sofa and closed his eyes. The clear deep-toned vibrations of the Koto brought back painful memories to him. His eyes filled with tears as he sought out in the dark room the face of his brother Keichi. His mind wandered over to his brother's cramped studio apartment in Los Angeles. Amidst the sound of the Koto, he heard the melodious voice of a child.

The music stopped and the diamond stylus returned to rest on its cradle. Keiji rose up from the sofa to reposition the stylus at the beginning of the music platter. When the music started again, he laid back on the sofa and covered his face with a soft velvet cushion.

The fall semester had finally come to an end and Keiji looked forward to spending Christmas with his parents in San Diego. After all the nights he spent studying, he was relieved that he would not have to open another textbook until classes resume in January. When the music stopped again, Keiji went to his bedroom to start packing his luggage for the trip home. He gathered sufficient clothing to last for two weeks. He closed the suitcase and went to the bathroom to fill a bag with a tube of toothpaste, a toothbrush and a comb. He carried the suitcase and the bag into the living room and set them by the door. He had spent the previous days buying and wrapping gifts for his family. He fetched two paper bags containing the wrapped gifts from his bedroom and set them on the dining table. Then he opened a cabinet at the bottom of a wall unit and retrieved a photograph album. He opened the album and fumbled through the pages until the picture of a girl appeared. Then he restarted the music and turned on the lamp sitting on an end table. He sat down to look at the photograph. A small child was perched on a saddle with her tiny hands clutching the mane of a horse. Her head was covered with a large white Stetson hat and her black hair covered part of her forehead. She wore a sheepskin vest and a flowery red scarf around her neck. Her round face had the fierce look of a samurai warrior.

Last summer, Keiji read an article in a magazine that a new disease was killing people in Los Angeles. The unknown disease had claimed the lives of eleven people. A few weeks later, he heard that twelve more people had died from it. The disease was also afflicting people in New York City and other part of the country. About the same time, his sister Atsuko informed him that his brother Keichi was very sick. When Atsuko told him that Keichi had only a few days to live, Keiji immediately flew back to Los Angeles to be by his brother's bedside. His brother was admitted in the Critical Care Unit at the Good Samaritan Hospital in Los Angeles. He had lost so much weight that Keiji could hardly recognize him. His father took him aside and told him that Keichi had harbored the unknown disease for a long time. At first nobody knew what Keichi was inflicted with. His family had kept his disease a secret. They had assured him that his brother's condition was not serious. Keiji was enrolled at the University of Texas at Arlington and was studying for a

Masters degree in Electrical Engineering. His parents keep Keichi's ill health from him because they did not want his brother's deteriorating health to distract him from his studies. He was really shocked when Atsuko later called him and told him the sad news. Visiting his brother at the hospital, Keiji saw his brother clutching the photograph of a little girl. His former girlfriend took the child with her when she left him. Before he died, Keichi gave him the photograph.

"When you see my little girl, tell her that I love her very much. Kiss her goodbye for me." Then he closed his eyes. His last words were: "Cheiko, I love you very much."

After Keichi's death, his parents sold their home in Los Angeles and moved to San Diego. Keiji returned to Arlington to resume his studies. Life in the small college town was not the same again for Keiji after he came back. He lost interest in his studies and no longer went to rowdy parties organized by fraternity groups. He spent most of his time in his apartment shooting at a target with a pellet gun. A pair of yellow pages telephone directory was stacked behind the target. The pellets had torn open a large hole in the center of the telephone books.

Keiji was confounded when his brother made his last wish to him. He had never met his brother's former girlfriend, although he had seen a blurry picture of them taken while they were in Seattle. He only knew her as Amaya, the nickname given to her by his brother. In Japanese Amaya signifies night rain. The nickname fitted her nicely as they met one night in a rainstorm. His brother was an artist and frequently exhibited his works in art galleries across the country. Keiji met Cheiko for the first time when he returned to Los Angeles to visit his sick and aging father. She was just a few months old then. He remembered holding her in his arms and playing with her while his mother prepared dinner. His sojourn in Los Angeles lasted just two weeks because he had to return to Arlington to attend summer classes. Soon after they came back from Seattle, Amaya and Keichi separated. Amaya took Cheiko with her and left Los Angeles without leaving any address.

Keiji carefully placed the photograph of Cheiko in his wallet. A long journey to San Diego awaited him the next day. He stopped the phonograph, turned off the light and went to sleep.

At dawn a motorist cranked up the engine in his car parked beneath Keiji's window. The sound of the engine coming to life awakened him. It was still dark when he woke up. The light beams of a car leaving the parking lot swept across the bedroom wall. He turned away from the window and covered his head with the comforter. When the radio came on, he opened his eyes and looked at the time. The doors of the apartment unit next to his opened and slammed shut as it occupants left for work. Soon after, other car doors opened and closed in a flurry as the morning commuters started their day. A few minutes later the sunlight started to bath the window curtains with a soft yellow light. An overhead door being raised open at a warehouse across the street signaled to him that a new workday had just begun. He turned off the radio and emerged from underneath the comforter. He went to the window and pulled aside the curtains to let the daylight in. The sunrays radiating in the bedroom brought into light a speck of dust as it danced in the sunbeam. He looked out of the window and found three cars still parked in the parking lot. Their owners must be working odd hours and did not have to get up like the rest of them.

After taking a shower, Keiji loaded his suitcase and the bag of gifts in his car. He walked around the car and checked the tire pressures, measured the oil and water levels, and topped up the windshield washer reservoir. He drove to a gas station to fill up the fuel tank. Afterwards he drove to a nearby restaurant to eat breakfast before starting the long trip to San Diego. He drank four cups of coffee so he could stay alert while driving.

Keiji estimated that the journey home would take him twenty-six hours. He planned to drive seven hundred miles on the first day, stop in Albuquerque for the night, and resume his travel to San Diego the next morning. He anticipated that he would arrive in San Diego late on Saturday night. Keiji checked his rearview mirror and the door mirrors to ascertain that they were not knocked out of alignment. He fastened the seat belt around him and pulled on the strap a couple of times to make sure that the clip had homed in securely. He then opened the road atlas and spread it on the front passenger seat. With a firm determination, he fired up the engine and set out on his lone journey home.

The music on the car radio started to fade out as he drove further and further away from the city. An hour later the radio became silent. He attempted to tune in to other stations, but was unable to pick up any radio signals. Driving at a steady speed, he cut into the barren countryside and drove through small, dusty and desolate towns. Several hours later he reached Abilene and continued on to Sweetwater. Just before reaching Sweetwater, he exited Highway 20 and headed north along Highway 84. He passed through a few dusty towns, drove into Lubbock and continued on to Clovis. He reached Clovis at two o'clock and decided to stop to eat and rest. He had driven over 400 miles on the first lap of his journey. His back was sore after sitting behind the wheel for more than six hours. He pulled into a gas station to refuel. After filling up, he pulled into the parking lot of a fast food restaurant. The long hours spent driving had wetted his appetite and he ate several pieces of fried chicken. After eating, he walked around the restaurant for a while to exercise his legs. Ten minutes later, he climbed back behind the steering wheel and drove west on Highway 60. He estimated that he would arrive in Albuquerque at around seven o'clock.

His car swallowed the two hundred and sixty miles of highway between Clovis and Albuquerque in a little over four hours. He arrived in Albuquerque forty minutes earlier than he had projected. He had been on the road for about eleven hours and he had traveled a total of six hundred and fifty miles. He exited the highway and headed towards a motel for the night. His feet were swollen and his body was stiff. His vision was blurry from looking at the road for long hours. Once inside his hotel room, he filled up the bathtub and relaxed his muscles in the warm water. After changing into a clean set of clothes, he left his motel room to look for a restaurant.

Keiji had no trouble falling asleep when he returned to his motel room after eating dinner. The room was warm and the bed was comfortable. He slept through the night without waking up. When he drew open the curtain the next day, he was surprised to see a dusting of fresh powdery snow on the ground and on his car. He checked out of the motel and went to eat breakfast in the same restaurant where he had dinner the previous night. Then he drove to the nearby gas station to fill up and purchase some snacks. While the gas flowed into the gas tank, he checked the oil level, the radiator cooler fluid level and the tire pressure. When the pump nozzle clicked shut, he removed it from the tank and hanged it back on the side of the gas pump. He went inside the gas station to pick up a bag of ice, some snacks, and a few cans of beverages. Before resuming his journey, he poured the melted ice out of the cooler and dropped the bag of fresh ice in it.

The countryside looked like a picture on a Christmas card. The morning air was cool and crisp. Keiji joined highway 40 and sped west towards the New Mexico/Arizona border. He felt that his car was not as responsive as the day before and kicked down on the gas pedal. The car still would not go faster. He speculated that his car was sluggish because the engine was still cold. There were hardly any vehicles on the highway. Occasionally a lonely car drove in the opposite direction. He had barely been driving for ten minutes when a slow moving trailer appeared in front of him. He cruised at a steady speed behind it until it drove onto the exit ramp and disappeared. A few miles later he reached the town of Navajo. Wanting to drive through the town as rapidly as possible, he pressed down on the gas pedal and sped across the town. As he barreled through a set of traffic lights at 60 mph, he caught glimpse of the posted speed limit. When he realized that he was driving through a speed zone, he quickly slammed on his brakes. But It was too late. A highway patrol car cruising in the opposite direction spotted him. It slowed down and turned around at the traffic lights behind him. Keiji slammed his right hand on the steering wheel. "Damn it," he cussed. He glanced into the rearview mirror and saw the highway patrol car complete the U-turn at the intersection behind him. Its lights started to spin and flash. The highway patrol car slowly gathered momentum behind him as it began to chase him down the road. In resignation, Keiji turned his emergency lights on and pulled over the shoulder. He rolled down his window, removed his driver's license from his wallet, and calmly waited for the patrol car to catch up with him.

The highway patrol car finally pulled up behind him. The officer came out and cautiously walked up to him. He glimpsed into the rear of Keiji's car before approaching him.

"May I see some identification, please?" the officer politely asked.

Keiji handed the officer his driver's license and waited. The officer looked at his driver's license. He looked up from the driver's license to scrutinize him.

"Where are you driving to?" he asked.

"San Diego," he replied.

"San Diego, California?" the Patrol Officer repeated.

"Yes," Keiji answered.

"You were doing 66 miles in a 45 miles zone," the officer sternly reprimanded him. Keiji stammered a few words of apology. The officer pointed his finger to the road ahead of him. "Out there, you will come across drunken Indians," he warned. Once again, Keiji apologized and thanked the officer for warning him about the drunken Indians. "You'll get yourself killed if you are not careful," he continued.

"Thank you very much for the warning," Keiji stammered. He waited for the officer to write him a speeding ticket.

"You'll shortly come across the New Mexico/Arizona border," the officer continued. "In Arizona the cops make their living from handing out speeding tickets." The officer's face grimaced with anger, but his voice had a paternal tone. He gave Keiji back his driver's license and beckoned him off. "Drive carefully," he advised him. Trembling with gratitude, Keiji wished the officer a merry Christmas. Thinking that the officer did not hear him, he stuck his head out of the window and shouted: "Merry Christmas."

Keiji was upset that he was caught speeding. After driving for less than ten minutes, he pulled up at a fast food restaurant to let his anger dissipate. He ordered a large coffee and sat quietly by the window. A group of men and children sat two tables away from him. The men's dark faces were furrowed with deep wrinkles. Their clothes were old, dark and soiled. The men's hats looked like they have been kicked around and trampled in the dust. He cogitated that they were farmers who spent long hours toiling in the fields under the hot sun. "Could these people be the drunken Indians the highway patrol officer had warned him about?" he mused. They appeared neither drunk nor dangerous. He only saw on their faces a look of helplessness and isolation.

When he crossed the border into Arizona territory, Keiji realized how serious the officer's warnings were. Parked out of sight behind large rocks and boulders, the Arizona highway patrol officers kept watch on the motorists who drove into and out of the State. About every two miles he saw a patrol car parked by the wayside. Like tigers on a prowl, the officers waited patiently for the unsuspecting motorists to drive over the speed limit.

Whenever their radars homed in on a speeding vehicle, they raced out from behind their hiding places in a cloud of dust. Not wishing to be ticketed, Keiji drove within the speed limit and kept his eyes on the speedometer. Within one hour of driving into Arizona, he had witnessed the patrol cars chasing after seven motorists.

At around eleven o'clock, traffic signs warning motorists of roadwork ahead of them appeared on the highway. Two miles later, a larger sign warned the motorists of a diversion. He reduced speed and drove carefully past a line of orange cones and white barricades. A section of the highway was closed to traffic and a road worker directed the flow of vehicles to a temporary roadway. A group of men worked behind the barricades. The men's heads were covered with feathers instead of hard hats. They donned animal hides instead of orange vests. They wore moccasins instead of work boots. They carried spears, bows and arrows instead of shovels, spades and picks. They rode horses instead of driving earth moving machines. They attacked the concrete highway with their spears and tried to move the concrete slab out of the path of a herd of buffalos. Keiji saw a buffalo pacing uneasily behind the workers and looking for prairie grass. The motorist behind him hooted and Keiji woke up from his daydreams. A worker flagged him on.

He reached Flagstaff at noon and stopped to refuel, eat and rest. It was cooler in Flagstaff and he put on a pullover to keep warm. He checked the road map again and calculated that he would reach Kingman at 3.00 o'clock. He estimated that if he maintains his driving speed, he would arrive in San Diego at 10 o'clock. He tapped the hood on his car and murmured: "Don't let me down." As he left Flagstaff the road curved around hills and valleys. An occasional car drove in the opposite direction, but for the most part the road was deserted. At times the monotonous driving made him sleepy. When he started nodding off, he rolled the window down to let the fresh air in. When the cold gust of air failed to keep him awake, he stuck his head out of the window. The chilly wind whipping at his face momentarily kept him awake. When he felt drowsy again, he rolled the window back up and turned up the volume on the radio. He rocked his body to and fro at the music. He moved on his seat so much that the car started to zigzag on the road. He stopped dancing to the music and pinched his arms instead every time his eyes closed. A milepost showing the distance in miles to Las Vegas appeared on the highway. He was now 90 miles away from Las Vegas. He thought about stopping in Las Vegas and trying out his luck at gambling. The prospect of winning big money at the blackjack tables tantalized him. Acting on impulse, he exited into highway 93 and drove towards Las Vegas.

There were hardly any vehicles on the narrow, undivided highway. The few vehicles that passed him were mainly pickup trucks. The highway cut through miles of desolate land covered with desert plants. He saw neither cattle nor human beings in the arid landscape. After driving for about an hour, the road became steeper and cut through mountain ranges. Then the road sloped sharply down, forcing him to keep his foot on the brake to control his speed down the tortuous road. He could now catch a glimpse of the Hoover Dam. As he drove closer to the dam, he saw a number of cars parked alongside the road. Sightseers were walking up and down around the lookout platform. He stopped to join the sightseers. Keiji felt dizzy when he looked into the depth of the gorge and he hastily returned to his car. More cars arrived and a traffic jam built up around the cliff's edge and prevented him from pulling out. When the bottleneck finally cleared up, he resumed his journey to Las Vegas. The sonic booms of military airplanes flying over the Nevada desert broke the tranquility of the desert. Whenever he heard a sonic boom, he looked up and scanned the pale blue sky for the presence of a fighter plane. He could clearly see the contrails of an invisible jet fading away in the clear blue sky, but saw nary a fighter plane.

It was still bright and warm when he reached the outskirts of Las Vegas. A few hours ago he had to wear a sweater to keep warm. Now he suffocated in the Nevada desert heat. He left a barren countryside with hardly anything standing on it and drove onto a long, dry and dusty street bustling with automobiles and people. The sights depressed him and he suddenly felt lonely. He wanted to turn around and drive to San Diego instead. Distraught and unable to decide on whether to stay in Las Vegas or turn back, he stopped at a McDonald's restaurant. The sight of several churches along the road convinced him that even sinners and gamblers attend church services. The gamblers, drug pushers, pimps and prostitutes were children of God too. The gamblers revered God when they were not gambling away their food and rent money. The drug pushers adored God when they were not selling their poison to children. The pimps glorified God when they were not enslaving defenseless young women into prostitution. The whores worshipped God when they were not engaged in fornication. God must have appeared to these people as the Almighty Dollar.

The food servers in the restaurant served him promptly. He sat at a table and ate his meal with trepidation. He was fearful of himself and of the City of Sins. He observed that the people around him ate their meals quickly, and he wondered why everyone was in a hurry to eat. The food servers probably took the diners' money quickly before the diners gambled it away. The diners on the other hand devoured their foods rapidly so that they had more time to spend gambling. The lure of gambling must be so strong that people didn't have time to sit down and savor their meals. He conjectured that money must change hands very rapidly in Las Vegas. When he walked back to his car a prostitute standing against a wall shouted: "Hey, Dude. Do you want to go?" Surprised, Keiji turned to the woman and asked: "Go where?" The prostitute sighed and replied: "Don't play dumb with me, Cowboy. You know what I mean." Keiji shrugged his shoulders and shook his head apologetically. He got into his car and drove off. Confused and exhausted by the long hours of driving, he aimlessly cruised along the strip. He was still undecided about whether to continue his journey to San Diego or spend a few days in Las Vegas. Images of a sea of silver coins dropping at his feet danced in front of his eyes. The clinking and clunking of the slot machines buzzed in his ears. He finally gave in to temptation and drove into a casino parking lot.

Keiji walked into the casino feeling somewhat apprehensive. He did not have much money to gamble away and he was worried at losing what little money he had. Gamblers stood in front of slot machines and sat around poker tables. Men and women sat in a semi-circle at blackjack tables, smoking, drinking and peeping at their cards. Tourists invaded the Russian Roulette pits and crowded around the crap tables. The sound of coins falling into the receptacles underneath the slot machines mingled with the screams of the gamblers. A woman screeched when the light above her slot machine lit up. A man pumped up his fist when the dices showed up his winning numbers. Two women danced and hugged one another when one of them won the jackpot at a slot machine. The Casino's employees, loaded with tokens around the waist walked up and down the aisles. They took the gamblers' bills and gave them cups full of tokens. Visitors crowded the change windows to exchange their money for gaming chips. Keiji walked up to a change window quivering. His hands shook as he removed a hundred dollar bill from his billfold and exchanged it for gaming chips. Carrying the chips close to his heart, he ambled along the blackjack tables until he garnered enough courage to join the other gamblers.

Hostesses walked from table to table and served drinks to the gamblers. After serving the cocktails, the hostesses stood in front of the gamblers and waited for tips. A gambler remarked that the cocktails were free and the hostesses should not be tipped. Nonetheless a patron tossed a $5 chip in the hostess' tray. "That's more than the cost of the cocktail," a gambler remarked to the tipper. A young woman walked up to Keiji and smiled at him, but he ignored her and continued to gamble. The pile of chips in front of Keiji rose up, diminished, and climbed up again. When the chips stacked up high in front of him, he removed and pocketed some of the chips. When the stack of chips dropped down, he took the chips out of his pockets and put them back on the table. When he lost all his chips he rose up from the table and left the casino. He had lost one hundred dollars at this sitting, but he consoled himself that he played long and hard before losing his money. He was seated at the blackjack table for four hours. He was now tired and hungry.

He went outside and looked for an inexpensive hotel to spend the night. The sidewalks were bustling with people. A number of prostitutes stood at street corners and teased the men walking by them. They approached the cars at the traffic lights to proposition the drivers. A white woman approached Keiji.

"Are you looking for a girlfriend?" She boldly asked him.

"I am looking for a hotel," Keiji replied.

"It's not hard to find a place to stay on the strip," the prostitute remarked. "Do you need a ride?"

"No, thank you. My car is right around the corner." The prostitute followed him and wrapped her arms around his.

"Did you win big tonight?" she asked, smiling at him.

"No. I lost one hundred dollars."

"Maybe you will be luckier the next time," she predicted. "Do you want to go? I'll do anything you want me to do."

"I need to find a room for the night," Keiji repeated.

The prostitute held his arm tighter and pressed her breast against him. "There is an inexpensive hotel three blocks away. I can take you there. The restaurant in the lobby serves good foods. What's your name?"

He told her his name. She followed him to his car. Keiji opened the passenger door for her. She directed him to a hotel along the strip. When they reached the hotel, she followed him into the lobby and sat on a sofa while he checked into the hotel.

"Any luggage, Sir?" the bellboy asked.

"No," he replied.

Once they were inside his room, the prostitute dropped her handbag on the dresser and undressed. Keiji took off his clothes. The prostitute took his hand and led him to the bathroom. She turned him towards the bathroom light on the wall and closely inspected his penis, looking for signs of venereal infections. Keiji had never slept with a prostitute before. He felt awkward standing naked in the bathroom and being examined by a woman whom he had met in the street.

"Do you examine the genitals of every man that you pick up in the street?" he politely asked the prostitute.

"You'd better believe it," she answered without taking her eyes off his genitals. She pulled back the foreskin on his penis to examine it more closely. Keiji uttered a painful cry.

"You are hurting me," he complained. The prostitute let go of his penis and washed her hands. "You are clean," she said.

The next day Keiji called Atsuko to inform her that he would spend a few days in Las Vegas before coming home. He told her that he would arrive in San Diego on Friday night, five days later than he had originally planned. After calling his sister he showered and changed into clean clothes. He slipped into a pair of blue jean and put on his cowboy boots. Then he went out to look for a place to eat. He had not eaten anything since he stopped at McDonald's the previous day. After eating breakfast he went for a walk along the strip. He looked at a young woman sitting on a bench at the bus stop. He wondered if she was a prostitute waiting to be picked up by a customer.

During the day it was harder to tell the ordinary people apart from the hookers. A woman paced up and down at a street corner. She seemed to be going nowhere and appeared to be waiting to be picked up. He learned a new phrase last night when the prostitutes approached him. He walked up to the young woman pacing up and down on the sidewalk and said: "Do you want to go?" The woman looked at him very hard and muttered: "You must be a psychopath!" She left him looking dumbfounded in the middle of the sidewalk. A car pulled up alongside her. She got into the car and the car drove off. He thought that he must have been the first man ever to be turned down by a prostitute. Disappointed at being turned down by the whore, he walked into a casino and lingered around and watched the gamblers. Late in the afternoon he went to a circus show. When the last circus act ended, he returned to the gambling halls and hopped from blackjack tables to slot machines, trying his luck again. He was emboldened to win back the previous night's losses. The nervousness that he had felt the previous day had dissipated. For a while his gambling strategy paid off and he won two hundred dollars at the blackjack tables in less than one hour. Then he started to lose again and by the end of the day he had lost all his winnings. When his new losses amounted to one hundred dollars, he ceased to gamble and left the casino to eat dinner. Since leaving Texas, he had been eating nothing but fast foods. He now wished for a hearty home-cooked meal.

A cool, windy night had settled over the city. The hookers had multiplied on the strip. At night it was much easier to tell them apart from the tourists. He noticed that the tourists kept walking along the strip whereas the hookers stood at crossroads and lined up along the sidewalks. A black woman planted herself in Keiji's path. "Do you want a blow job?" She asked him. Her question surprised him. He thought that the black woman was peddling hair blowers or was doing advertising for a hair salon. He smiled at the black woman and answered: "No, thank you. I don't use a hair dryer." The black woman frowned and blocked his path. "I am good, man. I'll give you the best blow job in Vegas," she boasted. Keiji walked around the black woman and ran his hand over his head. "I just had a haircut and I don't need a blow job. Perhaps, another time," he told the woman. A police patrol car stopped by the curbside and two police officers came out. They told the prostitutes that they were blocking the sidewalks and ordered them to move away from the street corners. The prostitutes dispersed, but came back after the patrol car drove off. The hookers were mostly young teenage women. They shivered with cold and stayed close to high walls and buildings to escape the chilly wind. Keiji left the crowd of prostitutes and walked into a restaurant at a street corner. The restaurant was empty except for a young man and two women sitting at a table. He thought that most people were busy gambling and therefore did not spend a lot of time eating. Keiji sat down by the window and ordered dinner. The two women smoked while their male companion ate. Shortly afterwards the two women went outside and stood in front of the restaurant. He then realized that the women were prostitutes and the man sitting at the table with them was a pimp. The waitress finally brought his dinner but when he gazed at his plate, his heart sank. He paid a great deal of money for the meal and expected to be served with something delicious, but the food was greasy and unappetizing. A hamburger and fries would have been much more enjoyable than the food he was served. A car pulled up in front of the two prostitutes outside. The driver briefly chatted with the prostitutes. One of them walked over to the passenger side and opened the door. The driver drove off with her. Keiji ate his dinner and watched the other prostitute outside. He thought that she was about nineteen years old. She was slender and had beautiful blonde hair. He wondered why a young beautiful woman like her would be engaged in prostitution. A few minutes later she came back inside the restaurant to warm up. She lighted a cigarette and puffed on it, then ordered coffee. A few minutes later she put out the cigarette butt and went outside to wave at motorists. Keiji paid for his meal and left the restaurant. The young prostitute turned to him as he walked back to his car.

"Do you want to go?" she timidly asked him.

At first Keiji hesitated. Then he asked her how much money she wanted to have sex with him.

"A hundred dollars," she answered. She had her two hands in her Jacket to keep them warm.

"I don't have much money. I'll give you fifty." The young woman seemed vexed that he offered her $50. "That's the going price," she said firmly.

"Will you take $75?" he asked her.

The woman got upset. "We don't negotiate the price. It's $100. "

"Alright," Keiji replied. She got in his car and they drove to his hotel.

The woman demanded payment first once inside his hotel room. He obliged by pulling out two $50 bills from his wallet and handing them to her. The prostitute took the bills and put them in her purse.

"Some men won't pay up after they are done," she explained.

"I understand," Keiji said. He unbuttoned his shirt.

"Do you mind if I smoke?" she asked.

"No," he replied. He slid his pants off and sat next to the woman on the bed. The woman dimmed the light and lighted a cigarette. She brought it to her lips and inhaled deeply on the cigarette. She turned her head away from him and exhaled a puff of smoke into the air. Then she leaned back against the headboard and put down the cigarette in the ashtray under the lamp. She took her blouse off without taking her eyes off him.

"You look very nervous," Keiji remarked. "Is this your first time doing this?"

"No," she replied.

She started to smoke again. She drew in two puffs of smoke then blew the smoke to her side. Keiji noticed that her fingers were trembling. She put away the cigarette and removed her bra while she stared at him. A round piece of soft padding fell off from her left breast. She let her bra hanged down on her stomach.

"I hope that you don't mind," she said, feeling slightly embarrassed.

Keiji was startled to see her scared bosom. Her left breast was mutilated. He surmised that she had a mastectomy to stop a cancerous tumor from spreading to the other part of her body. He looked away from her mutilated breast. She slipped out of her underwear.

"I am tired," Keiji stammered. "I don't feel like making love."

"Does my breast bother you?" she asked him. She stared at him as if imploring him to forget about the missing breast.

"No," he answered. He put his pants back on. "I am really tired tonight. You may keep the money. I'll drive you back to the restaurant."

"You can still make love to me," she pleaded with him. She looked sullen and dejected.

Keiji buttoned up his shirt and put on his shoes. She remained in bed.

"Are you upset?" she said. "You don't have to pay me if you don't want to."

"That's all right," he replied. "Keep the money. You took the trouble to come to my hotel room."

She slowly slipped back into her bra and her blouse. "Where are you from?" she asked, feeling a little bit more at ease with him.

"I am currently staying in Arlington, Texas," he replied. "I am a student."

"My brother works for Dr. Pepper in Dallas," she said. "He told me that he likes it very there very much."

"Your brother may soon be working for another company."

"What do you mean?"

"Southwestern Bell is looking at buying the company. They are thinking about calling the new company Bell Pepper."

"Are you serious?" she said, laughing.

"Southwestern Bell is not be the only company interested in purchasing Dr. Pepper. Pizza Hut is interested too. If the deal goes thru, they'll rename the new company Pepperoni."

"No. I don't believe it."

"Well, the Securities and Exchange Corporation will have to approve the merger. I heard that the U.S Treasury may also be interested. They'll love to call the new company Peppermint."

"You are pulling my legs," she pinched him on the arm and tried to snuggle close to him. "I thought about moving to Dallas too," she said.

"Why don't you?"

"I don't know. Dallas is a big city. Fear of the unknown, I suppose."

"Your brother lives there already. You won't be alone."

"My brother and I don't get along at all."

"That will be problem."

When he returned to his hotel room after dropping the prostitute back at the restaurant, Keiji pulled out the picture of Cheiko from his wallet. He sat on the bed and leaned against the headboard. He looked at the picture of Cheiko with sadness in his eyes. He reckoned that her niece was now two and a half years old. He reflected upon her mother's whereabouts.

"Kiss her goodbye for me," he muttered. He kissed the photograph and put it down on the nightstand. He got up and went into the shower room.

Keiji saw very few hookers walking the streets on the next day. "They must all be sleeping now," he mused. Once in a while he saw a lone hooker standing on the sidewalk and waving at the motorists. The tourists must be sleeping too as he saw few of them along the strips and inside the casinos. The pace in the streets was slow. It was as if the activities that the people engaged in on weekends had drained the energy out of them. It was also hotter during the day, especially during the afternoon. The casinos were the perfect place to cool down when he was not sightseeing or walking around the town. He visited the surrounding towns and parks and drove back to take a closer look at the Hoover Dam. On the way back he stopped at Boulder city to shop for presents for Atsuko's children. After shopping, he went to Caesar's Palace and ate a sumptuous dinner. He had no regret paying $32.00 for his dinner. It was the first decent meal he ate since leaving Arlington four days ago. Being a full-time student living on a limited budget, it was an extravagance that he did not engage in everyday.

At nightfall Keiji returned to the casinos to try to win back the money he had lost during the previous nights. When he suffered more losses at the blackjack tables, he switched to the slot machines. The machines gobbled down his coins faster than he could count them. After losing two rolls of tokens, he switched from playing the slot machines to playing the poker machines. He had no luck playing the poker machines either, but he had fun attempting to outsmart the machine. A Money Changer strolled by him with a token coin dispenser strapped around her waist. Keiji exchanged another $20 bill for the token coins.

"Having any luck?" the dark-skinned and dark-haired woman asked him.

"No," he replied, "but I am having fun." The woman pulled a business card out of her pocket and handed it to him.

"If you need companionship while in Vegas, please give me a call." Surprised, Keiji looked at the woman while she slipped the business card into his hand. The woman nonchalantly walked on and approached another group of gamblers. "Anybody needs change?"

The Money Changer disappeared amidst the crowd. Keiji resumed playing the poker machines, but soon moved back to the slot machines when his losses began to mount again. After playing the slot machines for an hour, he switched to playing blackjack again. His strategy was to win big at the blackjack tables, then retire for the night. The strategy, however, did not work. It was his third night on the strip and he was down by another hundred dollars. It was almost dark when he left the casino. The dark skin woman stood by the door and taunted men walking in and out of the casino. The woman recognized him and smiled.

"Did you have any luck tonight?" she said, handing him her business card again.

"No. I am a born loser," Keiji replied. "Would you like to go for a walk?"

They walked along the boulevard past the Stardust, the Silver Slipper, the Sands and the Flamingo Hilton. Young women lined the sidewalks and taunted the male passersby. The police officers stopped their patrol cars and rushed out to chase away the prostitutes who stood in front of automobiles at road intersections. Keiji passed a couple of tourists in front of them. The woman shook her head at the harlots and said to her companion: "This is really incredible. It's getting out of hand." A prostitute argued with a policeman on the other side of the boulevard. A few moments later the policeman led her into a police vehicle.

"Do you live in Vegas?" Keiji asked her companion.

"I work in Las Vegas four days a week," she replied. "The rest of the time I live in Lukachikai in Northeast Arizona."

"Northeast Arizona? You are a long way from home."

"It's about 380 miles away."

"Why come so far away just to work?" he asked.

"Jobs are very easy to find in Vegas. Besides, I can choose my own work schedule. I only work from Friday to Monday."

"What do you do during the rest of the week?"

"I take care of my children and my parents," she replied. "I also look after the family's business. We make rugs, blankets, quilts and jewelries on the reservation and sell them to tourists. The money we earn is not enough. I don't really have a lot of free time since the drive to Vegas takes me almost a full day. Sometimes I drive during the night."

They went to his hotel room. The Navajo woman spotted the photograph of Cheiko and picked it up.

"Is she your daughter?" she asked him.

"She is my niece."

"She is beautiful," she said.

She put the photograph back on the bedside table and disrobed.

"Do you have any children?" Keiji asked.

"I have two kids. My 10yr old son wants a video game set for Christmas. I can't afford to buy it for him on my meager salary. My 7yr old girl wants two Barbie dolls, new clothes and shoes.

"About the business card," Keiji started to say.

"Yes," she softly replied. She climbed on the bed and crouched down on her heels and waited for him to remove his clothes and join her.

"Your husband doesn't mind that you are engaging in this line of work?"

She laid down on her back when he climbed on the bed. "My husband doesn't know that I do this in my spare time," she replied. "Of course, I am doing this to supplement my earning. They don't pay me enough at the casino."

After they made love, the Navajo woman asked him if she could keep his underwear. "Why do you want to keep my underwear?" Keiji asked, puzzled at the unusual request.

"It's pretty and sexy," she replied, holding the red underwear at the top of her naked legs and admiring it. The Navajo woman eyed his suitcase. "Do you have a blue pair that I can have?"

"I do, but you can't have it. You don't expect me to walk around Vegas without wearing any underwear, do you?"

"Some men do. Why wear underwear if you have to take them off an hour later?"

"If you take all their underwear after making love with them, of course they won't have any left to wear."

The Navajo woman was vexed at his remark. "I did not steal anybody's underwear," she protested. "I asked my clients if I could have them and they gave them to me."

"I am sorry. I did not mean to say that you are a thief. What do you do with them?"

She shrugged her shoulders. "I keep them as souvenirs."

Keiji opened his suitcase. He retrieved a blue pair of underwear and threw it at her. "How long will you be in Vegas?" she asked him.

"I am leaving on Thursday," he replied. "I presume that you are going home tomorrow, is that right?"

"Actually I am going home tonight. I won't have to work again until Friday."

"Oh, that's right. You told me that." Keiji went to the bathroom to dispose of the condom and clean up. The Navajo woman followed him into the bathroom and watched him intently as he cleaned himself with a Betadine solution.

"What are you doing?" the Navajo woman asked, perplexed.

"It's just a health safety precaution," he explained. The Navajo woman picked the bottle of the antiseptic and said: "Can I have it?"

Keiji rinsed his genitals and washed his hands. "You should really carry your own, but I don't mind. You can keep the bottle if it is of any use to you." The Navajo woman spotted a bottle of cologne and a can of aftershave cream next to the sink. He took them too. As the woman walked out of his hotel room, she picked up a box of condoms lying on the dresser and dropped it in her handbag.

"Thank you for the bottle of antiseptic," she said. "You may have just saved my life."

When the Navajo woman left, Keiji picked up the photograph of Cheiko and put it back in his wallet. He took a hot bath and then settled down on the armchair to catch up on his reading. After reading for an hour, he put out the light and went to sleep.

The next day he slouched in bed until mid morning, sometimes reading, sometimes just listening to the radio. He had seen and experienced all the things that were to be seen or experienced in Las Vegas. He had now abandoned his dreams of winning large amounts of money at the blackjack tables. When the hotel cleaning lady knocked on his door, he ignored the knocks and went to shower. It was too late to eat breakfast, so he went out to eat lunch instead. After lunch he drove to the bank and obtained a cash advance of $500 against his American Express card. He had squandered all of next semester's tuition money on gambling and prostitutes. He figured that he would have to do some explaining to Atsuko later as most of the money for college tuition came from her. He dropped his dirty laundry at a dry cleaning store and asked the woman behind the counter if he could have them back the following day. The woman noted his request down on the service slip and handed him a receipt. He then drove south on Interstate 15 to the Mountain Springs summit to hike and sightsee.

At sundown he picked up a pizza and a six-pack of beer and returned to his hotel. He quickly showered and changed into a clean pair of jeans and slipped into a warm fleece sweatshirt. He turned on the TV and sat down to eat the pizza and drink beer. The program he watched was unexciting. He clicked on the remote and scanned the TV channels to find a more interesting program to watch. When he did not find any channel worth watching, he clicked the TV set off. He reflected that the TV programs were intentionally boring so as to force the hotel guests to leave their rooms and gamble. He opened his book and began reading where he left off the previous night. At around nine o'clock, he became tired of reading and left his room to go to the casino halls.

He parked his car near the Flamingo and walked to the hotel. He came across a large group of prostitutes standing at the corner of Flamingo road and Las Vegas Boulevard. The prostitutes laughed and joked among themselves while waiting for men to pick them up. They teased, chased and grabbed each other like children playing in a playground. The group of streetwalkers created quite a stir among the crowd of tourists. The crowd stopped to ogle at the young women. Keiji spotted a young prostitute dressed in a low skirt among the crowd of harlots. She wore a pair of red cowboy boots and her head was covered with an oversize Stetson hat. For a short moment the young woman in the cowboy hat and boots mesmerized him. He imagined her on his bed wearing only the red boots and fancied making love to her. As he crossed the street to pick up the young streetwalker, a gust of wind blew away her Stetson. She ran to the curbside to pick up her hat. Before he could reach her on the other side of the street, a motorist stopped and picked her up. Displeased at the motorist for carrying off the woman and interrupting his flight of fancy, Keiji walked into a casino to gamble the evening away. The Flamingo Hotel was not as crowded as the previous nights. Perhaps it was because it was the middle of the week or because the tourists had left town. He turned around and went to check out the other casinos, hoping to find one where he would have some luck. He finally settled in a less-crowded casino at the farther end of the strip. There were no prostitutes around to distract him. He spent two hours at the slot machines and then played blackjack for an hour. At first he lost ninety dollars, but later in the evening his luck turned around. When he tallied the chips, he was three hundred and twenty dollars ahead. He had recovered the losses of the three previous nights. Satisfied at his winnings, he left the casino and walked back to the Flamingo Hotel. Then he drove back to his hotel. On the way to the hotel, a group of four prostitutes waved him down. As soon as he pulled up alongside them, they all rush to him at once. He beckoned one of them into his car and drove off. Disappointed at not being picked up, the other three prostitutes went back to take their positions along the curb.

Once in his hotel room, he found himself face to face with a tall blonde woman with broad shoulders, large arms and muscular legs. The woman reminded him of a Russian spy in a James Bond movie. She quietly removed her clothes and dropped them on a chair. Keiji would have preferred a shorter woman, but she was the first one to rush to his car. He unclothed without saying a word. Then the prostitute pushed him down on the bed and aggressively performed oral sex on him. He was taken aback by her sudden move. In her haste to get it done quickly, she accidently bit him. Keiji uttered a painful cry and jumped out of bed.

"What's wrong with you?" he angrily shouted at her. It hurts!"

"I'll try to be more careful," the whore said apologetically. Keiji had lost interest in having sexual intercourse with her. He ordered her out of his room, but to his surprise the prostitute slumped on the armchair and sobbed.

"I am sorry," Keiji said. "Would you like me to drive you back to your hotel?"

"No," she said. "I can walk."

"Here's your money," he said. "You can leave my room now." He gave her a $100 bill. She snatched the bill and threw it on the carpet.

"I don't want to be paid," she blurted out.

Flabbergasted at the prostitute's behavior, he stared at her for some time. He felt sorry that he had flustered her and apologized to her again. He picked up the money and handed it to her. She dried her eyes and stared blankly at the wall in front of her. "I am a lousy whore," she said.

"I did not say that you are a lousy whore," Keiji protested. "I said that you were hurting me. You could have been gentler."

"If you want gentle sex, you should get it from your wife or girlfriend," she snapped.

"Well, I wasn't looking for violent sex when I picked you up. I am awfully sorry if I had misled you." Keiji slipped the bill into her fingers. He became impatient with her. "You've got your money, baby. What else do you want?"

"I am a lousy whore," she repeated. Her fingers slowly closed on the new bill. Keiji sat on the bed and waited for her to put her clothes back on. After getting into her clothes, she dropped the $100 bill into her purse and slowly walked to the door with her head down. At the door she turned around and said: "Have you been naughty?"

"Excuse me?"

The prostitute removed a knotted whip from her handbag and unfurled it. "Would you like me to flog your bare buttocks?"

"Hell, no," Keiji squealed, springing up on his feet. "You have caused me enough pain already. Good night." After the prostitute left, he bolted the door shut and went to the bathroom to examine his penis.

The next day Keiji went to a doctor to have his organ examined. The doctor prescribed him some ointment to prevent any infection around the teeth marks. After the visit to the doctor's office, he went to pick up his laundry. He took his car to the AAA car repair shop to have it serviced and checked up before he resumed his journey to San Diego. After eating lunch he spent the rest of the day driving around the small towns along Interstate 15 south of Las Vegas. When he returned from his exploration, Keiji went to the Flamingo Hotel to spend his last evening in Las Vegas.

The casino was crowded with Real Estate agents attending a convention. He sat at a blackjack table with three female conventioneers from Houston and two other male gamblers. The conventioneers talked, laughed and exchanged travelers' accounts with each other. They talked about the customs of the countries that they had traveled to. Keiji had lost all the $320 he had won the previous night. He was amused by the Realtors' travel accounts. When the card dealer flipped his cards over and revealed an Ace and a King, one of the conventioneers uttered the word 'caca!'

"Caca?" a gambler seated next to her repeated. "What does that mean?"

"It's Hawaiian for 'poo poo.'" the Realtor explained, laughing.

"Poo poo?" another gambler repeated. "Is that Hawaiian too?" That set off a roar of laughter among the three Realtors.

"It simply means that the lady is upset that the house had won this hand," another gambler explained. The remark set off another roar of laughter. Everyone except the blackjack dealer laughed. The blackjack dealer had his mind on the stack of cards and his eyes on the piles of chips in front of the gamblers. His shirt pocket was bursting with chips.

Keiji's aggressive play cost him another two hundred dollars. He lost his interest in the card game and looked around him for prostitutes. A lone woman sitting at the bar caught his attention. He watched her for a few minutes before finally getting up and walking to the bar. He sat three seats away from her and ordered a drink. He had learned since he arrived in Las Vegas that the bartender frequently introduced a client to a prostitute sitting at the bar. Sure enough, after a few minutes, the bartender introduced him to her. Keiji moved to the bar stool next to her and offered to buy her a drink. She ordered a glass of Perrier water.

"Where are you from?" Keiji asked the young woman.

"I am originally from Los Angeles," she replied.

"Oh!" he muttered.

"You've been to LA before?" she asked him.

"I grew up in LA," he replied, "but my parents moved to San Diego not too long ago." The woman was small in stature, had a baby face and spoke with a childish, melancholy voice. Her face was blanched white and her hair was raven-hued black. She wore little or no makeup.

"Is this your first time in Vegas?" she asked him.

"Yes," Keiji replied. He took a drink from his glass. "What line of work are you in?" he asked, without looking at her.

"I am in the business of entertaining gentlemen," she replied. Keiji turned to look at her. She smiled. "Would you like to be entertained tonight?" she asked.

"Sure." he murmured.

She left a handsome tip to the bartender and thanked him for connecting them. They left the casino and went to Keiji's hotel room. Keiji watched her as she unclothed and climbed on the bed. "Come lie down," she beckoned him.

"I don't feel like making love," he said to her. He took his shoes off and sat on the bed next to her.

"Let me take your shirt off," she said, moving closer to him and unbuttoning his shirt.

"Honestly," he said, stopping her from undressing him. "I am tired and I don't feel like making love. Can we just talk?"

"Lie down and I'll massage your body."

He turned his back at her. She stroked and teased him. "When did you arrive in Las Vegas?"

"On Saturday," he replied.

"So you have been screwing since then. No wonder you are so tired. I have just the right thing for you."

"What is it?" he said, turning to look at her face.

She leaned over him to reach for her handbag. He shuddered as she wriggled her naked body across him to reach for her handbag. She opened a small plastic pouch and pinched out a small amount of white powder. "What is it?" he asked her again, fearing that the white powder might be drug.

"Coke," she replied, smiling. She snuffed on the white powder and inhaled deeply. Then she moved the powder under his nose. "The finest that money can buy."

"No, thank you," he said, pushing her hand away from his nostrils. "I don't take this stuff."

"Try it," she insisted. "It will keep you alert and awake all night."

Keiji was frightened. He imagined narcotic agents bursting into his room and arresting them. He went to check that the door was bolted and locked. The woman mocked him for being so afraid of sniffing coke. "You have never smoked pot in your life?" she asked him.

"Never," he replied.

She climbed out of the bed and knelt down by the dresser. She spread a sheet of paper on the dresser and emptied the bag of cocaine on it. Then she pressed one nostril shut and pushed a small amount of the white powder into the other. She did this several times. Afterwards she showed Keiji how to do it. With fingers trembling, Keiji pinched a small amount of cocaine and stuffed it into his nostril. Seconds later he sneezed out the cocaine and shook the cocaine off his fingers. His nose was on fire and his eyes started to water.

"Don't waste it," she scolded him. "This stuff is expensive."

"How much does this tiny amount cost?" he asked, wiping his nose.

"I paid three hundred dollars for it." She climbed back on the bed. "Come lie down with me," she said. Keiji removed his shirt and he laid down next to her. She closed her eyes and cuddled against him.

"What's your name?" Keiji asked.

"Nicole," she replied.

"How did you get into this business?"

"When I was in high school, my hairdresser offered me $10 to have sex with him," she answered without opening her eyes.

"Did you?"

"I sure did. He gave me $10 for making love to me and I was thrilled." She sighed and moved her body closer to him. "He bragged to his friends about it. Thereafter all his friends were interested to meet me. Eventually I established a regular customer base and I started asking for more money."

"What is your name again?

"Nicole."

"Nicole? Is that your real name?"

"Yes. Some women like to use secret names to keep their identities secret. Nicole is my real name."

"That's a French name," he remarked.

"My mother is French and my father is Greek. I have a beautiful daughter that lives with me in Las Vegas." She opened her eyes and looked at him. "Would you like to see a picture of my daughter?" Keiji nodded at her. She crawled to the edge of the bed to retrieve her handbag again. She took a picture out of her purse and showed it to him. Keiji gazed at the Eurasian child in the picture.

"Isn't she beautiful? Her father is Japanese," she said. "I met him in Los Angeles. I was depressed and I had no friends. He gave me money and moral support. He took me to visit his mother even though I told him I was a whore. He wanted to marry me after the baby was born, but I told him that I did not want to get married. I took the baby and left him."

"What happened to him after you left him?"

She shrugged her shoulders. "I don't know and I don't care." She put the picture back in her purse and took out another picture. "That's my car."

"What kind of car is that?" Keiji asked, glancing at the strange-looking automobile. She laughed at the perplexed look on his face.

"It's a Cadillac with a Rolls Royce radiator grill and hood. I paid $10,000 to have this conversion done."

"For that price you could have bought a new car."

"It's not the same. Have you ever seen a Cadillac with a Rolls Royce radiator grill and hood?"

"No."

She glanced at his watch and exclaimed. "One thirty already? Oh, I have to go. My babysitter will be mad at me. She leaned over and kissed him. "Come with me to my apartment."

"Do you trust me?"

"I would not have asked you if I did not trust you," she replied, putting her arms around him. "I usually keep all my business meetings outside of my apartment. I am making an exception for you."

"Why?"

"I don't know. May be it is because you remind me of someone I used to know."

"Who was he?"

The question irked Nicole and she sat up on the bed. "You ask too many questions. Get dressed and let's go."

They left his hotel room and got into his car. Nicole directed him to the town of Winchester. Shortly afterwards she led him into a dark street and directed him to an apartment building. She hurried out of the car and ran to her apartment. A dark-skinned woman met them at the door. Nicole mumbled some apologies to the babysitter.

Keiji followed her into the apartment. She pointed him to the sofa. The babysitter gathered a bag, said goodnight to Nicole and left the apartment.

"Take a seat. I'll go check on her."

She went into her child's bedroom. A short moment later she returned and uttered a sigh of relief.

"I really should not leave her alone like this every night," she said. "Would you like a drink?"

He declined. She removed a metal box from under the sofa and put her money in it. Keiji stared at the box. He estimated that the box contained several thousand dollars. She closed the box and put it back under the sofa. Then she sat down next to him and removed the cocaine from her handbag. He watched her as she spread the cocaine on the coffee table and started to snuff the white powder. A few minutes later she led him into her bedroom. "Lie down and relax," she said to him. She unbuttoned his shirt and his trousers. Keiji turned over and she stroked his back. "Do you feel better now?" she asked. He turned over and she sat astride on him and made love to him. At that moment a child walked sleepily into the bedroom trailing a blanket behind her and rubbing her eyes.

"Mommy," she cried. She opened up her arms and paced up to her mother.

Nicole stopped making love and looked back at her daughter.

"Cheiko," she whispered, "You are awake!"

Nicole lifted her child on the bed. She clutched her against her bosom and rocked her back to sleep. She coddled her child's hair and looked at her with loving eyes. When her child felt asleep in her arms, she carried her back to her bed. Keiji followed her to the child's bedroom. The wall above the child's bed was covered with crafts and artworks. Keiji saw several photographs of the child on the adjacent wall. He stood dumbfounded in front of a framed photograph of a small child perched on a saddle. Her tiny hands hanged on to the mane of a horse. Her head was covered with a large white Stetson hat, and her black hair covered part of her forehead. She wore a sheepskin vest and a flowery red scarf around her neck. Her round face had the fierce look of a samurai warrior.

"She likes to paint," Nicole whispered, pointing at the paintings on the wall. "Just like her father." She put out the light in Cheiko's bedroom and returned to her bedroom.

"Do you mind if I take a shower?" Keiji asked.

"Sure," she said.

When he stepped out of the shower room, Keiji found Nicole sound asleep on her bed. The coke that she sniffed earlier did not help her stay awake. Exhaustion had finally taken hold of her. Keiji pulled a blanket over her naked body, put his shoes on and grabbed his jacket. He tiptoed his way into Cheiko's bedroom. In the darkness he leaned over her and kissed her on her cheek.

"I am taking you home," he whispered. "Your daddy loves you very much. He watches over you from Heaven and prays that no harm will come to you."

Keiji slowly caressed the girl's puffy cheeks with his finger. He gently lifted her into his arms and wrapped her in a blanket. The cocaine powder was still spread out on the coffee table. He glanced at Nicole who was still asleep on her bed. He clutched Cheiko tightly against him and opened the apartment door. Cheiko stirred in his arms. He closed his arms around her and bent his head over her to shield her from the cool breeze and hurried back to his car.

13 ANGUISH

"My hands shake whenever I slide open the patio door. My body trembles with fright at the thought that I will see your shadow lurking behind the glass. I took every precaution imaginable to keep you from entering my bedroom again. No, I have not forgotten the night when you came into my bedroom uninvited. I was too frightened to ask you to leave, too terrified to cry for help. Even if I had asked you to leave, I doubt whether you would have left. You knew what you wanted. I knew what you came for. What I did not know was that you were going to kill me after you raped me. You raped me. After you raped me, you raped me again. I did not have the strength to fight off your beastly behavior. You were a rapist with an instinct to kill. Your eyes glowed with the flames of destruction after you raped me. You had the strength of a beast. I was fragile like the petals of a rose. I still remember the knife. The blade was as wide as the palm of my hand and as long as my arm. I will never forget your intrusion into my life. I cannot forget those terrifying hours, the days of agony, and the nights of anguish. You stabbed me after you had satisfied your hunger for sex. Why did you have to stab me? Did I not let you have what you came for? Not once, but several times, you forced me to have sexual intercourse with you. I was too weak to resist and I could not have done anything to you for taking away my virginity. I would have forgotten your face if you did not try to kill me. Instead of going away after you had violated me, you proceeded to kill me. What devilish force put that knife into your hand and made you plunge it into my frail body? Were you afraid that I would tell someone after you left my apartment? Was it the reason why you decided to kill me? You left me lying in my bed, naked and bleeding to death. The nurse at the hospital told me that there were 12 stab wounds on my body. You left my apartment thinking that I was dead. No, I did not die. I almost came out of the hospital in a coffin instead of a

326

wheelchair. My mother sat by my bedside day and night to watch over me and pray for me. I still carry the scars of the stabbings on my body. I shudder when I think of those terrifying moments with you. Your shadow haunts me everywhere I go. I left college and went back to live with my parents and my little sister. My sister is only seven years old. She does not understand why there are evil men who prey on weak women. It is very hard for me to explain to her what happened to me. I am glad to be home and to be with my little sister. I missed her a lot when I was attending college. My father vowed to pump twelve bullets into your body, one for each of the stab wounds you had inflicted on me. He was angry when he said that, but I don't think he meant to do any harm to you. He is a very law-abiding citizen and he does not even own a gun. I love my father and I am more concerned about his well being than your crime and your punishment. I have become very cautious since you broke into my apartment and violated me. Every night, before I go to bed, I check all the doors and windows to make sure that they are secured. My little sister laughs at me whenever I bolt the doors and windows shut. I tell her that I don't wish for her to go through what I have gone through in your blood-soiled hands. She is too young to understand what a psychopath is. My mother understands my state of mind when I stay in my room for long periods of time. I dare not step outside for fear of meeting another person like you. I am leery of people walking around me in the streets or in the parking lots. I see your face in their faces. I see a knife in their hands. I see an evil mind in everyone that I pass by. I know that it's wrong for me to think that everybody is evil, mean and wicked like you, but your intrusion into my life is still in my mind. I am afraid to talk to or date another man. I am afraid to be stared at and be desired. Why did you have to stab me? I have never hurt you or cause any harm to your family. My country has been kind to you. The Apartment Management has been nice to you. They gave you a job, whether you had a green card or not. You have the means to buy all the things that you could only dream about in your home country. If you had asked for my help, I would have given it to you, even though I was only a student at the time. If you had asked my father for foods, he would have been delighted to provide you with a few bags of groceries. My mother would never refuse to help someone in need. She cares for the comfort and health of every human being, no matter where they come from or what their skin color is. She believes in helping people like you. My little sister is the most delightful child a person can have as a sister. Had you come forward and tell her that you were lonely, she would have been thrilled to keep you company and tell you a few fairy tales. If you had asked her, she would have taught you how to read and write English. She would even share her toys and foods with you. I know that I cannot live with the past all the time. I am only nineteen years old and I must forget that you raped and stabbed me. Dad told me that it would be easier for me to forget the incident if I have something to occupy my mind. Mom encouraged me to go out and get a job. I could not go back to school again and walk by the apartment in which I almost died. You would not have succeeded in entering my apartment if the Apartment Manager had acted upon my complaints. I reported to the Apartment Manager several times that the patio door lock needed to be repaired, but my complaints fell on deaf ears. Then you struck terror in me. Had the Apartment Manager followed up on my complaints, I would not have to go through this mental anguish every night. I was sad that it happened to me. I thought that I could never be a happy woman again. I felt nothing but bitterness and anger for the people who managed the apartment complex. They failed to provide for my safety while I was a tenant. It is sardonic that someone from another country would attempt to kill me. It never occurred to me that I would become another crime statistics. Why do we have people like you living among us? Why were you allowed to come to America and terrorize women? Our lives crossed in the apartment complex where I lived and where you worked. You must have known that the patio door latch was faulty. You intentionally did not repair the latch so that you can easily enter my bedroom while I was asleep. You had everything worked out and you just waited for me to move in. Why did you pick me for your crime? Why me, and why not someone else? There are hundreds of other women who lived in that apartment complex. You must have seen them walking back and forth on the campus every day. You picked me out instead. Why? Was it because I was a small, defenseless woman? Was it because you found me more attractive than the other women on the campus? Was it because I lived alone in my apartment? Was it because I had blue eyes and blonde hair? There were other women on the campus who had blue eyes and blonde hair and who were more attractive than me. I was wrong to think that the world I lived in was safe. I was too trusty of the people around me. I made the mistake of going to bed knowing that the latch was broken. I should have raised hell at the Apartment Manager's office to get them to fix the latch. I should have called all my friends and asked them to spend the night with me at my apartment. I should have gone back to my mother's house to spend the night there. It is too late now for me to think over what I should or shouldn't have done. I hope someone will learn from my mistakes. What matters to me now is that I am still alive. I thank God for allowing me to live, but sometimes I wonder if it would have been better if I had died. I spent long days and nights lying in pain in a hospital bed while you were comfortably lying on a mattress in a cell. While I agonized in a hospital bed, you were allowed to leave the jail to wait out your trial date. I had to relive the whole episode for justice's sake after I recuperated. When I testified against you in the courtroom, the defense lawyer made me recount those anxious and fearful moments with you. I was not afraid to tell him the truth. I was not afraid to recount to the jury and to the lawyers what you did to me because I did not want you to go free and rejoice in what you did. I wanted you to be punished for all the physical pain and mental anguish that you had inflicted me. I cried with joy when the jury found you guilty and the judge sentenced you to fifteen years in jail. I wish that the judge had sentenced you to life in prison. I feel better now knowing that you are kept behind bars and guarded day and night. I pray that the judge will not reduce your sentence to five years. You must not be allowed to roam our streets again so soon because you are a dangerous man. Our streets will be safe from you for some time. In about ten years my little sister will be of college age. It makes me feel good that you won't be around to hurt her or someone else. I am relieved that my college-bound friends can live in that apartment complex without fear. I will feel better too when I return to college to resume my studies which you so violently disrupted. I hoped all along that when they locked you away, you will disappear out of my life, but I keep seeing your face. Your shadow follows me everywhere. I see your hand brandishing a knife stained with my blood whenever I walk around a street corner. Sometimes I wake up in the middle of the night and see you in my bed. I always fear that one day you will escape from jail and take revenge on me for your sentence. The smallest noise around the house frightens me. When the wind blows and rattles the windows, I sense that you are trying to break into my room again. I jerk up when the cat meows or the dog barks. I am startled when the refrigerator motor starts up or the heat pump comes on. I think that I am going insane thinking about you all the time. I used to enjoy reading. Before you attacked me, I would come back to my apartment in the evenings and sit down by the window to read. I have not read a book since you struck terror in my life. Instead of reading, I stare at the blank walls and ceiling. Do you care what I am doing now? Do you care whether I will be able to live a normal life again? Do you care if I end up in a mental institution? I don't think that you care about whether I am alive or dead, or if I am in good health or sick. I don't think that you care about what I can or cannot eat. Since that horrible night, I have not been able to sleep peacefully. I sleep with the light on because I am afraid of being in the darkness alone. I sleep with my eyes open because I am afraid that when I close my eyes, I will see you when I wake up. I leave the bathroom door ajar when I shower so that I can keep my eyes on the doorway. I don't sit with my back against the door because I am fearful that you will lurk behind me. I have turned my mother's house into a fortress. My bedroom is a fortress within a fortress. I hid in it day and night, leaving my room only if I have to. There are four bolts on my bedroom door to keep you out. I never go anywhere alone anymore. My dad accompanies me whenever I go to the hospital for physical therapy. My boyfriend left me because of what you have done to me. My mother says that he was not true to his love, but I cannot blame him for not loving me anymore. I had 139 stitches to repair the damage that you did to my frail body. Yes, that's how bad it was! I am still in pain, emotionally if not physically. You were brutal, merciless and cold-blooded. I wept so much that tears no longer flow out of my eyes. Every day I ask myself: "What have I done to deserve all this?" I never receive an answer to my question. Maybe you know the answer. Tell me why was I subjected to all this pain and suffering? Why did you single me out? Have I wronged you? Have I interfered with your wretched life in any way? Have I stolen your bread or your beer money? Have I ever hurt your children or your wife? Have I ever stopped the flow of cocaine and marijuana from your country to my country? Have I told your government that I do not approve of the use of violence against your people? Did I ever get in your way? Mock at you? Spit at you? Push you around? Did I ever complain about the way you live? Have I spoken against your religious beliefs? Have I passed judgment against your people or criticize your government for the way it treats the poor peasants? Have I raised criticism of any kind against your country? Done or said anything that might have upset you? Do you know yourself why you stabbed me? Was there any need for you to stab me after you raped me? I suppose that knowing the answers to my questions will not change anything because what you did cannot be undone. In fifteen years or less, you will be a free man again, but I will remain captive to the painful memories of that horrifying night for the rest of my life. I don't care who your jailer is. I don't care whether your jailer is kind or cruel, cold-blooded or compassionate. I don't care whether you are getting enough to eat every day. I don't care whether you like being in jail. I don't care whether the prison guards beat you. All I care about is that the college campus is now safer without you. Now that you are behind bars, I want to return to college to complete my education. My mother would prefer that I wait a few more months, but I could not stay home every day and be a burden to my parents. I finally garnered enough courage to go out and find a job. I am glad I did for I met and fell in love with a man. He brought peace into my heart. I thought that I could never love again. I thought that a man could never love me and look at my scarred body. Our eyes met on the first day I went to work and we smiled at each other. He was the first man who had set eyes on me since my ordeal. I quiver whenever he talks to me or calls my name. I almost fainted when he asked me out for lunch. I swooped on him, but he caught me and prevented me from falling. It's wonderful to be in love again and to be desired by a man. Love had finally chased away my fear, my bitterness and my anger. It had meted out the revulsion that I had harbored in my heart for you for so long. It had freed me of the past and propelled me to the future. I now look forward to a new life without you in my shadow."

THE WE PEOPLE'S CHARTER

Preamble

We the People of the United States, in order to build a Better Nation, insure Peace among ourselves, eliminate Social Injustice, break down Racial Barriers, cultivate Love and Friendship, promote Fairness in Employment, and preserve our Environment, do ordain and establish this Charter for the all people of the United States of America.

Article 1

Section 1: We resolve to maintain a good health, both in spirit and body, so that we do not hurt our work productivity or ourselves. We recognize that inadequate sleep is a biological impairment that can affect our health and safety as well as the safety of others. We concede that drowsiness behind the wheel can be as dangerous as drunkenness. We will observe good sleep hygiene so that we do not fall prey to narcolepsy and create sleep-related accidents. Only by following good sleep hygiene can we hope to reduce the number of sleep-related driving accidents that occur on American roads each year.

Section 2: We promise to dispose of household waste in a more responsible manner and to reuse what are reusable, and we make a moral commitment to preserve the natural world. We realize that our valuable land

331

resources are being depleted, and we must strive to protect and save them for future generations of Americans. We will reduce our garbage to minimize ground water contamination. We vouch to sort our trash into recyclables, compostable and disposables in order to reduce by half the amount of garbage that we deposit in our landfills each year. We will avert air and water pollution. We will protect our forests. We will promote a healthy environment, espouse environmental friendliness, and achieve prosperity without pollution.

Section 3: We decry the invasion of our land by cheap products manufactured in foreign countries. We denounce the closing down of our factories and the loss of American jobs. We particularly feel a great loss in the disappearance of the tradesmen, among them the cobbler and the tailor.

Section 4: We demur the tainting of our soil, rivers and air with pesticides, insecticides and other chemical wastes. We object to the government dumping radioactive wastes on our land. We demand chemical-free water for drinking, ozone-free air for breathing, mercury-free lakes for fishing, contaminant-free foods, and oil-free beaches for our enjoyment. We pledge to keep our environment safe and clean for future generations of Americans. We resolve to set land aside to be used as parks, protect wildlife, and restore coastal areas. We fathom that lead is the most critical environmental health problem that faces our children today, and we vouch to shield our children from the hazard of breathing or eating Lead. We vow to educate families on the danger of lead paint, and we call for higher lead abatement funds for lead containment and removal programs.

Section 5: We frown on companies who screen out job applicants by the use of the applicant's family name. We are opposed to any form of discrimination in the work place. We will not judge each other on the basis of our skin color. We vehemently condemn racism in America. We must strive to coexist peacefully with one another without regard to our race, our country of origin, and our religious belief. We should live in harmony with the other animals on this planet and report any animal abuse to the authorities.

Section 6: We acknowledge that drinking and driving is a serious problem that continues to claim thousands of American lives each year. We recognize that teenage drinking and driving is an even more serious problem today in America. We resolve to do our part in reducing the slaughter of Americans on our highways by refraining to drive while intoxicated.

Section 7: We oppose the use of nuclear weapons for they will undeniably destroy our cities, contaminate our water sources, and damage the atmosphere. We ask our government to refrain from the use of weapons of mass destruction in the pursuit of international peace. We resolve to work together for eternal conciliation on Earth and to live in peace and harmony.

Section 8: We deplore the abuse and mistreatment of young children by parents, relatives or friends. We are deeply disturbed by the reality of child abuse, both physical and sexual in our fatherland. We are appalled and distressed that so many children in America are forced to live in wretched conditions. We bemoan the enslaving of children to further the sexual fantasies of adults. We oppose the posing of nude children to adorn the pages of pornographic materials. We cry out against child prostitution and demand tougher laws to put an end to this trade. We will take responsibility to safeguard the future of our children and protect them from predators.

Section 9: We recognize that the workplace has become a very stressful place, which may lead employees to deadly behavior. We recognize that murders remain the second-leading cause of death on the job. We will strive to identify employees with emotional problems to prevent violence and other hostile acts at work from happening. We realize that individually we cannot do much, but by working together as a group we may save a few lives. We implore business leaders and government to make the workplace safer for their employees.

Section 10: We grieve for the battered and abused women of our land, and we demand stiffer penalties for spouse beaters. We ask our city leaders and our government to provide more and better facilities and services for physically, sexually and emotionally abused women. We beg our fellow male human beings to show more compassion to their wives or girlfriends. We vow to step up our campaigns to combat and uproot domestic violence in America.

Section 11: We understand that not everybody in our world is fortunate to have friends, relatives or loved ones. We concede that that there are lonely people of all ages among every race in our country. We realize that loneliness is a disease that may lead to suicide, and that suicide is the eighth leading cause of death in America. We must treat suicide as a serious national threat, step up research to encourage intervention with people at risk, and work out a national strategy toward suicide prevention. We promise to help each other and provide company to each other, particularly to the sick, the poor and the old.

Section 12: We condole with those who are less fortunate than us. We will not vitiate our friends and neighbors, our teachers and our counselors. We will not demeanor the people we work with or do business with. We appreciate the right to be who we are, and we will show respect to those who choose to live differently.

Section 13: We proscribe all the licentious men who defile our wives, mothers and daughters. We damn them for disrupting the lives of the women they violated. We call for stiffer punishment for the debased men who heinously stalk and assault women. We ask our business leaders and our government to provide safer workplace and better facilities for rape victims. We vouch to respect and protect the weak, the innocent, the immature, the sick and the old.

ABOUT THIS BOOK

I wrote the stories in this book between 1984 and 1985. Soon after writing the last story, I decided to go back to College. After graduating in 1987, I submitted the manuscript to several publishing houses. There was no interest and I shelved the project. In 1991, I moved to St. Louis, Missouri. I enrolled at the University of Missouri – St Louis to pursue a Masters' Degree in Business. After completing the program in 1994, I edited and rewrote some of the stories. In 1995, I tumbled upon the book 'LIFE UNDER GLASS' by Abigail Alling and Mark Nelson. After reading the book, I rewrote 'Archernar the Clown' and used the Carlsbad Caverns as the new setting for the Colonists. The story as well as the book titles was changed several times. For many years, the manuscript languished in a cardboard box with other manuscripts. Then in 2011, I bought the 3rd generation Amazon Kindle. I began to wonder what my book will look like on Kindle. I started to toy with the idea of self-publishing my book and in August I uploaded my work to Amazon.com. To my surprise, they accepted my book and created a Kindle version. Soon after, I created a Print-On-Demand version using the self-publishing tools provided by the internet company CreateSpace. Finally, 26 years after I started writing these stories, I saw my book in print.

The statistics printed in this book were from the early 1980s. Much has changed since I wrote these stories. Baby Amy is now 28 years old. The National Debt has increased 10-fold, from $1.5 trillion in 1984 to $15 trillion in 2011. In Texas, anyone below the age of 21 is not allowed to buy, possess, or consume alcohol. However, minors can consume alcohol under the supervision of their parents or guardian. The acronym DUI is more commonly used nowadays although some States still use the letters DWI to refer to drunk drivers. The statistics in the stories were included to draw attention to a specific problem and they do not affect the plot in the stories. I won't be surprised if the statistics, such as the number of people killed in drunk-driving accidents, have increased in number today. But it is encouraging to know that American companies as well as the American people are enthusiastically involved in protecting the environment and saving ever-diminishing resources. Through this book, I tried for 26 years to bring these concerns to the attention of the public.